M000168285

THE
IMMUNE

DOC LUCKY
MEISENHEIMER

LJS&S PUBLISHING
ORLANDO
2011

Copyright © 2011 by
John "Doc Lucky" Meisenheimer
www.DocLucky.com

All rights reserved. No part of this book may be used or reproduced in any manner, including Internet usage, without the express written permission of the publisher, except in the case of brief quotations embodied in critical articles and reviews.

This book is a work of fiction. Names, characters, places, and incidents either are products of the author's imagination or are used fictitiously. Any resemblance to actual events, locales, or persons, living or dead, is entirely coincidental.

Published by LJS&S Publishing
www.LJSSPublishing.com

Contact Information:
Victoria Andrew, VP of Marketing
LJS&S Publishing
7300 Sandlake Commons Blvd, Suite 105
Orlando, FL 32819
(877) 969-6728
Victoria@ljsspublishing.com

ISBN: 978-0-9667612-2-1
LCCN: 2011925593

Book design by Lee Lewis Walsh, Words Plus Design,
www.wordsplusdesign.com
Cover art by Ron McDonald
Cover design by Kimberly Hawkins and Jason Synder

Printed in the United States of America

FOR

John VII, Jake, and Maximus

Read now for adventure, in the future for meaning.

ACKNOWLEDGEMENTS

Victoria Andrew, Andrew Arvesen, Fred Ehmke, Michael Garrett, Kim Hawkins, Ron McDonald, Mark Myers, Keria Myers, Micala Myers, my wife Jacquie, sons Maximus, Jake and John, parents John and Alice, niece Maylin Meisenheimer, Kathryn Mueller, Peggy Smith, Sigmarie Soto, Lee Lewis Walsh, and Darry Wright.

FACTS

1973   Herbert Boyer produces the first transgenic bacterial organism.

1991   Herman the bull becomes the first transgenic mammal.

2000   Transgenic rabbit fluoresces green.

2004   Florigen produces the first blue rose by genetic engineering.

2007   Translucent "see through" frogs created by Japanese scientists.

2011   Hundreds of genetically modified organisms now exist.

PROLOGUE

The Immune looked at the four large marine guards standing to either side of the massive metal door bearing the sign RESTRICTED ACCESS. His hand entered the right front pocket of his faded green and brown fatigues. His fingers lightly touched the hilt of the knife. He had shoved the blade through the base of the pocket so the handle wouldn't show. Not that it mattered. The Pope would more likely be searched upon entering the Vatican than any guard who would attempt to confiscate a weapon from The Immune.

Beyond the door, in an empty room, gagged with arms and legs bound to a chair, sat the infamous prisoner, Joseph Sengele: lunatic and unrepentant biogenetic creator of the airwars, whose continuing random attacks on humanity resulted in tens of millions, if not hundreds of millions, of horrific deaths worldwide. In a moment, The Immune would pass through the door and kill Dr. Sengele.

The Immune never killed a man before, but he had dispatched hundreds of Sengele's creations. Each represented to The Immune a small step to the ultimate goal of Sengele himself. Should the family of deadly sins ever consider an eighth, vengeance would make a fitting brother. Vengeance is a powerful, life-altering emotion, and no one in history could claim more metamorphosis from this sensation than The Immune. At this point, he knew not whether Sengele's death would alter the fate of the world, but he believed it would provide him some peace, and certainly a degree of satisfaction. The guards stepped back and the heavy metal door, straining on its hinges, opened for The Immune.

CHAPTER 1

GRAND CAYMAN

John Long slid over the water's surface off Grand Cayman. Even though the sun was setting, plenty of light penetrated the crystal clear water to illuminate the reef below. He glanced left at the trim female body in a white and silver swimsuit matching him stroke for stroke. A few strands of her brown hair loosened from beneath her yellow swim cap and swirled in the eddy currents behind her head.

He smiled with remembrance of the previous evening. He had proposed to Cassandra at The Wharf Restaurant. They were sitting at a table on the water's edge, throwing pieces of bread rolls to the tarpon that swam to the restaurant each evening. Their eyes remained fixed on the shimmering bodies of several five-foot fish swimming on top of each other. The surface of the water boiled as each tarpon tried to out-position the next for the tidbits cast from the restaurant patrons' plates.

Cassandra reached for the last roll, but it was already in John's hand.

"Let's split it," said John with a sly smile.

Her brown eyes sparkled as she smiled back. She took one end of the hard roll and pulled. As the bread separated, a glistening object fell from the roll and landed, spinning on her plate.

"Ohhh!" Cassandra gasped.

John looked at the ring, a heart-shaped cut diamond sandwiched between two deep red rubies, and said, "Thank God! I was beginning to think we'd fed the wrong roll to the tarpon. I imagined spending the rest of the weekend fishing."

She gave him a soft punch in the arm, then a long kiss, which lasted all night and through two room services.

Today, they arose just in time for an early evening swim. Cassandra was the ideal woman for him. He'd dated many women and she, unlike others, understood the pressures on a physician, especially one with a busy internal medicine practice. Additionally, she loved to swim, which was his passion.

As he cut through the water with his now fiancé, his medical practice seemed a million miles away, but tomorrow he would return to reality. An hour and a half flight would force him to reenter the world of medical forms. With all of medicine's issues, he couldn't think of one improved by paperwork. Yet, the government's answer to every problem was invariably another form. Then there were resolving staff issues, fighting denials by insurance companies, paying bills, and, of course, seeing the occasional patient should he get any free time. However, at this moment, John was at perfect peace.

He smiled as he passed over a large coral head covered with several black spiny sea urchins. The water was so shallow, he could easily see the colorful parrotfish swimming in and out. Occasionally, one would go vertical in the water to take a small bite of algae growing on the coral. John could hear a cacophony of clicks on the reef as hundreds of parrotfish repeated their feeding behavior.

John shouted to Cassandra, "Close your eyes and listen to the clicks."

Suddenly, John was lifted several feet as a large wave passed beneath. As the crest of the wave went by, the subsequent trough dropped John toward the coral heads below. John instinctively put his hands out to brace himself for impact on the outcrop of coral. Cassandra, who was swimming to his left, dropped harmlessly beyond the edge. John's right hand caught the edge of coral head, which stabilized his position but shifted his body uncomfortably close to the coral. He shoved to move himself into deeper water, but as he pushed, a sharp stabbing pain shot through his hand and radiated up the arm. Reflexively, he jerked his hand back. As he did, a sea urchin with long black spines dislodged from a fissure in the coral.

Embedded in his thenar eminence, the meaty muscle at the base of the thumb, was a broken black, urchin spine. A streak of blood appeared at the entry point of the spine and dissipated into the surrounding water. Cassandra was treading water next to him. She saw the grimace on his face.

"What's wrong?"

"The wave trough dropped me down on the coral head. I got stuck by an urchin," said John. He showed her his hand. One centimeter of the spine was sticking out from the skin.

"Ouch, that must hurt! We'd better go in," said Cassandra.

"Wait, sometimes big waves come in sets. I don't want to be over any coral heads if another passes."

Within seconds, they were lifted again by another large wave, this time even bigger than the first.

"Where did these waves come from?" Cassandra questioned. "The cruise ships already left, and it's too big for a wake anyway." A moment later, a third wave lifted and dropped them down.

John, while studying his punctured hand, said, "It's probably from some underwater landslide, seismic shift. Who knows."

They treaded water for several minutes. Other big waves passed, but none comparable to the first three.

Finally, Cassandra said, "It's almost dark. You're bleeding, and we're 200 meters from shore. I'd rather chance bumping into coral versus being bumped by large things that swim in the night."

"Yeah, chumming the water with my blood is like ringing a dinner bell out here."

After swimming back to their hotel, a swarthy Caymanian with blue eyes wearing a hotel staff shirt ran up.

"Are you people okay? Did you get caught in the big waves?"

"Yeah," said John, "we're fine. The swells passed under us. Was anyone injured?" John surveyed the disarray of lounge chairs on the beach. The waves carried some all the way to the back entrance of the lobby.

"No bad injuries," said the attendant, "just scrapes and bumps. Most guests already left the beach for the evening."

"Well, let me know if I can help in any way," said John. "I'm a physician."

Back in the hotel room, John managed to remove the spine with some difficulty. He sat down to watch the U.S. evening news as he wrapped a bandage around the injury.

An attractive blonde-haired reporter appeared on the screen. She was doing a remote report from the steps of the Capitol.

"Senator Bedford is the second senator from the state of Massachusetts to die from a heart attack this year. This brings the total to seven senate deaths this year. We have to go back to 1918 to find this many senators dying from natural causes in one year."

John mused aloud, "This could have the potential of being good, except they keep replacing them."

Ignoring John's cynicism, Cassandra said, "Oh jeez, I've got to call my stepbrother, Chunky. I haven't talked to him in three months. The last time we spoke, I told him things seemed to be getting serious. I want to let him know you popped the question and against my better judgment, I said yes."

John laughed, then asked, "You haven't talked to him in three months?"

"Yeah," said Cassandra, "remember, I told you before, he heads up a research team who studies bottle nose dolphins. It's hard to get a hold of him because he's always on a boat or on some remote island. For all I know he could be floating off shore right now. You'd like him. I guess you'll get to meet him at the wedding."

She smiled widely at John. Her attention switched to the phone as she connected. "Chunky, it's me! Guess what!" She walked into the other room, chattering happily.

John opened and closed his now bandaged hand and winced in pain.

CHAPTER 2

AIRWARS

One week later, back at his medical practice in Orlando, John settled into his daily routine of treating the many self-inflicted diseases of his patients. He finished listening to the emphysemic lungs of Mr. Jenkins. After draping his stethoscope over his neck, he said, "Mr. Jenkins, you're getting worse. I've been telling you for ten years to stop smoking. What can I do or say to help you quit?"

"Doc," said Mr. Jenkins, "since you put me on this here portable oxygen I kin walk clear cross the room without hardly gettin' tired. I jus' don't figur the need to stop smokin'. I'll be doin' jus' fine." This was followed by ten seconds of gasping coughs.

A knocking rattled the exam room door and a voice from the hall said, "Dr. Tobin is on the phone."

The request was the office signal to get him out of the exam room. John's staff used it if a patient was taking too long or if there was an office problem. He cracked the door and peered out. Cathy, his receptionist, stood looking pale and scared.

"Doc, you need to see this news report," she said.

He poked his head out the door farther, but as he did so, he noticed an eerie silence permeated the usually busy office. Missing were the typical sounds accompanying a hectic internal medicine practice. A chill ran down his spine.

"Terrorist attack?" he asked with apprehension.

"No . . . I don't know. Just come." She grabbed the white sleeve of his lab jacket and gave it a tug.

He followed her into the reception room where his patients and staff had gathered. All eyes remained fixed on the flat screen monitor hanging above the reception window. The only sound came from a newsreader, whose tone seemed to be a mixture of agitation and excitement.

" . . . and we'll be showing you that astonishing clip again from a rural area of Niquero, Cuba."

The screen filled with a jumpy B-roll clip, which looked like it was from a hand-held consumer video camera. Initially fuzzy, the camera refocused on a floating object. It hovered directly above weather-beaten wooden shacks built in a scattered pattern along a dirt road. The location appeared to be on the outskirts of what looked like a small village. As the camera continued to focus, the object appeared to be a large coal-black mass the size of a blimp.

John said, "What the heck is—?"

"Shush and just watch," interrupted Cathy.

John thought, if it's a blimp, its shape is grossly distorted. It had a ridged crescent top, and one end of the body was more conical in shape. Unlike a free-floating blimp, this object had hundreds of black hanging ropes, the thickness of a man's arm, in concentric rings attached to the base. John's first impression was of a Macy's Thanksgiving Day Parade balloon with a veil of dense ropes and absent handlers.

"Again," said the newsreader, "I must remind you, this clip is not appropriate for children."

John looked again at the shape. It reminded him of something, but he couldn't bring it to the front of his mind. As he was deep in thought, he ran his hand through his hair. His hand throbbed where the sea urchin puncture wound remained tender.

Suddenly it came to him. The pain from the urchin was bad, but nothing like the time he raced around Key West. During the four-hour swim, Portuguese Man O' Wars stung him six times. The first five were mild, but with the sixth, tentacles adhered and wrapped around his left arm. The pear-shaped, blue sac of the Man O' War looked like a small balloon stuck to his arm. The long tentacles stung him from the arm down to his lower torso. It felt like he had swum into a bed of electrical wires. To add insult to injury, his right hand received stings trying to peel tentacles away from his left arm.

The newsreader broke his train of thought. "This has to be the most disturbing yet amazing video I've ever seen in my twenty years in the news business."

John was familiar with Man O' Wars not only as an open water swimmer, but as a physician as well. Over the years he treated many stings from the common ocean inhabitant. He knew the crest on top of the air sac, blown by the ocean breeze, frequently moved colonies of hanging tentacles close enough to shore for encounters with surfers and swimmers. Each tentacle contained multiple poisonous nematocysts that paralyze any unfortunate fish brushing against them. Although rarely deadly to humans, the pain and sequela from the stings is intense.

"This looks exactly like a giant Man O' War," said John. "This has got to be a video hoax."

"You mean like the *War of the Worlds* radio show," said an elderly, bald-headed patient who was sitting next to John.

"Exactly! What we're seeing is impossible," replied John. "The thing is floating in the air, and look—" John pointed to the screen. "The tentacles are pulling it along the ground. It's moving on its own."

"Looks dang real to me, Doc Long," said Mr. Jenkins who followed them into the waiting room.

"Trust me it's not," said John.

John began pressing the buttons on the remote and flipping through the channels. With the exception of stations running critical programming, such as reality shows, all were either showing or talking about the clip.

"Dr. Long," said Cathy, "it's real! And more reports are coming in with other sightings, but you haven't seen the worst airwar clip yet. That's what they're calling them: airwars—"

"Look!" Mr. Jenkins yelled, holding his oxygen canister under one arm and pointing to the monitor with the other.

The news channel cut to the airwar passing the shacks. One of the tentacles pulled something through the door onto the wooden porch. The struggling creature was then pulled down the one-plank step. A small cloud of dust swirled as the writhing, tentacle-wrapped animal was dragged onto the dry, dirt road. John gasped as he realized the twisting object was a petite woman. The paroxysmal movements of the battle suddenly stopped as the body went limp.

"I can't stomach watching this again," said the elderly male patient. He stood and grabbed his walker. "I'm going home to my family." As he left the waiting room, two other patients followed.

Back on the monitor, five red tentacles appearing from the inside of the black outer curtain began to lift the paralyzed form slowly upwards toward the sac. John watched in horror as he noticed several other immobile and struggling human forms being lifted the same way. Presumably, others were unseen deeper inside the curtain, blocked from view by the density of the numerous tentacles.

Suddenly, entering the right of the screen, a military jeep came sliding to a halt in a large cloud of dust. Three swarthy soldiers dressed in brown and green fatigues leapt from the jeep. In unison, the men began firing automatic weapons into the airwar sac, which floated 75 feet off the ground.

At first, there appeared to be no effect, but then the sac began to shred in several places. The airwar began to collapse on itself.

"All right!" said John, and he began clapping, but then he noticed Carol, one of his nurses, shaking her head, frowning.

"It gets scarier," she said.

As John continued to watch the now rapidly descending airwar, he noticed something was exiting the shredded sac. At first, there were a few dozen. Only moments later, there were hundreds, then thousands of what appeared to be miniature airwars released into the sky. The juvenile airwars were twelve inches in diameter, the same size as a birthday party balloon. As the flock of newly birthed airwars passed in front of the sun, they were so numerous the skies darkened momentarily.

"Dang!" said Mr. Jenkins. "See ya'll later. I'm gonna go buy me some extra shotgun shells." He left the waiting room and John could hear him coughing all the way down the hallway.

The entire staff was now looking at John in silence, waiting for him to comment. He took his stethoscope from his neck and removed his white lab coat.

"It's Friday afternoon and I imagine the entire world is glued to their televisions," said John. "Waiting for patients who won't show seems pointless. Let's take the rest of the day off and, God willing, we'll be back at work on Monday."

CHAPTER 3

THE AIRWAR SCIENTIFIC COUNCIL

D ubbed the *airwar crisis*, the media fanned the flames of fear to the point widespread hoarding began and worldwide riots broke out in large cities. Congress immediately held an emergency session and passed a forty billion-dollar airwar crisis funding bill, eighteen billion directed at the airwar crisis, and twenty-two billion for special earmarks.

The entire world craved more information. An endless stream of airwar *experts* peppered the airwaves speculating on the etiology of airwars. Every social-political cause tried to lay claim to the airwar crisis. From greenhouse gases, ozone depletion, and deforestation to oil drilling and laboratory animal testing, every group tried to make the connection with their fund-raising efforts and the airwar crisis.

General scientific consensus was airwars were a genetically engineered species. Scientists weren't sure if this was intentional or accidental, but a worldwide search was underway to find the person or persons responsible.

In John's condominium, he and Cassandra watched the crisis unfold on television with undivided attention. Cassandra finally took a break to make sandwiches in the kitchen. John shouted new statistics to her as they appeared on the news.

"The Secretary of State just reported the fifth airwar sighting, and the death toll is now seventy-eight."

"I thought she said earlier the death toll was twenty-five thousand," said Cassandra.

"No, not from airwars. That's the number killed in the riots. Matter of fact, I'm feeling the urge to go rioting right now. Sounds like a good solution to the problem to me," said John facetiously.

Cassandra walked back in the room with a plate of sandwiches. "Well, you'll have to riot by yourself. I think I'll take my chances with the airwars. The odds are better."

"Not if airwars keep reproducing," retorted John.

The destruction of the five airwars resulted in the same outcome as the first. Torn air sacs, which were now known to be filled with hydrogen, released thousands of young into the sky. One of the airwars, shredded by incendiaries from a fighter jet, ignited with images reminiscent of the Hindenburg's fiery collapse. It was spectacular, but even with many juvenile airwars perishing in the fireball, scores escaped.

John and Cassandra stayed up late following breaking news reports. Around midnight, a female senator from Massachusetts, accompanied by other politicians and scientists, conducted a press conference. John and Cassandra watched the senator speak to the press.

"We believe, earnestly, that personal attacks on airwars must end immediately. Furthermore, the United Nations is obligated to create a multinational crisis team to address this epic disaster that—"

"John," interrupted Cassandra, "it's late. Let's do some end-of-world lovemaking."

"I knew there had to be a silver lining to this airwar crisis," said John. He clicked the television off.

On the second day of the airwar crisis, military sightings confirmed hundreds of full-size airwars. Sightings appeared limited to Cuba, Jamaica, Trinidad, and northern Venezuela. No new information was forthcoming on the source of the airwars. The human death toll from attacks elevated to the thousands. Confirmed destruction of seventy-five airwars was reported, but release of thousands of juveniles resulted. World leaders and scientists, who initially appealed for restraints, now demanded attacks on airwars surcease and recommended penalties for violators.

On the third day, John spent most of the morning watching the United Nations emergency session on television. Cassandra had gone shopping.

The U.N. president addressed the assembly, "The number of airwar sightings is now in the thousands. The death toll from direct airwar attacks is above forty-thousand. We have an unprecedented world crisis, and world leaders demand an immediate United Nations response. Although we haven't found the source for the original airwars, it's clear they only reproduce by destruction of an adult form. Therefore, we have no choice but to call for a worldwide ban on attacks on airwars."

A representative from Jamaica began throwing papers and files. He had to be escorted from the room by guards. Several other countries with confirmed airwars inside their borders also dissented.

Cassandra came in with a frazzled look. "The traffic is unbelievable for a Sunday. I've been sitting on I-4 the whole time. Stores are overrun. Everyone is hoarding. If I can't get coffee, there'll be a Cass-andra crisis making the airwar crisis look like small potatoes." She smiled at John. "Anything new on the airwars?"

John looked up from the television, "Yeah, the United Nations has formed an emergency council to disseminate world policy to all governments."

"Can the United Nations do that?" asked Cassandra with uneasiness in her voice.

"They just did. Someone selected a bunch of scientists, politicians, and military to run this Airwar Scientific Council."

"Who decided who gets on this Council?"

"I don't know, but not everyone is happy," said John and he pointed toward the television.

The ambassador from Lichtenstein was pounding his desktop as he was yelling. Scattered around the U.N. chamber, several other ambassadors were standing and yelling as well.

"Well, I'm sure it'll take weeks for them to get organized and make recommendations," said Cassandra, "Plenty of time to add anyone worthy who's been overlooked."

"I'm not too sure about that," said John. "For a new political organization, it seems pretty structured, and based on the rhetoric I'm hearing, it appears the Airwar Scientific Council is a closed club. Plus, the council has already voted on one action that, frankly, I'm a bit uncomfortable with."

"What's that?"

John tapped the keyboard of his computer tablet and said, "Look at this logo."

On the screen was a red square with the letters ASC in white in the center.

"This is the Airwar Scientific Council logo," John said with a frown. "Its now required on every press release dealing with airwars. ASC determined there's too much misinformation about airwars. It decided, as a matter of world security, press reporting on airwars must be limited to ASC-approved reports."

"Sounds like a violation of the first amendment to me," said Cassandra.

John shook his head, "This is the U.N. talking, not the United States. America, Canada, Britain, Australia, Japan, and a few other free press countries are having a cow, but the rest of the world press are marginalizing this opposition."

John stopped speaking and pointed to the television.

The lady senator from Massachusetts, who was now apparently an ASC member, was addressing the press. "I can assure you that everyone has complete freedom of the press. You just must report factually. I *am* sure none of you have a problem with reporting the truth."

A bald reporter wearing wire-rimmed glasses and a bow tie stood. "Who decides what's the truth?"

"ASC does, of course," replied the senator, with a slight roll of her eyes. "ASC is a highly qualified group of world scientists and leaders who are more than capable of discerning the truth."

Several other reporters stood and shouted questions, but the senator waved them off and walked off stage.

John looked at Cassandra and said, "Somehow I feel we're being required to ask the fox how the chickens are doing."

"Well, at least someone is doing something; that's somewhat reassuring," said Cassandra.

"Doing something and doing the right thing are frequently unrelated," retorted John.

By the fourth day, airwars had appeared in Europe, Asia, and Australia. ASC, backed by mounting scientific evidence, unanimously passed the airwar act. Any non-U.N./ASC attack or contact with airwars was determined to be an act of terrorism and punishable by death. There were a few weak protests from the United States press. Later that evening, ASC verified the presence of airwars in southern Florida, and the press capitulated.

On day five, virtually all countries had confirmed airwar sightings. World count of full-sized airwars reached ten thousand. Global citizen pressure demanded ASC try weapons of mass destruction on airwars.

A tall handsome man in his fifties named Otis Glavin appeared on television. His dark hair with some gray in the temples along with his steel blue eyes and deep voice conferred an air of authority. He was the spokesperson for ASC. Glavin read a one-sentence press release on the early morning news. "Due to the congregation of airwars near inhabited areas, it's unrealistic for ASC to support the use of large destructive weapons on airwars."

In response to the ASC position, early afternoon riots began breaking out in capital cities around the world. Spokesperson Glavin reappeared on the early evening news.

"ASC has reconsidered, with trepidation, to proceed with an experimental destruction of an airwar tonight."

Less than an hour later a thermobaric bomb obliterated an airwar hovering over Lake Cobly in the southern United States. Not a single juvenile was seen following the blast, nor were any of the citizens of the small nearby town, which was also annihilated by the explosion.

The media leveled criticisms that only cryptic warnings were given to residents before the blast, but Glavin responded that warnings were given and went unheeded.

Later the same night, a small nuclear blast outside Tel Aviv of undetermined origin destroyed three airwars, but a change in winds pushed the radioactive cloud into the city, making it uninhabitable.

Glavin read a final press release late that evening. "Due to extreme collateral damage, ASC has passed airwar resolution three. Weapons of mass destruction are to be placed under 'observational control' by ASC officials and are heretofore banned from further use on airwars."

Besides the criticisms leveled at the thermobaric bomb test, the media continued to create other problems for ASC with non-approved sensationalized headlines such as "Psychics detect telepathic communication among airwars. Scientist warns: alien super intelligent species bent on destroying mankind. Airwars: angels of God sent to punish sinners." Each new story caused greater panic and demands for more action by ASC.

On the morning of day six ASC began railing against media-produced misinformation. Glavin gave a seven a.m. statement.

"Half-truths, lies, speculation, and debate are clearly dangerous in times of crisis. Only ASC is qualified to provide accurate information. Therefore, ASC is now demanding worldwide passage of the airwar sedition bill."

The sedition bill essentially said non-ASC approved mention of airwars on radio or television would result in the revocation of the station's FCC license to broadcast. Printed columns regarding airwars without the ASC logo resulted in the jailing of the managing editor of the newspaper.

That evening, while watching the news, John became livid as he saw the sedition bill pass Congress with an override of a presidential veto. "I can't believe what I'm seeing, Cassandra."

"John, people are afraid."

"It's not right—makes me want to join a militia—and down a few airwars with them."

"Don't think of saying that in public," said Cassandra with concern, "Militias release thousands of juveniles every time they attack an airwar. That's why ASC is demanding global gun confiscation."

John pounded his fist into his hand, "That's a bunch of crapola too."

"Well, the press is hailing it as a step in the right direction," said Cassandra. She walked over and started massaging John's shoulders.

John pulled away. "Our press should be reviewing our constitution. They sometimes forget it's a linked chain that restrains the beast of government. You let even one link break and the beast goes berserk."

"Currently," said Cassandra, "I'm more afraid of airwars than the government. Complain all you want to me, but keep in mind members of the press have voiced your opinion and are now in jail."

The evening news continued with much fanfare. ASC demonstrated that regions with the least resistance to ASC directives had fewer airwar-related fatalities. This was followed by the approval of the "Save the Village" initiative. Although defending one's self might temporarily rescue an individual or family, the subsequent release of thousands of juveniles was worse for society as a whole.

Spokesman Glavin explained the "Save the Village" law in a press conference as John watched fuming. "I'm pleased to report anyone seen acting in personal self-interest will be detained and searched by local authorities. If deemed in the best interest of society, these terrorists will be immediately sacrificed to an airwar. A trial isn't needed; only the approval of an ASC official. This new policy can only help in our battle against airwars," he said with a smile.

A reporter stood and shouted, "Mr. Glavin, what about the fourth and sixth amendments of our bill of rights?"

Glavin pointed at the man and three young men wearing grey arm bands escorted the reporter roughly from the press conference.

Glavin looked at the shocked reporters and said, "Oh, it's another amendment *whine*. Like every fine *whine*, it needs cooling. Fortunately, we have a nice *whine* cellar for these *whines* called the federal penitentiary. This *whine* will be joining the others directly." He pointed at the reporter being dragged out the exit. "In closing, I'd like to finish with fabulous news of our first major victory against the airwars. ASC studies show the rate of increase in world-wide deaths from airwars is decreasing. Excellent! Most excellent."

Cassandra looked at John and said, "Doesn't that mean the death rate is still increasing?"

John answered by clicking the news off.

CHAPTER 4

SENATOR SNIVALING

I t had been one week since the first televised airwar attack. John was with Cassandra, sitting on his couch in his condominium. He was trying to catch up on dictations from the emergency room where he'd been working for the last several days. The television was on, but he turned the sound down. Cassandra came into the room carrying a *People* magazine. The cover displayed a giant airwar with tentacles wrapped around photos of celebrities who had perished in airwar attacks.

"John, do you want me to turn the sound up?" asked Cassandra.

"Why bother?" said John, looking up from a chart, "Nothing but the airwar crisis has been on for the last week. I'm sick of seeing the ASC logo in the corner of the screen."

"Well, they just flashed a number on the screen. It said we topped 100,000 deaths in the United States from airwars," said Cassandra.

"Feels like I've seen half of them in the ER this week," John said, flipping the last chart on a large pile.

"I thought you liked listening to the science updates."

"Yeah, but you have to wade through repetitive ASC mandates and tripe about how you're selfish if you fight back when an airwar attacks — what a bunch of crap!"

Cassandra nodded and said, "I agree, they're a bit redundant, plus they overdo those videos of juveniles being released."

"Yeah, the press makes it look like airwars are the victims. Go figure."

Cassandra snuggled next to John. "Well, they do give nice tips on how to avoid airwars."

John reached for the remote. "From what I see in the emergency room, their tips are bogus. I get my information from the Internet. That's the only media ASC doesn't control . . . speak of the devil."

John hit the volume button on the remote and a newsreader's voice blathered about an Internet video.

"The posting of this video by Noble Laureate, Dr. Koehler, yesterday was determined to be illegal today by ASC . . ."

Dr. Koehler's German accented voice synced with the video. "I have absolute proof airwar movements aren't random. Myself and other concerned scientists outside ASC demand access to airwars for research—" The clip ended abruptly.

A reporter standing in front of Dr. Koehler's lab appeared on screen. "Dr. Koehler was found dead today in his lab. Coroners report he suffered a deadly accidental sting from an airwar carcass, which he illegally acquired."

Senator Beulah Snivaling's image filled the screen. A U.S. senator, she now sat on the ASC High Council. A middle-aged woman with ash blonde hair in her early fifties, she was attractive for her age, but had the odd look of a face-lift done a bit too tight, giving her unnatural slitted openings for her green eyes. Botoxed to the max, she showed no facial expressions as she spoke.

John turned to Cassandra. "I've seen her on TV before. That's the senator from Massachusetts I find so irritating," John said and felt the muscles in his jaw tightening.

"Although Dr. Koehler was well-meaning," said Senator Snivaling, "his death was unnecessary and avoidable. ASC was already aware airwar movements are not random. In his ill-advised push for more fame, Dr. Koehler ended up dead. His family members, who remain in seclusion, issued this statement—you there! Sit while I'm speaking!" she shrieked nastily while pointing her finger at a photographer who changed positions.

"Wow!" said Cassandra, "she seems lacking in people skills. I wonder how she got elected?"

Senator Snivaling read from a yellow legal pad, "We urge all scientists to leave airwar research in the superior hands of ASC, so other families are not torn apart by tragedy as ours has been." Laying the pad down, the senator gave an expressionless nod and continued in a scolding voice, "Handling airwars is a serious business, not one for amateurs. Koehler's work created unnecessary panic and his findings were insignificant compared to ASC's current fund of knowledge." She then proceeded to list twenty recent deaths of other prominent scientists accidentally killed in their private research of airwars.

Cassandra touched John's arm, "That's a lot of dead scientists. Can airwars sting after they're dead?"

John nodded and said, "It takes several hours after the hydrogen sac has been ruptured for the tentacles to lose their stinging power."

Chairperson Snivaling droned on, "The Airwar Scientific Council has virtually unlimited resources and extensive safety features for handling airwars. There has *not* been a single sting suffered by ASC scientists. It *is* humanity's duty to report unauthorized research on airwars, not only for the safety and well-being of researchers, but also for the safety of society. There *is* an ASC hotline for any unusual airwar behavior noted. Call this hotline. Don't investigate it yourself." Snivaling smiled an emotionless smile.

The local news cut in with a report of a nearby airwar attack on a women's shelter, which involved several deaths.

"I'd feel more comfortable if you'd move in with me," said John, looking thoughtfully at Cassandra, "I know you have a month left on your apartment lease, but it took thirty-five years to find the perfect woman, and under the circumstances, I don't want something to happen to her now." He leaned over and gave her a kiss on the cheek.

She gave him a beaming smile.

"I'll bring the small stuff tomorrow. I won't worry about the furniture until the end of the month."

Before they went to bed, John watched Cassandra try to contact her stepbrother again without success, as she had done every night since the first airwar sighting.

"John, I'm worried about Chunky."

"You said yourself he'd be out of communication at times," he said, rubbing her back in a comforting way.

Cassandra, looking somewhat reassured, fell asleep in his arms.

John lay awake, troubled by thoughts of scenes he would again be experiencing at work the next morning.

CHAPTER 5

THE COLOSSUS

John spent most days in the expanded triage area of the local hospital ER. The city had a higher daily death toll and injury rate than other areas. Resistance to the confiscation of firearms was great in Central Florida. Attacks on airwars in Orlando were more frequent than other large cities. He fully understood local feelings on the repeal of gun rights. Although he turned in his shotgun and reluctantly even his childhood BB gun, which he doubted would have any impact on airwars, a defiant individualistic streak made him hide the Judge, his 45-caliber pistol that could fire a 410-shotgun shell. Even with death as a deterrent, some mandates were too misguided.

The airwars numbered few in Orlando, but all acted aggressively. Lists of the dead and injured were located on the "posting wall," an outside wall of the hospital running its entire length. A makeshift canopy ran the total span protecting hundreds of sheets of paper held in place with duct tape from the rain. Due to large numbers of victims, the posting organization was simplified into male and female sections, then into children, adults, and elderly.

The posting wall started near the hospital entrance and John hated passing it. He personally complained to the hospital's chief administrator, Mr. Goldman, about its placement. Early before his morning shift, John visited Goldman in his office on the top floor of the hospital. Goldman, a short, thin man, bald on the crown of his scalp, sat behind an oversized mahogany desk. He never directly looked at the person he was speaking to and sometimes even closed his eyes as he spoke.

"There's nothing the hospital can do," said Goldman.

"Well," said John, "it's morbid having the posting wall near the entrance. It's one constant scream of grief. Everyone who visits the hospital is exposed to it."

"I'd think you'd be used to screams," said Goldman.

"In the ER it's unavoidable," replied John, "but the posting wall is like an endless public funeral you can't escape from attending."

"I think what you need is a bit more compassion, Dr. Long."

"Compassion? I would think it would be far more compassionate to give the grieving families a bit of privacy."

Goldman looked out the window as if studying the cloud formations. "Dr. Long," he said, "the posting wall is an ASC requirement. Please don't forget ASC provides exclusive funding for airwar treatments and related services."

"Well," said John, "if they're funding the wall, it would be far cheaper to post results on the Internet. The posting wall is not only inefficient, but labor-intensive. Why don't you point that out to them?"

Goldman turned and looked directly at John for the first time.

"I have and ASC doesn't care."

"That's ridiculous. Why would ASC not care about cost?" asked John, then he paused in thought, ". . . Oh, I get it. Orlando is being punished by ASC for not being in lock step with their policies. That explains the barrage of videos about the wall we're subjected to on local news."

A blank stare from Goldman confirmed to John he was correct.

"Why don't you just stand up to ASC and take the posting wall down?" said John, "You know tempers are always flaring around the wall. People accuse each other of being anti-airwar, militant terrorists. ASC just wants a scapegoat to explain the aggressive behavior of airwars in Orlando. The posting wall is only a tool against the militias."

Goldman fiddled with papers on the desk and didn't look up.

"Dr. Long, I won't bite the hand that feeds this hospital. You have to admit it's blatantly apparent that other cities like San Francisco, which has virtually no attacks on airwars, have fewer human deaths."

John pulled out his cell phone, pushed a button, and spoke into the phone, "Colossus—San Francisco." A web page appeared on his phone and he said smugly, "It says here there are now over 100 Colossi in the Bay Area. I think I'll take my chances here in Orlando."

Goldman leaned back in his chair and closed his eyes, "Dr. Long, I'm well aware the Colossi first appeared in San Francisco, but you know as well as I ASC refers to them as *placid*. I don't know if I believe Colossi are fully mature airwars as ASC scientists do, but unlike common airwars, it's clear if you leave them alone they leave you alone."

"Well, to me, Colossi are massive adult airwars growing to three-hundred meters," said John, "and an accident waiting to happen. Everyone knows what happens if you tick them off. Remember the Zimbabwe video?"

Goldman shrugged, "ASC only shows that video as a warning to restrain citizens from attacking Colossi. With as many attacks on airwars around here, I'm quite glad there are no Colossi locally. An attack on a Colossus would be devastating to our community."

The *Zimbabwe Video* was widely circulated by ASC to emphasize the placid Colossus's aggressiveness, if attacked. The video opened with a swarthy, shirtless villager heaving a machete high into the hydrogen sac. The throw was an impressive feat in itself as the sac was, at a low point, fifty meters off the ground. The machete pierced the membrane of the sac and a tiny slit became apparent. The man stood in defiance, picking up another machete and now holding one in each hand.

He was trying to save the only object of value he possessed, his goat, now currently entwined in one of the black peripheral tentacles of the Colossus. The goat's bloodshot eyes bulged and mouth frothed. The only sign of residual life was a twitching hindquarter. The man decided to make a stand. It had a ridiculous quality, like an ant shaking a fist at a shoe stepping on it.

Although the injury from the first machete was comparable to a paper cut on an elephant, the reaction from the Colossus was severe. A tentacle snapped out and wrapped around the man's right forearm. The man screamed in agony as thousands of meganematocysts entered his skin. The airwar's meganematocysts were like bigger versions of the jellyfish or sea anemone stinging organelle, the nematocyst. Their hair-width points were barbed and hollow, injecting a man with painful poison. When an airwar stuck, the thousands of meganematocysts would fill a man with more venom than the bite of a diamondback rattlesnake.

The man spasmodically dropped his machete from his right hand, but held fast to the one in his left. He began hacking wildly at the other approaching tentacles. A spray of sweat mixed with tissue fluid from the creature flew in the air. For a moment he fended off the black tentacles of the outer curtain. Flopping about his feet were a half-dozen writhing tentacles. The now truncated, main branches reflexively snapped upwards in the sky.

Then the tentacle, still wrapped around his right arm, yanked upwards, forcing him to balance on his left foot. He couldn't deliver a direct blow, and severing the tentacle was his sole chance for escape. Another tentacle flanked him and slid in behind. As it contacted the machete-wielding arm, it coiled with a rapidity of a boa constrictor on its prey. The man screamed in agony again. The machete dropped as he was jerked four feet into the air. A gaunt man, he had sinewy muscles, which were bulging from battle. His pose and grimace was reminiscent of an Olympic gymnast performing an iron cross on the rings. Moments later he was engulfed by tentacles.

The Colossus then passed over the village. It moved forward at a speed a trained sprinter couldn't outrun, though many in the village tried. Tentacles were everywhere, exploring, probing, and coiling. If it was a living creature—from humans to livestock—its fate was the same. The black tentacles entered the small shacks and huts, dragging screaming victims out into the more dense inner red tentacles.

One hundred sixty-seven women, men, and children lost their lives in the seven minutes following. A lifeless village remained now sterilized of all humanity. The only evidence of the attack was a few dead bodies scattered from where the Colossus dropped them and the numerous human forms entwined at various heights beneath the airwar, which were rising in a slow ascent. From within the curtain of tentacles there came a chilling chorus of screams.

The small tear in the hydrogen sac already self-sealed. A sticky resin-like substance formed along the tear. As the two membranous flaps fluttered, they enjoined via the sticky substance. In a few minutes, this seal dried into a hard binding resin. No one observed the release of a single juvenile through the small tear.

John knew the video belied the euphemism "Gentle Colossus" granted to the oversized airwars by the press. Clearly, when provoked, the response was horrible. Yet, Colossi congregated in areas showing little or no resistance. Therefore, overall deaths due to the Colossi were extremely low.

The video became propaganda used extensively by the ASC to espouse what officials referred to as a passive battle against airwars. "Run, hide, do no harm" is the path to victory. RHDNH was the acronym seen everywhere from bumper stickers to billboards.

Goldman wouldn't budge on John's request to take down or at least move the posting wall. John left Goldman's office more frustrated than when he entered.

CHAPTER 6

A STAGE EIGHT

After leaving Goldman's office, John began his shift in the ER triaging the dead and soon-to-be-dead from the salvageable injured. There were no Colossi in Florida, so all envenomizations were from common airwar stings. In the triage area, the typical patients were young adults. They were most likely to escape an attack.

ASC released an antitoxin for airwar stings just days before. The antitoxin helped minor envenomizations, but not severe stings. Unfortunately, a common side effect was a transfusion-like reaction. One out of fifty victims died from the antitoxin. Private pharmaceutical companies petitioned ASC for the antitoxin production process. ASC refused and Senator Snivaling explained the denial in a press conference.

"Airwar antitoxin is far too important to entrust to private companies who would profit from its production," said Snivaling, "ASC always looks out for the common man."

Fair and equal was the distribution plan, with ASC officials as the top priority. ASC took a great deal of pride in supplying the antitoxin free. There was always a severe shortage.

John was on a mid-morning break checking news on the Internet. Although he knew the Internet was rife with bogus reports, it was more informative than ASC news. Network programming was nothing more than cloned presentations hour after hour. He cringed each time he heard of another ASC plan to "manage" the net.

The current buzz was a viral video of Ube Watabee, a Rwanda tribesman trapped by an airwar. The video showed Ube running and falling in front of an advancing airwar. Covered by black tentacles, he unmistakably struggled free without assistance. Although he had a few small scrapes from the fall, he claimed to have suffered no ill effects during his escape. The captivating portion of the video was a close-up of his skin showing no evidence of airwar stings.

John's eyes turned from the computer monitor to the television screen. ASC spokesman, Glavin, was holding a press conference with Senator Snivaling.

"Yes," said Glavin, "I can assure the press that the Ube video is a complete hoax. I'll remind everyone this is an extreme violation of our airwar sedition law. Anyone forwarding or disseminating this video will be arrested and prosecuted."

Glavin looked obsequiously at the senator, then stepped aside. Snivaling took the podium.

"ASC is offering a one-million dollar reward for information leading to the capture of the producers of this sham video," she said, "I'm personally disgusted with the crimes committed. These criminals will be punished swiftly and severely."

John's eyes returned to the computer. A second video of Ube was now surfacing. This time an airwar passed over an upright Ube as he walked through the curtain of tentacles. Ube passed to the other side unscathed. Although John realized this was a hoax, other reports had surfaced with similar claims. Even though it was impossible, the thought of it made John feel good.

John's attention shifted back to the television. Glavin returned to the podium. An aide handed him a red folder and whispered in his ear. Glavin nodded.

"I've just been informed in the last twenty-four hours, total human attacks on airwars decreased thirty percent with a corresponding decline in human fatalities worldwide. Even more exciting is the criminal, Ube Watabee, has been captured. He has fully confessed to the immunity hoax."

A wave of disappointment passed over John.

Glavin continued, "Ube is currently being transferred to an ASC facility. There he'll have psychological testing and a full confession tape will be available in a few hours."

Senator Snivaling, who appeared smugly pleased, leaned to the microphone, "The capture of this horrible man is an important victory in the run, hide, and do no harm battle," she said, "We must fight this as a collective society. One thought, one action, one world, one victory!"

"Dr. Long," interrupted a triage nurse, "there's a man who wants to see you." John looked up from the television. "Says he knows you."

The nurse maintained a stoic look. An unmoving detached countenance graced the faces of the hospital staff. It was the only way to cope with the daily horror.

"He's got a boy with him," she added, then glanced at the floor and shook her head, "He's a stage eight." Then she disappeared from the doorway.

John's stomach knotted up. It was hard enough giving bad news to parents he didn't know, but when he knew the family, he couldn't disassociate himself from the event. It was always heart-wrenching.

ER personnel triaged airwar stings on a one-to-ten rating stage. Children rarely survived a stage five and none survived past a stage seven, even with antitoxin. Matter of fact, due to shortages, ASC protocols banned use of antitoxin on kids above stage six. John hated the rule, but he understood the practicality. On the other hand, government dealt with statistics and he dealt with real people. "For the good of society" rang hollow when dealing with a dying child and the eyes of the parents were on you.

John walked back into the triage area and saw a tall man who appeared to be about forty. He had salt and pepper hair, strands of which were pasted to his forehead from sweat. His white dress shirt was plastered to his body from perspiration, revealing a swimmer's physique. His clothes were disheveled and stained like he'd been rolling on the ground, but he was still wearing a tie. The man was holding a limp figure of a young boy, maybe seven or eight years old.

"Bob!" said John, and motioned to a nearby stretcher, "My God! Bring the boy here."

John couldn't remember Bob's last name, but they both swam at the YMCA Aquatic Center with the master's swim team. John knew Bob and his wife owned a small gift basket business, Bob's Baskets and Balloons. He visited Bob's shop on a weekend a few months back. It was a small storefront in a strip mall near the hospital. Most of what he remembered of the shop was an animated, friendly, freckle-faced boy eager to assist him in his selection. Bob introduced him as his only child, Daniel, with pride only a father could emote.

"John!" said Bob, "I . . . please . . . Daniel needs your help."

John glanced at the limp figure. He was unrecognizable as the boy he met previously. Daniel was lifeless except for labored breathing. His face was red and bloated from stings, and there were large bruises on his swollen arms and legs. The father's eyes welled up in tears. John motioned him toward an empty treatment room. It was the only bit of courtesy John could offer in the busy triage area; just a moment of privacy. As they walked through the threshold of the treatment room door, John said quietly, "I think your wife should hear this as well."

Bob turned now with visible tears running down his cheeks.

"Didn't make it," he said choking the words out, "I couldn't pull her away. I could only save one of them."

Bob sobbed as he gently laid the boy on the treatment table. The yellowed plastic covers over the fluorescent lights suffused the room with a yellow glow, making the ill boy's skin look more sallow than it was in triage. John did a cursory look at the boy while taking his pulse, which was weak and thready. Sadly, John thought, *he didn't even save one.*

John put his hand gently on Bob's shoulder and looked directly into his eyes, "Bob, it hurts to say, but reality is, I can't help your son. He's too far gone. Antitoxin won't work at this stage, but I'll do my absolute best to make him as comfortable as possible."

"I want you to transfuse him," demanded Bob. His face looked as if it had turned to granite.

John, taken aback by the unusual request, paused, then said, "Bob, it doesn't work that way. A blood transfusion wouldn't benefit your son."

"I want you to transfuse him with my blood," said Bob unyielding, "We have the same blood type. Commingle our circulation; transfuse him into me and me into him."

"Bob," said John firmly, "not only would a transfusion not prolong Daniel's life, the toxins in Daniel would certainly kill you as well. The absolute best option for your son is letting me make him comfortable."

Bob responded by reaching into his pocket and pulling out a nine millimeter handgun. He aimed it at John's chest. His hand was trembling. "John, you're a good man, but I'll start shooting if you don't do this for Daniel."

"Put the gun away!" said John, eying the blue-steeled weapon, "If anybody sees that pistol, you'll be labeled a terrorist. Go directly to jail, do not pass go, do not collect $200. Your life will be over."

"If you don't transfuse Daniel, my life is over," replied Bob with a shrug.

"No!" said John, now raising his voice, "you'll carry on, but if I transfuse like you ask, you *will* both die!"

"Wrong!" said Bob, shaking his head stubbornly, "I'm immune to the stings."

John paused for a second and glanced at Bob's exposed skin. No edema, welts, or erythema was present. He had treated numerous heroic individuals who saved others from airwars. The one hallmark of these heroes and heroines was they invariably looked as bad as, or sometimes worse than, the victims they saved.

"You came in contact with tentacles?" questioned John.

"Yeah," replied Bob, "I had to run inside the curtain to get my boy."

"You went inside the curtain and came out?" said John with amazement.

John knew the curtain was the outermost specialized layer of tentacles, which were black like the hydrogen sac. The black tentacles were more mobile than the red inner layers and more toxic. They grabbed and attached to objects on the ground to pull airwars forward. If an immediate death occurred, it was typically due to massive stings from the outer curtain. Although not public knowledge, ASC released information to medical personnel indicating less effective stinging power inside the curtain. The inner tentacles, red to pink in color, although mildly poisonous, were more specialized in binding and lifting.

The outer curtain was the source of contact for most treatable stings largely because those passing to the inner curtain rarely got out alive. A person could wear protective garments, but airwars seemed to sense this and would bind and lift, then drop anyone wearing protective covering from a height of forty to fifty feet. Sometimes repetition of this process occurred until the victim was dead. Of course, there was no reason victims couldn't survive, if rescued, as the screams of victims inside the curtain continued for hours. These screams continued until death or to the point the victim transferred into the digestive chamber.

John looked at the dying boy. He weighed the resolve in the father's eyes against the trouble he'd be in if he agreed. The gun aimed at his chest factored in as well.

"Okay," said John, "I'll do it." He knew he would do the same if it was Cassandra lying there. "But please hide your gun!"

Bob appeared to be studying John's eyes to determine if this was a feint.

"Thank you," said Bob finally, then he handed the gun, butt end toward John.

"You keep it," said John, waving the gun off. Then he smiled and winked at Bob, "Besides, what would I do with another one?"

Bob gave John one brief smile back.

John exited the exam room and returned to the triage area. He knew it would be difficult to set up the transfusion by himself. He couldn't enlist the help of any other medical personnel. If it got out, the procedure would end and Bob would face certain incarceration. In addition, there was the problem of doing a commingled transfusion. He'd never done a direct transfusion; nobody did this in modern medicine. Commingling circulations might be a physiology experiment in a dog lab, but never as a human treatment.

Clearly, there were a list of risks a mile long, but he didn't know what they were, and he didn't have time to look them up. He also knew there would be hell to pay in the end, but he would just point to the dead man's gun and say he was coerced. Hospitals needed doctors too badly to revoke his medical license.

Even in the face of the negatives, John felt exhilarated. He knew he was pushing the limits of medical ethics, but for the first time, he was trying to accomplish something that might make a difference.

He knew deep down the procedure was doomed, but at least it was an attempt. Gathering the equipment for the transfusion took several minutes because he had to do it sub-rosa. Then there was a problem of disappearing an hour from triage without others noticing. Although five other doctors worked triage, his absence would eventually become apparent.

John draped his hand in a hot pack and approached the head triage nurse. Lifting the wrapped hand, he announced, "I just got a secondary. I'm feeling a bit weak. I'm taking an hour break, but I'll be back."

A "secondary" was a sting on medical personnel from tentacle fragments remaining attached to victims. Usually, secondaries were minor injuries due to minimum envenomization. The nurse seemed relieved he was returning after a break. Most personnel took the rest of the day off.

"Dr. Long," said the nurse with concern, "do you want one of the other docs to look at you? I think this is the first secondary you've ever had."

John knew he was a bit unusual in that way. He'd been lucky so far; in fact, the other docs deferred patients with tentacle debris for his evaluation.

"No, I'm fine. The hot pack is working well."

Medical staff used hot packs to denature venom that might remain high in the skin. If you could take the skin temperature to 118.5° F, you could denature one component of the poison, and this was the component responsible for pain.

"I'm holing up in treatment room seven for an hour," said John. "Please don't have anyone disturb me."

The nurse nodded and walked off.

As he rejoined Bob and his son in exam room seven, he placed a *Do Not Enter: Procedure In Progress* sign on the door and removed the hot wrap from his hand. John pushed a gurney with the box full of collected supplies into the treatment room. Bob climbed on a gurney as John hung IVs and tubing. Bob adjusted himself so he and Daniel were lying side by side.

The procedure needed an IV and John had trouble getting it started. The large needle needed for the transfusion, coupled with the swollen skin, required several sticks in the boy. John was out of practice as well. He hadn't started an IV in a decade. He thought in a few more sticks Bob would start reaching for his gun, but Bob looked on with stoic reassurance.

The procedure required two IVs each, one in the radial artery and one in a vein of the same arm. The artery of Bob connected to the vein in Daniel and the vein of Bob to the artery of Daniel. When he connected the tubes, the circulations would commingle. John coupled the tubes, looked at Bob, and said, "Are you sure?"

"Absolutely!" said Bob without hesitation.

John opened each valve and blood shot down the translucent tubes, forcing out the clear saline solution. Within seconds, each line was now supplying blood to the other.

John watched Bob closely for toxic signs, as he knew the venom in Daniel's bloodstream was now entering Bob's body. John figured if airwar toxins didn't kill him, a transfusion reaction would. Amazingly, after five minutes, Bob demonstrated no signs of ill effects and began a casual conversation. The light conversation seemed to ease the tension, but after a few minutes, both seemed to run out of things to say and they sat back in silence, watching Daniel's monitor.

After fifteen minutes of silence, there was a change in the vitals on the monitor. Daniel's pulse dropped from a tachycardic 178 down to a more reasonable 115, and his blood pressure increased from 40/0 to 80/40. The boy groaned.

"I'm getting antitoxin," said John and he stood to leave.

"No!" said Bob, raising his free hand, "He's improving. Let's not change a thing."

John knew they were dancing on the edge anyway, so he nodded agreement. Another twenty-five minutes passed, and the change was nothing short of miraculous. The boy was sitting up, crying in his father's arms. His vitals had almost normalized. He looked like he'd been beaten by a two-by-four, but it was clear he would survive.

"Bob," said John ecstatically, "I've got to let the staff know," he began removing the IVs, "This is a breakthrough. We need to notify ASC immediately. If we determine what this quality in your blood is, we could potentially save tens of thousands of lives. You're the real live Ube, not a hoax."

John was shocked to see Bob vigorously shaking his head. Just then, John's cell phone rang. He glanced at the screen. It was Cassandra. He let the voice mail pick up and made a mental note to call her back.

"No one must know," said Bob.

John was astonished, "For God's sake, why?"

"I'm a member of Mad Mike's Liberty Fighters," said Bob with a hushed voice.

John paled. Mad Mike's Militia was the government's biggest terrorist threat. Reward posters for members hung everywhere. The liberty fighters were reckless in their attacks on airwars. Glavin's press releases excoriated Mad Mike on a daily basis. John could relate to the militia's hatred of airwars, and Mad Mike had many Internet supporters, but their absolute disrespect of authority concerned him.

Bob continued, "Look, I know you think of us as monsters or terrorists, but we believe airwars must be killed not coddled."

"You release thousands more for each one you kill," retorted John.

"Not always. We had two clean kills where no juveniles were released and many others where less than one hundred escaped."

"Somehow it doesn't reassure me to know we're replacing each one with *only* one hundred new ones," said John with a slight amount of sarcasm.

"Well," said Bob, and he began cleaning his son's face with damp gauze, "We're improving."

The boy pulled away as the gauze touched the inflamed skin.

"Dad," whined the boy, "I want to go home."

"In a minute Danny boy," said Bob with a loving smile. He then looked back at John, "The government's idea of run, hide, drop your pants and bend over is worthless," he said.

John gave a slight laugh and replied, "Well, it's certainly not a testosterone-driven strategy, but it seems to be working. In the areas with complete adaptation of the strategy, the death tolls have dropped ninety-five percent."

"So deaths of hundreds rather than thousands are acceptable to you?" said Bob sarcastically, "What the government doesn't say is the Colossi are appearing in huge numbers in areas following policy, and I assure you they're not gentle giants when pissed off. At some point there'll be hell to pay. Don't be an idiot, John."

John felt the irony. Only hours ago he was in Goldman's office saying the same thing. Somehow being called an idiot made him feel obligated to twist himself into defending ASC.

"ASC's best minds believe this is the necessary policy to save lives," said John, but without feeling much conviction.

Bob retorted, "Of course, and if you disagree, ASC kills you. Look, I don't doubt they fully believe in what they're recommending. It seems compassionate; sacrifice the few to spare the masses, but it's reckless compassion and let me tell you, politicians are experts at reckless compassion. In this case, the government isn't fighting. They're doing a victory surrender."

"From what I know, it's the militias who are reckless."

Bob smiled and said, "You only know what ASC tells you under the pretext of preventing panic."

"Well," said John. "Panic isn't on my top ten list of desirable emotions. Bob, you're the key to a much-needed treatment. You may be singular in this respect."

"I'm not," said Bob with a smile.

John looked astonished, "You mean there are others?"

Bob nodded, "I've personally known two others, then there's Ube."

"You think Ube is for real?" said John with disbelief.

"Absolutely!"

"Dad!" interrupted Daniel, "my face burns — bad." His face was cherry red from the stings.

John opened a cabinet and pulled out a white aerosol can of lidocaine spray.

"Close your eyes, Danny," He said and sprayed a light coat over the boy's face, "That should help shortly."

"Thanks, Doctor Long," said Daniel, "It feels better already." He pulled on his dad's tie. "Dad, can we go now?"

"Not yet," said his father.

John looked at Bob and said, "But why on earth would someone cover it up?"

Bob laughed, "Think of it. You can't have a bunch of guys immune to stings thinking they can attack airwars, releasing juveniles all over creation."

"Well, I suppose, but at least you can try to contact ASC."

Bob shook his head and said, "Well, both the guys I mentioned did. Jeff Bowen disappeared with his family at gunpoint in the middle of the night. Steve Able got a late night phone call warning of what happened to Jeff. He left his apartment and went to his neighbor's house, only to see his residence raided by ASC agents. His name appeared on a government terrorist list the next day. He's now with Mad Mike's Liberty Fighters."

"How do you know I won't turn you in?" asked John boldly.

Bob smiled as he picked up his son from the gurney. "Because you're like most, frightened. You want to believe the government can legislate every problem away. That's a comforting thought for the masses because it doesn't require any personal responsibility, but deep down, self-interest motivates us all. You still question whether we're going down the right path. Otherwise, you wouldn't have kept your gun — by the way, my deepest thanks. You've burdened me with a debt I know I can never repay."

John contemplated what Bob said and knew at least part of it was true. He watched in silence as Bob carried his son out of the hospital. The boy gave a slight wave to John as the sliding doors of the ER opened. John realized the remarkable event he experienced would alter the airwar crisis. He just needed to decide how to use the discovery.

CHAPTER 7

THE MORGUE

John's mind was swirling as he tried to digest all that happened. He scribbled notes on a paper attached to a white plastic clipboard. As he walked back to the triage area, the local news interrupted programming with a special report. Hospital monitors displayed news teams tracking airwar attacks near the hospital. As he looked at the screen, he realized several reports were emanating from Cassandra's neighborhood. His pulse quickened as he remembered her comment of spending the day packing at her apartment.

He pulled his cell phone. An unplayed voice message from Cassandra popped on the screen.

"Play message," he commanded the phone.

Cassandra's screaming voice came over the speaker, "Get back. I've got a knife; get back. They're breaking down the door. Help, John, help!" Then the message cut off.

John hollered at the head triage nurse, "Cassandra is being attacked by an airwar." He tossed the clipboard on the nurses station. It slid off, hitting the floor, shattering in several pieces. "I gotta go." He bolted toward the parking lot exit.

On John's arrival at Cassandra's, everything was in chaos. Police, ambulances, injured, dead, and grieving surrounded the apartment complex. A policeman told John three airwars attacked the area. Several residents managed to outrun or otherwise escape. Those who had stings were sitting or lying on the curb of the street, attended to by emergency personnel. Bodies of victims who hadn't survived were lying side by side farther down the road. Gray blankets borrowed from nearby ambulances covered the distorted and swollen faces of the deceased.

John scanned the injured for Cassandra, but she wasn't there. He then jogged over to the dead victims. A police officer started to stop him, but he deferred to John's white coat and his ID badge from the hospital. John could feel the palpitations of his heart as he lifted each blanket from the faces of the ten dead, but Cassandra's wasn't among them.

He sprinted up to her apartment. The threshold was splintered as the door was busted from its hinges. There were obvious signs of a struggle in the living room. Several partially packed cardboard boxes were overturned; their contents strewn over the floor. A kitchen carving knife lay on the floor next to wet streaks of blood. He called her name and checked the entire apartment, including the closets and cabinets. She wasn't there.

John noticed a thin man with stringy long hair and a shaggy beard staggering by the open front door. The man was drenched in sweat. John recognized the man as a resident of one of the apartments near Cassandra's.

"Hey," shouted John, "have you seen the woman living in this apartment? Her name is Cassandra."

The fellow seemed to be in shock.

"I hid . . . all you could do was hide," he babbled, "I heard her scream . . . nothing I could do . . . I was hiding. They would have got me too . . . Must have been a hundred of them." He waved his arms wildly in the air. "They carried off so many . . . I heard her scream . . . yes . . . yes . . . nothing I could do . . . I was hiding."

John grabbed the man by his shoulders and shook him. "Did you see Cassandra?"

The man wiped his forehead on his sleeve and seemed to calm down.

"No," said the man, "I only heard her screaming." He surveyed the mess in the apartment and shuddered, "One of them got her, I'm sure. Airwars carried off twenty or thirty people besides those dropped left for dead."

Then he began to rant about Mad Mike's Liberty Fighters.

"It's their fault. None of this would be happening if we were just to leave them alone. I'm in the Love the Airwars League, for God's sake. I mean them no harm. The government was here. They shot at terrorists and captured at least one. That's why airwars were here! The government needs to protect us from those terrorists. The airwars are gentle animals just wanting to be left alone to live in peace." He stopped his tirade and began sobbing. John, with a dark black hole sucking on his heart, headed back to the hospital.

John waited by the posting wall and kept checking his cell phone. He called in every favor he had with staff and administration trying to locate Cassandra, but her status was unknown. John walked to the temporary morgue, which in reality was a converted gymnasium near the hospital. It had no listing for her.

John tried to talk his way into the morgue, but even as a doctor, the stocky, gray-haired guard denied him access. No deceased relative, no entry, was the policy. The guard at the door was empathetic, but firm.

"Doc, I understand you wanting to search," said the guard, "but there're hundreds of bodies, and even more missing people. We can't handle everyone looking for a loved one prowling around. I assure you every body has a confirmed identity before they're accepted at this morgue. If your friend isn't on the list, then she isn't here."

From the chaos John observed looking through the gym's glass doors, he had little confidence in the precision of the morgue records. John understood the policy, though. Yet, he didn't relish the idea of looking through hundreds of dead bodies. He also maintained hope Cassandra was alive. If she showed up injured at the hospital, he wanted to be there, so he returned to the posting wall. The hourly postings passed one by one, then on the fifth posting, Cassandra's name appeared. *Deceased; ID confirmed.* Darkness closed in.

John awoke to the grim face of Dr. Lee, a new ER doctor just out of residency. His employment at the hospital began a mere six months previously. John was one of the medical personnel who had done his staff appointment interviews. Dr. Lee spoke with some reverence to the more senior staff member he was tending.

"Dr. Long, you went vasovagal on us."

Great, I fainted, thought John, then he remembered the posting and became nauseous.

"Someone bring me an emesis basin STAT!" shouted Dr. Lee. It was too late. John vomited over the side of the gurney. Dr. Lee called out with less intensity, "We need custodial services."

"Sorry," John groaned. His head flopped back on the gurney.

"Nothing a mop can't fix, Dr. Long," said Dr. Lee and put his hand on John's shoulder, "I'm sorry. The entire staff extends their deepest sympathies. Whenever you feel you're up to it, you can leave. We just pulled you straight back, no testing, no paperwork involved."

John nodded understanding. Paperwork had become 95% of medicine these days. ASC just added another level of paperwork with the airwar toxicity swab. Every patient who came through the hospital received an oral swab; if positive, quarantine officers took them to offsite holding stations. It was the most stupid ASC edict. A five-page form was required on every positive. In John's experience, the extremely rare positives for the toxicity test always appeared the healthiest. If they wanted truly toxic people, they should check the morgue.

Several screams from down the hallway interrupted John's thoughts. A small mob rushed in through the triage door and knocked a man off his gurney. The man writhed on the floor as the newcomers shrieked for help.

"Dammit!" said Dr. Lee, "Dr. Long, I've got to run. New batch of victims." He paused, then added, "Oh, by the way, Goldman in administration said take all the time off you need, but the S.O.B. also asked if you could keep it to one day, since we're in crisis mode." Dr. Lee darted down the corridor.

John, with his head in a dark fog, stumbled back the two blocks to the morgue. The same stocky guard was there. John showed him a copy of the posting. The guard glanced at John's name tag on his white lab coat.

"Says here the deceased's last name is Shelly," said the guard, "Your name is Long. You related?"

John tried to speak, but the grief was overwhelming. Words wouldn't come out. The guard appeared to soften as he saw the anguish on John's face.

"Never mind," said the guard, "go on in." He pulled the door open for John to enter.

Inside, John was almost overcome with the smell of decomposing bodies. Clearly some had resided in the morgue too long without embalming. A squirrelly, short man wearing a long lab coat and safety glasses approached him. The man held a clipboard binding hundreds of pages. He looked at John and said in a mechanical voice, "Morgue concierge . . . sorry for your loss . . . name of victim?"

John couldn't speak; he just pointed to Cassandra's name on the posting he held.

The man shuffled through his papers, saying to himself, "Not here . . . not here . . . not here either . . . She doesn't seem to be on the log in list."

He paused for a moment, looking somewhat perplexed; he checked the name again on John's sheet.

"Great, this is putting me behind," he mumbled.

Then his face brightened and he pulled out some blue papers rolled up in his back pocket. He thumbed through the new papers and his face lit up in a beaming smile.

"Ah, here she is, on the ASC autopsy list," he said, "Thought I'd have to do a manual check. Takes forever, you know. Dodged another bullet, I did." Then he laughed.

John didn't see the humor in his situation. He gave the concierge a hard glare.

The concierge returned to his mechanical voice, "Row twenty-three, gurney K, do *not* remove items or body parts without an attendant." He turned abruptly and walked to a crying woman who had just arrived, "Morgue concierge . . . sorry for your loss . . . name of victim?"

John began moving down the many rows looking for row twenty-three. The rows, in keeping with current government efficiency, had no visible numbers, so he began counting. When he came to the twenty-third row, he went down to the gurney with the letter K. He couldn't help but notice he was standing under a basketball goal. Black sheets of plastic looking like over-sized garbage bags covered all the bodies on the gurneys. John took a deep breath and pulled the covering back. Underneath laid the naked body of a large, bloated African-American male with a full beard and a number of tattoos. John began cursing loudly.

A young male attendant wearing a short white lab jacket ran up to him.

"Sir," he said in a nasally voice, "I empathize with your loss, but please, no profanity here. Others are in mourning as well."

"Sorry, I lost control," said John, looking around at the scores of other mourners. He felt bad about his outburst.

The red-headed, freckle-faced attendant smiled and said, "That's okay. I understand." He looked at the man on the table and said to John, "Was he your significant other?"

"No," responded John curtly, "I don't know who this is."

"Well, it can be difficult to identify loved ones after airwar stings," said the attendant, smiling empathically, "You may want to look for a familiar mark or perhaps a piece of jewelry you recognize." He pointed to a flaming snake tattoo in the man's genital area, "Do you recognize this?"

"No!" John angrily replied, "I'm looking for my fiancé." He paused and added with emphasis, "*A woman.*"

The attendant looked confused and said, "Sir, this is a man."

John bit his tongue and said in a slow steady voice, "I'm trying to find my fiancé who's supposedly in row twenty-three on gurney K, *a woman.*"

"This is row twenty-four," said the attendant with a knowing smile, "You need the previous row."

John was sure he counted correctly, "Are you sure? I took great care in my counting."

"Yeah," said the attendant, still smiling, "but you probably counted row thirteen, and we have no row thirteen. Our senior administrator thinks it's bad luck. Don't know why; people in this place are just as lucky on row twelve as thirteen. I think—"

A shriek of anguish interrupted him. Three rows away a thin middle-aged woman had just located her son.

The attendant continued to rattle on undisturbed. "I think he does it so people are always begging for more attendants. The more attendants under him, the more power he has. Two days ago, Pete advised him he could reduce attendants by eighty percent if the rows got numbered and added a row thirteen. He fired Pete. So I guess, indirectly, row thirteen is bad luck. Anyway, it's job security for me," he said and smiled a big grin.

John got a feeling he was in a horrible, surreal dream. He wanted to scream, but he held his composure. He looked at the attendant and asked, "Could you please take me to my Cassandra?"

John stood with the attendant at row twenty-three, gurney K. He reached and pulled back the black plastic cover over the body. Lying before him was a badly bruised and swollen body of a female. John knew if he hadn't been a physician and hadn't experienced multiple autopsies in the past, he would have probably passed out again. During an autopsy, pathologists remove the brain by cutting the scalp and peeling it back over the face. Then a saw slices the skullcap, which is popped off, exposing the brain. They hadn't bothered to pull the scalp back or to replace the cutoff skullcap. John reached to pull the scalp back off the face, but the attendant grabbed his arm. John stopped, looked at the attendant, and said, "I've got to be sure," and the attendant released his grip.

The face revealed was grotesque and twisted from bruising and swelling. He looked at the misshapen body. It looked like Cassandra, but the numerous contusions made it difficult. He was trying to think of identifying moles or marks, but then he noticed a shiny object on the ring finger. It was a heart-shaped diamond sandwiched between two rubies. It was the engagement ring given to her on their trip. John's heart sank. He again felt a dark hollowness in his soul as the last bit of hope expired.

John started to remove the ring, and the attendant cleared his throat, "Ah, doctor . . . umm . . . you need to leave the ring. I'll need it in the future . . . umm, I mean . . . for further ID."

John noticed the attendant slip his hand into his lab coat pocket as he was saying this, almost as if he was reassuring himself something was there. John thought he heard high-pitched sounds of metallic objects bumping together.

John stopped and moved slightly toward the attendant, who had now removed his hand from his pocket. John suddenly shoved his own hand in the attendant's lab coat pocket and retrieved several rings, necklaces, and other small jewelry items. John defiantly held the jewelry up in the face of the attendant, then put them back in the attendant's pocket. He then went back to Cassandra's body and began removing the ring. The attendant started to back away as if he was leaving.

"Wait!" said John brusquely, "I'm not finished with you."

The attendant stopped and looked like a dog caught crapping on the living room rug. John resisted the urge to slug the fellow in the gut.

"Why was Cassandra autopsied?" demanded John.

"Are you going to tell?" said the attendant with his head hung low, "I only *borrow* from those without families. I didn't know she had a fiancé. That's not listed in the records. The others will take from anyone, not me." He lifted his head and stuck out his chest, giving it a thump, as if he were proud of his disclosure.

"So you believe your ill deeds are excused by more wicked actions done by others?" John said with a steely stare.

The attendant looked at him blankly.

John, frustrated, angry, and not at the moment interested in getting in a discussion of morality, said, "Forget it. Tell me what I want to know about Cassandra."

The attendant looked around to see if anyone was within earshot. The middle-aged woman was three rows away, but she was weeping so loudly over her son, she presented no danger of hearing their conversation.

"Some bodies come in tagged *airwar death*," said the attendant in a low voice, "and they've all been autopsied by ASC as part of a study. ASC wants to avoid any public backlash from the random autopsies, so we can't mention them. She must have been logged in through the ASC receiving room because she still had a ring on."

"Her engagement ring," said John as his eyes started to water up.

"Whatever," said the attendant with a shrug, "If she came through the standard check in, I assure you she'd have been divested of her ring long before she got to this main holding area." He patted the pocket of his lab jacket containing the stolen items. "The ASC bodies like your fiancé are always the worst. We leave the jewelry items on just in case a relative shows up for ID, but we always remove them on checkout before burial. You won't find any report on her death other than the tag on the toe."

The attendant bent and read the toe tag aloud, "Airwar Death," and he glanced back at the body, "The bad ones look pretty much the same."

John was acutely aware of this fact as he sent many a victim to this very morgue. He wiped his eyes with his hand and appeared to have regained his composure. "Okay, what about the study? What was ASC looking for?"

"How the hell should I know?" said the attendant, "I'm just a minimum wage dead body clerk," and he sarcastically added, "ASC doesn't report to me on a regular basis regarding their classified studies."

John frowned at the attendant. The attendant assumed a cowering stance, realizing he over-stepped the line.

"Leave me!" ordered John, and he dismissed the attendant with a flick of his hand. John figured at this point it didn't matter what kind of autopsy data ASC was collecting. He only hoped their findings would help end the crisis.

John proceeded to a large window counter at the back of the morgue. A sign above it read *Gym Equipment Check out and Towel Return*. A notice on white poster board was taped below the sign. *Victim Deposition* was handwritten in black marker. Behind the counter working on a computer was a short, obese woman in her late forties. Her blonde hair was done in a bee-hive hairdo. She looked at John over her reading glasses and motioned for him to hand her the posting.

"I'm here to make arrangements for my fiancée," said John, handing her the death posting.

Without a word she looked at the posting page and began typing on the computer.

"Deposition has already been arranged," said the clerk without looking up from the monitor," the body is to be cremated tonight."

"Who made the arrangements?" John said with surprise.

The clerk glanced at John's hospital ID badge, then looked back at the monitor, "Are you her stepbrother?"

"No," said John. "I'm her fiancée."

"Well," she said with a slight annoyance in her voice, "her stepbrother, who is listed as next of kin, made the provisions already."

"Could you give me his contact information?" said John, "The number I have for him doesn't work."

The clerk frowned as she saw the line forming behind him.

"Look, doc," she said, now clearly irritated, "all my records say is, arrangements by stepbrother. There's no contact information listed. Your name is not on her file, so I couldn't give you contact details even if I had them. Now, if you don't mind, others are waiting." The clerk motioned to the lady behind John to move forward.

John stepped aside and pulled out his cell phone. He tried the one number he had for Chunky. An out of service signal was all he could get. In a way, John was relieved he didn't have to inform Chunky. Although John wanted to arrange a private funeral and burial, he didn't feel like fighting over the deposition of the body. At this point it wouldn't make a difference to Cassandra. He shuffled out of the hospital in the black shroud of night, not caring what he might meet in the darkness on his way home.

CHAPTER 8

PASSIVE WARRIORS

John arrived at his condominium shortly after midnight. He couldn't sleep. At six a.m. he took 20mg of diazepam, causing him to doze for the next twenty-four hours. For the next week he remained absent to the world, not leaving his condominium. Multiple calls from the hospital were ignored. He lived on Ramen noodles, diazepam, and root beer.

On the eighth day he finally broke free from his sedative-induced haze. He began walking to get away from the condominium and the various reminders of Cassandra. His appearance looked more like a homeless druggie than a successful physician as he wandered downtown. His hair was unkempt, his eyes swollen and red from crying. He wore nothing but flip-flops, a light blue t-shirt, and matching surfing shorts, which he'd slept in for the last week.

John's emotions swung repeatedly between grief and absolute rage. After a couple of hours, only from pure Brownian motion, he ended up at Lake Eola in the downtown park. The giant central fountain was flowing in the twenty-acre lake framed by an early morning cloudless blue sky. It seemed bizarre, with the world in crisis. Somewhere, some way, someone was making sure the fountain ran. He could take no joy in its beauty today as blackness crowded out any pleasant feelings.

In front of him, several hundred "passive warriors" from the "Love the Airwar League" had cast their clothes aside. With the exception of pumpkin orange arm and headbands, the passive warriors all laid prostrate on the ground, completely naked. This display was presumably to demonstrate passive unity in the city to the airwars.

Over the last few days, airwars had been using the lake as a drinking station. The airwars would glide over the water surface, let down a tube called the central siphon and take on water. ASC discovered airwars electrolyzed water into hydrogen and oxygen. Electrocytes, similar to those found in electric eels, were contained in specialized tentacles. These long serial arrays created voltages needed for electrolysis in small organs under the hydrogen sac. The sac collected hydrogen, and oxygen was released. Lighter than air, hydrogen allowed the creatures to remain airborne similar to early zeppelins.

John thought of the televised press conference the night before. It was the first time he watched television in over a week. ASC spokesman Glavin was at the podium. "For the last two days the heroic members of the Love the Airwar League have placed themselves in the paths of airwars coming to drink," said Glavin.

A B-roll clip of airwars passing over the unclothed bodies was shown.

"As you can see, the airwars are lifting their tentacles to avoid these *passive warriors*," said Glavin, grinning widely, "This is a remarkable confirmation that our Run, Hide and Do No Harm policy is the correct path to follow." He raised his arms to the heavens.

John reached for the remote, but before he could turn the television off, Glavin pointed directly at the screen.

"Should one err and join the militia filth—this is what happens," said Glavin, with vitriol.

Clips from the Zimbabwe Colossus video started running. John turned the television off with disgust. The last thing he wanted to watch was a lecture on how to get along with airwars . . .

Now, absolute rage replaced the black despair. He loathed airwars. He wanted to kill, but he knew the futility in that action.

Ultimately, he wanted fewer, not more, airwars. He hung his head again and felt impotent as melancholy returned.

A middle-aged man with a gray beard wearing only round, wire-framed glasses and an orange wristband called to him, "Brother, shed your clothes and become a passive warrior with us. The key to victory is passivity."

John turned and walked away. Somehow, lying naked in the paths of airwars didn't seem a great strategy, even though it was the current politically correct action.

As John was winding his way through all the naked bodies, he noticed several airwars appearing between buildings on the edge of the lake. The reflection of the sun off the water through the trees gave a greenish aura along the edges of the black airwars. The aura appeared similar to the corona discharge seen in Kirlian photography. The first group of five passed over the horizontal bodies without incident. As one in a second group began to reach the water's edge, three large solid black vans screeched to a halt on the road next to the lake.

Several militiamen, wearing fatigues with American flag armbands and their faces covered with black sock hats, jumped from the van. The men and women all carried automatic weapons. In unison, the group aimed at an airwar and released a deadly hail of projectiles into the airwar's hydrogen sac. The airwar's sac immediately caught fire, but not before hundreds of coal-black juveniles released into the air.

The terrorists continued a stream of fire into the air and juveniles were popping and disappearing like bubbles in the wind. John counted; he could only detect three floating out of range. The burning carcass made John smile even though he knew three more would replace it. Still, he had to admit he enjoyed the show. The "passive warriors" had begun to sit and were screaming profanities at the militia. John thought, *perspective is the only difference between a hero and a terrorist.*

As he continued to watch, John felt a deep vibration. As sound added itself to the vibration, he realized it was a large, gray Apache helicopter. He looked forward to seeing more burning airwar carcasses, but the flying vehicle passed several of the black monstrosities without engaging them.

The "terrorists" were back in their vans as the helicopter approached. Two rockets abruptly fired from the helicopter. One directly hit the middle van, which immediately exploded into a fireball. The other hit the sidewalk, shearing off a hydrant, which resulted in a strange scene of smoke and fire surrounding a fountain of water.

The other vans, wheels shrieking, sped away in opposite directions. The helicopter followed the left van, creating unusual vortexes in the smoke and spraying water as it passed. Then both the pursuer and pursuee went around a building and were lost to sight, but machine gun fire could be heard for the next few seconds, followed by one explosion.

Most of the "passive warriors" were now sitting or standing, watching the end of the spectacle. They all seemed to turn as a single unit as one solitary scream pierced the air.

A twenty-something, red-headed female wearing nothing but an orange headband and a peace sign necklace was entwined in tentacles, but she wasn't screaming. Her mouth was making movements like a goldfish out of water. No sound, only frothy sputum came from her lips. The scream came from her tall blonde friend who could pass for a runway model. She also wore an identical headband and necklace and stood less than five feet from her entrapped friend.

The scream was short-lived as tentacles engulfed the blonde. From that point on, it was madness. On one side floated scores of airwars, on the other was the lake, and sandwiched between were hundreds of "passive warriors." The passive warriors, now no longer passive, were running helter skelter, naked and panicked.

It was a phantasmagoric dance of black with orange. Adding the running, naked bodies to the dancing colors made John think the sight would have been quite comical, except there were injured and dying people everywhere. John, for a few moments, disassociated himself from the scene, but a shadow passed over him and he realized he was in grave danger himself.

As with the passive warriors, his position was also between the airwars and the lake. Unlike the others, John ran toward the lake. For him, water was safety. He could easily swim out to the middle, outflank the airwars, then run to safety. He kicked off his flip-flops as he was running and stripped away his light blue shirt. He was still wearing surfing shorts, and this wouldn't slow him down too much in the water.

As he ran into the bluish-tinged water, he noticed airwars were floating above the lake, tentacle tips barely touching the lake surface. The airwars weren't in his planned escape path, though. As his head dipped below the water surface, the screams behind him seemed to vanish into a muffled background of moving water.

The water enveloped his body, which gave him a sense of security that he didn't feel on the land. He remembered a poster Cassandra had given him for his birthday, a picture of a swimmer doing butterfly. The inscription read, *The meek may inherit the earth, but they'll never rule the water.* The thought of Cassandra and his loss began fueling a raging anger. He lifted his head to get a directional bearing, but all he could see was an advancing curtain of black tentacles. The tentacles parted somewhat, revealing a red inner layer.

With a defiant curse, he put his head down and swam straight forward, infuriated, toward the red. He had no plan. He was only enraged. He felt a tentacle pass over his back. He waited for stings, but none occurred. Tentacles loosely grabbed at his extremities, but wetness of his body, coupled with slime on the tentacles, allowed him to release himself easily.

It was dark in the middle of the airwars tentacles, not pitch black, but like dusk. Only a small amount of reflecting light passed through the hundreds of tentacles.

Then he heard a sucking sound. A bubble gum pink tentacle with linear striations its entire length, dissimilar to other tentacles, was touching the water's surface. It was the diameter of a fire hose, and the base flared like a funnel. The tube's expanded end engulfed water, and a peristaltic wave carried the water as a one-foot diameter bulge up the tube. It looked like a hanging boa constrictor that swallowed a basketball, and the basketball was ascending through the inside of the snake.

This must be the central siphon, thought John. He grabbed the tube and figured if he was dying anyway, why not agitate the creature along the way?

A bolus of water entered the end of the tube just below where John wrapped his arms and now his legs. *If I can't kill it, at least I can make it thirsty,* thought John. Instead of blocking the bulge of water, the swelling pushed him up the slippery tube. Riding the wave was like sliding up a fire station pole. After a relatively quick sixty-foot ride, he almost lost his grip when his body slammed into what felt like a giant sac of wet flour.

He looked over. It was a lifeless naked man suspended in air adjacent to the siphon tube. The blow caused the body to rock back and forth in the cradling red tentacles.

As he passed the body, he looked up and realized he was nearing the end of his ride. The airwar siphon ended in a water storage chamber that resembled a giant pink cow's udder covered with thousands of narrow elongated teats. It was the size of a large bathtub.

Adjacent to it was a large deep purple sphincter, slowly dilating. The sphincter opened into a purple sac-like structure, slightly larger than a minivan.

On the opposite side was a translucent white five-foot tube, six inches in diameter, which looked like a corrugated drainage pipe. It hung from what appeared to be fleshy bellows the size of an extra large sofa. The tube maintained a pipe-like appearance by rings in the wall along its length. It reminded him of a giant trachea. In man, rings of cartilage support windpipe walls to keep the lumen from collapsing. Air rushed in and out of the tube each time the bellows compressed.

John realized, when the traveling bulge finally entered the water chamber, he would slide back down the siphon until he hit the next bolus of water. He doubted he'd be able to maintain his grip if this happened. As he reached the base of the water chamber, he let go with one hand and grabbed the air tube.

Between rings, the translucent membrane was compressible. He pressed down and in with his fingers, getting a grip on one of the rings. The membrane was flexible and didn't tear. Although rubbery in consistency, it wasn't slick like the siphon tube.

As the water entered the chamber, the bulge disappeared, and he started sliding back down. His grip on the air tube stopped his downward progression. He released his other arm and got another handhold on the air tube. Now he lay at an angle under the airwar, hands gripping near the top of the air tube, legs wrapped around the siphon tube.

He gave a couple of tugs on the air tube and it seemed to be able to support his weight. In one last move, he released his legs and swung entirely to the air tube. He pressed his toes between the membranes above the lowest ring. The bottom ring was thickest; he could rest his entire weight on it securely. He hung there for a moment and thought, *now what*?

He looked down through darkness. He could barely see water below. If he fell from this height, he might survive hitting feet-first. Otherwise, a seventy-five foot drop into water was like striking concrete if you didn't punch an entry hole. The collision would knock him unconscious and he'd drown.

John took time to study the central base where he was hanging. The siphon tube and water chamber were in the center. On the opposite side, the sphincter opened wider. It began to emit a purple phosphorescent glow. Unfortunately, he learned the reason why at that moment.

The previously encountered body arrived at the opening. The sphincter began the process of slowly sucking it up, legs first. The lifeless corpse suddenly had one last spasmodic opposition to being swallowed. An arm wearing an orange wristband pounded violently on the purple sphincter without effect. The body sucked upward until only the head remained out of the opening.

John looked directly in the upside-down face of the man. He recognized him as the gray-haired passive warrior who had invited John to join him only minutes before. When the man appeared to notice John, he said nothing, but an expression of surprise and confusion merged with terror. With a loud pop, the head disappeared through the sphincter.

A green, gelatinous substance extruded out the sphincter and dripped as the glowing, purple sphincter clamped down. John, paralyzed from horror, could only watch as walls of the digestive chamber moved with the struggle of the passive warrior. The entire digestive chamber phosphoresced an intense purple, which began to fade as the struggle slowed to a standstill.

From John's estimate of the digestive chamber size, it could hold between eight and ten bodies. This explained why airwars let some bodies hang in the tentacles and if there were too many, why they would drop others to the ground.

Thanks to John's medical experience, he was able to disassociate himself from the previous drama. He immediately shifted his full attention to his own dire situation. On closer inspection, the bellows seemed to have many branching tubes spreading to all areas of the external hydrogen sac, like veins on a leaf. The base of the water chamber was smooth at the siphon entrance. Two feet out from the entrance, tiny worm-like tentacles hung like thousands of earthworms. These covered the entire water chamber base.

John reached out and grabbed the fringe of miniature tentacles. They weren't slippery or wet, nor did they move. Some ruptured and popped when he squeezed hard. As the small gas pockets burst in the worm-like appendages, the sound reminded him of popping that occurs when breaking air blisters in bubble wrap.

John thought, *These must be the organs that electrolyze water into hydrogen and oxygen.* Squeezing these firmly provided a good handhold. He felt, if he had to, he could move around under the airwar sac, holding on to the fringe while wrapping his legs around either the air tube or siphon tube.

John also observed, in the clear area surrounding the siphon tube's entrance, four smooth softball-sized lumps equidistant apart, like cardinal points on a compass. He had no clue to their function.

John noticed the airwar finished taking on water, or at least peristaltic boluses stopped ascending. He was thinking of sliding down the siphon tube when it suddenly coiled.

The tightly curled tube was seven to eight feet in diameter and looked like a large coiled fire hose. It hung three to four feet beneath the base of the water chamber. John reached one leg over and pushed on top of the coil. It didn't budge.

Holding onto the mass of appendages in the fringe, he swung, put both feet on top of the coil, and pushed down. The coil didn't unwind. He slid one arm down around the four-foot section of siphon tube, which was the neck between the water chamber and coil. He straddled the coil and sat down.

It looked like he was riding a velocipede, the old style bicycle with one large front wheel. After a few moments, it was evident the siphon wasn't going to uncoil from his weight, and he decided to move back to the air tube.

Once he was securely on the air tube, he began to reanalyze his situation. The only way down besides jumping was sliding down the siphon as it uncoiled. It might be another 24 hours before the airwar took on water again.

How could he better secure himself? He was wearing surf shorts and nothing else. His phone was long gone, and his wallet and keys were lost during his swim and aerobatics. The shorts did have a drawstring made of a cotton cord. He thought he might be able to secure this for a better handhold. John figured it was better for his shorts to fall than him. He pulled out the cord and looped it around the air tube.

He began pulling the cord tight, which reduced its diameter between two support rings. The whooshing sound of air passing through the breathing tube changed to a higher pitch. As the cord tightened, the pitch of the airflow became a high whistle. When he constricted the lumen to a diameter of a couple of centimeters, the airwar started jerking. Tentacles began writhing spasmodically. John smiled maniacally and thought, *So you like breathing, Mr. Airwar?*

He wrapped the cord around his wrist several times and pulled hard. The loop constricted, blocking all airflow. The bellows kept contracting, at a rapid pace, but no air passed.

Below John, tentacles were writhing like a pit of snakes that had hot grease poured on them. The bellows pumped so furiously, small tears at the base of the hydrogen sac formed. He could hear a steady hissing. John held fast, never releasing his tight grip on the cord.

John estimated less than three minutes passed since wrapping the cord around the air tube. The last twitching of tentacles had ceased two minutes before. The coil of the water siphon suddenly released downward. John thought this would be his chance to escape, but he didn't want to release his chokehold yet. His dilemma ended when he noticed the sensation of descending.

He looked down. The airwar was gently floating toward the water. The only sound was the hissing tears in the hydrogen sac where the bellows attached. The sac was losing hydrogen at a rate fast enough for the airwar to drift downward. He wrapped the cord around the air tube a few more times, tied a knot, then looked for an exit point.

From above, lifeless tentacles looked like a plate of giant red spaghetti on the water's surface. He didn't want to end up trapped between tentacles and the hydrogen sac base. As the airwar's breathing tube descended to fifteen feet above the water, John saw an opening between the tentacles and dropped through. The drop plunged him several feet under water, then he began swimming.

As he looked toward the surface, it was obvious the mass of tentacles was blocking his exit. John swam at least twenty meters, then began to see flickers of light between tentacles. He aimed at a sliver of light and dolphin-kicked hard, forcing two tentacles to the side and passed through the interface to air. After several breaths, he resubmerged, swam fifteen more meters underwater and popped out to a tentacle-free surface.

As it was, he ended up only ten meters from shore. Although airwars were visible in the distance, the attack was over and they appeared to have moved on. General mayhem was occurring around the lake, which was typical following an airwar attack, but the developing crowd in front of him seemed unusual. As he stepped from the water, the crowd cheered.

For a moment, he didn't understand the reason for cheers, then he looked back at the floating airwar carcass. He suddenly realized he single-handedly killed an airwar. The sac was deflated, but intact, and not one solitary juvenile was released.

Not knowing how to respond, he waved to the crowd and shrugged. The cheers heightened. He noticed several cameras, phones, and video cameras aimed his way. He thought, *I'll be on the Internet shortly if I'm not live now. I guess I'm the next Ube.* Five armed marines pushing through the crowd immediately broke that thought.

"Sir, you must come with us!" ordered the largest, a sergeant with a chiseled body who was sporting a blond flat-top haircut.

A marine on either side grabbed his arms firmly, while the other two created a path in the crowd with pointed rifles. The sergeant, pistol drawn, ran point directly in front of him. The crowd began to boo. The marines walked, half-carrying John to a large gray-colored military van with side doors that slid open at his approach. John hesitated entering for a moment, but found himself lifted and shoved through the opening as the doors slid shut behind him.

CHAPTER 9

ADMIRAL BECKWOURTH

Admiral J.P. Beckwourth ran one of the Navy's most successful recruiting campaigns. Perhaps this wasn't too surprising because his family owned one of the largest public relations firms in the Los Angeles area. As a public relations prodigy as a young man, he delivered two multimillion-dollar accounts to the family business at the age of eighteen.

His parents were devastated when he left the firm to join the Navy. His namesake, a relative several generations removed, never received deserved recognition for serving his country. This remained a sore point with the family. However, Beckwourth made good use of his PR talents and rose rapidly up the ranks. Now, after nearly thirty years in the Navy, they were proud of "our son, the Admiral." In the public relations arena of swaying opinion, he followed one rule—find what people want and deliver it.

Admiral Beckwourth had a problem. Only a few days previous, he was recruited to the directorship of ASC public relations. His duties now included curing all accumulated headaches of ASC.

Previously as a non-ASC naval officer, he ran some successful propaganda campaigns for the High Council. During the same period, internally produced ASC propaganda efforts were failures. His vocal criticisms of those programs, coupled with his successes, earned him an offer to become an ASC member.

He was now privy to all behind-the-scenes machinations, and only then were his eyes opened. The added knowledge was horrifying. When ASC High Council members approached him, they were concerned with his reaction, or perhaps, loyalty.

Other public relations leaders had declined recruitment and ASC extremely desired the Admiral's expertise. The recruiters needed not worry. The Admiral was a master at grasping the big picture. As the ASC master plan was unveiled, he easily made his choice. He realized he'd be required to do disturbing, morally reprehensible activities while accomplishing his goal. ASC made clear his only option was to succeed, and in this goal, he was in total agreement.

New information made him realize he'd have to revamp all of his original opinions and strategies. Ignorance, or even willful ignorance, allows for rejection of responsibility. Knowledge obliges burden of duty. It was clear the task was to be borne on his shoulders alone.

The High Council members who brought him onboard said, "These are our goals. This is what's not happening; now fix it. Our survival, and now yours, depends on it!"

Admiral Beckwourth had little respect for politicians. The current situation cemented his views. However, this was a world crisis of a singular nature. He guessed in an odd way he should be grateful he was chosen because no one else inside ASC was capable of performing the responsibility he accepted on himself.

The government's Run, Hide, Do No Harm campaign was a miserable failure. Even though ASC completely controlled the press and their propaganda fund made presidential campaign budgets appear to be pocket change, only fifteen percent of the population embraced it. Seventy percent remained undecided, but could be swayed. Using the incessantly played ASC cant, "Save our children, don't assault airwars," he maintained shaky support. The problem was the remaining fifteen percent were strong individualists. Not only were they opposed to centralized world government, nearly all militias' ranks came from this group. Furthermore, the militias were responsible for ninety-nine percent of attacks on airwars. Thanks to the Internet, militias organized quickly after the first airwar appearance.

The hastily formed ASC wisely decided not to call their leadership a "world government," although essentially it served as such.

Their biggest challenge was their inability to rein in the militias. Countries like North Korea and China, which controlled Internet locally, didn't have an issue. However, in free countries, ASC couldn't censor the Internet as they did radio and television.

Before the crisis, the admiral considered governmental interference with the Internet a direct attack on freedom. He always feared the general public wouldn't fully recognize the Internet's importance as a pillar of liberty and would lackadaisically cede control to pernicious government regulations. Ironically, with the admiral assuming his current position, the Internet had become a giant pain in the ass for him.

ASC clearly wanted him to reduce militias' attacks on airwars. This was currently their top priority. The admiral smiled to himself. The extraordinary ability of militias to avoid ASC-controlled military campaigns served to make ASC more dependent on a public relations alternative.

The admiral sat at his computer doing data crunching. He needed something militias wanted, supplementary to what he could provide now. He was looking for a bargaining chip to influence their behavior, but he wasn't sure what militias craved.

As columns of data streamed across the screen, he noticed a couple of aberrations on the hourly attack on airwar numbers. There were two significant drops in militia attacks on airwars, each for a few hours. It was a worldwide effect. Why was that? He tried to correlate this to releases of different ASC propaganda ads, but there were no causal relationships to dips.

Oddly, he found a direct correlation to the media account of Ube Watabee's capture and exposure of his immunity hoax. He knew the account was an outright lie because he wrote the report himself. However, the dip in militia activity didn't make sense. Why would this particular headline make militias less likely to attack? The admiral reasoned it must be something else. He double-checked his data, but it remained the only event correlating to the drop.

He paged Captain Howe in the data room. The data room had fifty staff members continuously crunching numbers for any trends the admiral might need. "Howe, get me the most commonly searched word on the Internet during dips on airwar attacks."

Only moments later, Captain Howe's voice came over the phone with a one-word response, "Ube."

The admiral frowned. The answer was clearly Ube and he kept trying to reframe the question to understand the answer. Coming up blank, he did a routine check of ongoing stats. He was shocked. Current attacks on airwars had suddenly bottomed out. Worldwide, it was the lowest hourly attack count yet.

He was exhilarated. He knew he'd get credit for the drop even though it wasn't his doing, nor had he a clue to the cause.

He checked the news; no breaking stories and nothing on Ube. Plus, anything new would have crossed his desk long before airing. He looked again at the Ube numbers. He noticed the Ube report release time was at the nadir of the second dip. The plunge in attacks started hours before. He then had a thought; if it's not our media, it must be the Internet.

Admiral Beckwourth logged onto a highly visited, but "illegal" anti-airwar blog. He selected the most recently posted video. A man was emerging from the water, and a collapsed airwar floated in the background.

While he was viewing the video, Colonel Vickers entered the admiral's office. Colonel Vickers, assigned by the Air Force to aid Beckwourth during the crisis, was a no-nonsense military type. He wasn't an ASC member, nor was anyone else under Admiral Beckwourth's command. The colonel rarely spoke and never smiled, but he followed orders with military precision.

The colonel looked to be in his mid-forties. He maintained a short-cropped military haircut with beginnings of gray showing in the temples. He kept himself in good shape, and appeared not the type one would want to pick a fight with in a bar.

The admiral motioned to Vickers to join him watching the video, but before he could walk around the desk, the admiral's phone rang. Beckwourth checked the caller ID, then answered.

"Yeah, I'm watching the video now. Did he actually kill it?"

Colonel Vickers, privy to only the admiral's side of the conversation, stood silently.

"Any word on how he did it?"

"Well, I'll be a son of a bitch! If we'd all known that in the beginning, maybe we wouldn't be in this situation."

Colonel Vickers began to move to the door, but the admiral held up a finger, indicating he wanted him to wait in the office. The admiral continued speaking.

"Okay, don't panic! This isn't a disaster; it's fantastic!"

"The hell you say! Have him brought in here."

"I don't care what they want, I'm running this end of the show and if they don't like it, they can kiss my ass!" Vickers flinched slightly as the admiral's clinched fist suddenly pounded the desk.

"Bring me that Ube guy, too"

"Stewart did what? . . . Frickin' idiots surround me!" The admiral looked at Vickers, mouthed the words, not you, and continued speaking.

"Okay, what about our Immunes?"

"Okay, good. I'm emailing you parameters. Bring those meeting the criteria to me."

"Well, tell them they weren't prisoners. Tell them it was a quarantine for their own protection. Then tell them they're heroes."

"Yeah, I know all about foreign purges—I argued against them vociferously. The extractions make me cringe and are nothing more than inhumane torture. An hour ago I didn't have power to stop the purging or processing, but now I do." He hung up the phone.

Admiral Beckwourth smiled and thought, *I may be the greatest PR guy in the world.* He scribbled on a notepad, handed it to Colonel Vickers, and said, "Get started on this. I'll explain later."

Without a single question, Vickers saluted and exited the room. The admiral picked up the phone. He had several other calls to make. This was going to piss people off because he was about to crap on the current ASC dogma. He didn't care. This plan would work. The High Council would be happy and he'd get breathing room. He punched a speed dial.

"Yes, this is Admiral Beckwourth," he said into the phone, "I need to speak to the senator . . . yes, it's an emergency."

CHAPTER 10

TERRORIST

After manhandling him into the van, marines grabbed and restrained John. His arms, now folded behind him, had plastic ties binding his wrists. The soldiers patted down his dripping, light blue shorts and, satisfied he didn't have a weapon, backed off, leaving him lying on the floor. A small man in a military uniform with captain's bars on his shoulders spoke in a demanding voice, "Terrorist, where's your gun?"

John thought, *What's going on? Maybe they found his gun hidden in the condominium. They might be trying to entrap him.*

"I have no idea what you're talking about," lied John.

The officer was so furious, he was shaking. He was partially balding, and his comb-over was standing up. As he reached up to smooth it down, he winced. John noticed he had a bandaged left hand and a dressing on the left side of the neck.

"We know you have a gun," said the officer, "Do you know the penalty for owning a gun?"

"You've got the wrong man," said John, "I'm Dr. John Long. I'm an internist and not affiliated with any terrorist group. I see from your injuries you've been in the fray with terrorists, but please don't project militia's defiant actions on me."

"I just saw you attack and kill an airwar," screamed the captain, "You're a terrorist! You know there's a world ban on attacking airwars. WHERE'S YOUR GUN?"

The man's jugulars were bulging so much John thought the captain's neck wound might start bleeding. His fingers were tapping on his gun holstered to his side. He looked as if he was deciding whether to shoot John right then.

"Do you know how many deaths were caused today by the antics of you and your ilk?" the captain said with a shrill voice. "Well, I'll tell you, two hundred, and the toll is rising." His finger flicked the snap of his holster open.

"Sir!" said the sergeant with the flat-top haircut. He spoke with such force the captain hesitated.

"Look, I'm not a part of Mad Mike's Liberty Fighters," interjected John, "Do I look like I came to attack airwars?" He nodded down to point out his still-dripping pale blue shorts, "I clearly don't have a gun."

"So you say," said the captain snidely, "I have a feeling our interrogators will have you singing a different tune in a few hours" and, he added, "That's, of course, if I don't shoot you here and now."

John took a deep breath and tried another approach, "Look, my fiancée was killed by an airwar a week ago. I wandered down to the park and—"

"—you thought, I'll just kill an airwar for revenge?" screamed the captain, "Why, I lost my wife and two sons, and you don't see me attacking airwars." The captain thumped his chest, "I follow the law. I don't create mayhem. I don't cause the birth of thousands of those bastards, but you do."

"There were no juveniles that I saw," said John.

"That's not the point," screamed the captain. "You are . . . are . . ." He seemed lost for the appropriate word, "Gobshite!" The captain pulled his gun from the holster and waved it wildly in the air.

John wanted to wake up from the nightmare. The whole episode had a dream-like quality. He was about to be mistakenly shot as a terrorist while wearing only a pair of wet, light blue surfing shorts by a man who called him an expectorated wad of tobacco. Gobshite was an arcane term he heard used once in his life. A 102-year-old patient of John's uttered the word after being informed he needed a rectal exam.

The sergeant sitting next to the captain put his hand on the captain's shoulder. The captain jerked away. He gave a venomous look at the marine. The marine, showing no reaction to the captain's stare, said, "Sir, you need to take this call."

The soldier tapped a monitor above the sliding door and it flashed on. A tiny camera embedded in the monitor allowed video conferencing. A frowning woman's image appeared on the screen. John immediately recognized Senator Snivaling.

"I'm Captain Flinch, Madam Senator," he said to the screen. His voice dropped lower and into a stilted military style, "Senator, we're currently transporting the terrorist to the hole."

John read about these "holes" on the Internet. Holes were former jails converted into interrogation areas for presumed terrorists. Executions occurred in the holes as well. John struggled from the floor of the van to a sitting position.

"I'd just as soon shoot him now," said the captain, "I witnessed him kill an airwar. He doesn't deny it."

"No!" said Snivaling, "don't kill him or take him to the hole. He *is* an Immune."

The captain nodded and asked, "Do you want me to take him to quarantine?"

"Absolutely not!" she said in a sharp voice, "Take him immediately to the processing unit."

"It would be my pleasure," said the captain with a grin.

John looked at the marines in the van. Unlike the captain, their faces didn't register any reaction to the order.

Snivaling then said, "Captain, after the—"

"Senator Snivaling," interrupted John, "my name is Dr. John Long. I'm not a terrorist. I'm a medical doctor. There's been a complete misunderstanding, which I'm sure I could explain if you would give me a few moments to—"

"YOU SHUT UP!" shrieked the Senator, "Gag this man if he speaks another word. After processing, I want extractions delivered to me personally by you, captain. Do you understand?"

The captain appeared shocked by the Senator's vitriol and nodded without speaking.

"Senator, there's no information to extract from me," said John, "I'll happily cooperate and explain what happened if you—"

"How dare you speak when I clearly told you to SHUT UP," screamed Snivaling, "Captain, do I need someone else to do your job?" Her face contorted into a sneer.

The captain slapped John on the side of his head with the gun. Pain wracked John's skull and he saw stars, but remained conscious.

"Captain, please repeat that correction to impress on the doctor that when I say shut up, I mean SHUT UP," said Snivaling with a hiss.

The captain struck John again. This time John slipped away into darkness.

CHAPTER 11

THE PROCESSING UNIT

John didn't know how long he was unconscious. He awoke to a splitting headache and the sergeant holding pressure with a handkerchief to the side of his head. As John moaned and opened his eyes, the sergeant released pressure.

"It looks like you've stopped bleeding," said the sergeant. He threw the saturated, makeshift bandage on the floor next to John and returned to his seat, "Doc, I didn't know a small cut could bleed so much."

"Yeah, scalps bleed a lot. There are quite a few blood vessels up there," said John, hoping he could strike up a conversation with the sergeant, "Thanks for your help."

The sergeant nodded. Two other marines were sitting with the sergeant, eyes fixed forward, not looking at John. He couldn't see the captain. He had moved to the front passenger seat in the vehicle.

"How long was I out?" John asked the sergeant.

The sergeant looked toward the front to see if the captain was paying attention. Then he said, "Oh, not long, five minutes max."

"What's the processing unit?" asked John.

"I haven't a clue," said the sergeant with a shrug, "Some interrogation facility I guess. Never been there—"

"Sergeant Clark," The captain's angry voice interrupted from the front of the van, "Did I ask you to carry on a conversation with the prisoner?"

"No Sir," replied Sergeant Clark, fixing his eyes forward, away from John.

John sat in silence for the next twenty minutes with the van speeding to its destination.

The van came to a sudden stop, and the sliding side doors opened. A gated chain link fence topped with coiled barbed wire blocked their passage. Beyond the gate, John could see one solitary windowless building looking similar to a warehouse. Behind the building, multiple wood fences gave it a stockyard-like feel. Additionally, a dark brown, three to four acre lake abutted the side of the building.

A peculiar stench filled the air; the odor of benzene mixed with an animal smell. He hadn't smelled benzene since organic chemistry lab in college. The animal smell he couldn't place, but it reminded him of the large animal housing at the zoo, only worse.

The marines with Captain Flinch escorted him to the gate. John's wrists remained bound. The gate opened, and two large men, both wearing black hoods, appeared. Each grabbed one of John's arms. They began roughly ushering John to the building. Sergeant Clark started to follow.

"Where the hell do you think you're going, soldier?" said Captain Flinch, "Your mission is complete. You and your men return to Central immediately."

"Yes, Sir," Sergeant Clark gave a salute. John noticed the lower half of his neck flushed red.

"Let's go!" said Captain Flinch as he caught up to the masked men.

The party of four entered the building through the only door John could see. John was woozy from the blows to his head and occasionally stumbled. The guards firmly held him upright. As the group walked in the dark hallway, the strong smell of benzene and an associated repugnant animal smell nearly overcame him.

John heard a multitude of inhuman screams coming from the direction they were heading. As they entered an arena-sized room, it became obvious; it was a swine farm. Rows and rows of swine lined up one against the other, each in their own metal-railed stalls. The screams John heard were squeals from hundreds of pigs compressed in the large warehouse.

They walked down the main aisle, passing pig after pig. All the pigs' needs were addressed—food, water, and veterinary care. Continuous music played in the background to subdue and calm them. Handlers managed every aspect of the pigs' lives, from feeding to cleaning the defecation. The handlers provided a perfect worry-free society for the pigs.

John had worries, though. The little group had reached the far end of the warehouse. Captain Flinch shoved on a heavy metal door, which opened into a long darkened corridor about eight feet wide. Even with multiple large vents in the ceiling sucking the odor from the passageway, the smell of benzene now overpowered the smell of the swine.

As they proceeded down the corridor, John noticed numerous animal skins covering the walls. What appeared to be benzene was dripping from porous pipes on the ceiling edges. The benzene trickled down the hides, collecting in long troughs at the base of the wall. The walkway of the corridor was slightly sloped left. Small channels three inches wide cut across the walkway every eight feet or so, draining the right trough into the left. The left trough ran the length of the corridor to an oval collection pool fenced with large, slightly separated, two foot square, white, marble blocks on the near and far sides.

The collection pool was three times the width of the corridor and was located in a rectangular vestibule. This opened into a large round room about fifty feet in diameter. The periphery of the room was lined with medical devices and computers recessed into the wall. The floor of the lab was white and clean like an operating room. Narrow three-foot walkways in the vestibule on either side of the black bottomed collection pool gave passage to the lab. UV lights lit the area and cast a purplish-blue haze over everything in the room.

In the room's center hung a semiconscious naked man held vertical by chains shacked to his wrists. The chains attached to tracks in the ceiling. The shaking prisoner was standing in what looked like a small black children's wading pool containing several electronic devices attached to the rim. The pool was split in half by a white plastic divider. The divider separated the prisoner's feet. Directly above him was a fixture, which appeared to be an oversized showerhead.

As they entered the round room, John was shoved past the hanging man to one of two round black tables placed symmetrically in the room about six feet away and a forty-five degree angle from the "wading" pool.

"Lay down," ordered one of the hooded men.

"Why?" said John belligerently.

Without any further discussion, the two hooded men forcefully lifted John and slapped him onto the table. He was then bound with cable ties to straps built into the table.

A man wearing a blood-stained white lab coat and a Plexiglas face shield stepped out from behind the hanging prisoner. He flipped the faceplate up. He had dark black oily hair with thin eyebrows which looked like they'd been plucked. A sutured laceration extended from his forehead to his cheek. Its placement made it look like a *renommierschmiss*, a German dueling scar, and didn't make the pock-marked face any more appealing. He ignored John's presence.

"So, Captain Flinch," said the man, "we meet again. I hear your final indoctrination was completed yesterday and I see you've already begun fulfilling your role nicely. Let me officially welcome you to the ranks of ASC, and I hope you have no ill will over my initial objections to the circumstances of your allegiance test."

As he was talking he removed the faceplate and held it up to the light. Identifying blood streaks on the Plexiglas shield, he wiped them off with the sleeve of his lab coat.

"I still feel your own hand should've done the task even though you were technically the cause," he spit on a resistant streak and wiped again, then he continued, "But I would have to say you proved your mettle to me with our little foray the other day." He motioned to the wounds on Flinch. "I'm sure you'll advance to second tier rapidly, as long as I know I can rely on you."

He pulled off his bloody rubber gloves and reached under the lab coat, pulling out a black handkerchief from his left back pocket. As he walked to an oversized briefcase leaning against the wall, he dabbed beads of perspiration from his brow. Opening the briefcase, he removed a quart-size jar appearing to be made of green depression glass and handed it to Captain Flinch. Flinch opened the jar and poured out what looked like dried green lima beans into his hand.

"Captain Flinch, you must take one of these every morning," said the man.

"Thank you, Captain Stewart, I'm greatly indebted to you," said Captain Flinch slavishly.

Captain Stewart gave Flinch a small bow, "I understand this next extraction is for Senator Snivaling as well? She already requested the Ube extraction."

He reached into his lab coat pocket and handed Flinch what appeared to be a small aerosol can with a blue cap. On the side of the cap in marker was UW. He went on to say, "I don't know why she needs more than one; it's not like she'll ever get within a mile of an airwar."

"I don't know, sir," said Flinch, "I'm just following orders. She wants me to wait and bring this extraction, too."

"Oh, so you're watching?" Stewart said, somewhat patronizingly. "Most can't stomach it."

"I'll be fine."

"Okay," said Stewart, giving Flinch a devilish grin, "then, if you don't mind, I'll complete this extraction." He turned to the hanging man.

"Excuse me, sir," John raised his head from the table he was strapped to, "My name is Dr. John Long, and I'm a physician. I believe there's been a terrible misunderstanding," John twisted his head so he could get a better look at Captain Stewart, "I'm more than happy to provide you any information you desire without resorting to torture. Senator Snivaling incorrectly believes I'm part of a terrorist organization called Immune. I assure you, I'm not a member."

Captain Stewart turned, looked at him for the first time, and said, "Oh, I recognize you. You're the fellow who killed the airwar with your bare hands—impressive. Now I see why the senator wants your extraction. Ironically for you, doctor, I'm a lawyer."

Before John could respond, Stewart turned and walked away from John to the hanging man in the center of the room. Stewart reached into his pocket, took out a metal probe, and touched it to the now unconscious prisoner's right testicle. An electrical arc flashed from the probe to the man's skin. The prisoner jerked violently and screamed, then a shower of benzene discharged over him. After a minute, Stewart looked at a meter on the side of the collecting pool and said to Flinch, "Well, that's it. We should be down to less than ten percent remaining. The rest we'll do in residual extraction."

What followed was horrifying. Stewart picked up some odd-looking stainless steel surgical instruments from a nearby table. He then proceeded to remove the skin from the prisoner as calmly as if he were removing skin from a holiday turkey. The poor soul screamed, jerked, and gyrated, but Stewart was skilled at the process. John then realized skins he'd seen on the corridor wall were human, not animal. There wasn't going to be any torture to extract information; they were extracting something from the man's skin.

When only the skin from the man's head, hands, and feet remained, Stewart stopped his dissection, but the man continued his wild screaming. Captain Flinch was off to the side, vomiting. Apparently, he wasn't fine with watching.

"It's not a job you acquire a taste for," Stewart said, laughing at Flinch, "You enjoy it the first time or you never do. I'll place you in the *didn't* enjoy it category." He laughed again, "That's more job security for me, I guess."

Stewart walked to the wall and pushed a button. Doors behind the screaming man opened, and chains on the ceiling lifted him from the pool and moved along a track to the opening. Beyond the opening, a pit ten feet deep by thirty in diameter came to view. It was filled with a dozen large pigs.

The chains carried the writhing man over the pit, then the shackles suddenly released, dropping him into the midst of the swine. The reaction was immediate and more terrifying than seeing Stewart working with his skinning knifes. The swine tore into the man, ripping him to shreds and eating him alive. His limbs tore easily from his body by the five hundred pound beasts. Stewart laughed at Flinch, who resumed his vomiting.

"Want to bet on the time?" Stewart said to Flinch.

Flinch's face was pale and he looked near passing out.

"The record is two minutes, thirty-five seconds, but I guess this group isn't hungry enough to get the record." Stewart grinned. After a few moments, Stewart announced, "Three minutes and eighteen seconds. Not bad."

He pushed another button. A side door in the pit opened and the swine ran through it. Other than a few bloodstains on the floor, there were no signs the prisoner ever existed. Stewart looked at John and said, "I'll get hungry ones for you, Doctor. Maybe you'll get the record."

Both hooded men began moving toward John.

CHAPTER 12

EXTRACTION

J ohn attempted a valiant escape as his bindings were cut. Unfortunately, his captors were experienced in transporting the unwilling. John quickly found himself in shackles; arms pulled above his head by chains. His feet were in the blue pool and, looking down, he could see several measuring probes and coils in the base. Upon lifting his head, he met the smiling features of Captain Stewart. Stewart stuck his face three inches from John's nose.

"Doctor, I have to cause extreme pain so your sebaceous glands will release the needed protein," said Stewart, "Benzene will solubilize and wash it into the collecting basin. I'll then extract the protein from the benzene. I hope you'll be cooperative." Stewart laughed.

"I can't believe Senator Snivaling knows what you're doing," said John.

"Not only does she know, she placed a special order just for you," Stewart said and poked John in the chest.

"Impossible," said John, "There's no way a United States senator and ASC official could be aware of what goes on here."

"Now that's a laugh," said Stewart, "Not only is she aware, but she personally developed the residual extraction process. You didn't know it, but before she replaced her deceased husband in the senate, she was a biochemist. Before Snivaling, we were tossing bodies to pigs after we extracted only ninety percent of the protein."

Stewart picked up an apparatus off the dissection instrument table. It looked like a hot glue gun with three tips. He pulled the trigger, and the tips glowed orange. He smiled.

"The last ten percent we couldn't recover by the live stimulation wash technique," Stewart continued, "She postulated a slow benzene drip over several days might capture another seven to eight percent, and she was right. When we tried using the drip on skins without a previous live stimulation, we recovered less overall than the combination."

"Why on earth kill people?" said John. "You could harvest more protein later."

"Good try, Doctor, but we already attempted that," said Stewart. "After the benzene wash, whatever was making those glands produce the protein stopped working. So we extract what we can get and discard the offal. So sorry." Then he laughed and said, "Not really," and laughed again.

"For God's sake, what protein do you want from my skin?" John shouted.

"Doctor, my question and answer time is over," Stewart turned, "You may direct further questions to our porcine friends shortly." He then started laughing loudly.

Captain Stewart motioned to one of the hooded men and commanded, "Prep him and strip him."

The "prep" was a bucket of ice water tossed on John. The hooded man grabbed John's pale blue surf shorts and stripped them down. As the shorts caught on his feet, they turned inside out, revealing the red inner lining. The man bent farther to get a better grip, and John wrapped his legs around the man's neck and squeezed.

John thought, in a movie, the henchman would pass out. He would free himself, then kick Captain Stewart's ass. This didn't happen. The hooded man's cohort slugged John once in the solar plexus, and John, for the second time in one day, lost consciousness.

When John awoke, he was lying on the ground outside the processing building. His shorts were back on, and his hands remained bound behind his back. He looked around and didn't see Captain

Stewart nor the hooded guards. Captain Flinch was standing over him talking on his cell phone.

John couldn't hear the conversation on the other end of the line, but on this end, the captain was saying a lot of "yes sirs" and "no sirs." The captain pulled a knife from a sheath strapped to his ankle. John tensed.

"Dr. Long," said Flinch in a formal tone, "there appears to have been a slight misunderstanding. You have my apology. I'll be removing your restraints."

At that moment, the van that brought them pulled up. Captain Flinch turned toward the van and shouted, "We're heading to Central ASAP." He then looked back to John and said, "Dr. Long, I was following orders. I'm sure you understand. I've been instructed to aid you." He bent down and cut John's restraints.

"Well then," said John, "send the limo on its way. I think I'll walk."

Captain Flinch, who seemed disappointed in the change in John's status, said, "That I can't allow. I'm under orders to deliver you to Central."

Sergeant Clark, now out of the van, extended his hand to John to help him to his feet.

As the three were walking toward the van, Captain Flinch asked, "By the way, just how did you kill the airwar?"

John, who was seething, hesitated, then spoke, "Well, the airwar had me trapped inside. I tried everything, but nothing worked. Then I thought back to my medical school days."

Flinch was listening intently as John continued, "I located the airwar's rectum, and I shoved my head in it. I held it there until the airwar died of constipation. I'm naming it the 'Flinch maneuver.' I hope you enjoy the reverse eponym; I plan to make it famous." Sergeant Clark smiled and suppressed a laugh. Captain Flinch stalked ahead and sat in silence the remainder of the trip.

It was a two-hour drive and John tried to glean some information from Sergeant Clark. The only answer he could get was, "Sorry, sir, I'm not at liberty to discuss anything with you at this time." The other marines' response was the same.

Once the van reached Central, it was another thirty minutes before they entered the building. Three checkpoints needed clearance. The first checkpoint presented the most difficulty because the pot-bellied Sergeant Baker wanted ID verification for everyone. This was impossible for John, as he was clothed only with the light blue surfing shorts with no form of identification. Captain Flinch's entreaties, then veiled threats, had no impact on the sergeant.

Sergeant Baker's speed seemed to become inversely proportional to the degree of flushing on Flinch's face. Finally, after several minutes, the sergeant had seemingly satiated his power lust.

"Everyone can pass except for Mr. Blue shorts," said Sergeant Baker, "He must remain outside the gate until he presents proper identification."

"Sergeant, you open this damn gate and let all of us pass," screamed Captain Flinch, who looked on the verge of apoplexy, "If you don't, all hell's breaking loose."

"Captain," said Sergeant Baker smugly, "I must remind you your rank doesn't supersede checkpoint security protocol. If your current behavior continues, I have every right to detain you as well."

John, who was enjoying the show, couldn't help notice Flinch's hand shifting to the grip of his holstered pistol. Sergeant Baker noticed this, too, and motioned with his left hand. Two sentries appeared with M-14s aimed at the van. At that moment, a jeep from Central skidded up to the checkpoint. Colonel Vickers vaulted from the back seat and stalked toward the sergeant. The sergeant immediately snapped to attention and saluted.

The colonel, without returning the salute, demanded, "Corporal, why have these men not been checked through?"

"It's Sergeant Baker, sir."

"Not anymore," said the colonel.

John noticed beginnings of a slight smile on Captain Flinch's face.

Sergeant Baker began to speak, "Sir, I was—"

"Pass these men through—NOW!" interrupted the colonel harshly. He waved to the gun-bearing sentries, who immediately opened the gate. At the next two check points there were no delays. John could hear his heart pounding, but sat motionless as he was whisked to his fate.

CHAPTER 13

THE IMMUNE

The building they entered was large, chunky, and square with a gray stucco external finish. A private airstrip stretched from behind the building. Parked in lots on either side of the facility were multiple armored military vehicles of various types. Although there were several glass doors at the entrance, windows appeared to be blocked and sealed.

In the entrance's vestibule, a row of turnstiles with electronic ID card readers blocked their way. Colonel Vickers, who continued to escort them, preceded John through the turnstile. Vickers stopped and tapped a code in the card reader. Following an audible click, a green light appeared and he motioned John to follow.

As John passed through the turnstile, he noticed two things. First were modified forklifts on either side of the entrance holding massive concrete and steel barriers. It was apparent, at a moment's notice the building could be sealed. The other was a scattering of applause from service men and women who happened to be performing duties or passing through the large entrance hall.

John looked at Captain Flinch, who was now smiling a big toothy grin. Flinch's grin suddenly disappeared when he seemed to realize those clapping were looking at John. Unsure how to react, John did nothing; he just followed Colonel Vickers. Sergeant Clark and one of the marines from the van continued to flank him. John noticed they were giving each other sidelong glances seeming to indicate neither knew what was going on.

Captain Flinch caught up to Colonel Vickers and, on the pretext his talents required him elsewhere, excused himself from the entourage. Flinch then saluted the colonel, turned, and as the colonel passed, flipped John a one-finger salute and quietly said with a hiss, "Watch your back, asshole."

John was happy to have Flinch gone as the group changed corridors, but Colonel Vickers hadn't spoken a word or even acknowledged John's existence except at the turnstile. Colonel Vickers was John's height, around 6'1". He, unlike some of the other officers in the building, was carrying a sidearm. John also noticed he was in the Air Force. Looking at other service men and women in the proximity, he noted they were a mix of the various branches of service. John could only assume "Central" was a multi-branch command center.

The group continued down a long hallway with several large offices branching off each side. Most doors remained open, and John could see considerable ongoing activity within. Halfway down was a large corridor branching off from the main hallway. John noticed this corridor was under construction. It was packed with several busy workers. Their procession was stopped at the hall's end by a set of large metal double doors. A sign next to the doors read *Bay 1*. A single armed guard stood at the door and saluted Colonel Vickers. Vickers pushed both doors open at the same time.

Bay 1 was a rectangular room, eighty by fifty feet with a twenty-foot high ceiling. Banks of fluorescent lights lit the room, giving it a bright white appearance. A refreshment table had been hastily set up in the center of the room. Although its top was covered with white banquet paper, the table underneath was clearly an office desk pulled from another room. A cooler filled with soft drinks sat on two plastic chairs next to the desk. On the desk, with stickers from the local supermarket affixed, were cheese and fruit trays, plus a platter of sandwiches.

Approximately fifteen officers of varying ranks were standing in the periphery of the room. Seven men and two women, all wearing disheveled street clothes, were near the refreshment table. Most carried anxious looks and none were eating.

The room was quiet except for humming of one of the fluorescent bulbs. John entered the room and everyone turned. A low murmur started. A man looked up from a clipboard he was writing on and, in a booming voice everyone in the room could hear, said, "Dr. John Long, welcome! I'm Admiral Beckwourth."

Admiral Beckwourth was about 6' 2" with an average build and a bit of a middle-aged gut starting to show. He appeared to be in his mid-fifties. His hair was a mix of black and gray with signs of receding. He was wearing reading glasses and, without the pearl-handled revolver he wore by his side, John thought he looked more like an accountant than a high-ranking officer.

The admiral walked up and extended his hand to John and they shook. John noticed the admiral shook his hand vigorously, then the admiral turned to the rest of the room.

"Ladies and gentlemen," said Admiral Beckwourth, sounding more like a carnival barker than an admiral, "I'm pleased to introduce to you Dr. John Long, soon to be the most famous man in the world. I and the press refer to him as 'The Immune'."

Turning to the nine civilians in the middle of the room, he continued, "Like you, he's immune to the stings of the airwars. However, unlike you, he's discovered a secret for killing airwars without the release of juveniles. He's the world hero *du jour* and he's been selected to be the standard-bearer of the World Immune Corps."

John's thoughts became distracted when Admiral Beckwourth mentioned his immunity to airwar stings. Everything happened so fast, but reviewing recent experiences, it was clear he sustained no injuries from the airwar. He also thought of his triage duties at the hospital. He was the only doctor never to receive a secondary sting. He wasn't sure if he was immune to the sting's poison or if the airwars didn't sting him. Either way, the thought of it was quite remarkable.

John's attention was jogged back to the admiral's speech when he once again mentioned the Immune Corps. John thought, *What the heck is the Immune Corps?* He hadn't heard of this organization, even on Internet blogs.

"Don't worry," said the admiral, as he saw the quizzical look on John's face, "I'll explain everything momentarily." Then the admiral seemed to notice John was wearing only light blue surfing shorts. With a tone as one addressing a foreign dignitary when a culturally sensitive subject is being broached, the admiral said, "Is your attire your preference or did somebody fail to offer you clothes?"

"Thank you," said John, who now had goose bumps from the cool room, "A shirt and pants would be nice."

"Get this man suitable clothes," ordered the admiral and snapped his fingers at one of the servicemen. Then, to no one in particular, he said, "No wonder airwars are kicking our butts. Nobody thinks!"

Changing gears, the admiral announced to the civilians, "Okay, I know you have questions, but first I'm showing you a short video. This is classified material you'll never see on the evening news."

The admiral motioned to a screen in the back of the room. A laser projector hung from the ceiling John hadn't noticed when he first entered. As the admiral pushed a remote's button, he said, "Please, please, feel free to have food and drink."

Nobody moved toward the food table. All eyes were fixed on the screen.

CHAPTER 14

THE IMMUNE GENE

The film opened with ASC spokesman, Glavin, recapping the last ten days of the airwar crisis. He read statistics indicating worldwide death tolls were much higher than ASC news releases previously suggested.

John whispered to the admiral, "How can he justify appearing before the press corps and reporting something utterly different?"

"Glavin doesn't think," whispered back the admiral, "he reads. He's not even a tier two. He's a man with a pretty face people want to believe. His job is to tell the press what we want them to hear, which has little to do with the truth."

John wanted to ask what a tier two was, but he also wanted to hear Glavin's report.

"Current ASC strategy is not effective in many Western countries," Glavin droned on, "Militias in America and other democracies continue to attack airwars. The result is these countries experience the highest toll in human lives lost. On the other hand, the strategy is working well in totalitarian societies. For instance, North Korea has virtually no attacks on airwars and correspondingly the lowest human death rate."

The admiral leaned over to John, "ASC has to love those iron fisted dictators. The only bright spot in a dreary campaign."

Glavin continued, "Today ASC is celebrating its name change from the Airwar Scientific Council to the Airwar Security Council. Senator Snivaling, Chairperson of ASC High Council, had this to say regarding the name change."

Snivaling's face filled the screen, "The name Airwar Security Council reflects the more powerful command our organization wields in this singular crisis. As of today, all world governments have wisely ceded ASC absolute authority regarding laws on airwars, and by extension, these laws affect all facets of peoples' lives. Like a mother knowing what *is* best for her child, we know what *is* best for you." She gave a patronizing smile and a small head tilt to the screen. "And like a good child, we expect you to obey — or suffer consequences." She smiled again and pressed her fingertips together.

John cringed and cursed under his breath, "I can't believe she's been elevated to chairperson."

"So," said the admiral, "you've met Senator Snivaling?"

"Yes . . . well no, not in person."

"Well, she's even more charming in person," said the admiral, grinning.

"Yeah, I bet," said John with a disgusted look, "like maggots in road kill."

"Are you *sure* you haven't met Snivaling?" said the admiral, laughing.

Glavin reappeared and reviewed new policies. All governments now enforced ASC laws. Governments not following enforcement rules were subject to immediate nuclear attack on the capital city. Surprisingly, this had little political resistance; fear supplanted academic discussion worldwide.

Glavin went on to explain Mad Mike's Liberty Fighters were the best-organized militia, but other airwar resistance groups were forming alliances worldwide.

Although the military easily crushed any militias they engaged, militias were likened to airwars. When the military destroyed one, even more militias would appear. Moreover, they were extremely adept at avoiding military confrontations.

The video switched to a recent joint ASC-United Nations closed meeting. A delegate from Uganda was speaking through an interpreter. "America, you'll be the destruction of the world if you don't control attacks on airwars."

This was followed by malicious remarks from the socialist side of the aisle on the failure of the capitalist mentality.

The admiral leaned over to John again and whispered, "Watch this great PR guy."

John was surprised to see the admiral appear on the screen.

"It's true there have been one million deaths in the U.S. directly related to airwar attacks," said the admiral, "but hundreds of millions are currently dying from disease and starvation in totalitarian and socialist countries due to policies unsustainable in times of crisis." The admiral pointed across the aisle, "Who's in worse shape?"

A loud murmur filled the chamber. Beckwourth waited for the noise to subside before he continued speaking, "Ideological bickering is unimportant. What's important is . . . the run, hide, sacrificial surrender slogan is useless." He pounded his fist on the podium; the thud resonated throughout the hall. The delegates went silent and all eyes were on him.

"Words are powerful and we're using the wrong words. In the United States the phrase 'estate tax' was used for decades without any political consequence, but a simple name change to 'death tax' repositioned the issue and made it a political lightning rod."

There were many delegates nodding in agreement.

"We must do the same," said Beckwourth, "The new ASC slogan will be *evade, seclude, defend by restraint*. Americans will find this slogan acceptable, although it won't resolve the problem of the militias." Light applause echoed throughout the chamber.

Back in the video room, Beckwourth said to John, "If you're losing the game, don't play the losing strategy harder—"

"Change the strategy," interjected John.

"Umm . . . no, change the rules," said the admiral with a thoughtful look, "The opposition is always preparing for a change in strategy, rarely a change in rules."

John gave the admiral a blank stare, thinking, *Who is this guy?*

Glavin returned to screen and began talking about the biology of airwars. Considering all the scientific minds of ASC studying these creatures, surprisingly little information was provided that John hadn't already discovered on his own.

Glavin did mention the unique quality Immunes possess wasn't limited to toxin. A protein in skin oils made Immunes unlikely to be stung when in contact with tentacles. A similar circumstance occurs in nature with clown fish and sea anemones. Unlike other fish that are stung and eaten by anemones, a clown fish's specialized mucous covering allows it to pass through poisonous tentacles unharmed. Immunes were even less prone to be stung in the water, as the protein solubilized somewhat and would reach the tentacles before skin contact. John realized this was why he hadn't received a single sting in his aquatic encounter.

Glavin remarked research on isolating and manufacturing this protein was ongoing, but even with full ASC support, researchers expected any production to take months or years.

John noted Glavin made no mention of the "processing units."

Glavin went on to say researchers calculated the Immune gene sequence occurred approximately one out of 100,000 people. It appeared to be an unusual, spontaneous mutation; airwar immunity wasn't an inheritable trait. It was estimated there were 50,000 individuals worldwide who were Immunes, of which 20,000, age and health-wise, might be physically capable of fighting airwars.

The testing was simple for the trait. A moistened swab was rubbed on skin. When dipped in indicator solution, it changed color. Governments had done massive testing surreptitiously. John recognized this was the airwar "toxicity" swab test required at the hospital for the "benefit" of the patients.

ASC categorized Immunes as highly suspect individuals. This was due to a high percentage gravitating to terrorist militias. Governments worldwide had been quarantining Immunes for that reason. Sadly, due to a 'communication error,' several countries purged their quarantine facilities. Glavin estimated only 10,000-15,000 would be available to the World Immune Corps.

John noticed the other Immunes were looking at each other with uncomfortable expressions.

The video jump cut to Glavin addressing a press conference. He had excitement in his voice. "ASC is releasing the name, photos, and a video of the man singularly responsible for the sad state of the world. He's the confessed creator of the airwars. This lunatic is now in the custody of ASC. His name is Dr. Joseph Sengele," Glavin spat out the man's name like it was putrid meat.

Sengele appeared as the quintessential mad scientist. The doctor used a research biology station located on a remote island to do genetic engineering experiments resulting in the creation of the airwar species. Video clips of Sengele's laboratory showed technicians studying intermediate airwars, immature specimens with hydrogen sacs varying from three to ten feet in size.

Dr. Sengele's face filled the screen. He was tall and thin with a gaunt skeletonized face. The hollow dark sockets around his eyes appeared demonic. His hair was unkempt, and his eyes were bloodshot. To top it off, he had a small Hitleresque mustache. Hollywood couldn't have provided an actor that better personified evil. If his natural looks weren't enough, the ASC videographers had taken pains to have his key lighting come from below. The shadows created in the deep bony recesses of his face made him look ever more ghastly. As he spoke, his eyes rapidly darted around looking to the camera, then off camera, but his words came forth slow and precise.

"I'm Doctor Joseph Sengele. I'm personally responsible for genetically engineering the airwar species and setting them free," Sengele spoke without emotion in a matter-of-fact way, "Airwars will cleanse the earth of humanity. That's my goal."

John watched rigidly. His jaw muscles repeatedly clenched. The admiral seemed to be carefully observing John's reactions.

Sengele continued, "I sacrificed my associates to 'my children' so they could feed and grow."

Clips of several deceased lab assistants were shown within the tentacles of the airwars. Only weeks ago, these scenes would have been shocking, but the public was now desensitized.

Sengele was noticeably not contrite or remorseful. He finished by looking off screen and saying, "Is that it?" He emoted such an *are-we-done-yet* attitude John wanted to throw something at the screen.

Glavin returned, "Interrogations of Sengele are ongoing, but ultimately he'll be tried for crimes against humanity and punished accordingly."

Glavin provided no further information about Sengele other than he was a loner without friends or family, which seemed understandable to John.

John was seething with anger. His only thought was, *This psychopath is responsible for the death of Cassandra.* John didn't know what kind of punishment ASC proposed, but he could think of some unique ones. He regretted he wouldn't have the opportunity to perform several of his ideas on Sengele personally.

"Now for astonishingly good news," reported Glavin.

John was surprised to see himself vanquishing the airwar on Lake Eola. Editors took the liberty of adding a soundtrack to the video clip. *Ride of the Valkyries* played as John swam into the airwar. *Also sprach Zarathustra* highlighted his dramatic exit from the water, which was shown in slow motion. John thought the producers made him appear heroic, although it certainly didn't feel so at the time. He smirked when the film cut short his ignoble escort to the van.

"The press has given Dr. Long a sobriquet," said Galvin excitedly, "The Immune. The Immune is now the leader of the recently formed World Immune Corps. The Immune Corps *is* mankind's silver bullet in the airwar crisis. Immunes will lead us to victory against the airwars."

Platitudes followed about heroism and the importance of following the mandates of ASC. The new battle cry of Evade, Seclude, and Defend by Restraint repeated endlessly. The film ended by imploring loyal citizens to follow this creed so the "professionals" of the Immune Corps can best do their job.

CHAPTER 15

PERSPECTIVE HISTORY

The film ended and John scanned the room. Gathering from the expressions, up to this moment, no one in the room realized they'd joined the Immune Corps.

"Nice piece of video work," said Admiral Beckwourth to John in a hushed voice, "if I do say so myself. I was working on it until you walked into the building." The admiral cleared his throat and announced, "Dr. Long, now known worldwide as 'The Immune,' will be leading our little group, which will be known henceforward as the First Immune Attack Force. You'll be killing airwars shortly." He said this with a smile and an arching wave of his hand.

"I know many of you are upset about your quarantine experience, but there's been an extreme paradigm shift. I'm now the ASC liaison to the Immune Corps. I fully understand the importance of Immunes and no matter how bad your previous treatment was, I assure you your star has risen. Of course, joining the Corps is optional. Any of you can walk out that door and go home."

A tall skinny man in his late forties stepped out from the center of the room. He wore wire-rimmed reading glasses and had a receding hairline with light brown stringy hair tied in a small ponytail.

"What happened to Ube?" he said.

"Before I answer," said the admiral, "I want to make one thing clear. You can trust me and I'll always tell you the truth." He smiled a big grin and added, "or at least as much truth as you can get from a public relations man."

The admiral became somber.

"Ube is dead. I can't tell you how upset I was finding he was part of the Immune purges. I knew nothing of his execution, nor was I in a position to prevent it."

The admiral pushed a button on the remote, and the projector clicked off and the lights of the room turned on.

"Now things have changed," said the admiral, "I have power and resources. I assure you, purging will never happen on my watch. Tonight the news will run a brief report of Ube's 'accidental' death. The story will go unnoticed, as the announcement of the Immune Corps formation will supplant it. You won't hear the truth of his death from the controlled media. I'd ask you to keep this to yourself for obvious reasons."

"How do you know about Ube's news release, and why should we trust you?" retorted the skinny man.

"I know about the news cover-up because I wrote it," said the admiral. "That's my job. If we're going to win the battle against the airwars, propaganda is required to maintain stability. You can trust me because I'm telling you the truth about the report."

"So we're to trust the prevaricator because he tells us the truth about one of his lies?" said the skinny man.

The admiral smiled and said, "I prefer the word *disinformation* over lie. It's only a lie if historically I can't make it true."

"Historically, it's still a lie," said the skinny man.

The admiral ruffled through pages on his clipboard and after a moment he seemed satisfied the conversation was worth pursuing.

"You're an English professor, correct?"

The skinny man nodded.

"Well, it depends on whether you're talking physical history or perspective history," said the admiral.

"I don't follow you; history is history," said the professor.

"Incorrect," replied the admiral, "Humans only record perspective history. By definition, it differs from physical history, the actual event, because the recorder's perspective judges the event. For example, a man in a hotel room remembers an earthquake as terrifying and another man swimming in the hotel pool didn't even note the tremor. Described as a hero by his fellow compatriots, a sniper is nevertheless described as loathsome by his opponents. Of course, the winning side determines the recording of the historical record. Ultimately, humankind bases records solely on perspective history, not physical history."

"So lies undiscovered become truths," said the professor.

"Professor," said the admiral, "I think you've got it."

"Now," said the professor, "I'm still not clear how that should make us trust you mo—"

"Do you got any mustard?" interrupted a tall, aloof-appearing man with straw yellow hair. His mouth was half-full of a sandwich he'd taken from the food table moments before.

Everyone turned and stared in uncomfortable silence.

"It's a ham and cheese sandwich," he continued and pointed to the sandwich he held in his left hand with one large bite taken from it, "You gotta have mustard with a ham and cheese. American mustard, you know, not that foreign Guido don mustard that art dealers eat."

"You mean Dijon mustard," corrected the admiral.

"Yes. Yes," the blond-haired fellow said, snapping his fingers and pointing at the admiral, "That's the stuff. I hate it."

"I believe others besides art dealers like Dijon," replied the admiral as he pointed to the mustard on the table.

"Yeah," said the blond fellow, "you're right. People who buy art, too. That's it in my experience, and nobody else can stand the stuff." He held his sandwich in his mouth as he twisted the cap off the mustard squeeze bottle.

The admiral looked at the professor and said, "And what if this man ends up writing the history of mustard?"

"Yeah," said the professor, "I get it, but even if we do trust you, how do we know ASC won't replace you on a whim?"

"Good point, but that won't happen," said the admiral, "Not as long as the Immunes succeed. We have a linked survival, you and I. If the Immune corps go down, I'm going down with it."

The admiral continued, "I'm positive ASC hasn't taken the correct approach handling airwars. Although, I do agree we need to stop militia attacks to prevent the release of juveniles. We must fight back some way. The world needs heroes. Eventually, someone in ASC will figure out a way for a final solution, but we need time. The Immunes can give us this time. They can stabilize the current panic, and that will make the difference. The world needs a rallying point and the Immune Corps will be the uniter." The admiral pointed his finger at John and said, "And this is the man who is leading you!"

CHAPTER 16

FS MANEUVER

The evening news had ended an hour earlier, and the admiral took a moment to consult with Captain Howe for a review of the current statistics. Captain Howe looked like a GI Joe doll with brown hair. His only distinguishing feature was a pink port-wine stain birthmark covering the left side of his neck.

"Admiral, you guessed correct," said Howe, "Following our news release of the formation of the Immune Corps, worldwide attacks on airwars decreased eighty-five percent. Congratulations."

The admiral turned to the Immunes. "I'd like a show of hands of those wishing to join the Immune Corps," announced Admiral Beckwourth.

Every hand shot in the air except for John.

"Thank You," said the admiral, "If you would please follow Captain Howe to conference room B, he'll brief you on your upcoming training." He then turned to John, "Dr. Long, if you don't mind, I'd like to speak to you privately before you leave."

John nodded, but secretly felt like heading for the exit.

As they went back down the hallway, a marine finally brought John fatigues.

"Soldier, what took you so long?" admonished the admiral.

The soldier began explaining the requisition process in minute detail and the admiral, exasperated, finally waved him off. John put the uniform on in the middle of the hall. The fatigues were at least three sizes too big; he had to hold his pants up as he walked.

As they came to the corridor off the main hall, John noticed a sign above the entrance now read *Immune Corps Authorized Personnel Only*. The admiral's office was the second door on the right. A laser handprint reader was mounted to the door. The admiral positioned his hand and a red beam passed beneath. A computer generated voice then said, "Welcome, Admiral Beckwourth." The door lock clicked open.

John noticed the admiral's office was sparse on furniture. Two mauve fabric guest chairs sat in front of a large mahogany desk, and a massive black leather executive chair towered behind. Adjacent to the desk was one gray metal file cabinet and a neatly organized bookcase. The walls were bare except for a black-framed photograph of a battleship. On the desk were four computer monitors tracking multiple media outlets. The only personal item on the desk was a dried up Venus flytrap plant and a little desktop ultraviolet grow light, which unnecessarily saturated the quite dead plant with purple light. The dead plant seemed incongruous with the tidiness of the office.

The admiral didn't go behind his desk. He sat on a guest chair and turned it to face John. The admiral seemed to notice John staring at the dead plant and said, "Never wanted to feed it. I mean, it doesn't seem natural; a plant moving and feeding on animals. Maybe I'm developing a touch of botanophobia. Still, I can't bring myself to toss it. It was a gift from a recently deceased nephew." The admiral paused and seemed to be waiting for John to join the conversation thread.

John, feeling annoyed at himself for not leaving when he had the chance, looked at the admiral, but didn't speak.

The admiral appeared to contemplate John for a few seconds, then said, "You don't talk much, do you?"

"Considering today's events," said John, "and that I'm in mourning, well, this doesn't serve to make one an engaging conversationalist. Additionally, I can't think of a single thing I've ever learned from talking."

The admiral gave John a perplexed look. He moved to the front of his desk, opened a drawer, and pulled out a manila folder full of papers. John couldn't help but notice the file tab had his name on it. After the admiral perused each sheet, he looked up at John. "I'm sorry, your file doesn't have any listings for living or recently deceased relatives. Was it a friend you lost?"

"Yes," said John, "she was my best friend. My fiancé."

"Airwar?" queried the admiral.

"Yes."

"Recently?"

"A little over a week," John said, slumping forward as the reality again embraced him.

"My God," said the admiral in a genuinely compassionate tone, "I'm sorry. I had no idea you were under such strain. What was her name? Can I help in any way?"

John replied with his head hung low, "No . . . no, arrangements were taken care of . . . thanks for your concern, but I'd like to avoid the subject for the time being."

Then John lifted his head and gave the admiral a steely glare.

"You managed to conveniently avoid discussing the processing unit with your Immune recruits."

The admiral closed John's file and set it on his desk. John thought the admiral seemed to be carefully considering his next words.

"Yes," said the admiral, "you're correct. Of course, I've been briefed on your unfortunate experience. What occurred was unthinkable. I assure you the processing unit is no more." He reached and turned off the UV grow light.

"Now in response to my obvious omission, consider this adage. If the crap is out of the colon, flush it, don't stir. Otherwise, the smell only worsens. However, if you feel it's necessary to inform the others, I'll do it. I'll also answer any questions, as long as it doesn't violate ASC policy."

John thought for a minute and said, "What were the processing units trying to extract?"

"The Immune protein," said the admiral, "ASC can't manufacture it, but they could extract it from the skin of Immunes. Sprayed on a non-Immune's body, it temporarily protects from airwar stings. Every ASC official wants a can of the stuff, but one aerosol can equals one dead Immune. This was the real reason the Immune purges occurred. In the United States, I had just enough influence to hold ASC off, except for charged terrorists. Now Immunes are heroes. Extractions will never be an issue again."

John frowned, "So you approved of the processing units before discovering the latest value of the Immunes? Or maybe I should ask, do you have a can of the stuff?"

The admiral looked dismayed, then said, "First, I wasn't aware of the processing units until eleven days ago at the time of my ASC indoctrination. I opposed the 'quarantine' of the Immunes even before I knew of the extractions. Between you and me, I'm the reason the extractions ended, and no, I have no need nor desire to pack a Brown or a Blue."

"What's a Brown or a Blue?" asked John.

"The cans of extraction have either brown or blue lids. Browns come from swab positive Immunes. The sensitivity of the test is ninety-nine percent, but the specificity is ninety-three percent, which means the test identifies almost everyone who is an Immune, but seven percent are false positive."

John's brow furrowed as he did the math, "So this means seven out of a hundred brown lid cans don't work," he said.

"Correct, seven percent are duds," said the admiral, "That's why everyone wants a Blue. The blue cans are from Immunes who have survived documented encounters with airwars. The Blues are always one-hundred percent successful and accordingly carry higher value. Now that the extractions have stopped, the Blues are considered even more valuable."

"Valuable to who?" asked John, "I've never heard of Browns or Blues even on banned Internet sites."

"Only ASC members qualify for cans, but not everyone eligible has one." The admiral pointed at himself. "The existence of Browns and Blues is, for obvious reasons, a tightly kept secret."

"A nasty evil secret," retorted John, "Who decides who gets the Blue lidded cans?"

"You'll only see tier ones and High Council members with a Blue. Final extractions ended up as antitoxin. The final ten percent extraction wasn't potent enough to prevent stings, but delivered intravenously, it reversed some toxic effects. I assure you, there'll be no more extractions on my watch. I've required cremation of any deceased Immunes, skins intact."

"So are you tier one?" asked John.

The admiral shook his head. "I only rate a Brown. I'm tier two. The only way I could get a blue on my tier is to steal it. I don't pack a can of either color. Even if I felt the need, the idea would be abominable."

The admiral motioned to John, who had been standing the entire time to sit in the other guest chair. John hesitated, then sat. The admiral moved to the file cabinet and pulled one of the metal drawers. He rooted around a moment, then pulled out a can with a brown topped lid. John felt a surge of anger.

"It's not mine, John," said the admiral, "It's a spent can," he handed it to John, "Push the top."

John took the brown cap off and pushed the white spray button. The can sputtered and a few drops of fluid came out. It had the smell of putrid meat and benzene. John twisted his face in disgust.

I just wanted you to see one up close," said the admiral, "It's really not different from an ordinary aerosol can."

John studied the can for a second, then asked, "How do the ASC tiers work?"

"There are three tiers," replied the admiral, "The lowest is the third tier, who would be someone like your new friend Captain Flinch."

John scowled at the admiral.

"Sorry, I was being facetious," said the admiral, giving John a smile, which wasn't returned.

The admiral took the brown can from John and set it on the desk next to the UV grow light. He continued speaking, "Flinch understands the big picture, but he's not privy to every detail. Tier threes like Flinch serve largely as aides. My position required precise knowledge of the machinations of the big picture, so ASC brought me in as a tier two."

The admiral stood and turned his back to John. John couldn't see the admiral's face as Beckwourth continued speaking, "I did go through informational shock, to say the least . . ."

The admiral paused for nearly thirty seconds, then continued, "It turns out there isn't much difference between a tier two and tier one, except tier ones are voting members. Then there's the High Council; they decide the voting issues. I report directly to the High Council, so I have more political clout than most tier ones."

John, feeling agitated, stood and said, "The High Council needs to arrest Captain Stewart. He's a dangerous, sadistic, psychopathic murderer." As he stood, his oversized fatigues slipped down to his thighs before he could grab them.

"That's not happening," said the admiral, turning and looking at John with a sad smile, "Stewart sits on the High Council."

John shot back, "What about Senator Snivaling?"

"You already know she sits as the chairperson of the High Council, and High Council members can't be impeached."

"Who decided that?" said John, looking incredulous.

"Surely you jest," replied the admiral with a laugh.

John answered his own question, "The High Council."

The admiral nodded and said, "If not tended closely, justice ends up being a reflection of the conscience of those in power."

"Stewart and Snivaling have no conscience," retorted John with scorn.

The admiral smiled and said, "And I rest my case."

"I can't ignore what happened and do nothing," said John.

The admiral clapped his hands, "Great! Then join our World Immune Corps and lead the First Immune Attack Force. You'll get to kill airwars with the blessings of ASC."

John thought the admiral appeared to be studying his face to get a hint at what he was thinking. The admiral quickly added, "If you do well, you might even get a shot at Sengele himself."

John delighted in the thought of killing Dr. Sengele, but then shook his head and said, "I don't want to take orders from the High Council."

"You won't," said the admiral, "The Immune Corps is an independent entity. All divisions of the World Immune Corps will report directly to me."

"Ultimately, the politicians will want power over the Immunes," said John.

"That's why I'm setting up the Corps as far removed from ASC High Council control as I can get. The problem with politicians is that they always come to believe power is wisdom." The admiral smiled at John and gave a slight head tilt as if saying *your move.* Then he added, "Plus, you'll get a uniform that fits."

John smiled for the first time and said, "Okay, admiral, I guess I wouldn't mind killing a few airwars. I'd love a shot at Sengele, too, but I'm certainly not the leader you need, or in that frame of mind."

"Look, that's what I thought you might say. That's why I announced it without asking you first. Sadly, I didn't know of your loss, but it doesn't change things."

As he was speaking, the admiral picked up John's file and wrote a notation inside the front cover. He then tossed the folder back on his desk. The folder slid into the Venus fly trap, knocking it a few inches. A few of the dried up leaves fell from the plant to the desktop.

"John, the corps needs a leader, and you're the most famous Immune in the world. He has to be a larger than life hero, and you fit the bill perfectly. I hate to sound trite, but because of Ube's 'accident,' you're our one hope. Sure, eventually someone will do something outstanding that'll make him or her a red penguin too, but it may be weeks or months. I don't have the luxury of time. I need a standout hero, yesterday, and you're the first Immune to kill an airwar without releasing juveniles, and this makes you the hero *du jour*."

"It's not that I don't want to help fight the airwars," said John, "I'd love to kill every last one, then finish off Dr. Sengele for dessert. I have no military leadership experience, nor do I care for public exposure." John sat back down in the chair and waited for the admiral's response.

The admiral made a raspberry sound with his tongue and lips.

"John, leading is mostly about public relations. Think of this as a coach-athlete situation. I train you, I set up competitions, and I make sure you always win. You do your job, then sit in front of a camera and smile. As far as avoiding public exposure, forget it," said the admiral. He got up from his chair and pulled open another file drawer. He picked up a stack of files six inches thick and dropped them on the desk with a thud. The admiral motioned to the pile.

"This is from a news clipping service. The entire file drawer is full. You've been famous for less than a day and look at the volume of articles. Every news organization is currently plowing through your life history. By tomorrow, they'll know everything from the sexual orientation of every one of your elementary school teachers to your favorite brand of toilet paper and how many squares you use each time you wipe. Keep in mind, you'll always be the first man to kill an airwar without releasing juveniles.

Your only chance of controlling public exposure is me. ASC controls everything but the Internet. However, even there we have an advantage. Your current hero status makes it possible to voice certain subjects off limits; for instance, those causing you emotional pain. Well, with your current standing, few would take those topics on."

"Okay," said John, "Perhaps there's one item you could help me with. My fiancé was a private person. I know she wouldn't like the press sifting through her life, and personally, I want to keep our previous relationship privileged. There's a rage from my loss which I desire to direct privately."

The admiral grinned and said, "Okay, done! Here's our story. You lost a loved one to airwars, no mention of your fiancé. This loss nourishes your resolve to battle the creatures. Everyone relates, especially those who have also lost a loved one." The admiral picked up John's folder and scratched through the note he'd written on the inside cover.

John thought the admiral seemed to have switched to public relations mode.

The admiral rubbed his hands and said, "Your only request for your sacrifices is your private memories are left untouched. I'll make investigation of your loss an act of disrespect. Ten minutes after we've finished talking, it'll be taboo worldwide. I'll even call off my research team on your private life."

"Thank you," said John.

The admiral slapped John's file folder on his leg, "My researchers clearly didn't do a thorough job the first time, so why go there again?" the admiral paused, then added, "Of course, there'll be those who find the taboo a challenge. I'll need to develop an FS maneuver. Perhaps we'll let it slip your loss was a second cousin."

"What's an FS maneuver?" asked John.

"It's the keystone of public relations campaigns," said the admiral, "An FS maneuver is a deception hiding an underlying agenda. You can easily recognize an FS maneuver in its simplest form as a component of advertising."

The admiral moved around his desk and opened a drawer. After shuffling through some files, he pulled out the back cover of an old magazine. On the cover was a beautiful model at the beach, playing volleyball with one hand and smoking a cigarette with the other. Two handsome male models vied for her attention.

"We all know 'sex sells.' If an ad shows a supermodel wearing a bikini and smoking a cigarette, the FS maneuver is offering the sexual image of the 'possibilities' of smoking, obscuring the agenda of selling cigarettes, which in reality, addicts you, ruins your health, then kills you."

"So what's up with the second cousin?" asked John, feeling confused.

"Well, the deception is the invented second cousin. It'd take time-intensive investigation to look into what appears a boring family relationship. We'll name him John Smith, the most common first and last name in the United States. This further impedes investigation. The media won't pursue it. The underlying agenda is to have them look over the fact you lost your fiancé, which would be mesmerizing to the gossip mongers on the Internet. The bloggers would be unrelenting in their quest for more information."

"Okay, I think I'm beginning to follow you," said John.

The admiral smiled and rubbed his hands together, "We're going to FS maneuver the pants off the small amount of independent press that's left."

The admiral continued to elaborate, as it appeared this was a highly interesting subject for him. "John, the world reeks of FS maneuvers and those who are skilled at creating them end up controlling society."

"Therefore," said John, "an FS maneuver is a bit of advertising trickery?"

"No, no," the admiral's tone turned serious, "It's more than that. FS maneuvers start wars and they can end wars. FS maneuvers change the course of history." He began waving his arms in the air.

John, seeing the admiral was becoming agitated, tried to tone him down by changing his thread of thought, "What does the acronym FS stand for?"

The admiral paused and seemed to calm down. He folded the cigarette ad and filed it back in the drawer. Then he looked at John like a teacher might at a star pupil who has asked an insightful question.

"The FS stands for Fortitude South. This was the greatest covert disinformation operation of World War II. It allowed the Allies to pull off D-Day. Many heroic men never recognized by the history books sacrificed their lives to pull off this FS maneuver. From dummy rubber tanks and double agents to fake radio transmissions from a nonexistent army, the authentic point of attack caught the Germans by surprise. Therefore, you see what I mean when I say FS maneuvers change the history of the world."

The admiral's face fell as he finished. He drew in a deep breath and let out a sigh. "Sadly, FS maneuvers seem to start more wars than they . . ." and then the admiral went silent. An uncomfortable pause followed, then he said, "Sorry I digressed. I have a tendency for that. We were talking about you leading The Immune Corps."

"Okay," said John, nodding. "I guess you have a leader. I hope your FS maneuver skills are up to the challenge."

"You're looking at the best public relations guy in the world," said the admiral, "Only politicians create FS maneuvers better than me."

John smiled cynically and said, "I haven't decided if that's a good quality to be bragging about or not, so, if I'm leading this so-called Immune Corps, do I have a rank? Will I be considered a third tier ASC?"

"No," said the admiral, "you aren't military, and as I said previously, we want to keep Immunes away from ASC. Your title from this point forward is 'The Immune.' We're labeling everyone else in the Corps as 'Immunes.' It's a PR thing. We need a hero, quick. We'll focus largely on you and your team, the First Immune Attack Force. In a few months, the world will live and breathe by your daily exploits. We don't need multiple little heroes; we need one big one."

"What if something happens to me?" said John, thinking aloud, "Wouldn't this be psychologically devastating if you're creating a hero as a rallying point? A war can be lost on something like that; a man called Goliath comes to mind."

The admiral stared in John's eyes for several seconds as if he was sizing him up for a chess match, then said, "Yes, you're sharp. I keep forgetting you're a physician—it would be devastating. That's why actors have stunt doubles."

"So," said John with disbelief, "you'll have stunt 'Immunes' play me, then I take credit?"

"Something like that," quipped the admiral.

"No," said John stubbornly, "absolutely not. I can't work that way."

The admiral laughed and said, "You, yourself, recognize the danger of something happening."

"Well, change your public relations model," said John firmly, "I plan on killing airwars."

"I can't," said the admiral, "The whole initiative builds on creating a living legend, not a dead one."

"Look," said John, "those are my terms. I'll be your public relations puppet, but when it comes to killing airwars, this puppet's strings are severed."

John looked intently at Admiral Beckwourth in silence, then the admiral smiled and spoke, "Well, I guess it makes my job easier if I'm working with a genuine hero. I only have to figure some way to keep you alive after tomorrow."

CHAPTER 17

FIRST IMMUNE ATTACK FORCE

When the admiral indicated he had power and resources, it was clear the next day he did. John's world changed overnight. His entire schedule was organized from the moment he opened his eyes. In the morning, with help of five assistants, he dressed and showered.

John discovered his first task each morning was in front of cameras. He read inspirational messages from a teleprompter, which were satellite uplinked around the world. He also gave orders and encouragement to other Immune Corps forming around the world. The comments were not of his creation. A team of writers overseen by Admiral Beckwourth did advanced preparation of John's statements.

John had been going non-stop in front of a green screen for two hours when the admiral walked on the set. John hadn't spoken to the admiral yet and he waved to get his attention. Admiral Beckwourth motioned to the camera crew to take a break, and he approached John.

"Admiral, where're the other Immunes?" inquired John, "I hope they're not being tortured as well?" Then he smiled at the admiral.

"Sorry, John," said the admiral, "publicity is a necessary evil for your job. You might as well get used to the idea. By the way, the film crew has already brought me your first video segments—you're a natural in front of the camera."

"Thanks," said John.

"The rest of your team is being briefed on your airwar downing technique," said the admiral, "The other Immunes won't have the same press responsibilities as you."

John stood from the stool he was sitting on and moved away from the hot HMI lights. The admiral followed him to the side of the set.

"So how did you pick this so-called team of mine?" said John as he wiped perspiration from his brow.

"Well," said the admiral proudly, "it's a highly select team, the best in the world. Since the only technique we know in downing an airwar is using your water route, we selected good swimmers."

"What were your other selection criteria?"

The admiral was silent.

"So we're a group of ordinary people who happen to be good swimmers and immune," John said incredulously, "No special forces, no ninja warriors. A few of those might be helpful."

The admiral smiled, "As I said, a highly select team, the best in the world."

"By whose standards?"

"Mine," said the admiral, "And my opinion is all that counts or will be reported in the news." The admiral gave John a sly smile. "Let's go to breakfast."

A seven-minute breakfast followed where John was briefed about the day's planned activities. Captain Howe stopped by the table, introduced himself, and provided John with recent poll numbers.

"Polls from this morning give The Immune Corps an approval rating of ninety-seven percent," said Howe.

John began to think perhaps the admiral was indeed a PR genius.

"How can this be? We're less than 24 hours old and I haven't even met members of my team," said John.

Howe then showed John an image recognition ranking. John's image was now more recognizable than the current president. John noted he lagged behind several, living and dead, sports stars, singers, and actors, but so did all the world-changing scientists.

"Look here," said John, "Nikola Tesla ranks a zero on the image recognition ranking. That's sad."

"John," said the admiral, "in America, the most lauded and compensated skill continues to remain the ability to entertain. If a ball was needed to kill airwars, it would make my job far easier."

The most mind-boggling poll number was fifty-three percent felt Immunes were winning the battle against the airwars. Ironically, there hadn't been an official kill by an Immune Corps member, except for John. The most pleasing statistic was the level of attacks on airwars dropped to an all-time low. Presumably, numbers of juveniles released was correspondingly lower as well.

Next on John's agenda was a visit to a large conference room, which had a sign over the door reading *First Immune Attack Force Briefing Room*. The space reminded him of a fancy theater with arena style seating. The room could hold several hundred people, and technicians, military personnel, and press filled two-thirds of the seats. He could smell fresh paint and glue in the air. The seats appeared brand new and John figured that this room didn't even exist 24 hours before. He believed this to be another testament to the power of Admiral Beckwourth.

At the front of the room was a stage with a large screen behind it. On stage sat two desks and a podium facing the audience. The desktops were clear except for a briefing folder and a monitor. Ten other desks were on the floor in front of the stage. These desks faced the stage. Each had an occupant, whom John recognized as Immunes he'd seen yesterday.

Admiral Beckwourth already moved on stage behind the podium. Everyone in the room appeared to be waiting for John. When he entered the room, the admiral announced, "This is Dr. John Long, 'The Immune'."

Everyone in the room turned and looked at John. Scattered applause occurred around the room. Most of the world had seen video of John downing the airwar. John cringed; he didn't care for rock star status.

"The Immune will lead the First Immune Attack Force," continued the admiral, "He'll be working with these ten Immunes and a support group of four hundred."

John looked around the room. It appeared half of the "support group" was media.

"We have hundreds of sister Immune Attack teams forming around the world," said the admiral, "This group, the First Immune

Attack Force, is our flagship team. The press will closely follow them. The First Immune Attack Force has eleven members, unlike other squads fielding ten."

As the admiral was speaking, John sat in a nearby seat in the first row. The admiral stopped speaking and looked toward him.

"The Immune's desk is here," said the admiral in a commanding voice. He motioned to the desk beside him on stage. All eyes were on John as he walked up front.

"John, I'm afraid you'll have to get to know your team on the fly. We're pressed for time." The admiral immediately went into planned activities for the day, which John already heard at his breakfast update. This gave him a moment to study the people he'd be entrusting his life to.

There were eight men and two women. John thought, *This is one more than yesterday.* Overnight an Immune was added to their group.

As he moved his gaze from face to face, his eyes stopped at the last desk on the right. A resonance of familiarity flickered in his mind. The man was definitely not present at the first meeting. Five to six days' growth of black and gray facial hair covered the lower half of his face. His clothes were unkempt, and his uncombed hair looked oily, like it hadn't been washed for several days.

The man looked up and realized John was staring at him. He gave a small wink, one suggesting familiarity. Then John realized it was Bob. He'd last seen him in the ER with his son. He wondered if Admiral Beckwourth knew of Bob's previous affiliation with Mad Mike's Liberty Fighters. He decided to keep quiet until he had a chance to speak with Bob privately.

John finished his study of the other faces. Occasionally one or the other would lift their eyes from their monitors to look at him. The expressions ranged from admiration to mistrust. None of the other faces resulted in even the remotest recognition by him.

The monitors jumped to the current day's training exercise and John's eyes fixed on the screen. The crux of the exercise was John demonstrating his airwar takedown technique. John thought, *Well, the admiral must have embraced the do-your-own-stunt idea. The admiral seems to have more confidence in me than I have in myself.* Although John was certain he was an Immune, he wasn't confident he could repeat his previous act. Beginner's luck kept rolling through his mind. John wouldn't only be performing before the First Immune Attack Force, but broadcast live, in front of the entire world.

John knew the admiral was taking a huge risk. If John failed, world morale would drop instantly, the admiral would be demoted, and the Immunes would end up quarantined again, if not purged for the "common good." The positive side was, he'd be dead and wouldn't have all these worries. The monitors simultaneously going off and lights coming on broke this happy thought.

Admiral Beckwourth glanced at his watch and said to nobody in particular, "Good, we're eight minutes ahead of schedule." Then he looked up and announced, "The team will meet at 0900 at the bus bay. Until then, the Immunes can get acquainted with The Immune; the rest are dismissed."

The theater seats immediately started clearing. The admiral looked out to the ten remaining Immunes and said, "You were briefed on The Immune earlier. Please introduce yourself to him, your nickname if you have one, former occupation, hometown, and your 100 freestyle time. Keep it brief. We have to depart soon."

Luke Haley, the skinny English professor whom everyone already nicknamed, "Prof," came forward. He took off his wire-rimmed glasses and, gesturing as if he were speaking in a lecture hall, said, "I'm an English Literature professor from UCF. I struggle out a sub-minute 100 free, but back in the day I could do a 49."

The admiral pointed to the man with straw blond hair who wanted mustard the day before. He looked to be in his mid-twenties. The man had mistrust on his face. He stood and addressed the group instead of John, as if he had some kind of superior position.

"Ron Suggs. My friends call me Birdman." He then stretched his arms out and revealed an abnormally wide arm span. This, in conjunction with his aquiline nose and slightly pointed head, did give him the appearance of a large bird. "I'm Head Assistant to the Assistant Athletic Trainer at Eastern Kentucky University, 49.7." Instead of sitting down, he continued speaking, "How did The Immune get to be leader? Shouldn't we vote for our own leader?"

John thought he heard the admiral softly curse under his breath, but externally he appeared composed. The admiral lifted his hand and said, "All Immunes who wish Dr. Long to lead this group raise their hands." Everyone, with the exception of Suggs and John, raised their hands.

This didn't appear to deter Suggs, who continued to speak, much to the consternation of the admiral. "Sir," Suggs looked at the admiral, "Are we meeting at 0900 in AM or PM?" There were a few scattered laughs from the Immunes. At first the admiral appeared as if he might explode, then he realized Suggs was serious, so he let out a deep sigh and said, "That would be AM."

"The 0900 PM events are only scheduled on October 32nd," quipped Prof.

"Thanks, let me write that down," said Suggs as he sat down. Then he pulled out a pad and made a notation. The room was quiet, as nobody knew how to react.

The admiral shook his head sadly, pointed at the first woman, and said, "Since the Immune, Suggs, took so long, I'll finish introductions. This is Sue Redmonds." An exotic woman in her mid-twenties who appeared to be of Euro-Indian descent, stood. She was dark olive skinned with thighs and hips like a professional figure skater. "Her friends call her DS. She's a Massage Therapist from Ventura, CA. Although she was a competitive diver, she swims a 1:05 100 free."

Next was an enormous, heavily muscled young man with a shaved head who appeared to be 6' 5". "Ray Grouse. His nickname is Sumo. He's a senior collegiate swimmer from USC. His hundred time is a 45.1." John noticed he had a Speedo logo tattooed to the side of his muscular neck, and he was always smiling like he'd just finished playing a prank.

"Hey, hey, hey!" interrupted Suggs. He pointed at Prof and said, "Are you trying to make me look the fool? There's no October 32nd except in leap years, and I'll just bet it's not a leap year."

General laughter broke out among the Immunes. John even noticed the admiral smile. Suggs nodded, pointed again at Prof, and said, "See, we're on to you." Then Suggs started erasing in his notebook.

The admiral, distracted from his introductions by Suggs, motioned with a keep-it-quick swirl of his finger for the next two Immunes to introduce themselves. The first was Chip Travis, a pale, unemployed thirty-something from Memphis, TN whom everyone called Mr. Eddie because he looked like the kid from the old sixties TV show *The Munsters*. The other was Joey Bear, a quiet artist from Kansas whom everyone called Booboo. His baby face, with wide brown eyes, and a small-framed body made him look younger than his twenty-four years.

The first person in the second row introduced himself as Roger Fernandez. He was a black haired, swarthy 23-year-old who seemed to have a layer of baby fat evenly distributed over his thick muscles. He was nicknamed Cupcake. His nickname resulted in chuckles, but after he gave his time as 49.1, the admiral interrupted and said Fernandez reported his 100 meters time, not yards. There were a few low whistles from around the room.

Rachel Spooner was the other female on the team. A college student and triathlete, she was an incredibly attractive brunette with hazel eyes, high cheek bones, and flawless skin, and at nineteen, the youngest on the team.

Fred Hemke, nicknamed Dude, a 55-year-old Japanese-American international investor, was the eldest of the group. His close-cropped hair was black, but mixed with gray. He was square-jawed with heavy sun-damaged lines cut into his face from years of swimming and surfing. His short but muscular body could swim a 53-second 100 freestyle. Finally, John's friend Bob, whose last name was Rund, rounded out the members of the First Immune Attack Force.

"This is your team, John. These are the best Immunes in the world," said the admiral with sincerity in his voice.

"For being the world's best, we all appear to be Americans," said John, observing out loud.

"Yes," said the admiral, "there are faster, better qualified, swimmers, but I need English-speaking Immunes for the flagship team. There can't be any chance for miscommunication within the squad. There's no room for foreign languages, dialects, or accents. Besides, once ASC says you're the best, everyone will believe it. And in the next few minutes, you'd better not only believe it, but also be it, because your life depends on it."

CHAPTER 18

ACCOUTREMENTS

T he admiral glanced at his watch and said, "Okay, to the transport." Two side-by-side doors on the right hand wall of the
room swung open to the outside. Only three strides away
was a bus painted military green, waiting for the Immunes. The
team quickly formed a queue and entered the vehicle.

John and the admiral were last to board. The front seats
remained unoccupied. The right seat next to the window had his
name spray painted in black on the back seat cushion. A mesh bag
hung over the seat with his name on it as well. Others were unclip-
ping similar bags over their seats. John noticed several other military personnel in the bus, but he only recognized two, Captain
Howe and Sergeant Clark.

"Please change while we're driving," said the admiral standing
at the front of the bus, "We're only a few minutes away." The admiral then sat by John. John looked over his shoulder. Everyone was
undressing and storing their clothes in the mesh bags, and it didn't
appear the Immunes were putting a uniform on. He turned to give
a quizzical look at the admiral.

"Sorry," said the admiral as he realized John didn't know the
drill, "I forgot you weren't in team orientation. The uniform is a
Speedo."

John looked back again and realized the Immunes were wearing a red Speedo with a yellow lightning bolt on the side panels.

He'd been given the same suit to wear under his clothes when he dressed this morning.

"That's the only print style in stock that fits everyone," said the admiral, smiling, "I wanted everyone to match for the cameras."

The admiral motioned to John to start changing as the bus pulled out. When John opened his bag, he noticed items in the base. Included was his surfing shorts–drawstring cord, the original one he used to kill the airwar, and two four-foot long locking plastic cable ties, normally used for mounting air ducts. Rounding out his gear was a handle attached to a weightlifter's glove, and most strange, a headband with alternating black and clear glass, dome-shaped decorations. These "decorations" numbered twenty and ran around the circumference.

"That's your video camera," said the admiral. "Ten miniaturized cameras alternate with ten LED lights. We want to see how you do it. The micro batteries supply fifteen minutes of bright light and video transmission.

John held up the glove. The admiral fit it over John's right hand. "Push the button with your thumb," directed the admiral. He pointed to a red protuberance that looked like a miniature hilt. John pressed with his thumb. Blades sprang out from either side. The dull edge of one blade struck his slightly curved finger with a stinging slap as it joined the other blade. Immediately the blades divided again, and John was suddenly holding a knife with an 8" blade.

"Sorry about the smack to your fingers," said the admiral, "I should have warned you. You'll get used to opening it with your fingers out of the way."

"I suppose the other button amputates my fingers as the blade closes?" said John humorlessly.

"No, either button opens and closes, so you can use your index finger to open as well. Technicians felt it might be helpful if your thumb got torn off."

"Pleasant thought," said John.

He pushed the button again. The blade withdrew silently into the handle. "Well, you'd think the creators could've made it open as easily," he said to the admiral.

The admiral smiled and said, "You're looking at the most sophisticated knife ever designed, constructed, and soon to be field tested in under twenty-four hours. They cost a mere $100,000 each."

"I suppose the test isn't a whittling contest."

"John, you could whittle an eight-inch iron rebar into a flute with this knife. I hope you won't need to use it, but Immunes have saved victims by cutting them free. Airwars ignore minor trauma caused by Immunes. I wanted you to have the best."

"Why the glove?"

"We had to attach it to something. The armament gurus figured the best location was the hand, but they had to make it so you could also grip and swim."

"Well, what if airwars have my right arm tangled?" questioned John.

"You pull the knife off the glove with your left hand."

"How? Is there an electromagnetic release?" John furrowed his brow as he examined the knife handle more closely.

"No, just pull it off. It's a Velcro attachment."

"You mean a $100,000 knife is attached by a thirty-nine cent piece of Velcro?" said John.

The admiral shrugged, "Some things you can't improve upon."

"I suppose plastic cable ties are the same principle?"

The admiral nodded, "We also added your surfing shorts draw-string as additional weaponry backup."

"Well, I'm glad for high-tech backup," said John, smiling.

The admiral glanced at his watch. "Okay, once we stop, you'll have to move fast. World news airs in fifteen minutes, and I want this live. When you're ready, dive in and do your thing. If things go wrong, ditch the video band by breaking any glass lens. An alarm will go off, and we have a backup plan."

John picked up the headband and examined the attached tiny camera lenses and lights.

"John, make sure you break a lens. It shuts the camera off. We can't afford to show failure. Drop your weapons, get out, and tell the press tentacles knocked them from you. We'll regroup in the red command truck and go from there."

"Okay, wait!" John held up his hand like a crosswalk guard, "Three things. First, it sounds like you expect me to fail, so what's the backup plan? Second, I'm assuming, based on our attire . . ." John motioned to the others in Speedos, "I'll be attacking from the water, which screws with your time schedule. I'm positive airwars won't appear siphoning on cue. You do remember the siphon I need to ride to get to the air tu—"

"John, we're going through a giant learning curve," interrupted the admiral before John reached his third concern, "I'm hoping you succeed as before, but our experts give you a twenty percent chance." The admiral glanced at papers on a clipboard. "Success prediction increases to thirty percent with all eleven attempts."

"Eleven?" questioned John.

"Yes, if that's how many tries required to succeed," said the admiral with a resolved look on his face.

"And what if I die in the first attempt?"

"Well, that's why the others are suited up," replied the admiral matter-of-factly, "It's better press if you succeed, but the show must go on."

"So we're expendable?"

"Sadly," said the admiral, "but remember, you declined the stunt double."

"How could you've used a double this time?"

"Couldn't," said the admiral, "We need you once on film. After that, we would've faked the rest."

"So either way, I'd be in this position?"

The admiral smiled and said, "Yep, and it's almost time for the stunt show to begin!"

CHAPTER 19

THE BIG SHOW

The First Immune Attack Force was traveling down a two-lane road in the middle of nowhere. Heavy, tall trees and brush lined the sides of the road. As the bus rounded a bend, trees gave way to an open area of grass and a small lake of twenty acres. The seven to eight acres of field gently sloped six hundred feet down to the lake edge. The bus pulled on the edge of the field and stopped.

On the opposite shore thick cattails merged with a pasture scattered with a few solitary grazing cows. On the right and left-hand sides of the lake, a heavily treed forest abutted the edges. The lake was undeveloped, not even a single dock or boathouse. The location would have been quite serene except for the hundreds of soldiers and press jamming the area.

The activity, noise, large cranes and lifts, and military equipment reminded John of the midway at a fair. Moreover, where on a midway you might see the giant Ferris wheel dwarfing the other rides, there were a dozen airwars floating in a tight group.

John was stunned. One of the first "facts" the ASC promulgated about airwars was they couldn't be restrained. If airwar movements were impeded with nets or ropes for more than a couple of minutes, the hydrogen sac self-destructed, releasing juveniles by the thousands. Flame-throwers, dousing with liquid nitrogen, toxic gases, large explosions or any direct external damage to the sac resulted in the same effect.

John wondered how these airwars remained herded in place. A one hundred foot clear area surrounded the airwars. Masses of military and equipment were at the free zone's periphery, so it was hard to tell what was keeping the monstrosities in check.

He heard the answer before he visualized it. A low background roar everyone had to talk over got John's attention. It sounded like the wind right as a squall line hits. Then, as he looked at what he thought were large satellite dishes surrounding the airwars, he realized these weren't satellite dishes like the others scattered on the field. They were massive fans evenly spaced around the periphery. These wind machines were keeping the airwars in place by blowing them there.

As an airwar pulled his tentacles along the ground, fans at the other side would rev up until it stopped or moved back. *Ingenious*, John thought, *but not practical for fighting millions of airwars.*

"Admiral, are you sure the sacs won't disintegrate?"

"Well," said the admiral, "we've held some at an ASC test facility for as long as ninety-six hours. So far, no problems. Although they're not dead, airwars can't hover because, without water, they can't continue to produce hydrogen for the sac. These have been here six-to-ten hours, and they should be thirsty."

John thought, *So that's how the admiral can keep a time schedule for broadcast news.* John realized the admiral was appointed his position for a definite reason; he was a clever fellow.

"So," asked John, "how are you freeing only one, or are you releasing the whole lot at once?"

He didn't have to wait long for an answer. As soon as he stepped from the bus, the show apparently started and everyone knew their part, except for John. Scores of cameras turned toward him.

At the pool, John never felt self-conscious wearing Speedos. After all, he'd worn Speedos his entire swimming career, but walking in an open field wearing only tennis shoes and what the Aussies call a "banana hammock," made him feel a bit uncomfortable.

This feeling quickly passed as he observed two fans closest to the lake slow down. One nearby airwar immediately passed toward the lake. As the other airwars followed, fans revved up, impeding their way.

The admiral and John walked to the water's edge where Colonel Vickers was standing. He had been there most of the day organizing and he gave the admiral a brief update.

The admiral then turned to John, "If you live, smile a lot and wave as you exit. If you fail, stay low in the water as the backup requires us to try to kill all the juveniles released," he instructed.

John then noticed several odd-looking machine gun turrets on military vehicles on not only this side, but also now moving into position on the pasture side.

"Five-thousand rounds a minute," the admiral answered without waiting for John's question, "The backup plan shreds everything a foot off the surface of the water. So don't wave for help."

The admiral gave a slight bow, gestured with his arm as if he was admitting John into a grand ballroom, and said, "Good luck. The whole world is watching."

John thought, *That's it, no instruction, no last minute trick play,* yet then again, he was creating the instruction book on the fly. The admiral was probably right again. *Don't think it; just do it.*

He kicked off his tennis shoes and waded into the lake. It had a sandy bottom, as many Florida lakes do. The water was crystal clear and cool, most likely spring fed. He thought it would be a nice place to swim if a giant mutant monstrosity wasn't hovering over the lake twenty-five meters in front of him. *Oh, well, it would be refreshing for twelve seconds or so,* then he did a slight dive from his knee-deep position.

As he came to the outer curtain, his thoughts turned to Cassandra, which filled him with intense anger toward the beast. His lack of caring whether he lived or died, coupled with this anger, gave him the fortitude to enter. Again, he experienced not a sting, nor an untoward movement from the tentacles. It almost seemed peaceful in a way, because, as he penetrated deeper, the harsh roar of the giant fans and the voices shouting over them began to dim to a mild hum in the background.

John quickly saw what he was looking for. The siphon tube was already at work, taking on water. John swam toward it, gently pushing tentacles away, which didn't resist his efforts. Suddenly, just as John was reaching out for the tube, he felt a disturbance in the water behind him. All at once, the tentacles became wildly alive. The siphon tube rolled up six feet in the air, too high for John to reach. His heart skipped a beat as it became obvious the disturbance in the water was coming at him.

CHAPTER 20

BACKUP PLAN

The admiral watched from the shore as John swam out. *God, this looks good,* he thought. The airwar had produced no waves on the lake surface and from the angle John was at, it looked like he was swimming on glass. *Without hesitation, beautiful strokes, perfect now, just don't die, and we may pull this off.*

He looked around. Most had eyes or cameras fixed on The Immune and were awe struck by the bravery of the situation. As the admiral watched, John passed through the outer curtain. The admiral turned and headed toward the large red command vehicle parked one hundred feet away.

He hadn't passed the halfway point to the command van when he noticed shocked faces. He turned to see writhing tentacles and splashing. A great life and death struggle was clearly occurring. He raced to the command unit.

The gun turrets began shifting. The admiral knew John had only moments to live if he didn't act fast. The moment he saw the struggle, an unexpected possibility flashed in his mind. He realized the backup plan was about to kill John before the airwar ever did. In less than thirty seconds, everything above the lake would be shredded. The admiral hadn't been quite honest about the one-foot clearance.

He pushed through the door of the command post so quickly he knocked Captain Howe to the ground.

"Backup commencing in ten seconds," reported a technician to the admiral.

"All views now!" screamed the admiral. He shoved a soldier from the nearest monitor. Ten different camera angles displayed on the big screen. Tentacles were everywhere. "Is he entwined? Is he entwined?" shouted the admiral. Then an arm flashed on one of the views, knife in hand. There were no tentacles wrapped around it. "Stop the backup!" screamed the admiral.

"Sir," said Captain Howe, rising from the floor, "you can't order that. Only General Cleevus can. It's protocol."

A corpsman offered, "Sir, I have him on if —"

The admiral snatched the microphone from the solider. "Cleevus, it's Beckwourth. Stop the backup!"

"Beckwourth," said General Cleevus, his voice crackling over the speakers, "protocol states an attack on an Immune resulting in an aborted mission initiates backup. Following backup, mission commences until Immune supply is exhausted. I can't sto —"

"It's not attacking The Immune," interrupted the admiral, yelling, "It's got a gator."

The countdown voice in the background droned on, "Zero — backup commencing."

Guns began rapidly firing in the distance.

CHAPTER 21

SAURIAN CONCERNS

John knew something was going terribly wrong, but he wasn't sure what. Behind him, a great struggle commenced and it was approaching, fast. His thumb hit the red button; the blade opened. He held the knife in the air above his head, poised and ready to strike as he treaded water. One thing was certain; the airwar was attacking something. From the size of the turbulent wave, it was big. He wondered if some poor soul tried to follow him on a small boat. Then it all came into view at once.

John saw teeth, scales, and tail rotating like a spinning log in the water. The giant tail slashed and ripped tentacles away from the four-meter long beast. Although the thick scales offered some protection for the saurian, it was clear the airwar's tentacles were finding enough unprotected areas to inflict significant injury. The ferocious jaw snapped right and left, ripping and shredding all tentacles in its path. However, the cost was severe, stings on unprotected mucous membranes, which were swollen and frothing. Each time the gator stopped his roll and attempted to dive, new tentacles entwined and impeded his escape.

For a moment, John felt remorse for the creature. That was, until the enormous reptile noticed John. In one desperate lunge, the gator attacked as if John was the source of its suffering.

John had no idea how fast a large, cold-blooded animal was until that moment. He didn't have time to use the knife.

Fortunately, it didn't matter as he was whisked eight feet in the air, just as the massive jaws snapped shut in his previously occupied position.

Something had pulled him from the water by his knife-holding hand. He was now dangling, arm straight over his head. He looked upward to locate his savior and was surprised to see his knife blade deeply embedded in a thick tentacle. The power of the alligator's lunge forced the tentacle on to his blade. A reflexive ten-foot recoil from the impaled tentacle carried John upward with it. He was held in place due to the blade embedding horizontally so the flat side bore the weight rather than the cutting edge.

John watched the death throes below until the gator abruptly went still. John's weight shifted, resulting in the blade angling. The sharp edge began cutting through the tentacle. Before John could twist the blade flat, it sliced through, and he fell.

He hit hard. For a moment he saw stars and had a floating sensation. As he regained his orientation, he realized he was lying on the gator. The floating sensation was real. Red tentacles were lifting the reptile. He glanced toward the siphon and it remained coiled several feet above the water's surface. After some contemplation John decided to ride this unique elevator. If the destination was the gastric sphincter, he should be able to grab the fringe next to the water chamber.

Suddenly gunfire erupted. He reflexively ducked low on the gator's back. A thought flashed to jump in the water below, but before he could react, the gunfire ceased. He wasn't sure whether the pause was good or bad, but he decided to continue his ride. Occasionally, the random tentacle would grab or touch him, but he easily pushed away or twisted them off without any untoward reaction from the airwar. It was a slower ascent than the siphon tube, but he could now see his goal.

His plan, when he reached the digestive sphincter, was to grab the fringe of the water chamber and wrap his legs around the siphon tube. Then he would transfer to the air tube as he'd done previously. Unfortunately, he was approaching the digestive sphincter from the side opposite the water chamber. He feared he might not be able to reach the fringe. He was too high to drop off, and he certainly didn't want to join the gator in its upcoming journey through the gastric sphincter.

John considered the angles for a moment and thought he might have one chance. The gator, now held in a horizontal position, would have to change to vertical to pass through the sphincter. If he held to the downward end of the gator, as it was sucked upward when he approached the sphincter, he would shift close enough to grab the fringe. He would only get one opportunity, otherwise he would fall or end up swallowed.

The tentacles shifted the gator closer to the sphincter, which was now phosphorescing purple and slowly opening to receive its next meal. The gator head would enter first and John crawled toward that end, but two large tentacles wrapped around the head blocked his reach of the fringe.

He would have to slide to the tail end and hope nothing would block his reach as the position switched. The tentacles held the head and mid body. The tail hung down slack in the back. John was able to squeeze between the tentacles to the base of the tail before the airwar began shifting the gator's position.

Using his knife, he made a cut in the gator directly behind the leg. He thrust his hand in the incision, gripping flesh and skin as a handhold. The gator then tipped down in a full vertical position. John, holding with one hand, wrapped the other hand around the tail. His legs grasped the distal tail like a gym climbing rope.

It was an uncomfortable position. Blood from the incision was running down his arm and dripping on his face. The sharp scales cut into his other arm and legs. The gator's head already passed through the sphincter. He could tell he'd be able to reach the fringe, but only with the hand remaining burrowed under the skin, supporting most of his weight.

If he released the grip, he risked falling. He'd have to wait until the last second to grab. About half the gator's body had now passed, and the upper hand was nearing the fringe. He squeezed tight with his legs and other arm. He could feel a sharp pain in his right thigh, where a scale edge was cutting through bare skin.

John grabbed and missed. Another foot of the gator disappeared through the sphincter. His second attempt, he gripped the fringe firmly. The gator sucked upward and the sphincter orifice was only a foot from his head. In less than five seconds he'd be passing into the gastric chamber. John released his other hand and grabbed a handful of fringe while holding the tail between his legs.

He held for an instant, then his legs pulled upward before he could release his straddling leg hold. When the last of the gator's torso passed the sphincter, the tapering of the tail caused a rapid disappearance of the remainder of the gator through the sphincter. This also, unfortunately, included John's right foot.

John was now stuck in a precarious position of hanging from the fringe by his hands, with his left leg hanging free and his right foot in the sphincter. A tremendous vacuum sucked on his foot, pulling him slowly into the purple glowing sphincter. Fortunately, tentacles didn't assist the sphincter's progress and his handholds were hindering the advance. This was good temporarily, but his hands were beginning to tire.

He tried using his free leg to push the trapped leg loose, but he couldn't get any traction on the slippery mucous surface of the sphincter. The green slime extruding from the opening around his ankle was too slick. He also didn't want to accidentally shove his free foot in, next to the other trapped appendage.

He felt another inch or two of his leg slide farther in, and he considered his options. He could just say screw it all and let the air-war digest him, but his desire for vengeance against Sengele was too strong to concede defeat.

If he let go suddenly, the falling force of his weight might pull him free. Of course, he would plunge seventy-five feet. The impact on the water would likely knock him out, and he'd drown.

He could slice up through the water chamber into the hydrogen sac. This would cause the hydrogen to leak and the airwar to descend. Unfortunately, the trauma would cause sac disintegration, releasing juveniles. John was sure the admiral would shred everything in that event, which included him.

He thought he might stab a tentacle, but he doubted the reflex recoil this high would be strong enough to pull him free.

The acids inside the gastric chamber began burning his foot and John began to think the admiral's backup plan might be the better way to exit this earth.

CHAPTER 22

BECKWOURTH'S STALL

The guns stopped firing and the admiral let out a deep sigh. The guns aimed well above the airwar. They were set high to kill released juveniles, then they would arc down toward the water's surface, obliterating everything along the plane of the bullets. The first salvo was well above the airwar and the firing ceased before it reached the uppermost portion of the hydrogen sac.

The admiral noticed his fists were clenched and he stretched open his fingers, but the angry face of General Cleevus on the monitor interrupted the moment of relaxation. General Cleevus's head was smooth shaven and both his scalp and face were beet red. His jugulars bulged from the sides of his neck. Beads of sweat dotted his upper lip.

"Beckwourth, this was your call, not mine," said the general, "I hope to hell it was the right one, because it's your ass on the line. You broke protocol, and you know ASC doesn't like broken protocol."

The admiral thought, *Yes, he's right. I'm running barefoot and blindfolded through a cow pasture and if I don't come out with clean feet —* he knew the dire consequences of that. Nevertheless, some quality about John Long made him push all his chips in the pot. The admiral knew the protocols for today's event intimately because he wrote them. This wouldn't help him, though, if he deviated from them without a positive result. He had now cast his lot with John Long surviving and he'd have to play it out to the end.

"General, you must have confidence in The Immune." The admiral smiled in the camera above the monitor. "He's alive, and we have him on the monitors. I don't want to go to backup without my approval."

The general frowned and looked ready to protest.

"Yes, I know it's not protocol, but I'll take full responsibility," said Admiral Beckwourth.

Back in his own mobile command post the general pondered the options. He glanced at the monitors showing The Immune's video feeds. Nothing could be seen but a forest of tentacles. A successful mission by The Immune would result in him sharing the glory. If not, the admiral would take the fall since he was ranked higher on this exercise. Even so, the general controlled the gunnery so a failure would include a reprimand. He would still be better than Beckwourth, who ASC would crucify. The general nodded his acceptance, but the admiral already moved away from the camera to better view the ten video feeds from The Immune's headband.

The Immune seemed to be moving upward, although clearly not by the siphon tube visible several feet away on one of the views. The admiral wished the techs thought to add an intercom system. He assumed it would have been done automatically, but they produced exactly what he asked for and nothing more. Indeed, it was amazing. Anything he requested, he could get under twenty-four hours, regardless the cost. Next time he'd be more specific in his design plans because he'd like to hear what the hell was going on.

"Admiral Beckwourth," said Captain Howe, interrupting the admiral's thoughts, "the general wants to know how you know The Immune is alive. The changing of the positions of the video could be from the tentacles moving his corpse upward. He also wants to know why you think it was an alligator, not The Immune, being attacked by the airwar."

The bright red flushing on Captain Howe's neck indicated General Cleevus hadn't asked his questions as respectfully as Howe relayed them. Beckwourth knew more blood flowed through the birthmark as Howe got angrier. The more blood flow, the darker red it became.

The admiral was aware the general was looking at the same video streams. Although he could hold the general off briefly, at some point, the general could initiate backup. If he did, there would be no evidence The Immune was, or wasn't, alive. The admiral realized he was in a precarious position. He would have to stall the general until he could prove The Immune was on course.

"Look at the videos," said the admiral, returning to the microphone and camera, "You can see the alligator struggling."

The admiral knew the general couldn't see anything of the struggle. The video was too dark without enhancement, and it would take techs several minutes to fix. The admiral hoped the general hadn't checked yet; this would buy a few minutes of time. The general's eyes narrowed in the monitor. It was clear he already viewed the replays.

"Beckwourth, you know there's nothing to see," said General Cleevus, "It's too dark, and my tech boys say The Immune is dead and heading toward the gastric sphincter. It's better to shred now than letting the world view our latest hero being digested."

"Perhaps The Immune found another way to the air tube," said the admiral, with his most confident smile, "The siphon is clearly not working."

"Oh, so you think your Immune has suddenly discovered how to control the airwar's tentacles?" The general arched his eyebrow. "Perhaps he asked it to carry him up to the air tube so he could choke it to death. No, Admiral Beckwourth, it's clear The Immune is deceased and his body is being transferred to the gastric sphincter . . . look!"

The general pointed to a monitor in his mobile command. The admiral shifted his gaze to a similar monitor in his command post. The sphincter came into view.

"If The Immune was in control, why would he be heading toward the gastric sphincter, not the air tube?" continued General Cleevus.

The admiral didn't have an answer and as time went on, he was beginning to think the general might be right. As the views kept changing, it was difficult to follow. He wished he'd aimed a few cameras looking down so they could see The Immune's body, but they all directed away.

"Look, general, the way the monitors are moving," said the admiral, "Don't you think it's The Immune looking around? This proves he's alive."

The general was looking at the monitor and the rapidly approaching sphincter.

"Well," said the General, "if that were me and in a few seconds I was going to be an airwar meal, I'd be trying evasive maneuvers. Admiral, you've had your chance. You have ten other Immunes you can expend before this mission is a failure. I know you spent a lot of political capital pushing to make this guy a hero, but you should've tested his mettle before committing. ASC will go easy on you as long as one of the next ones is successful. We have eight more minutes to get this on world news if we start the backup now."

The admiral was hoping the general would keep talking. This was buying time. His gaze remained fixed on the banks of monitors looking for any sign of life.

"Okay, boys, that's enough," said the general, "Let's commence with—"

"Roll that back on monitor seven," interrupted the admiral with a shout.

Monitor seven replayed. The camera lens was approaching tentacles that seemed to be blocking its way, then a hand came into view and deliberately moved the tentacles apart.

"General," said Admiral Beckwourth, "would you agree The Immune is alive?"

"Yes," he said thoughtfully, then added, "But for how long?"

Suddenly, views on the monitors went spinning.

"The Immune has fallen or the video band is off," said one of the techs.

The admiral whispered an expletive under his breath.

"Well now, what do you want me to do, Beckwourth?" said General Cleevus gruffly.

"We wait!" said the admiral.

"Well," said the general, "you've proved your precious Immune is alive, but he's in no position to complete his mission. Matter of fact, it looks like he'll be sautéed in gastric juices shortly.

If the tentacles brought him that high, I'm sure they'll finish their job. Unless you have a different opinion, I think if we shred this thing, it'll give your Immune a more compassionate death than he'll be receiving momentarily."

The admiral was trying to put the pieces of the puzzle together to form a different outcome. He kept coming up with the general's scenario, then he had an idea.

"General," said the admiral, "he could've been riding on the back of the dead alligator. The siphon isn't working. He would know the air tube is in the vicinity of the sphincter. It would be a brilliant maneuver," and only to massage the general's ego, he added, "I'm sure you would've done the same."

That seemed to placate the general for a few moments. Then the general responded, "Beckwourth, I think you're giving this particular Immune more credit than deserved. Your alligator theory at best extreme, and to paraphrase Occam's razor, you shouldn't suggest that for which there's no proof. If you had even a shred of alligator evidence, I'd sit back and let this whole scenario run its course until The Immune's remnants are defecated out."

"General, I'm sure you're aware of the extraordinary times we're living in, so nothing should surprise you. As far as the talent of The Immune, I remind you he'll always remain the first to single handedly down an—"

"Sir, we have an image from the video band," interrupted Captain Howe, "It's definitely on him. The tentacles appear to be passing the headband around. We were able to freeze an image of The Immune."

An image of The Immune filled the monitor. He was up to his knees in the airwar's sphincter, both hands grasping the fringe holding him horizontally under the airwar.

Both the admiral and the general were silent for a few moments, contemplating the image.

"Captain," asked the general, "how old is that image?"

"One minute and seventeen seconds," answered Captain Howe.

The general said quietly, "Admiral, as much as I'd like to believe your Immune has everything in control, I can't believe after looking at this image anything is going according to some possible plan you might theorize. I now beg you to let me commence with the backup. Not because of the need to press forward, but for compassion's sake."

The admiral couldn't speak. He knew it was over. He was upset about the loss of John Long, but he was more upset at himself for emphasizing the importance of this one individual. The admiral realized this might be an unrecoverable error for himself and his plans.

CHAPTER 23

A TIGHT SPHINCTER

John was having trouble coming up with a great solution. His lower leg was on fire from the digestive juices, and his hands were in agony from holding him in place. He then had a thought, what would be the reflex on the sphincter?

His current position had him sucked up to his right knee. The sphincter was strobing a luminous purple in anticipation of the upcoming meal. His hands were cramping and he bent his left leg as far away from the orifice as he could. As he pushed his left foot against the under surface of the airwar to gain better position, it slipped and went straight into the sphincter opening.

It felt like an inquisition rack. His knuckles were white from gripping and he had only seconds of hold time remaining against the unrelenting sucking force. He knew he had only one option. He let go with his right hand and reopened the knife in one move. His left arm was screaming in pain as he felt small tendon fibers tearing. The sphincter had sucked him in above the knees.

He thrust the knife to the hilt and pulled out. John got his reflex reaction. His legs ejected forcefully, swinging him like a pendulum, his feet arcing 180 degrees, hitting the underside of the airwar with enough power to bounce him back to the sphincter. His right foot amazingly reentered the sphincter, but not for long.

The foot immediately spewed forth, followed by the gator. The carcass slammed his thigh from its forceful regurgitation, twisting his one handhold to its limit. John screamed in pain. He grabbed and grasped the fringe with his free hand, then wrapped his legs around the siphon tube. He tried to relax his left hand to relieve the pain, but it had cramped in place. He realized the cramp had saved his life. He slowly worked his left hand and finally loosened it from the fringe.

John looked back to see the gator being rapidly transferred by the tentacles toward the outer curtain.

John felt as if he'd been in the airwar for hours, but he knew it must have been only minutes. It seemed extra dark, so he reached up to the video headband to adjust the lights, and he realized it was missing. His headband must have dislodged during the struggle.

John needed a moment to rest, but realized the commanding officers wouldn't know if he was alive. They might assume the worst and shred him with the beast. He also knew the admiral was a schedule freak and he needed an airwar kill for the news. The admiral had ten Immunes waiting to go and his patience might be limited.

John transferred himself to the air tube, then, after looping one of the locking plastic ties, he pulled it taut, constricting the air passage. The reaction was similar to his first airwar kill. Thrashing tentacles, followed by hydrogen leaks at the base of the bellows and a gradual descent.

Unlike his initial experience, he couldn't find an opening in the tentacles floating on the surface. When he was six feet from the surface, he dropped onto a coiled pile, which bounced up and down like a rubber raft. He pulled on the tentacles trying to find an exit.

The sac continually pressed his head farther downward. There remained three feet of crawl space between the sac and the tentacles on the surface. In seconds he was about to become an Immune sandwich.

At the last moment, he found an opening and he reached straight down to his shoulder. Nothing seemed to impede. He would have preferred to squeeze in the opening feet-first, so he could take a last gulp of air before submerging, but at this point he was lying flat on the tentacles, and the hydrogen sac was four inches above him. No time and no room to maneuver, he forced his other arm through the tight opening, took a breath, and submerged his head. It took thirty seconds of vigorous wiggling, pushing, and tugging to free his body.

Finally liberated, he looked up. He could see no exit from the tentacular masses above. Far away, he could see rays of light, but he knew he couldn't swim that distance with his lungs screaming to inhale. He began swimming for the light, hoping to discover an opening. He swam for twenty meters, but the light was too far to make. Only the throbbing pain in his left arm superseded the extreme discomfort in his lungs. He knew he was seconds from slipping into unconsciousness.

He decided to make one desperate attempt for the surface. He pointed his arms above his head, kicked like a dolphin, and shot upward toward the ceiling of tentacles. His pointed hands hit between two tentacles, which easily spread, followed by another layer and finally a third. A brilliance of light hit his face as his head exited the surface above the floating mass. He inhaled deeply, the most satisfying breath of air he had ever taken.

CHAPTER 24

WELL DONE

Admiral Beckwourth nodded to General Cleevus his recognition of the general's wishes. The general looked up to give the command for backup to commence. This would effectively sterilize the air above the water's surface of anything larger than the size of a gnat.

"What's that?" someone shouted.

All eyes in the command post looked at the large central monitor. An external view of the airwar hovering over the lake filled the screen. From the outer left curtain fifty feet in the air, remains appeared, dripping with green ooze. Tentacles tossed the carcass out, which was that of a large, quite dead, alligator.

The general's jaw dropped.

"Maybe I should wait a moment longer," he spoke to himself aloud.

For nearly a minute the general's gaze remained fixed on the rippling water where the alligator entered. A low cheer interrupted his contemplation. His stare shifted to the writhing airwar tentacles. There could be no mistake. This was the airwar's dance of death. It was identical to the video of John's downing of the first airwar at Lake Eola. The airwar began to descend and the cheers changed to nearly hysterical screams of happiness.

Back in Admiral Beckwourth's command center the only person not cheering and clapping was the admiral himself. He was shouting to get any of the techs' attention. "Sir?" Captain Howe finally responded.

"Stream this to the wire," shouted Beckwourth, "As is, no edits. The world has to see it like it happened."

The decibel level of the cheers went up a notch. The Immune had been spotted surfacing among floating tentacles.

"Boys," said Beckwourth grinning widely, "we've got ourselves a real hero. Now, let's let the world know about it."

As John surfaced, the bright light of the sun temporarily blinded him and he sensed something was wrong. All he could hear were screams. He blinked and, as his iris adjusted, he could see a crowd on shore waving and jumping. He then realized he was hearing cries of jubilation. As he swam to shore, the other Immunes were there to greet him. The admiral previously planned and choreographed John's aquatic exit for maximum public relations benefit. All were smiles and high fives except for Suggs.

"Well," said Suggs, as John exited the water, "it looks like you're Mr. Big Shot now. It may be okay for the rest of these stooges to be your handmaidens, but I plan to shine beyond your immense luck with skill." Suggs thumped his chest.

"Please ignore King Pomposity," said Prof, "You did fantastic."

John wanted to offer the hero position to Suggs. John knew the bigger the hero, the larger the burden borne. Once again, he didn't feel like a hero and certainly, he agreed with Suggs, luck was a critical factor. The spotlight, which he knew he was now the focus of, was another aspect he'd like to pass on as well. A mob of thirty to forty network cameras, and twice as many still photographers, surrounded them.

From a bird's eye view, it looked like a busy beehive with him, the queen bee, at the center. Large HMI lights rolled up and flooded him and the other Immunes with brilliant light. Questions shouted out from the mob as intense as brokers making buys and sells on a commodities trading floor. Suddenly, lights went out, and a cave-like silence fell over the field.

CHAPTER 25

THE PROBLEM WITH APPEALS

I t quickly became apparent the extra lights, all turning on at once, overheated the large generator powering everything in the field. The generator entered an automatic shut down cooling cycle. All military power requirements were carefully planned and they were well under maximum output. Of course, nobody calculated the press plugging into the same system.

"Where's the backup generator?" screamed the admiral, in the now dark command post.

The answer was silence. No one mentioned to the admiral his request for a backup generator was denied. Twenty-four hours ago, a clerk, recruited to the military from the healthcare insurance industry, automatically checked the denied box on the requisition form. A form letter was sent, which explained a request for appeal was possible at the next appeal board meeting in four weeks.

"How long until the generator is back up and running?" said Admiral Beckwourth, angrily.

"Five to ten minutes, sir," answered Captain Howe. His birthmark on his neck flushed a dark red.

Admiral Beckwourth looked out of the command post. He happily noted several of the news crews had their own power supplies. They were operating independently of the generator's power grid. *Good, we're live and worldwide,* he thought.

That's when the authentic screams started. The admiral wasn't hearing screams of joy, like moments before, but screams of terror and pain. The sudden silence that initially spread over the field was not only due to ceased conversations, but secondary to the large fans spinning to a slow stop. Released from their wind-driven bondage, the eleven remaining airwars were heading for the lake, taking several unfortunate souls with them.

The bulk of the airwars headed for the press and the Immunes. The admiral watched a mad dash of camera operators and microphone-wielding newsreaders push toward The Immune.

"Immunes, in the water," screamed John.

The First Immune Attack Force all jumped in concert into the lake. Swimming out a few meters, the Immunes then turned and looked back on the mayhem. Several camera operators and reporters lay crushed on the ground from the stampede. One camera operator foolishly stopped, turned, and filmed the approaching airwars until they were only feet in front of him. Dropping his camera, he tried to escape. He wasn't quick enough. John watched tentacles flank and engulf the man. His screams joined the shrieks of several other rising contorted bodies in the inner curtain of the airwar.

The airwars hit the lake within seconds of each other, siphon tubes dropping. John knew there was no following a perfectly choreographed master plan of the admiral's. This was to be a chaotic battle for survival, airwars versus Immunes. John swam toward the airwar nearest him.

A female reporter screamed and struggled at the water's surface. A large tentacle entwined her waist. Her screams for help were unintelligible. As he approached, he discovered why; she was Chinese. Water plastered her straight black hair to her forehead. She struck at the tentacle with her fist, each time recoiling with pain from the stings.

John dove and came up on her side closest to the offending tentacle. His arm lifted, and the knife blade snapped into place. With one smooth motion, he severed the tentacle and freed the reporter from the truncated section. She shook free from his grip, and he watched her swim erratically toward the shore. She stopped once to glance back. The intent look made him uncomfortable. It was one of reverence.

More shrieks came from inside the curtain. He swam within. An obese, balding man was using a still camera with a large telephoto lens as a club. He repeatedly beat off advancing tentacles. One already wrapped around his right upper arm, but was too small to lift or subdue the heavy man.

The Immune's knife once again swished in the air, and the distal end of the tentacle dropped to the lake's surface. The Immune slashed at several other advancing tentacles as he pushed the obese man through the outer curtain to safety. The man could barely swim, but due to his obesity, appeared unsinkable, so John left him and again reentered the curtain.

No others were in reach of saving, but John could hear screams and moans of victims higher. The siphon was taking on water, so John latched onto a peristaltic wave and rode it up.

He passed closely to three victims, one, which was moaning and not moving. A blonde female was kicking, but without making a sound. The highest was a gray-haired man who neither moved nor made a noise. John passed within two meters of each, but could do nothing to help them as he rode the siphon up. He could see several other figures at various levels of struggle, but he couldn't differentiate male from female. There were also the shrieks and moans from others outside his vision.

This time he was quick. His other plastic tie was lost, but he had his cord. In seconds he had the cord wrapped around the air tube, but hadn't constricted it yet. The siphon had coiled up, and he decided to transfer back and see if he could tie it off while sitting on the siphon coil.

He reached to grab the fringe, but missed and instead grabbed one of the four six-inch dome protuberances that sat in the twelve, three, nine, and six o'clock positions around the entrance of the siphon tube. As his fingers dug in, it felt as if he was grabbing a cloth bag filled with modeling clay. The airwar suddenly shifted its direction. He released his grip. The airwar stopped the movement change and resumed its original path.

John swung out and grabbed the knob again, this time digging his fingers in hard and deep. The airwar shuddered with the direction change and was now moving fast in the opposite direction.

When he released, the same reaction occurred as before. The speed slowed, then returned to the original direction. The finding fascinated John, but a scream returned him to reality.

The gray-haired man John was certain was dead was making one desperate effort to avoid being consumed by the sphincter. He was already swallowed to his hips. John pulled the cord taut around the air tube and tied it off. He watched the sphincter regurgitate the man as if the body was causing the airwar to choke. He heard several screams and splashes from below. The tentacles entering their spasmodic dance of death released all victims both live and dead.

As before, small hydrogen leaks at the base appeared, and the airwar began a slow descent. John thought of the stunned victims below. He was confident some survived the fall, but all would drown if the airwar deflated on top of them.

John looked back at the protuberance, which altered the airwar's direction and speed. He grabbed and sunk his fingers in deep. It didn't respond as before. Tentacles consumed in a chaotic dance below seemed nonreactive, but then he felt movement. It was slow at first, followed by a definite shift in position. After a few seconds, when he was sure the airwar cleared the victims below, his grip released. The airwar's lateral movement stopped, while continuing its descent.

Fifteen feet above the surface, John observed a large hole in the massed tentacles and dropped through. He easily swam beneath and beyond the floating tentacles.

As John popped to the water's surface, he noted several waverunners and small boats rescuing survivors. A nearby airwar began its dance of death, and John smiled, knowing another Immune joined him in the elite airwar killer club.

A waverunner with a single rider sped toward him.

"Sir," said Sergeant Clark, "the admiral requests I take you to shore. You've done well."

"Are there any airwars remaining not addressed by an Immune?" said John squinting and trying to assess the progress of the ongoing battles on the lake.

Sergeant Clark pointed toward the closest airwar. Several screams were coming from within.

"Take me there," commanded John.

"Sir, my orders are to take you to shore."

"Are you refusing to assist me with so many lives in the balance?" John asked incredulously.

"No, sir, I would never —"

"Good!" said John, "let's go!" He pulled himself up behind the sergeant.

John dove off as the waverunner reached the curtain, using the momentum to carry him almost to the siphon. It appeared the siphon was taking the last few boluses of water as the boluses seemed smaller. John wrapped his arms above the last bolus and noticed the tube was coiling up behind him. When he reached the top, he remained seated on the coil and experimented with the protuberances.

It was as he thought; grabbing each one changed the airwars' direction toward the protuberance he was squeezing. The harder he squeezed, the faster the airwar moved. If he squeezed two at the same time, the amount of squeeze also varied the direction as well as speed. Light squeezes changed directions; heavy changed speeds. Once again, screams below refocused him on the task at hand.

This time he had no cord or ties. He grabbed one protuberance and squeezed as hard as he could. The airwar lurched and picked up speed. Then he released, swung to the air tube, and began choking it with his arms. This time, although the tentacles entered their dance of death, momentum was carrying the airwar beyond the splashes below. Once again, he found an opening as the sinking airwar dropped to the water, and he escaped with ease.

When he broke through the water's surface, the scene on the lake had changed. There were now five deflated, expired airwars floating on the lake's surface. One to his left was in the midst of the death dance. Small watercrafts were zipping back and forth between the airwars.

On land, power appeared to be back on and some semblance of organization was returning. Scores of emergency vehicles littered the edge of the road. John started swimming to the closest airwar remaining airborne, but Sergeant Clark cut him off on a waverunner.

This time the sergeant had a different attitude. It hadn't gone well for him, returning without The Immune as ordered.

"Sir, The Immune is ordered to accompany me," he said in a demanding voice.

John had never been ordered in his life and the emphasis the Sergeant put on the word 'ordered' made him defiant.

"So what are you saying?" said John, "I'll have to fight you to get to the next airwar?"

The sergeant's face fell and his firm in-control attitude evaporated.

"Sir," said the Sergeant, "please don't kill the messenger. Colonel Vickers demoted me to corporal, on the spot, when I showed without you. If I come back empty-handed, I'll end up in the brig, or court-martialed."

John felt a twinge of guilt for Sergeant Clark.

The sergeant, seeing a glimmer of hope in John's pause, added, "The admiral says he needs your urgent advice on an Immune that's in extreme danger." John wasted no further time and climbed up behind the demoted Corporal Clark.

Less than a minute later John was standing, dripping, in the command center next to Admiral Beckwourth. Both were looking closely at a monitor.

"We've been following this for the last several minutes," said Admiral Beckwourth, "We're receiving a signal from a video camera inside the curtain. We believe the camera is attached to a steady cam harness worn by one of the victims. The cameraman is likely deceased as the camera hasn't moved."

"What I want to show you is this," said the admiral. He pointed to an image on the left of the screen. An object entwined in tentacles maintained a slow upward movement toward the sphincter. In the darkness, it was hard to discern, but it was too bulky to be a man.

The admiral turned to a technician who was staffing one of the many monitors. "See if you can freeze and enhance another still image."

The frame froze and the pixels of light twinkled on the screen, enlarging and clarifying the image. Although the image was fuzzy in grayscale tones, it was now clear what John was seeing.

Tentacles entwined and plastered the Immune Suggs to an obese man. Although Suggs' knife blade was open, his arms were bound to his sides by tentacles also encircling the obese man. Their position was that of a sixty-nine pose, Suggs' face jammed in the crotch of the obese man. Had the situation not been so dangerous, John would have liked to enjoy the ego-bloated Suggs' predicament a bit more.

"Is he alive?" asked John.

"Yes," said Beckwourth, "Suggs is, but we doubt his current traveling companion is with us." The admiral then began firing off several questions to John, "Did you ride the gator up this way? How did you know to let yourself be partially swallowed by the sphincter, or did you get swallowed entirely and use that to your advantage? Is Suggs emulating your strategy at this point?"

"Uh . . . no," said John with a surprised look, "Suggs is in deep shit!"

"So," said the admiral, "this isn't a strategic maneuver Suggs is executing?"

John studied the image again and said, "No. He's in *really* deep shit!"

Admiral Beckwourth pushed a button on the control console, and General Cleevus's face appeared on the monitor.

"Sadly, General Cleevus, it was as I feared," said Admiral Beckwourth, "Our Immune, Suggs, isn't executing a strategy. He's being eaten."

"What about The Immune?" said Cleevus, looking confused, "Didn't he use a similar strategy?"

"Apparently there are subtle differences between being eaten alive and an effective offensive plan," said Beckwourth, "While the airwar is in this position, can we do a backup without risking other lives?"

"Whoa, whoa," said John, "What do you mean, backup?"

"We frag them," responded General Cleevus, "It would be a much more humane death. Don't you agree?"

"Somehow I don't think the general is as concerned about the fate of Suggs as he is anxious to try out his new toys," replied the admiral sarcastically, "Unfortunately, remaining airwars are poorly positioned. He can't shoot without killing people. Protocol allows him to kill entwined Immunes, but create no collateral damage."

"I can bring the airwar down," said John.

"Absolutely not," said the admiral, "The siphon is up, and we're fresh out of alligator elevators. It's best to shred them now. Our window of opportunity is limited."

"If the airwar shifts position, even another fifteen meters, we can't backup without collateral damage," said the general.

Bob walked up, dripping, and interrupted them. He wore a big smile. He snapped his knife blade open, then shut it as he spoke, "Got one. It felt gooood."

"Loan me your knife," said John, giving Bob a thumbs up.

Bob gave John a quizzical look, but handed him his knife. John dashed out of the command center toward the lake.

Corporal Clark was sitting on the waverunner at the water's edge as John ran up. John pointed with his knife to the airwar about to feed on Suggs and yelled, "Take me to that one!"

"Are you sure it's okay with the admiral?" Clark said suspiciously.

"Absolutely!" lied John.

John hopped on behind Corporal Clark.

"If the airwar moves, look for a floating Immune," shouted John in corporal Clark's ear. "He may be unconscious."

John dove under the outer curtain. The knife in his left hand slowed his swimming. He transferred it to his teeth and swam with one knife in his mouth and the other velcroed to his palm.

As he reached the middle, it was clear the siphon remained high up and coiled. He looked for two large tentacles that were adjacent to each other. Finding a suitable pair, he took the knife from his mouth and stabbed it deep into the center of the first tentacle. The reflex reaction caused the tentacle to recoil, pulling him upward ten feet. The knife blade in his right hand clicked open. He thrust this knife deep into the adjacent tentacle. He ascended another ten feet in the air. He kept repeating this process, alternating tentacles, but each time the recoil elevated him less and less. Finally, John reached a point three meters below the siphon coil.

John could easily see Suggs, who was alternating shrieks, curses, and sobs. Suggs was one meter from the now slightly dilated purple sphincter.

John's last stick and recoil lifted him less than six inches. He shifted climbing technique to using the knives as ice picks, stabbing a tentacle, pulling up, and stabbing the next a little higher up. His previously strained muscles in his left hand and forearm screamed in pain each time he pulled himself upward. The last ten feet took as long as the previous sixty.

Suggs heard John approaching. He lifted his head from the obese man's crotch and began to scream for help. His head was about to enter the airwar's glowing purple sphincter.

"Suggs, close your eyes and hold your breath," shouted John. Suggs' screams stopped. His head disappeared in the sphincter, as well as the legs and thighs of the obese man.

John could reach the fringe now with his left hand, but was afraid the airwar might not regurgitate Suggs if he started choking it. Instead, he swung toward the sphincter and stuck the knife in deeply.

The reaction was violent, more than he remembered with the first airwar. Suggs and the body expelled like a rocket, a tracer of green ooze following. The two bodies separated, and John could hear Suggs screaming all the way down, then silence. John swung back, grabbed a motion protuberance, squeezed hard, and the airwar began moving in that direction. John continued squeezing until he felt the airwar moved enough for recovery teams to spot Suggs.

The knife remained stuck in the sphincter muscle, which was continuing to react. Body after body spewed forth with ever-increasing force, always followed by a stream of green slime. Finally, the sphincter expelled the last of the bodies. The sphincter's color changed from purple to a dark red. Its surface looked like a bag of gyrating worms, similar to cardiac fibrillation where the heart muscles contract randomly with no organization.

Suddenly, John heard a loud ripping sound from above. The airwar began descending rapidly, which was followed by the report of machine gun fire in the distance. He knew the hydrogen sac must have disintegrated from the stress of the knife in the sphincter. John wished he would've had the foresight to pull the knife out. He figured he had only seconds to react before the space he was occupying would be shredded by thousands of projectiles.

John knew he had only one option. Hitting the water at a bad angle usually guaranteed some degree of injury, and he was jumping through tentacles. He let go and fell. He only hoped he would land in an opening and hit feet-first. He was lucky on both counts. He went deep; both ears hurt with the increased water pressure. John swallowed. He heard a high pitch squeal as both ears equalized pressure. Then he swam underwater to the surface. He easily made it to the edge of the tentacles. After a few long strokes he was able to wade out of the water.

The machine guns were firing, but the barrels remained aimed upward at an angle. A few remaining airwar juveniles were disappearing like bubbles popping in a breeze as they hit the ceiling of lead projectiles. As the last juvenile burst, the guns ceased firing. The admiral walked up to John.

"Quite an afternoon, John. A complete success in my book. Yes, an absolute success." The admiral grinned widely.

John looked around the field. It looked like a tornado blasted through. John wasn't sure what the admiral used as a measurement of success, but he knew what he valued. "How's Suggs?" asked John.

"Oh," said the admiral laughing, "he'll be fine. His head looks like he had the chemical peel from hell. But, hey, people pay good money for the same treatment at a dermatologist's office."

"Where's he now?" asked John.

"He's on one of the ambulances heading back to our base. His only other injury was his ego. It deflated more than the hydrogen sac of that airwar that swallowed him. Sadly, unlike the airwar, I'm pretty sure his ego reinflates." The admiral began waving his hand to get the attention of nearby camera crews.

"My God," said John, "there must be at least a hundred dead," as he surveyed the carnage.

"John," said the admiral, ignoring John's concerns, "you've surpassed all my expectations in only one day. I was trying to construct a hero, but I don't need to now. You're the real deal! Now, I just have to get you to act like one. John, as we walk back to the bus, smile and wave at the cameras."

Although far fewer in number, there were twenty members of the press shadowing their walk toward the bus. Everything up to that point seemed natural to John, almost comfortable in execution. Nevertheless, responding to the press—this was difficult. It took conscious effort to force a smile and wave toward them. It was even more difficult to smile as John was forced to walk around a dead soundman, boom pole gripped in his hands.

"Admiral, this is a giant catastrophe any way you spin it," whispered John to the admiral as they walked.

"Nonsense, John," said the admiral, "this is only a small brush stroke in the big picture," then he grimaced, "Although, undeniably it's not without sacrifice, and sadly there will be more." The admiral took a deep breath and let out a sigh. "Ultimately the end justifies the means." The admiral then motioned his hand, indicating he wished not to discuss the subject anymore. They walked in silence for a few more steps waving at the press.

"A word about Corporal Clark?" said John as they approached the bus.

"Oh, never mind that," said the admiral, now smiling again, "The corpsman has just experienced classic Colonel Vickers, expressing his charming personality. I say Corporal Clark remains a sergeant, and I'll make sure he's awarded the Navy and Marine Corps Medal."

As John entered the bus, it was to a round of applause and cheers from the seven remaining Immunes. Booboo and Spoon suffered minor injuries; Booboo a corneal abrasion of the eye and Spoon a banged-up knee. Both rode back in an ambulance at the admiral's orders.

John waited patiently for the cheers to subside. Then said, "The admiral was correct when he said this team was the best, and I'm extremely proud to be part of it." John gave them thumbs up and said, "Strong work."

He then flopped in his seat. His energy seemed to leave him at once. He didn't move nor speak on the ride back.

CHAPTER 26

THE COMMON ROOM

The admiral met the team in the common room on their return. The only missing Immune was Suggs, who was still being treated at the medical clinic.

"I can't tell you the importance of the success of this first mission," said the admiral. His tone became somber. "Although Central will support and protect you as much as we can, some of you will undoubtedly die in future encounters."

"If you're asking for volunteers, I nominate Suggs," said Prof. There were a few scattered laughs.

The admiral ignored the comment and continued, "You'll be well taken care of as you reside here at Central. All of your needs will be addressed including, 'arranged dates' with any sex desired."

There was silence from the Immunes as all were contemplating the ramifications.

"What about beer?" said Sumo, breaking the silence.

"There's absolutely no restriction on alcohol and recreational drugs in the First Immune Attack Force, except when you're on call," said the admiral with a smile.

"Well then—what the hell are we standing around making chit chat? I got serious business to take care of with a Mr. Bud and a Mr. Wiser."

The admiral kept smiling and didn't move. He only raised his eyebrows and looked at Prof.

"I've got a feeling we're getting our call schedule right now," said Prof.

"Correct you are," said the admiral, "Call is twenty-four hours a day, seven days a week. I think everyone understands my meaning. Prof, I'll leave it up to you to explain it to Suggs. It may take a few days, but I'm sure you'll prevail."

"If there's no beer, then I volunteer for the first suicide mission," said Sumo in a serious tone.

"I'm afraid you'll have to survive only with the amenities of the Common room," said the admiral.

In the common room full-time chefs manned grills and anything from a peanut butter and jelly sandwich to prime rib was available around the clock. Masseuses and estheticians remained on call for them 24-hours a day. There was ping-pong, billiards, foosball, a poker table, plasma screen televisions, and a wall of the twenty most current arcade games for their pleasure. A library, weight room, bowling alley, and indoor swimming pool were in the process of being installed.

The alcohol restriction wasn't a problem for most of the Immunes, but it eventually became a problem for Sumo and Suggs. Sumo listed on his medical history questionnaire that he drank one beer every two days. What he didn't say was the one beer was a mini keg. So he was effectively drinking two and a half liters of beer per day. When the Immunes' prohibition started, Sumo needed hospitalization for a week when he went into DTs.

Suggs was also an alcoholic consuming at least five mixed drinks every night. When confronted by the medical team, Suggs responded, "I'm not an alcoholic, I'm a professional drinker."

Ultimately, the admiral took care of Suggs by planting Disulfiram in his food, then challenging Suggs to a drinking contest. Administration of Disulfiram is common in treatment of alcoholics by making them extremely ill when they drink. Most of the Immunes enjoyed seeing Suggs change every hue of green, but the fun ended when he began projectile vomiting.

The first stream caught the admiral in the chest, then Suggs turned and nailed Prof in the face. He also took out two arcade games and the billiard table. The last hurl arced through the air. It landed on the hot grill at the snack bar. The steaming fumes caused a chain reaction, with four other Immunes losing dinner. From that point forward the Immunes refused to eat anything from the grill, which was now dubbed the vomitron.

The admiral finished his speech, telling the team that the missions would be frequent and media coverage intense from here on out. Then he recommended the Immunes either enjoy the common room or retire to their apartments.

"Are there any other choices?" asked Prof.

The admiral gave Prof a salute and walked away whistling to himself.

Every Immune chose common room R&R except for John. He, as well as the other Immunes, was provided an apartment at Central. Everything was new except for original oil paintings on the walls. John mentioned he liked the art of Sir Edwin Henry Landseer. It was obvious the paintings were original Landseers. One he recognized—a large piebald dog stood watch over a child he'd saved from the sea. John remembered past emotion when first viewing a reproduction. Currently he had no capacity for sentiment as his soul was filled with vengeance.

The paintings weren't the only extravagant objects in the apartment. His bathroom faucets were gold and the floor was Italian marble. The rest of the apartment dripped in luxury, but John couldn't care less. All he wanted was to drain his brain of intelligent thought and to become numb. John turned toward the high definition, 3D screen that filled the wall.

As the display lit up, he saw his image fill the screen for the five o'clock news opening. He changed the channel and saw a video of himself. John tried several Internet feeds, but it was the same, nothing but him. Frustrated, he turned the monitor off and went to bed.

CHAPTER 27

PR MAN

A purple tentacle wrapped itself around Cassandra's neck. She struggled and clawed at it. A spotlight of purple emanating from the sphincter illuminated her naked body. Tentacles bound John, and he couldn't move. Cassandra didn't speak; she only stretched her arm out to John as she was lifted toward the sphincter. The sphincter became putty-like and engulfed Cassandra. John struggled, but his bonds continued to restrain him. Evil laughter chortled from behind. Suspended and held by tentacles was a throne, upon which sat the demonic Dr. Sengele. Using oversized hedge clippers, Sengele began cutting the tentacles suspending John. John struggled, then began to fall.

John awoke as he fell from bed and hit the floor. He struggled as he felt bound, but it was only the bed blanket wrapped tightly around him. He was drenched with sweat from the nightmare. He looked up at the clock; it was two minutes to 5:00 a.m., so he didn't return to bed. He knew attendants would be banging on his door at five sharp. He was right. The banging started precisely at five. He opened the door and five assistants entered and began his prep for the day.

His scheduled first task was to be in front of a bank of video cameras, but the admiral wanted to speak with John first. John was escorted to the admiral's office for breakfast.

A small round table with a white tablecloth was set up between the admiral's two guest chairs. A sumptuous meal had been prepared, but John didn't hunger for food. He was more interested in being fed information.

"When do I get taken to Sengele?" blurted John as he walked into the office. He was still shaken from the nightmare.

"Hey," said the admiral, looking surprised, "hold on there, big fella. I didn't say one successful day with the Immunes would score you Sengele. Sit and have breakfast." The admiral motioned John to the other chair. "I said you might get a shot at Sengele over time. Currently, only High Council members know his location. In addition, his interrogations continue. We wouldn't want you taking out what could be a great resource of information."

John sat in silence, lost in thought. The admiral took the opportunity to change the subject.

"What happened yesterday exceeded our wildest expectation."

"Not to rain on your parade," said John, "but at my count, we killed only seven airwars. As I said yesterday, it was catastrophic. The airwars must've killed a hundred people in that field."

"One hundred and sixty-seven to be exact," replied the admiral, but his smile remained.

John shook his head and said, "Well, by my calculations, if you're calling this a victory, this must fit the definition of a Pyrrhic victory."

"Oh, not so, my world hero. There's more to victory than a casualty count. Yes, we lost one hundred and sixty-seven brave souls, but tens of thousands die each day from airwar attacks around the world. Our losses are inconsequential."

"Perhaps not to the families of the victims," said John.

The admiral ignored the comment and continued, "The seven airwars were killed without a single juvenile being released. Hope has returned to the world, and you, John, are now the world's favorite defender. Perhaps you noticed you made the news?"

"I noticed nothing on the idiot box but me, and just when I thought TV programming already sunk to its nadir, this happens." John pointed to himself.

"I'd call it a PR rout," said the admiral, grinning. He motioned to a monitor on his desk. "I'd be happy to show you the media clips from last night."

John frowned. "So this is a public relations victory?"

"The most important kind," said the admiral, "John, do you realize, with the exception of Mad Mike's Liberty Fighters, world-wide attacks on airwars have dropped to zero? People have faith now. The common man is again listening to the government. The world's military can now concentrate on Mad Mike."

"Why don't you recruit him?" said John, "His militias can work with the Immunes."

The admiral paused and shook his head, "The militias have absolutely no trust in ASC's leadership. ASC can only control the militias by killing them."

"That's ironic," said John, "as militias recruit some of the bravest. Mad Mike was fighting airwars when ASC could only cry run and hide. Consider, too, every Immune alive could kill twenty airwars a day, and it would take a hundred years to rid all the monstrosities. It's not right that ASC's new efforts lie in killing our fellow man."

"John," responded the admiral dogmatically, "these Mad Mike guys are renegades. They don't care how many juveniles are released. They could seriously disrupt my plans, and that would be catastrophic. Ultimately, it's of little consequence. I figure the military will have them rounded up in a week."

A corpsman with a steaming pot of coffee entered the office. Both men declined the coffee. John wanted to continue to debate the militias. He was a bit perturbed the admiral was more concerned about his plans than the lives of those men. However, the admiral used the interruption to quickly change the subject to the previous day's stats. Seven airwars had been downed. There were two clean kills by John, a third considered dirty because of released juveniles, but technically it was clean because the backup obliterated every freed juvenile.

Bob, Dude, Prof, and Sumo each killed an airwar using John's technique. Five other airwars ended up escaping. With two, the siphon tubes ascended before Cupcake and DS could catch a ride up. On one, Mr. Eddie and Booboo fell from the siphon tube when they both tried to ride at the same time. Mr. Eddie's thumb caught Booboo in the eye during the fall. With the fourth airwar Spoon fell when she lost her grip on the fringe. She hit the water hard and tore cartilage in her left knee, but otherwise was okay. The last airwar to escape didn't have an Immune attack.

One hundred and sixty-seven people died, and over two hundred others sustained injuries. Not all were from airwar stings. Eleven deaths were due to trampling from the stampede.

The events of the previous afternoon appeared on the news worldwide. Estimates showed viewership was near three billion. John, who was already a hero before the exercise, was now considered a living legend. The admiral likened the event to hitting a grand slam home run at the bottom of the ninth in the seventh game of the World Series, down three runs with two outs, two strikes and no balls.

"Yes, John," said the admiral, "you've changed the world overnight, or perhaps I should refer to you by your formal name, The Immune."

John preferred "John," or maybe formally, "Dr. Long," but to be attached to a sobriquet like The Immune made him cringe.

John saw the admiral noticed his expression.

"Ah yes," said Beckwourth, "the reluctant hero with an unassuming personality, the average Joe to whom everyone relates." The admiral paused to wipe his mouth with his napkin, then threw it on his plate.

"John, you're this PR man's dream. I know you don't recognize your importance in the big picture, or even what you've already accomplished. I want you to know, before you came on board, ASC strategy was in shambles. Politicians and military politicos had an agenda, but were clueless how to accomplish it. The High Counsel was on the brink of complete failure, putting them in total jeopardy. You saved the day. ASC now has the confidence of the masses. Our current strategies are moving along well."

John raised an eyebrow. "Okay, what's our current strategy? As I previously said, the small number of Immunes can't begin to make a dent in the millions of airwars."

"What we're doing is buying time at the moment for ASC to arrange a final solution," said the admiral, "Patience is key. If we control the masses, it goes a long way toward that goal."

"Well, from my perspective, ASC is too slow. I've personally acquired more information about the airwars in the last day than all the supposed brilliant member scientists of ASC have since this crisis began. From my readings on the Internet, I now question the qualifications of many of those in charge."

"John, let me assure you ASC loves you at this point. I'd strongly suggest keeping political feelings to yourself." The admiral stood from the breakfast table. "You do have a distinct advantage over ASC scientists. Lab jockeys are not in a position of risk-taking as you are. Discovery is frequently the by product of daring action, wouldn't you agree?"

John did have to agree to that, if necessity is the mother of invention, then danger was the father of action.

CHAPTER 28

PSYCHIC RELIEF

The next few weeks came and went swiftly. Although each day was a different experience, the overall itinerary was the same. Mornings began with filming televised propaganda and video messages to other Immune Corps around the world. Then it was breakfast briefings followed by transport of the squad to where the admiral felt the need was the greatest. This translated to the location that would provide the maximum public relations impact.

The team was an eclectic mix and John got along extremely well with everyone, even Suggs. Suggs warmed up to John after John saved his life. Suggs was regarded by the team as a harmless blowhard. Everyone except Prof ignored his constant boasting. Most of his brags centered around his airwar takedown ranking on the team, which stood consistently at number three. Much to the endless agitation of Suggs, Prof repeatedly combined Suggs' limited mathematical skills and improvised statistics to demonstrate Suggs had the worst record.

John maintained the most takedowns on the team, but he had an advantage of solo missions, which were only glorified press junkets. He might do two to three of these a week after their regular daily mission. After John, Bob was the best downer.

Besides the admiral, John had become the friendliest with Bob. John never spoke of Bob's previous association with Mad Mike, but he did inquire about Daniel, Bob's son. Bob weakly said he'd been killed in another airwar attack, but he would always be eternally grateful to John for giving him a few extra days with his son.

When John wasn't around, Bob could usually be seen with Dude in a never-ending political discussion. Neither Immune was enamored by ASC. Although John didn't disagree with them, he just didn't care about following politics. His energies remained solely focused on downing more airwars and getting to Sengele.

Booboo was the least aggressive of the group. He had the fewest kills and the most injuries. He had fallen from airwars so many times it was amazing he survived with no more than sprains or minor contusions. Suggs said he fell on purpose just to get more attention from Spoon, who seemed to fawn over every little injury Booboo sustained. Spoon and Booboo were inseparable, but it was unclear to the team whether they were romantically involved. Regardless of his shortcomings, Booboo always had a smile and was eager to return to the fray even after an injury. His post mission cartoon drawings raised morale and were loved by everyone.

Sumo spent most of his time hanging out with Cupcake in the common room, taking advantage of the billiard table. If he wasn't shooting pool with Cupcake, he was helping Prof harass Suggs. They both performed that pursuit with great gusto. Sumo also made it clear his sole motivation for ending the airwar crisis was so he could return to drinking beer.

Mr. Eddie, or Kentucky Blue as Prof called him, was the loner in the group. Keeping to himself, he passed most of his time in his apartment listening to classic rock. His eyes always seemed bloodshot and, except for frequent visits to the snack bar, he was seldom seen in the common room.

DS was the social butterfly of the team. She talked with everyone, even forcing Mr. Eddie to interact with her. And if a rumor was being spread, she was usually the source.

Besides the admiral, the only non-Immunes who had access to the common room were Sergeant Clark, Captain Howe, and Colonel Vickers. The colonel would occasionally make an appearance at the snack bar, but he never spoke. The captain and sergeant would interact with the team members, but Howe was too busy to spend much time with the team. Sergeant Clark only seemed to appear when DS was around. It was well known he was seen on more than one occasion making a late night exodus from DS's apartment.

The admiral stayed largely aloof from the team, except for John. The admiral controlled the mission location, but John ran the logistics for the actual assignment. He would give John geographic details, numbers, and locations of airwars. John would work out an attack strategy with the other Immunes, then the squad was off.

John repeatedly proved himself a strong leader. None of the other members of the First Immune Attack Force questioned his leadership abilities. All were happy not to have to deal with his additional administrative work. Of course, Suggs was the exception. Suggs was in constant negotiation for a co-command rank in the First Immune Attack Force. The admiral became skilled at ignoring him.

As time passed, The First Immune Attack Force developed a bit of cabin fever. Even though their needs were well taken care of, other than missions, the Immunes never left Central. Prof referred to himself as the prisoner of Camelot. Continuous pressure from the team led the admiral to acquiesce to a weekend of liberty.

It was a Friday afternoon, and the admiral and John were meeting privately in a post-mission debriefing in his office.

"Against my better judgment, I've arranged a flight for the entire squad to Key West for a day off and a reprieve from the no alcohol rule," announced the admiral.

"Great," said John, "the team needs the break. I'll let them know right away. You go on and arrange a solo mission for me."

"Sorry," said the admiral, "I can't play mother hen. I have a meeting at sea, and I'll be out of contact. You're the only one whom everyone will listen to, and of the entire group you need a break the most. You've been running on emotion only. Take a day to find yourself."

John pounded his fist on the admiral's desk. "This is ridiculous. These are grown adults who risk their lives every day. The First Immune Attack Force doesn't need a nanny. My time would be better spent killing Sengele's creations, but I'll go if that's the only option given."

He could see the admiral smiling at him for having caved into his wishes.

"Just try to make sure there are no incidents," said the admiral, "The Immunes have their political detractors, such as your friends, Senator Snivaling and Captain Stewart, who both pine for the good old days of the extraction centers. The public loves the team, but Snivaling and Stewart's love, I assure you, is only skin deep."

John could feel a bristling of hair on the back of his neck with the mention of the senator and Captain Stewart. "There'll be no incidents. I'll make sure we keep a low profile."

"I'm sure you will . . . I'm sure you will," said the admiral, maintaining a devilish grin as John left his office.

And the team did keep a low profile, or at least as low as you can keep having a hundred-plus paparazzi and crowds of onlookers following every movement. In less than twenty minutes of strolling on Duvall Street, the squad had become completely frustrated. The Immunes were so compressed they could barely move from shop to shop. The overflow of the crowds into the narrow street shut down traffic. Like a herd of antelope, the team kept together out of necessity. The press and fans desiring autographs and photos would consume any one member culled from the herd.

Suggs made the matter worse when he noticed a side street filled with weathered eclectic shops. Peering down the lane, he saw a garish purple, wooden sign, which read *Madam Curie, Spiritualist and Advisor*. Suggs announced he had heard of her, so she must be good. He insisted the team accompany him for a consultation as he had an important personal question that needed answering.

The team groaned in unison, but suddenly everyone's attention was pulled to Prof, who began jerking spasmodically. The spasms ceased with his head arched back and arms spread, palms and face lifted to the sky. In a low, moaning voice he said, "Suuuuugs, I have a message from beyooooond. I speak with the spirit Thomas Tusser."

The crowd became hushed. Only the sounds of clicking cameras were heard.

"Oh, great professor," said Sumo breaking the silence, "who's Thomas Tusser?"

"A looooong dead poet," replied Prof in the same groaning voice. Then Prof straightened, glared at Suggs, and in a pedagogic voice exclaimed, "Who said a fool and his money are soon parted!"

"That's a load of crap!" retorted Suggs with his face puckered up like he had bitten a sour lemon, "You're no psychic. I *have* heard of Madam Curie. She's famous."

"Suggs!" said Prof, rolling his eyes, "you're an imbecile. Of course you've heard of Madam Currie. She won the Nobel Prize for discovering radium."

"See!" said Suggs, grinning with satisfaction, "I knew it. Now I don't know much about spirit names, but if she discovered the ghost Radium and won a noble prize for it, she must be good."

Prof, now exasperated, said, "Suggs, go in and give the con lady your money so we can get the hell out of here."

Mystical symbols and the street address "number 83" adorned the front of the shop. The team squeezed into the small reading room. Paparazzi and onlookers jammed the door opening and filled the storefront window with faces and cameras. The crowded bodies blocked the natural light, which darkened the room. Suggs sat at a small mahogany table. The table was clear on top except for a centered crystal ball gradually rotating on an electric wooden stand. The only light in the room came from beneath the crystal. Its beam, scattered by multiple inclusions, made an eerie dance of lights on the ceiling.

An elderly woman swept into the room from behind a curtain of orange beads. Her deep facial wrinkles, observable even under heavy make-up, looked incongruous with her dyed, coal-black hair. She was wearing a purple wrap highlighted with silver flecks and rhinestones. The gold bangles, which covered both arms, made a metallic ringing sound with every movement. A look of astonishment crossed her face as she became aware of the media circus in the front of her establishment. As she recognized the marketing possibilities, the look was rapidly replaced with a toothy grin, revealing missing and yellowed teeth.

Before Suggs could speak, she gazed straight into his eyes and announced in a thick east European accent, "Vhat's zis I sense, you ave lost a loved one recently, no?"

Prof rolled his eyes and whispered to John, "That's a safe divination. Who hasn't lost a loved one to the airwars?"

Suggs looked like a deer in headlights and said nothing. Madam Curie continued, "Vhat I am sensing eez a name beginning with an M or, R, or perhaps a C. Eez zat correct?"

"Notice how mediums always only channel a letter first," Prof whispered again to John, "Why don't the spirits just give their name right off? Spirits must have a good sense of humor jerking the psychics around like that."

Suggs shook his head. Without missing a beat, Madam Currie made a sweeping gesture with her arms to the Immunes in the room and said, "Not you, blondee boy. I feel ze spirit of a lost loved one in zis room."

The suggestion made John think of Cassandra, and he involuntarily winced. John could see the Madam immediately noticed his momentary facial expression. She addressed John, "Madam Currie feels ze spirit of your loved one nearby. You vere close to zis person, vere you not?"

John mildly angered by violation of his emotion, refused to take the bait. He pointed at Suggs and said, "He's the one with the money, and he was highly referred to you by a Mr. Tusser."

Prof snorted, and there were a few muffled laughs. The word *money* seemed to refocus Madam Currie's attention back to Suggs.

"Vell, young man, 'ow can Madam Curie be of assistance?"

"Yes . . . well . . . what I'm trying to say is . . ." Suggs seemed to be at a loss for words. He then blurted out, "Could you ask your famous spirit, Radium, my question?"

More laughing came from the Immunes.

The madam's brow furrowed in anger, and now in a distinctly non-European accent she spit out, "Don't mock me, boy, or I'll throw a hissy like you've never seen before, and I'll toss everbody outa this here room faster than a frog tongue on a fly."

Suggs appeared startled by her tone. He said apologetically, "I'd never mock you, Madam Curie." He pulled a fifty-dollar bill from his pocket and laid it on the table.

Madam Currie's smile returned. She lightly touched her fingertips together, and in a return to her European roots said, "I vill be happy to consult ze spirit Radium for you. Vhat is your question?"

"Well," said Suggs, "I noticed Dr. Invincibilis' tattoo parlor down the street, and I wanted to know what kind of tattoo I should get? I think—"

Prof, who appeared to no longer be able to contain himself, interrupted, "Suggs, you dragged us in here for that idiotic question? I'll tell you the tattoo you should get and where you should put—" but before he could finish, Madam Curie snatched the fifty and began pounding the table with her fist.

A long tirade of expletives and rants followed. From what John could piece together from the diatribe, it appeared as though Madam Currie and the good doctor had been an item in the past, but now had irreconcilable differences. She was under the belief that Invincibilis sent Suggs to humiliate her in front of the paparazzi.

She finally screamed at Suggs, "Boy, the spirit, Radium, has told me only a dumb, blind cracker would get a tattoo from that torn down coot Invincibilis. The doctor otta make better use of his tattoo gun by shoving it up his ass." She then stomped out through her beaded curtain, breaking one of the strands as she passed.

The room was silent for a moment except for the small orange beads rolling on the floor. Prof broke the silence by looking to the sky and saying, "The spirits have spoken—now let's get the hell out of here."

A brief, early afternoon thunderstorm came to the Immunes' aid. The pelting shower thinned the crowds and paparazzi enough that the team could retreat to the "historic" Parrot Joe's Bar, built the previous year. The admiral had the foresight to reserve the two-story building made of fabricated weathered wood. A plastic sign with antiqued glazing hung over the entrance, dating the establishment from 1910. Every opening of the building emitted the sounds of old Jimmy Buffett songs.

Access was only allowed for the Immunes and military personnel hand-picked by the admiral. John couldn't help but notice a high percentage of the military were of the attractive female type. Even with liberty, the admiral had come up with a plan to sequester the team, or at least the male members.

Due to the necessity of banding together, after performing a head count, John was surprised to discover one of the team was missing. John asked Sumo, who was actively taking advantage of prohibition's repeal. Sumo, without looking up from his beer, pointed to one of the many monitors scattered throughout the bar. Over fifty percent of the monitors displayed a live feed of Suggs being inked by the bald-headed Dr. Invincibilis. Surrounded by cameras and adoring young women, Suggs' expression suggested this might be the happiest moment in his life.

John thought, *Death by smothering attention; a risk of celebrity.* Weighing the dangers of airwar tentacles versus press adulation, he figured Suggs was currently at high risk, but his thoughts on coordinating a rescue were distracted by Sumo. Sumo already drained his first pitcher of beer and was acting as if it served only as a warm up. Scanning the room, John eyed a bubbly brunette whose most impressive attributes couldn't even be concealed by a drab naval uniform. As he approached, she flashed a smile worthy of any toothpaste ad.

Seaman Carol Withers gushed like a junior high cheerleader meeting the captain of the football team. John ignored the gushing, and with a brief introduction, inserted her between Sumo and the next pitcher of beer. John watched Sumo eye the froth-filled pitcher, then the winsome girl, then the beer. An inviting touch of her hand won the battle and Sumo appeared to become absorbed in her chatter and smiles.

John scanned the bar. The rest of the team appeared not to be abusing the liquid two carbon spirits. Most carried on conversations with the new military faces except for Booboo and Spoon, who were laughing together as they followed Suggs' progress on the monitors.

Camera views rapidly cut from Suggs' grimaces as the tattoo gun moved up and down his chest to the bald scalp of Dr. Invincibilis. His scalp, covered with an elaborately tattooed Franciscan cross, was beaded with droplets of sweat. In the tattoo parlor, over the buzzing of the tattoo gun, "In-A-Gadda-Da-Vida" could be heard playing in the background. The overwhelming excitement of following Suggs' reality show resulted in John slipping into an uncharacteristic mid-afternoon nap.

John awakened to Suggs' grand entrance into Parrot Joe's. In his most regal-sounding voice, Suggs announced he was unveiling his new tattoo. John watched Suggs' face fall as he realized, blocked by MPs, his fawning followers remained outside. Only a few curious military personnel, John, and Prof turned their attention toward Suggs.

Looking disappointed, Suggs almost appeared as if he might return to the street, but instead he pulled off his T-shirt revealing a blood-tinged gauze bandage on his left upper chest. Puffing out his chest, he peeled the bandage away while performing a 180-degree slow turn. Permanently embedded in the skin were three blue vertically aligned Chinese characters that moved up and down as he relaxed and contracted his pectoralis muscle.

惧
卜
者

After the unveiling, John watched everyone turn back to their drinks or conversations, except for Prof, who whistled, and in a sarcastic tone said, "Let me guess what it says."

"Courage, bravery, intrepidness," exclaimed Suggs before Prof could make a snide comment.

"Brilliant!" Prof chuckled, "Three synonyms, just brilliant. You had them tattoo three synonyms on your chest. This is so marvelous, it captures your personality perfectly, only —"

An attractive Asian-American officer inserted herself between Prof and Suggs. Her attention was focused on the Chinese characters. As she read, the right corner of her mouth twisted into a slight smile. She paused, looking at Suggs for a moment as if trying to make a decision, then she began to move on.

"Wait, wait, wait," begged Prof, "You can't tease me with that little display and expect to walk off without telling me what made you smile."

"Wisely," said the officer, flashing an impish smile, "I'm letting a sleeping dog lie."

"Officer, I should let you know that this is clearly a matter of national security," said Prof in a serious tone, "I must know what you read."

"Well, there may be a translation issue," she said with a grin, "but I don't want to get involved."

"I knew that tattoo guy didn't look like a real doctor," said Suggs, now agitated, "I told him exactly how to spell intrepidness. I looked it up before I went in. He misspelled it, didn't he?"

Suggs began spelling out loud, "I N T R . . ."

The officer gave Suggs an incredulous look. Prof rolled his eyes and said, "See what I have to deal with on a daily basis? Just what does it say?"

Now the entire bar had come to a silence except for the tune "Margaritaville" playing in the background.

"Kindergarten Dance School," blurted the officer, grinning.

A moment of silence followed, then Prof fell from his bar stool to the floor in convulsions of laughter. As if this were a signal, the party started. There were toasts to Suggs, jokes about Suggs, and pantomimes of Suggs. Every patron of the bar was participating, except for Suggs. He bee-lined to the bathroom and locked himself in a stall, leaving only a trail of expletives floating in the air.

Later, John heard the officer admitting to Prof that she was of Filipino descent, born in Georgia, and couldn't read a single Chinese symbol. Prof made her promise, on the threat of death by airwar, that she would never reveal this to Suggs.

After a couple of hours, the party reached a feverish pitch. John was beginning to worry that things might be getting out of hand when Sumo climbed onto the bar next to five empty pitchers. He was holding an inebriated Seaman Withers in his arms and announced that he had proposed and she accepted. Everyone cheered, except John, who was trying to figure a way out of the new predicament. Suggs ended up being the answer.

After hours stewing in the stall, Suggs suddenly re-entered the bar with the plan of slugging the first person who mentioned his tattoo. Sumo and Withers were now off the bar, and when Sumo saw Suggs, he announced he and his new fiancé were each having Kindergarten Dance School tattooed as an engagement gift to each other. A slugfest ensued, resulting in the whisking of the First Immune Task Force back to Central. Seaman Withers was assigned a mission at sea, and Sumo, the next day, remembered nothing of the proposal or why he and Suggs both had black eyes.

On the admiral's return, no comment was made to John; only a slight rise of his eyebrow during the report. But no further liberty days were ever again granted to the First Immune Attack Force.

CHAPTER 29

HOMICIDE

D ue to ever-increasing responsibilities, frequent flights by the admiral were now necessary to the new seat of world government, dubbed ASC City, located outside Washington, DC. In addition, his presence was required one or two days every other week at undisclosed locations. He described these as administrative meetings and was reticent when questioned about them.

Overall, the admiral was absent twenty-five percent of the time. Regardless of his length of absence, he would always check in each day with John. Somehow, the admiral always managed to have the day's mission planned. John regarded him as an amazing man, but difficult to comprehend. They frequently had late night discussions on the importance of unwavering ethical standards and morality. The admiral's actions sometimes contradicted his avowed philosophy.

Perhaps the most bewildering event occurred when the admiral returned a day early from an ASC City trip. Captain Flinch had been skulking around Central all morning. John nearly bumped into Flinch's rapid exit out of a machine shop doorway. Flinch sneered at him, turned, and walked away.

John hadn't seen Flinch since the day Flinch first escorted him to Central. The sight of Flinch brought back horrible memories of Snivaling, Stewart, and the processing unit. He mentally tried to excuse Flinch's associations, rationalizing that Flinch, distraught from his loss of his family to airwars, was acting irrationally. He found out later, airwars killed Captain Flinch's family in a women's shelter where they were hiding from Flinch.

Shortly after his brief encounter with Flinch, John followed Suggs into the common room. John noticed someone stuck a sign onto Suggs' back that read *Please don't feed me, I might reproduce.* Prof and Sumo were in the corner snickering, so John had a good idea of the sign's origin.

"Suggs," said John, approaching him from behind, "Great job on downing that airwar yesterday." John patted Suggs on the back and surreptitiously removed the paper sign.

As no good deed goes unpunished, Suggs treated John to an incredibly detailed narrative of the event. Prof and Sumo were bursting at the seams with John's predicament. John looked around the room for someone to rescue him. There was only Spoon and Booboo sitting on a couch, their foreheads touching, lost in their own little world, oblivious to John's predicament.

John was relieved when Mr. Eddie entered the room and said, "Admiral's back. Saw him heading for his office."

"If you'll excuse me, I need to touch base with the admiral," said John. Then he leaned and whispered to Suggs, "You know, Prof and Sumo are 'very' interested in your airwar downing technique, but are too embarrassed to ask your advice. Perhaps you could educate them both. Don't take no for an answer. Prof and Sumo are proud men and don't want to impose on you."

Suggs beamed as he strode over to the two conspirators whose smiles suddenly evaporated.

As John approached the admiral's office, he could tell something was amiss. The laser handprint reader adjacent to the door was detached from the wall, hanging by wires. The door had forced entry marks along the door jamb. The door stood slightly ajar.

"The secret is out; you're a traitor to us all," said Captain Flinch, his voice hissed from inside the office.

A single gunshot rang out. John burst into the room to find the admiral with his pearl-handled pistol in hand, a thin wisp of smoke emitting from the muzzle. Captain Flinch lay face-down on the floor, an exit wound still pumping blood out of the back of his head. A crowbar was on the desk next to the dead Venus flytrap plant, even more dried out than before. The grow-light, plugged in and lit, lay beside him on the floor.

The admiral looked at John and shrugged as if to suggest *all in a day's work*. He bent over Captain Flinch and began rifling through the officer's pockets. He blocked John's view as he retrieved an item and slipped it into his own pocket. From the bulge in the admiral's pocket, it looked like a cylindrical object with a blue top exposed. Then the admiral removed what appeared to be a thin children's storybook from Flinch's hand.

"The best way for two men to keep a secret is for one of them to kill the other," said the admiral, turning to face John, "No sense in you getting involved. You head on out, and I'll explain everything later."

John walked out the door, shaken from the event as several armed military police ran into the office. Nobody tried to stop John's exit.

All day he waited for the military police to question him, but this never occurred. Nor was there any mention of the incident by anyone. It was as if the event never happened. The admiral called John to his office later that day.

"John," said the admiral, "I told you I'd explain later and I've previously sworn that I'd always be truthful. The only exceptions are if it violates ASC security and I'm afraid this entire incident does."

"What did you take from Flinch's pocket?" John demanded, not satisfied, "Was it a blue? Tell me that it wasn't Ube Watabee's extract."

"Sorry," said the admiral, shaking his head, "ASC security."

"Okay," said John, still fishing for information, "What about that kid's book with the cats and rat on the cover?"

"That I can tell you," said the admiral, smiling, "It's a children's book called the *Three Samurai Cats*. It's based on an old Japanese folk tale. It was a present to my nephew. He drew pictures on the inside cover and gave it back. Said it would bring me good luck during my assignment. I promised that sweet kid the return of his book once the crisis ended. Sadly, he passed away."

The admiral then pulled the rolled up book from his back pocket and opened it. There were crayon drawings on the inside cover.

"John," said the admiral softly and with sincerity, "I don't know what you're thinking of me currently, but I'll tell you this. I had no choice with Flinch."

"Just make sure you never share any secrets with me," said John, with a wry smile.

The admiral laughed, and John never brought up the incident again. John did note that from that point on, the admiral always carried the book in his back pocket and on at least one occasion, he seemed to be making a notation in it.

CHAPTER 30

MOTION PROTUBERANCES

All the Immunes on the First Immune Attack Force had become proficient at downing airwars. A mission could be planned and executed anywhere in the country, but the team always returned to Central on completion. On a good day, under the right conditions, John's team could down as many as forty airwars. The record was sixty-seven on Lake Calm, outside Atlanta. John himself had taken out eight on that day.

Following the mission, the dog and pony show began. Interviews, photos, autographs, and frequent marriage proposals were a constant reminder of their superstar status. John weathered the glorification well, recognizing it as inescapable. One day a young boy asked John to autograph his new action figure doll, "The Immune." John felt compelled to confront the admiral.

"I need to know two things. First, that our efforts are saving lives, and second, I want to know you're not personally profiting from this merchandising." John waved a boxed "The Immune" doll in the admiral's face.

"The answers are definitely yes and no with qualification," said the admiral with a smile, "Yes, you're saving lives. Look at the stats. Worldwide deaths from airwar attacks are plummeting. Juvenile releases have declined, even considering the persistence of the militias."

The admiral took the action figure from John and removed it from its box. After a brief examination of the toy, he pressed a button on the back.

"Hold your breath, Suggs," said a voice from the doll, "I'll save you."

The admiral laughed, "John, it says here there are nine other awesome 'The Immune' phrases. Do you want to hear them all?"

"I wasn't joking, admiral," said John.

"Oh, lighten up, John. If you were a comic book hero, there's no doubt you'd be the number one character franchise in the world. The Immunes are technically a governmental organization and, therefore, public domain when it comes to merchandising. So no, I'm not receiving any financial gain whatsoever."

The admiral handed the toy and box back to John. As he did, he pointed to a small advertisement on the box for the Admiral Beckwourth action figure, then he grinned.

"John, at this point in my life, wealth isn't a motivator, but I do profit when you and the other Immunes rise in celebrity. Don't forget, I'm the ASC liaison to The Immune Corps. Currently, I have more political clout within ASC than the President of the United States, plus he's not even a member. I assure you, having ASC on my side is vital. So your icon status helps me in my job, and since fame begets fame, I only hope the Immune bobble heads, lunchboxes, and bandages continue to be a success."

The admiral reached in his pocket and pulled out a yo-yo bearing a three dimensional flasher image of Suggs on each side. He tossed the toy to John. "Learn a few tricks. Relax some. There can be more to life than killing airwars and trying to get at Sengele. Oh, keep the yo-yo. I have the entire First Immune Attack Force set."

The admiral was whistling to himself as he walked off. John stood fuming and promised himself he would redouble his efforts to find the location of Sengele.

Although not at ease with the celebrity aspect of his job, John was even more disgruntled with the limited biological information ASC provided. John firmly believed science would be the ultimate answer to the airwar crisis.

John frequently wondered aloud why ASC didn't provide the Immunes more information on the biology of airwars. Certainly, after he discovered the "motion protuberances," ASC must have put huge resources into studying the effect.

The admiral assured him many biologic discoveries had been uncovered about the navigation system, but none of the information would benefit the Immunes. John debated this point with the admiral on more than one occasion. He argued, if he understood more of the biology, perhaps he could find suitable applications in the field. The admiral adamantly responded Immunes needed laser focus on their missions. Trying new tactics and experimentation might cause extreme setbacks, so John backed off.

After each mission, the team would dutifully report any findings or observations to the assigned ASC scientist, Professor Doak. Professor Doak was a thin man with black hair combed straight back, which was held in place by heavy hair grease. His one distinctive feature was a large nose with dilated pores. He always wore a white lab coat and Buddy Holly style black-rimmed glasses. He was the most phlegmatic individual John ever met. Rumor was his wife up and disappeared right before the airwar crisis. DS said she would have run away, too, or cut her wrists if she was married to Doak.

Professor Doak would interview each Immune post-mission. He always referred to himself in the third person. He would say, "Professor Doak would like to know" and follow it with a question. Doak would diligently type their comments into a laptop and occasionally ask a clarifying question. All information flow was one way. Other than asking questions, Professor Doak, or Professor Dork, as Suggs referred to him, never spoke or interacted with any of the Immunes, except once.

The Immunes had become adept in moving airwars by squeezing the "motion boobs," as the team now called them. They were useful, as John discovered, to move airwars away from dropped victims. However, it was also practical for transporting the Immunes to advantageous drop-off points. On more than one occasion, Immunes reported sticking injuries when squeezing the protuberances.

Once, John removed a small copper wire that imbedded itself in Sumo's index finger pad. John, as per protocol, reported the incident to Doak. Professor Doak took the one-centimeter wire and placed it in a sterile plastic bag. Doak looked over his glasses at John.

"Dr. Long, please remember you're no longer a medical professional," he said in a droning voice, "Your role is as an Immune. A public servant. Nothing more."

Doak then held the little plastic bag up, wiggling it in front of John's face and said, "My concern, not yours."

Incensed, John was trying to come up with a witty retort when he realized Doak was correct. John was in reality a glorified public servant. The Immune Corps, like other government agencies, had an immense budget, great power, and, although busy, were ineffective. The simple truth was airwar numbers hadn't decreased.

Instead of arguing, John clicked his knife open and stared at Professor Doak. Doak paled as white as his lab coat, then ran from the room. John smiled to himself, thinking *Being a public servant isn't so bad. Government employees are impossible to fire.*

John was expecting a reprimand from the admiral at the next morning's team briefing. He was surprised when the admiral ignored John's intimidation of Doak, but brought up the wire issue.

"ASC scientists have discovered, immediately above the 'Long protrusions' is a sac-like gizzard," said the admiral. The eponym "Long protrusions" was the term used by ASC to name the motion protuberances, presumably to honor John.

"Airwars transport small indigestible parts from the gastric area to the small sacs. Items not rendered digestible by grinding of the gizzard end up transferred back to the sphincter for expulsion."

The admiral opened a box which contained a ring, watch, and cell phone components that looked like a ball-peen hammer had previously pounded them.

"Sometimes sharp objects will work out of the gizzard sac into the 'directional joysticks' below." The admiral had his own term he liked for the protuberances.

"You might get a small cut or abrasion, but that's it. Don't waste time trying to retrieve gizzard debris. Immunes should focus on the mission of downing airwars."

The admiral paused and gave John a look of consternation, "As a side note, Professor Doak has been transferred out of Central. Post-mission ASC interviews will surcease."

Clapping and cheers erupted from the squad. John shrugged in response to the admiral's glare.

John knew he wasn't quite accurate in his vocalizations that new data on the biology of airwars wasn't forthcoming from ASC. Daily news always seemed to be confirming new "discoveries," and each day Dr. Joseph Sengele would verify the discovery in yet another video confession.

John also knew if he was considered the hero of the world, then Dr. Sengele was the antichrist himself. In-depth, investigational reporting by ASC had shown Sengele was the embodiment of evil. The Internet was rife with proofs of his wickedness. Daily Internet posts would go viral on Sengele's association with the Klan, devil worship, and animal cruelty. John thought the accusations were almost as bad as those in a presidential election.

What enraged John most was Sengele's continuous inflammatory comments regarding the Immunes.

"Immunes are an unanticipated genetic quirk and an unfortunate occurrence if you ask me," said Sengele in his most recent interview.

In none of his many televised confessions did he ever show a modicum of remorse for the deaths attributed to his airwars.

In John's opinion, Sengele made Captain Stewart look like a saint. ASC's use of the airwar crisis as the rationale for gutting constitutional rights made sense regarding Sengele. The Sixth and Eighth Amendments of the Constitution need not apply to Sengele. The televised facts were overwhelming on Sengele's guilt, so a trial was unnecessary, and cruel and unusual punishment was the only fitting penalty for his crimes against humanity.

Demands from around the world ran the gamut from Sengele's immediate execution to public torture. Many supported the notion that John himself should be the executioner, and John, frankly, loved the idea. In fact, he tried to use his growing influence to discover Sengele's undisclosed location. This remained at ASC's highest level of security, which he couldn't penetrate. Sengele was the one person John could channel his hatred at for the death of Cassandra. In an odd way, it was good. It gave him vengeful energy to keep downing airwars.

The latest scientific discoveries by ASC had the most significance in the crisis since the formation of the Immune Corps. First was a revelation that airwars had an abhorrence to salt water. This report seemed somewhat dubious to John because part of the genome came from Man-O-Wars, whose natural environment was salt water, but Sengele himself confirmed the fact on video.

"Why would I use my genius to create a creature to eliminate humanity and have it spend two-thirds of the time in areas barren of humans?" said Sengele in a monotone voice, his eye darting back and forth as he spoke, "Clearly inefficient. So, of course, I genetically engineered them to avoid salt water. You can force airwars over salt water by squeezing the 'Sengele knobs.'" 'Sengele Knobs' was his own term. It was reported that he was appalled with the name 'Long protuberances,' which honored The Immune. "But, otherwise airwars will shun bodies of salt water."

Based on this discovery, ASC ordered migration of the entire world's population to coastal areas within 800 meters of the water's edge. The decree would have appeared pointless without the coexistence of another airwar aversion.

Apparently, a specific oscillating electrical pattern was noisome to airwars, but only if a significant body of salt water was on the other side. A wire fifty feet high was strung on telephone posts parallel to inhabitable coastal areas. A half mile from coastal shorelines was determined to be its maximum distance of effectiveness. The oscillating wave pattern ran continuously through the wire. Within this protective band between sea and wire, airwar attacks dropped to near zero. The only drawback was Colossi tended to accumulate along the wire's perimeter.

Many communities tried to protect themselves with the wire alone, but unless the town was coastal, airwars would cross. Countless numbers resisted this forced migration. The President of the United States wanted more time before implementing such a drastic plan.

"I understand the crisis," said the President, "I'd like to have the opportunity to examine input from scientists who disagree with the ASC findings. Perhaps we could find a less draconian path that wouldn't be ruinous to countries and economies."

John watched the immediate ASC response on television. Senator Snivaling appeared worldwide with ASC spokesman Glavin. Snivaling did the talking.

"ASC scientific findings are common knowledge and undisputable amongst reputable investigators," said Snivaling, "Any opinion to the contrary is not science, but seditious."

Glavin stood behind her, nodding the entire speech like a bobble-head doll.

"Population redistribution is such an important cause it must be undertaken immediately without further discussion. Foot dragging would be disastrous on epic proportions."

The President and other leaders acquiesced to ASC's power. So began the greatest human migration in the history of the world.

The only exception for forced migration was an inland city named ASC City. Located several miles southwest of Washington, DC, small complexes of buildings and homes surrounded a 150-acre lake. The lake, initially drained, was, at considerable expense, refilled with seawater. A perimeter wire was installed and virtually every ASC member transferred there to conduct business more efficiently. Long-time residents of the community, at the outset, were required to host ASC officials. Then, these same hosts, only a short time later, were asked to relocate to the coast in the name of world security.

An unanticipated side effect of the forced migration was an increase in world wide popularity of militias. Unified under the banner of Mad Mike's liberty fighters militias hadn't let up on attacking airwars. Generally, militia limited their attacks to rescuing victims. ASC controlled military responded to these attacks with so much ferocity complaints arose. Some soldiers even refused to fight militias citing humans weren't the enemy.

The "Winchester incident" caused a paradigm shift in ASC's military strategy. A company of United States military encountered a militia attacking airwars near Winchester, KY. The airwars had struck an elementary school. The screams from scores of entrapped children made the soldiers shudder. Instead of attacking the militia, they joined them, assaulting airwars instead. Several soldiers then deserted to join the militia. Although the rescue of several children occurred, the release of thousands of juveniles was the result.

ASC's response was to proclaim worldwide bans on gun possession now extended to the military. The only exception was the Grey Youth Guard. The Grey Youth Guard protected ASC City and served as enforcers for ASC policy. All encounters with militias from that point on involved either air attacks, and/or the ASC Grey Youth Guard. The Guard was known best for their young ages, grey armbands, religious-like devotion to the cause, and mercilessness. It was exceedingly motivating for town residents to start their coastal migrations upon the appearance of Grey Youth Guards.

The admiral knew the First Immune Attack Force loyalties leaned more toward Mad Mike than the Grey Youth Guard. He constantly admonished the Immunes to keep political opinions to themselves.

"I must remind you to not bite the hand that feeds," said the admiral at an early morning briefing in the auditorium.

"What if the mouth connected to the hand that feeds is eating your offspring—what then?" challenged Prof.

"They're the ones in power," said the admiral, frowning, "and for me to keep my essential position I must remain always cognizant of who wields the power."

"Sounds like you care more about your career than what's right," said Bob cynically.

The admiral became stone-faced. For a moment he felt the pressure was unbearable. He then said, "My duty is to do what is best for humanity, and the Immune Corps is an absolutely vital component in this missio—"

"I have an important question, admiral," interrupted Suggs, standing behind his desk.

The admiral put his hand to his forehead and began rubbing his temples. "Go ahead Suggs ask your important question," he said with resignation in his voice. He didn't think he could tolerate another Suggs question.

"The Internet says the Immunes haven't decreased airwar totals, and the militias have video proof of complete kills without 'juvie' release." The admiral looked up, astonished that Suggs said something relevant. Suggs continued speaking, holding up a printed page from a website. "The Internet also says I'm ranked as the favorite Immune in Japan for girls between the ages of nine and twelve. Don't you think we should do a mission in Japan?"

The admiral waited for the moans from the team to subside. "ASC does now concede complete kills are possible, but I remain terribly concerned about the continued release of millions of juveniles from attacks by militia. As for your question, the tweens of Japan will have to survive without you ad infinitum."

"Okay," said Suggs, nodding in agreement, "if you're running ads about me in Japan instead, I guess that's alright."

"Suggs, my IQ drops ten points if I walk within five feet of you," cried out Prof.

"Well, mine drops thirty and you don't even have to be around." Suggs twisted around looking at Prof.

"Wonderful comeback, Suggs." Sumo laughed, "You have succeeded in making Prof speechless." Prof was laughing so hard tears were streaming down his face.

"Stop it—now!" the admiral roared. The briefing room fell silent. "Keep this imbecilic banter in the common room where it belongs. The admiral pounded his fist on the podium. "These briefings may influence the outcome of the world and they should be treated as such." He was livid.

"I do occasionally have something important to say that may impact yours and others' lives. Although I've been successful in keeping ASC out of the Immunes affairs so far, Captain Stewart has pushed a motion through High Council."

The admiral heard a cough from back of the room that sounded distinctly like "*bullshit*." The admiral frowned, but kept speaking.

"The High Council believes the First Immune Attack Force shouldn't be surfing 'illegal' Internet sites. Captain Stewart has conveniently provided a security program to lock out illegal web sites on Central's computers. The program is being installed as we speak."

The briefing room erupted with all the Immunes shouting their opposition.

"Silence!" yelled the admiral. "This is not a Beckwourth decree, it's an ASC decree. I've completed my orders. Captain Stewart has been informed his security programs are applied and running as per his specifications. I'm done with it."

Bob stood and said, "Admiral, this—"

"Bob, don't say another word," interrupted the admiral with uncharacteristic sternness in his voice, then he pointed at Bob. "You're all clever and intelligent boys and girls." He glanced at Suggs, shook his head slightly, and continued, "I'm sure I'll be fine *not* knowing whatever you decide. Then he marched out of the briefing room."

John watched Bob and Dude take less than twenty minutes to hack the security program and log into his favorite "illegal" site. The three Immunes crowded around the monitor looking at the home page of AirwarsStings.com. The site listed nearly 500 ways to prevent airwar stings.

"John, do you think any of these work?" asked Bob.

"No," said John with a smile, "they're all bogus, but check out number 124 under 'Natural Protections' on the list."

Bob scrolled down the site on the monitor to number to 124.

"Bathe in toad urine!" exclaimed Dude, "You got to be kidding, thank God I'm an Immune."

Bob laughed and said, "Even if it were true, how would one find enough toads to collect that much urine?"

About ninety percent of the listings linked to product purchase sites. The spray "UnSting," promised for $49.95 it would protect from airwar stings, grow hair, clear psoriasis, and take away age spots. The site had extensive before-and-after pictures and a money back guarantee.

Bob pointed to a link at the bottom of the page. It was a drawing of Sengele. "Hey, click on that."

"No need," said John, frowning, "that's the Sengele Cult site. When I feel my rage slipping, I go there to recharge my batteries. Best not to go there unless you want to get pissed off."

John knew The Joseph Sengele Cult had gained traction in the fringe of society. Cult members, dressed in dark gothic attire, called themselves Sengele's ambassadors and tattooed Sengele's face in red on their right cheek. They claimed if you were an ardent follower of Sengele's teachings—it wasn't clear to John where these came from—the tattoo would protect you from airwar stings.

John had first-hand evidence that this was false. He'd saved a Sengele ambassador, who was trapped and screaming in an airwar. Swollen and bruised from stings, the young ambassador spoke to John.

"Thanks man," said the young man, "You saved my ass for real . . . holy crap you're The Immune."

"No problem." replied John, "Just glad I could help."

"The other ambassadors are never going to believe me."

John gave him a sad smile, and then began to walk off.

"Hey, you're a Doc too, right?"

"Yes," said John, looking back.

"Well, do you think you could tell me where I could have this tattoo removed?" He pointed to the Sengele tattoo on his cheek.

"Sorry, I don't know," said John, pleased with the young ambassador's decision, "but it would be worthwhile to share your experience with other Sengele ambassadors. The tattoo clearly is not protective and your role model is a—"

"Doc I couldn't agree more," interrupted the young man, "This tat is worthless, but it's my own fault. I didn't have it inked by a certified Sengele tattoo artist. I'm going to have it removed and redone certified this time. What do you think doc?"

"I think," said John pausing, "a belief, unflappable by a hurricane of contrary facts, defines 'willful ignorance'."

He then turned and walked away.

CHAPTER 31

FIREWORKS

D aily mission locations were based on an ASC importance scale, which corresponded to the site the admiral felt the team could get the most media exposure. The admiral seemed to believe his power in ASC rose and fell with the popularity of the Immunes. John had observed ASC was constantly reaching for more control of the Immune Corps. The admiral appeared to be quite adroit at blocking ASC advances.

Missions by now, although still risky, had largely become routine. John and the other members of the First Immune Attack Force were increasingly frustrated because assignments didn't involve more rescues. Although the team now wore special rescue harnesses, the squad rarely made use of the apparatus. Even with declining airwar attacks on humans as the migration to safe coastal zones progressed, there were ample missed opportunities for the Immunes to intervene. One particular occurrence caused controversy within the First Immune Attack Force.

A group of thirty airwars attacked a small town that ignored migration orders. About half of Fairview's population ended up injured or in airwar tentacles by the day's end.

That same evening, the First Immune Attack Force's assignment was a ceremonial downing of eleven airwars in front of the ASC press corps. It was to memorialize the one-hundred thousandth airwar downed by Immunes world wide. A small fireworks display launched at dusk commemorated the Immune event. The last pyrotechnic shells were memorable as they erupted. The upper pattern shell formed an outline of an airwar sac, and rockets below produced swirling coils looking exactly like the death dance of an airwar. One incredibly loud salute shell, symbolizing an Immune, erupted in the middle of the display, and the flaming likeness of the airwar faded into nothingness. It was an unforgettable image. The Immunes were shocked when they saw the same display in a heart-breaking story on the late news.

The storyline of "Fairview, the town that wouldn't listen" followed the account of a community that ignored ASC's decree on relocating to the coast. It chronicled the tragedy of not heeding ASC mandates. Its focus was a heart-wrenching interview by a petite blonde woman, eyes bloodshot from grief.

"I lost my husband and my two baby boys," she said, wailing, "Stevey and Chris were only two and five." She wiped her eyes with a large white handkerchief handed to her by the reporter. "Those bastards—those sanctimonious town council bastards—convinced my husband to stay. It was listening to Mad Mike's propaganda that caused this," she said in a shrill voice, "He was supposed to protect us. Where were Mad Mike's men when my babies were dying?" She began sobbing again.

The camera cut to a beautiful blonde reporter who, in a somber voice, said, "This reporter has learned the town requested an Immune team for help, but there weren't any within one-hundred miles. Spokesman Glavin from ASC has issued this press release."

Glavin's face filled the screen.

"This was an unnecessary tragic loss of life easily avoided if only Fairview leaders would've followed ASC's migration policy." Glavin pointed to a large map behind him showing migration paths and safe zones.

"Immunes can protect migration paths, but they're spread too thin to shield those who refuse to leave their homes."

The news feed returned to the reporter and the crying woman.

"Mrs. Roberts, what will you do now?" asked the reporter in a concerned voice.

"I'm leaving for the coastal safe zones." She began crying again, then she walked off camera.

"Good advice for us all from a mother who has lost everything," rattled off the reporter, "Back to you, Stan."

The news segment cut to the anchor desk.

"Thank you, Betty, for such an informative report." The anchor lifted a sheaf of papers and straightened it by hitting them on edge. "A final note to this sad story. We understand a militia did approach the town to assault the airwars illegally. These renegades came across some of our heroic Grey Youth Guards answering the town's cry for help. The militia proceeded to ignore the town and conduct a cowardly attack on those brave young men. Happily, an air strike obliterated the marauding militia. Our condolences go to the families of the Grey Youth Guard who were also all killed in the air strike. We'll end our report with some frightening clips as a reminder of the extreme importance of migration policy."

A clip ran of airwars siphoning from a lake at dusk outside Fairview. The screams of the trapped victims could easily be heard. At that moment a small, but unmistakable fireworks display of a writhing airwar appeared in the upper right corner of the screen. It looked as if it was a mile or two in the distance.

"What kind of crap is this?" screamed Prof, jumping to his feet.

John, who was reading in the far corner of the common room, looked up when he heard several expletives being hurled at the giant screen.

"Give me the remote," said John. He replayed the end of the story three times. Clearly, John was seeing the Immune's fireworks display they attended, but filmed from a distance.

"What's the emergency?" the admiral said as he rushed into the room, "I was paged there's an emergency in the common room." Everyone crowded around the large screen remained silent. The admiral gave John a quizzical look. John didn't say a word, just replayed the final seconds of the story.

John watched the admiral's neck flush and jugulars bulge as Beckwourth comprehended the implication. The admiral took the remote from John and played the entire story from the beginning. He said nothing. All the Immunes, including John, watched for a reaction. As the story ended, he clicked the monitor off and said, "Those dumb bastards! If you excuse me, I'll be ripping some people new assholes."

"So . . . you didn't know about this?" said John in a calm voice.

"Oh, I knew about the fireworks celebration," said the admiral, "I set it up. I also knew about the Fairview incident, even told our media to run the story. It was total safe-zone propaganda, but nobody told me it happened frickin next to us. The big picture is complex, and I can't have incompetents running the show. I assure you, I'll have a head on a silver platter in the morning," and he stomped out of the common room, madly pushing buttons on his cell phone as he left.

For a moment it was quiet, then Bob spoke, "He seemed more upset by the communication breakdown than for those poor people."

"He's got a lot on his platter," said DS. "You can't expect him to know everything. It's a heavy load."

"Yeah, the platter will be even heavier with the head he's adding!" quipped Prof.

"Look," said Bob, frowning, "I'm not criticizing. I guess I'd be getting better satisfaction spending more time saving people than doing paparazzi missions." Paparazzi missions were Immune slang for missions serving as a show for the press. "We might as well do morning talk shows instead."

"Don't forget fearless leader," Dude said as he motioned toward John, "With the exception of Suggs, I don't think anyone would want to be in his shoes." Dude was referring to John's daily press feeds. Eight camera stations were permanently set up next to the common room. Each morning started with interviews. John would move from camera to camera, averaging eight live and taped news feeds an hour. John hated it.

John complained about his PR responsibilities once, but only Suggs volunteered to help. The admiral gave Suggs a chance, but he cleared his throat seven times in a two-minute interview and said, "You know," a record thirteen times. From then on, the admiral limited Suggs to print interviews. Suggs loved those because he could talk about himself longer. Additionally, print articles included photos, which Suggs would clip and post on the common room walls. One morning every posted photo had a tiny Joseph Sengele mustache added. Suggs immediately accused Booboo because he was an artist.

"If I did it," said Booboo, "I'd have drawn a better mustache, but why bother? I couldn't make the subject any more ridiculous looking."

Suggs started moving toward Booboo, but Spoon stepped between them and gave Suggs such a look he backed down. This only served to increase the heckling.

One photo headline, computer altered and rewritten, read, *Sengele's moron twin brother discovered among First Immune Attack Force.* Suggs read it and screamed, "This is totally bogus. I can't be his twin. I've never, ever had a mustache!"

"Suggs, you're correct," replied Prof, laughing, "The headline is spurious. A moron requires an IQ of at least 50, and clearly the editor assumed too many IQ points." John entered the room to a shoving contest. He calmly inserted himself between the two battling Immunes. The altercation immediately stopped without anyone saying a word.

CHAPTER 32

THE HIGH COUNCIL

The following day the admiral was summoned to an urgent meeting of the High Council in ASC City. Initially, the team believed it was about the fireworks incident. Later the squad discovered it was a power play by members of the High Council to wrench control of the Immune Corps from the admiral. Under the guise of a failed propaganda campaign, the admiral was called to task.

The admiral sat alone at a small wood table barren of objects except a solitary microphone and his briefcase. In the High Council Hall he faced fifty members seated in a semicircular pattern on four stepped levels. Behind each High Council member sat two ASC members who served as their aides. Senator Snivaling sat at the center of the semicircle on the highest level next to Captain Stewart. Behind Snivaling was ASC spokesman Glavin and an ASC member the admiral didn't recognize.

"Although the success of the Immune Corp is without question," said Senator Snivaling, addressing the High Council, "I believe there are many deficiencies regarding the admiral's handling of the militias. Admiral, you have full access to all military maneuvers and control ASC propaganda, yet the militias are extremely elusive and stronger than ever."

"The militias may appear strong," replied the admiral, with a small shrug, "but their effect is inconsequential. The migration efforts are going well, which is the number one priority for ASC, or at least that's what I'm told by my superiors. I might also—"

"Well," said Captain Stewart, interrupting, "the High Council are your superiors' superiors, and I don't find the militia's continued existence so inconsequential. I find your apparent lack of concern regarding the militias disturbing." The Captain waved a sheet of paper in the air. "My fairness proposal ASC501 initiates an in-depth investigation of the admiral's records and computer files regarding the militias."

A few High Council members pounded their fists on the tables in front of them in support.

"I've always felt that Immunes could be used better," added Senator Snivaling, "ah . . . elsewhere."

Stewart laughed along with many others on the High Council and shouted his wholehearted agreement.

"I also propose an amendment allowing the Immunes to fight militias alongside the Grey Youth Guard," Stewart said, staring at the admiral as he spoke.

"Immune training is to kill airwars," said the admiral, leaping to his feet and bellowing so loudly council members could hear him without the aid of the microphone, "not men! The Immunes aren't military. Hundreds would die unnecessarily." The admiral could feel rage coursing through his veins.

Captain Stewart clearly pleased to see the admiral upset, brusquely said, "I, and many other High Council members, feel this is an acceptable risk."

Snivaling then added, "We have Grey Youth Guards ready to follow the Immunes into battle, and like the marines, no man will be left behind. Every fallen Immune would receive a hero's funeral; the cremations would stop."

"Would the Immunes' funerals be with or without their skins?" said the admiral sarcastically.

Senator Snivaling now leaped to her feet, her voice screeching, "How dare you suggest we would place Immunes at risk solely for an extraction. At least half of us on the High Council, including myself, have been heroically living in ASC City without a blue cap this entire crisis."

She shook her finger at the admiral, "We *have* borne this heavy burden in admirable silence, even though we know many lesser tier-ones among us have blue caps. I *am* positive any Immune felled in battle would be honored knowing their extract found good use in the protection of my esteemed High Council colleagues."

There were scattered claps from around the council room. She continued, "Clearly their inconsequential lives would have ended serving a useful purpose."

She gave a sickeningly, sweet smile to the other council members, which was returned by multiple nods of agreement.

The admiral regained his composure during Snivaling's outburst and again sat down. He leaned to the microphone and addressed the High Council in a level voice, "I must remind you I've delivered *exactly* what ASC requested of me. Regardless of minor inconveniences, such as the militias, the overall strategy is playing out well. Remember, survival is the ultimate goal of everyone in this room. Changing strategy mid-game could be disastrous for everyone." This seemed to strike a cord with several High Council members.

Stewart, aggravated that the admiral regained support, retorted, "Your Immune Corps has served its purpose well, but propaganda-wise, it doesn't matter whether there are one hundred or twenty thousand Immunes. Currently, militias are ASC's biggest headache, and they must be addressed aggressively. Therefore, I ask the High Council to vote now. Should Immunes be required to fight the militias?"

Discussion was stopped, and an anonymous electronic vote commenced. The results immediately flashed on the great screen in the High Council Hall; the vote was a tie. The admiral presumed exactly one-half of the High Council members were lacking blue caps. He requested a private audience with Senator Snivaling while the potential directive was being re-debated.

On the next ballot, the admiral's position won by a switch of one vote. The Immunes wouldn't fight the militias. Following the vote, Senator Snivaling didn't appear too disturbed her side lost. The admiral was pleased, but he didn't leave unscathed. Stewart, searching for a chink in the admiral's armor, managed to pass his proposal to investigate the admiral's anti-militia propaganda campaign.

"Admiral, my investigators will be visiting you shortly," said Stewart, "You have nothing to fear, admiral, it's only an investigation." He smiled wickedly at the admiral.

"My experience is government investigations are like statistics," retorted the admiral, "The outcome is often dependent on the investigator." He turned his back to Stewart and walked out of the High Council hall.

On his return to Central, the admiral made no mention of the ASC votes, although John knew every Immune was aware of what transpired. Even the secrets of the processing units, extractions, and brown and blue cans had long been common knowledge among the First Immune Attack Force.

"Keeping a secret is like holding ice in your hand," the admiral would say to John. "With enough time, both slip away." John hoped this maxim would eventually hold true for Sengele's secret location.

The admiral addressed the team at the morning briefing. It was a rare closed meeting. Only the Immunes, Colonel Vickers, Captain Howe, and Sergeant Clark were in attendance. The admiral leaned against the front of the stage. John watched everyone gather in a small crowd in front of the admiral as he spoke.

"The fireworks incident represented a grievous error in communication," said the admiral, "I assure you somewhere on an isolated military base, there's a colonel currently cleaning latrines. I've reviewed the present policy of Immune deployment with ASC High Council. Even though I'm well aware of the First Immune Attack Force's noble desires to do only rescue missions, the team plays a more important role as standard-bearers in the fight against airwars. The First Immune Attack Force is not to be disturbed from our current high profile missions. This is ASC policy."

"No, that's the Beckwourth policy," said Bob, "ASC's is 'Down Airwars, kill militia, and please be so kind as to die on the way'" Bob drew his finger across his throat as if it was being cut, "Both policies suck, if you ask me."

The admiral appeared to ignore the interruption and continued, "The importance of The Immune and the First Immune Attack Force can't be over-emphasized. I know you'd relish downing airwars all day long—"

Claps broke out from around the room.

"But you eleven folks are the window to the world of the Immunes. You're the world's best Immune team, and you know it. There's an average thirty percent death rate with other Immune squads. So far, none of you have ended up in an urn, which attests to your skills—"

"Or dumb luck, in the case of Suggs," said Prof with a chuckle.

"I have skills," shouted Suggs, "I'll have you know I have the—"

"Third highest kill score on the team," several immunes chanted along with him in chorus. Sumo slapped Prof on his back, laughing.

"Well, I do," said Suggs with a slight pout.

The admiral pulled out his cell phone and looked at the time.

"We can make this a ten minute briefing or a two hour briefing. It's your choice."

"Ten would be fine," said DS.

"Wise decision. Additionally, you've downed more airwars than any other team, and I think you'll all agree that this statistic was earned, not given." The admiral raised his fist in the air and continued speaking with emotion in his voice. "We needed heroes to rally around during this crisis, and The Immune and this team has provided. The world lives and breathes on your daily exploits, and it's paid off. We've managed to move seventy-five percent of the world's population to the coastal safe zones where deaths from airwars are essentially zero." The admiral tapped a button on his phone, and the theater screen lit up with a map of the world. Population densities were color -oded, with black representing the densest. A band of black nearly bordered all the world's coasts.

The admiral continued, "Mad Mike's militia and allies represent the only remaining worldwide resistance to ASC policy, and with each success from you, the less activity we see from them. Public relations announcements from The Immune have motivated millions to follow ASC instructions for their own protection. The Immune has more credibility than Washington, Lincoln, and the Pope rolled into one."

John felt Sumo grabbing him in a bear hug. Sumo gave him a wet kiss on the cheek. "My hero," he said, squealing in a high voice. John shoved him away. The admiral waited for the laughing to die down.

"You guys and gals are saving the world, and if you think I'm mother-henning you for your own sakes, you're wrong. The world needs you. God forbid, should anything happen to the team or The Immune, we'd have chaos in the streets. So, yes, you'll continue paparazzi missions, as you call them, and you'll smile for the cameras, and yes, I'll always worry about your safety, twenty-four seven, so don't expect a break from protocol from here on out."

That afternoon, there was a break from protocol.

CHAPTER 33

NOT A DRILL

The Immunes gathered in the common room. John was reviewing strategy with the team for the afternoon's mission. The squad had a planned ninety-minute flight to get to the assignment somewhere in Tennessee. Press coverage was to be limited, but a documentary crew would be present. The admiral was expecting less than ten airwars.

Sumo would be missing from the mission because he violated the alcohol ban following the morning briefing. He somehow acquired a quantity of beer. John found him in the common room bathroom intoxicated and semi-conscious.

"I only had one . . . case," slurred Sumo. Then he passed out in John's arms.

Abruptly, Central's alarm blared. The First Immune Attack Force had experienced alarm drills, but a genuine alarm never occurred. At first, John looked incredulously at the others, wondering if it was in error. Finally he shouted, "Let's move!"

The alarm lights were color coded, blue, red, and green. The flashing color determined the reporting location. Blue was the jet bay, red-heliport, and green-bus terminal. The light strobed red. As the team exited for the heliport, the admiral, Colonel Vickers, Captain Howe, and Sergeant Clark, joined them.

"What the heck is going on?" said John, running alongside the admiral.

"I've just called an emergency mission," replied the admiral.

"Would this be what you'd describe as a break in protocol?" said John, feeling smug.

"*Touché*," replied the admiral without smiling.

They continued their jog toward the big gray Chinook, its twin rotors already spinning. Each Immune took their place in the helicopter, and it lifted off immediately.

John noticed the two media helicopters, which always accompanied them on missions, were grounded, and there seemed to be no preparation for getting them airborne.

"What, no press on this one?" shouted John over the thumping of the overhead blades.

The admiral shook his head and motioned for everyone to put on their headphones. As the final Immune adjusted his headphone in place, the admiral spoke, "We're close, only forty miles out from Central. We have ten Colossi headed north." The admiral looked down to the glowing battle tablet on his lap and began tapping the screen.

"Current intel believes Mad Mike's raiders are attacking this group. This is the first time we're aware of militias targeting Colossi. This has the potential for release of millions of juveniles. It's imperative we down every Colossi before Mad Mike's terrorist band arrives."

It was quiet on the helicopter for the longest time. The admiral appeared focused on his battle tablet. Finally Dude broke the silence.

"We've never done a Colossus takedown." He was lightly running his thumb along his open knife blade. "How do we know that we can down Colossi the same as regular airwars?"

"ASC has never had you attack Colossi because they don't violate safe zones," interjected Captain Howe, "Their behavior has been for the most part benign. If we leave them alone, they leave us alone; it's a good plan. ASC scientists say they down the same as the common airwar."

"So other Immunes have downed them in the past?" questioned Spoon.

"No," Captain Howe said, shaking his head, "I said they were off limits. You've seen videos of what happens when a Colossi goes berserk from an attack."

"Well," said Prof, "how can you be sure ASC scientists know what they're talking about?"

"ASC scientists report a ninety-seven percent certainty," said Howe.

"That being said," retorted Prof, "I'm one-hundred percent certain I'd rather have an ASC scientist like Doak the Dork show me how it's—"

A sonic boom interrupted Prof.

Another sonic boom followed.

John and the other Immunes peered out the windows of the helicopter at the vapor trails. It was rare to see military jets these days. The Immunes flew in a special transport jet, but these were fighter jets. Most had been decommissioned because the military didn't want any rogue pilots trying to take out airwars. John knew there were rumors that Mad Mike's supporters had jets, but this was largely Internet speculation. The speculation ended with a loud explosion.

Far in the distance, John could see a dogfight unfolding in the sky. The sky was clear blue except for crisscross vapor trails and one slowly dissipating cloud. It was all that remained of a jet whose opponent's missile reached its target. John noted no survivor's parachute emerging from the cloud. The battle in the air continued to rage even as the Immunes reached their objective.

CHAPTER 34

COLOSSI

As the First Immune Attack Force approached their destination, the squad could see a group of the largest airwars any had ever seen. The large hydrogen sacs obliterated the lake view below. It was as if the Immunes were above a gathering storm of giant black clouds. Although John and the other Immunes had seen many videos on the Colossi, none had seen one in person.

"My God!" said Spoon, "look at the size of those."

"They must be at least one-hundred and fifty meters," said Booboo, frowning.

"Look at that one," said Prof, pointing out the window, "You could put three football fields on it. Why, I think it might be even bigger than Suggs' ego."

Strangely sedate, Colossi typically congregated around coastal safe zones, but never entered past the oscillation wires. Although an attack by one could destroy an entire town, unlike the less mature airwars, Colossi seemed to be content to feed on livestock and wild animals beyond the safe zone. John knew there were, of course, many stories of Colossi snagging people if victims ventured beyond oscillating wire. News reports regarding Colossi were largely limited to those attacking inland towns. Colossi were a great motivating force in the migration movement.

As the First Immune Attack Force exited the helicopter, John thought the team looked like a bunch of New York tourists with their head craned back looking at skyscrapers.

"Man, oh, man!" whispered Cupcake to Bob, "We'll be working three times as high as we're used to."

"Hang on tight," said Bob, with an acerbic smile, "If you slip and fall from up there, your next mission will be from inside a aerosol can with a blue cap."

Booboo looked a little pale, but Spoon was massaging his shoulders and whispering encouragements in his ear.

Gunfire rattled through the air. John noticed the air battle was not the only ongoing battle. In the not too distant hills, dark black columns of smoke were peppered throughout the trees. This wasn't some small local militia. This was a full-fledged army advancing toward the airwars. An army of the Grey Youth Guard of equal size or larger was separating the Immunes and the Colossi from Mad Mike, at least for the moment.

"We think this group might include Mad Mike himself," said the admiral, looking up from his battle tablet toward John.

"We weren't expecting such a large force," interjected Captain Howe.

The Admiral glanced at the glowing screen and tapped the surface. He looked up at the sky and said, "Neither side seems to have air superiority, but on the ground we outnumber them. Mad Mike's army, on the other hand, has one focus, these Colossi."

Captain Howe frowned, reached over, and showed the admiral a screen on his tablet.

"Someone has spread our troops too thin," said the admiral, shaking his head with a disapproving look, "Mad Mike's men may be able to punch through."

"Admiral, the Immunes don't have much time," said Howe.

"John," said the admiral, looking up from his battle tablet, "you need to down these Colossi now. If Mad Mike gets to them, you'll be fighting the offspring for years to come."

The admiral looked back at his tablet and began rapidly tapping the screen again.

All the Colossi were hovering over the lake. Some were siphoning, but the majority had finished. John ran into the water up to his knees and dove. This lake was cooler than the air temperature due to the body of water being spring-fed. Even though the underwater visibility was incredible, John kept lifting his head Tarzan-style to look in awe at the sheer size of his prey.

As he swam through the outer curtain, it felt similar to any other mission. He did notice the interior was darker, as there were more tentacles blocking the sunlight, but innovative headband LEDs automatically adjusted for the darkness.

As he pushed through the masses of tentacles to the center, he had his first view of the siphon. It was four times as big as the common airwar. During his approach, he felt a sudden undertow. He realized the siphon was drawing so much water it was pulling him toward the opening. Because siphoning corresponded to the peristaltic waves, there were gaps in the undertow. John realized timing the siphon grab was critical because, if too soon, he might be sucked in.

After the next bolus started rising, he sprinted toward the tube. He could feel the pull of the current toward the base of the siphon tube. Quickly he wrapped his hands around the tube and locked his arms in place by grabbing each wrist with the opposite hand. He could feel the lower half of his body yanked downward as the end of the tube sucked in yet another bolus of water. As the bolus moved upward, the rising forces overcame downward, and John began his longest ride on an airwar siphon tube to a height of 200 feet.

John wondered how far he could see from this height. Currently, he could see only a jungle of tentacles highlighted by his headband. When the lights reflected from the air tube, he whistled to himself. The air tube, like the siphon, was greatly oversized.

He was carrying a newly-released TC developed for the Immunes. TC was an acronym for "trachea choker." The device was like a large locking plastic tie with an electronic mechanism that could tighten the strap remotely. This allowed the Immune to get out of the airwar before the asphyxiation started. Even though the TC was the largest one made, it was a tight fit around the Colossus air tube.

John was glad that the TC could be set off remotely as he studied the size of the mammoth hydrogen sac. He knew it was tough to hold one's breath long enough to swim from under a normal-size airwar. Immunes from other teams had drowned, caught beneath tentacles of downed airwars. It was now standard for Immunes to carry extra air. This Colossus was so large that it would be impossible for a trapped Immune to make it out without oxygen inhalers.

Oxygen inhalers looked like a snorkel mouthpiece with a small metal cylinder attached. It was good for four to five inhalations of pure oxygen. This would be plenty of air for a good swimmer to get out from under an airwar, even a Colossus. Although the First Immune Attack Force always carried inhalers, the reality was, most airwar downings were now done over land due to the availability of the remote TC.

Using the tentacle retraction climbing technique John developed, Immunes climbed using modified knives. Following the application of the TC, Immunes descended using a tentacle as a rappelling rope, cleared the curtain, and activated the TC by remote. The method completed attacks on airwars quicker, but it was riskier than the siphon tube technique. Worldwide, several Immunes would die each week, typically from falls.

Having secured the TC, John grabbed a nearby tentacle to start what would be his longest descent. Fortunately, the slight mucous surface on each of the tentacles prevented friction burns. John slipped silently from tentacle to water. It took forty-five seconds of swimming to exit beyond the outer curtain.

John looked up at the airwars. None of the other Immunes had appeared. He swam to the shore, and the admiral was standing near the edge with Colonel Vickers and Captain Howe, each working their battle tablets. John motioned to the remote attached to his utility belt as he stepped from the water.

"No," said the admiral, looking up, "We'll down them after all the TCs are in place."

"Yeah," said Howe, "It's too risky to do them one at a time. It might trap an exiting Immune."

John nodded in agreement. When the ten Colossi were downed, the lake surface would be nothing but a mass of tentacles. It would be hard to swim from under them, even with the inhaler.

Colonel Vickers, wearing headphones and looking at the tablet monitor, spoke to the admiral, "Nine of the TCs are in place, and Spoon says she's adjusting hers now. She's slowed down because of the size."

John could see now at least half his team swimming back to shore.

"Satellite feed shows a small band of Mad Mike's forces have broken through," said Captain Howe with a grimace, "They're coming right at us."

CHAPTER 35

PARADIGM SHIFT

John watched the admiral frown and ignore his battle tablet. The admiral rubbed his temple and said, "Can't General Cleevus redirect forces to attend this group?"

"The general says no," said Captain Howe, shaking his head, "The fighting is more intense in some zones than expected. He also said ASC dumped him with large numbers of adolescent thugs to battle an army of seasoned soldiers."

"Is it possible to do an air strike at this point?" said the admiral, looking toward Colonel Vickers.

"Sir, our air forces are currently occupied," replied Vickers.

John's eyes shifted to the multitude of vapor trails in the sky. A serious fight was going on above, but it was impossible to tell who was winning

"How are we situated?" said the admiral, seemingly unfazed by the negative reports as he turned to Sergeant Clark.

"Sir," said Clark, "we have six fully armed soldiers and four lightly armed technical staff, not counting you, the captain, and colonel—we also have the Immunes."

"The group that has broken through numbers at least twenty," said Captain Howe, "Unfortunately, they're likely better armed and more battle savvy than our men. Perhaps we should abort the mission. There's no need to put the Immunes at risk."

Before the admiral could respond, Bob, who just exited the water, said, "We Immunes are at no risk from Mad Mike. He doesn't seek out humans to kill as do the *grey baby brigade*. He has the same mutual enemies as us."

"For not killing humans," replied the admiral, "he's doing a fair job of lying to rest many of the Grey Youth Guard."

"I didn't say he wouldn't defend himself from a gang of armed juvenile hooligans," said Bob irritably.

"Well," said the admiral cynically, "I'm not sure he'd be saddened by a little collateral damage to the First Immune Attack Force. Bob, face it, we're dealing with an illegal militia who carries illegal weapons and refuses to comply with the ASC, the current world governing body. I doubt there's any high moral ground preventing them from killing Immunes."

"Since when did America wad up the Constitution and give it to ASC to piss on?" said Bob, now visibly perturbed, "There are some who feel individual liberties are more important than ASC."

The admiral appeared out of character when he haughtily stated, "Not when the greater good is at stake. Sometimes individual liberties require sacrifice in times of crisis."

John saw Bob rolling his eyes.

"Central planning is the answer to get us out of this horrible situation," said the admiral, ignoring Bob's eye roll, "This is a paradigm shift. The Constitutional guarantees appear quaint contrasted to this world disaster. Strong world government leaders with absolute power, who have placed themselves at high risk serving the people, are needed to prevent decimation by the airwars, and so far we're doing a pretty good job."

"The job is being done well because ASC says we're doing well," responded Bob angrily, "which ultimately means you. I never believed any of the garbage you dump to the media, but now you're speaking it to us."

Two explosions from above silenced Bob. John turned and looked high in the distance. Two smoke clouds marked the spots where missiles again found their targets.

Bob continued, "Regarding our leaders, who elected them? Clearly, the people didn't elect them. I never notice any airwar deaths in the ranks of our 'risk taking' ASC leaders. Frankly, that doesn't surprise me. The only thing surprising me is our leaders haven't attacked property rights. ASC already controls the press, guns, and the judicial system. Perhaps we're seeing the real reason for the migrations. War and crisis are always the best times for government to destroy personal liberties."

"Property rights remain intact because this is a paradigm shift," said the admiral in an arrogant tone "Centralized government is good; you've painted it wrong."

"The paintbrush I use is history, and history paints the same picture repeatedly," said Bob, "Large centralized governments always cause internal collapse and ultimately destruction of the masses. All governmental evils are justified and rationalized, as necessary, to maintain the all-powerful, all-knowing, current leaders for the good of society."

Again Bob was interrupted by another explosion. This time John could see a deployed parachute above the falling aircraft debris.

"Don't forget the main tenet of our constitution is life, liberty, and the pursuit of happiness," said Bob, not wanting to drop the debate, "This was specifically referring to the individual, not society or government. There's something ominous about ASC even if we do kill every airwar. What's left is a self-appointed central world government you astonishingly believe will return civil liberties once the crisis is over."

"You're paranoid," said the admiral. He then poked his finger on Bob's chest, "It's a paradigm shift," he said.

John was shocked. He began to think the admiral was baiting Bob. Maybe he suspected Bob's past association with Mad Mike. Perhaps he was trying to make Bob slip up in the heat of the argument.

"Excuse me, gentlemen," said John, "May I say something?"

"No, John," said the admiral, "I want the militia hugger to finish what he has to say."

Another blast rocked the sky. John noticed several jets appeared to be retreating with others in close pursuit.

"Admiral, as far as your paradigm shift goes," said Bob, "Pundits say that before every financial crisis, too. It's a new economy; it's a paradigm shift. Old fiscal rules of common sense don't apply. We'll make money forever on Internet stocks, real estate, tulip bulbs, etc.; you just add your new economy category *de jour*.

It's a paradigm shift. The end is always the same, and the government was always complacent because their political coffers were being filled by the standard bearers of the false economy."

"This is different," said the admiral with a smug voice.

John noted the sky was quiet for the first time. The air battle shifted elsewhere. The loudest noise currently was coming from Bob and the admiral.

Bob appeared livid. He started shaking his finger at the admiral. "Until the collapse, then each political party points their fingers at the other. Then the industry begs for a bailout. The government complies because it was typically their policies or lack of law enforcement that let the 'new economy' develop in the first place. Of course, politicians cite compassion as justification. 'Oh, look at the good people who'll lose jobs if we don't intervene.' Then they label it a government bailout. It's another example of reckless compassion. What it should be called is a taxpayer confiscation-redistribution plan. Government has no money. The money always comes from the people, either through new taxation or inflation or more commonly, both."

John stood watching the political discussion continue. It seemed surreal. Here were two men arguing politics with a raging battle behind and above and ten Colossi in front. The admiral, who seemed to be intentionally antagonizing Bob, suddenly snapped out of the little drama.

"Look, we're not going anywhere until these Colossi are downed. We can't chance Mad Mike's crew releasing millions of juveniles."

Suggs, who just joined the group, joked, "Isn't that called job security for us?" Nobody laughed.

Suddenly, an alarm sounded from the captain's tablet, and the screen glowed red. Howe looked up and said, "Sir, we have an issue. Spoon is reporting a premature TC activation in her colossus."

CHAPTER 36

DISREGARDED ORDERS

John noticed the entire Immune crew was out of the water except for Spoon. As he looked toward the lake, he could see one Colossus in its death dance.

"She's trapped up high," said Captain Howe, "She can't slide down, and she says her inhaler was knocked from her belt."

John looked at the other Immunes. The Colossus was a good three hundred meters from shore. No boats were available, and other Colossi blocked the helicopter from making a drop.

"She's gonna die," whispered Suggs.

John knew if Spoon ended up trapped, she wouldn't have enough air to swim to safety. There was clearly no way for her to hold her breath that long. He couldn't swim to the Colossus; it would take more than five minutes, as other Colossi blocked the way. John looked at the admiral. The admiral frowned and shrugged. Beads of sweat on his forehead indicated his lack of rescue ideas.

"Well," said John, "I've got to try something." He looked out to the lake. The Colossus he attached his TC unit to was fifteen meters from shore. John snatched several inhalers off other Immunes' belts and clipped them to his own.

"John!" said the admiral, "don't try anything stupid. I can't risk losing you."

John ignored him as he ran into the water.

"That's an order!" roared the admiral. He saw John's face slip under the water and knew John could no longer hear him. The admiral felt a combination of rage and fear. He spun around and looked at the rest of the Immunes. Most looked distressed and anxious. Only Booboo was animated and looking eager for action.

"Admiral, let me help!" hollered Booboo.

"Good man!" shouted the admiral, "Go stop The Immune! He'll get himself killed!"

Booboo ran madly toward the water. The admiral noticed the other Immunes looked at each other with surprise.

DS said, "Admiral, Booboo is a fast swimmer, but he can't catch John. What were you thinking?"

"He'll catch him," said the admiral, "You'll see. I've never seen him swim so fast."

John passed the outer curtain of the Colossus. The siphon tube wasn't apparent, nor did he expect to see it. He pulled his knife and thrust it into a nearby tentacle. The force of the upward contraction almost pulled his arm from the socket as he rose nearly twenty-five feet in the air. The reflex contractions from the Colossus were extreme compared to a common airwar. Each knife thrust tore at his rotator cuff as he was yanked upward. Finally, he viewed his destination, the motion protuberances at the base of the siphon.

John clicked on his headband speaker only to hear screaming and shouting. Spoon was screaming in terror for someone to help her. But Spoon wasn't the only one who had dread in her voice. The admiral was yelling, and John could tell the admiral feared for John's life. From the beginning, John remained fueled solely by vengeance. He didn't care if he lived or died. He knew the admiral was mindful of this fact.

The admiral's apparent lack of concern for Spoon made John wonder if his friendship with the admiral was a good circumstance. The admiral always gave orders to everyone with military aplomb, no matter what the risk. He seemed reluctant to give those same orders to John. John was afraid someday their friendship might get in the way of a higher need, such as now.

"Spoon!" said John, "can you hear me?"

"John!" sizzled the admiral's voice over the speaker, "abort! . . . abort now! That's an order, John! Abort!"

"No!" shouted John. "I'm not coming back without Spoon. Your screaming puts me more at risk because I can't communicate with her."

"John," pleaded the admiral, "it's a lost cause. We can lose an Immune, but not you."

"Admiral!" said John firmly, "you can keep it up, but you know me well. Is there an infinitesimal chance I'll heed your orders?

The lack of response from the admiral was an adequate reply.

"Spoon, can you hear me?" repeated John.

"Yes," Spoon answered in a stressed squeaky voice, "The Colossus is sinking. I'll be underwater in twenty seconds."

Dammit, thought John. *I'll never reach her in time.* He kicked the air tube in anger, which bounced like a large balloon off his foot. An idea flashed in his head.

"Are you near the air tube?"

"Yes!"

"Can you get on it?"

"Yes," said Spoon with terror in her voice, "My feet are in the water. Oh! God! Please someone help me! Tell Booboo I love him."

"You'll have to tell him yourself," said John in a reassuring voice, "Grab the air tube and cut a small slit in the membrane, then shove your head inside."

"No!" roared the admiral, "the Colossus must be destroyed."

"Quiet!" snapped John, "The Colossus is dead; no juveniles will be released. Spoon, there'll be enough air to breathe until I get there, okay?"

Back on the shore the admiral and colonel were standing next to each other. The Immunes were whispering to each other in a small group immediately behind them.

"Brilliant!" said Colonel Vickers, giving an uncharacteristic compliment. He turned to the admiral.

"Yes," said the admiral pessimistically, "The Immune is smart. Now Spoon will live long enough for them both to die together." The admiral's stomach knotted up. He thought, *Nothing is going according to plan. All the Colossi should have been downed by now, and If John dies, this could be ruinous for everyone. Where the hell is Booboo?*

A stray bullet from the battle in the distant forest hit the shore a foot in front of the admiral's feet. Mud spattered on his shoes and pant legs.

"Jeeze!" yelled Vickers jumping back.

The admiral remained motionless, lost in thought.

John grabbed a motion protuberance and squeezed hard. The Colossus lurched forward. John pulled out a one-inch monitor that looked like a cyclist mirror from his video headband. He could follow his progress from parked helicopter external cameras. He was moving at a rapid speed, but two Colossi blocked the one he needed to reach. He aimed at the point between the two, not knowing what would happen if the Colossus rammed the others. Fortunately, the two Colossi bounced away, letting his ride pass through with an associated deceleration.

He sailed directly above the downed Colossus, now floating on the surface with its tentacles spread. From John's view it looked like a shriveled, black cucumber sitting on a pile of black and red spaghetti. He slid down a tentacle and rappelled, pushing off from the side of the deflating hydrogen sac as he reached it.

John arrived at the floating tentacles, but couldn't squeeze through them. He tapped his knife, and the blade clicked open. He began slicing his way through the barrier. It took several minutes to hack through to open water beneath. The last half was under water, so he had to use up two of his inhalers to cut through.

The Colossus blotted out the sunlight, so it was almost pitch black beneath. Only his headband light gave him any visibility. All John could see was a mass of twisted tentacles forming what appeared to be a giant cap on the water's surface. Spoon remained stranded somewhere in the darkness beyond the reach of his light. The external camera feed and audio went out once he swam below. Only static and an occasional word came through. He couldn't tell if any of the words came from Spoon.

It had been two minutes, and he was no closer to locating Spoon than when he first entered. He was down to two inhalers. The floating tentacles above were so twisted he couldn't orient himself. It was like being in a dark forest with a flashlight.

Suddenly, outlined on the tentacles, the shape of a familiar object came to view. It was the siphon tube. He began swimming and following it, not knowing whether this was going away from or toward his goal. If he was swimming toward the end, he'd have to abort because there wouldn't be enough air to swim back, retrieve Spoon, and swim out again. Even if it led to the siphon base, he wasn't sure they would make it out alive.

John then saw a faint white glow in the distance. It was cylindrical in shape and it glowed from a bright light in the middle. As he got closer, he could see it was the air tube with the head of Spoon stuck in the side. Her headband lights were ablaze on maximum power. The TC sealed off the end of the tube. The membrane of the tube had retracted, making the supportive rings stand out.

John swam up to the tube, slashed a hole in the base next to Spoon, and pushed his head through. The air had an acrid smell, and Spoon was breathing rapidly. John imagined carbon dioxide by now replaced most of the oxygen.

"Excuse me, could you direct me to the aisle that has croutons?" said John.

Spoon cried, then said, "Sorry, mister, I'm on break. Come back in ten minutes." They both laughed nervously, then Spoon said, "Is there a plan or is this another fly by the seat of your Speedo operation?"

"More the latter," said John, "We'll have to deal with the darkness. We need to follow the siphon tube to its end. Unless we find light from the edge, we could end up swimming in circles."

"Do you have an inhaler?" asked Spoon, maintaining her composure well under the circumstances.

John felt for her hand and pressed the full inhaler in her palm until she gripped it tightly. He kept the mostly spent one. "Yeah, one for you and one for me."

"Is that all you have?" Spoon's eyes got wide.

"No," said John, "I had more, but they were lost with my luggage."

"Crap!" said Spoon. "How much oxygen do *you* have?"

"I have one, and it's almost full," lied John. He pressed the inhaler into the translucent membrane so Spoon could see the projection of its outline. "I took one inhale before I joined you."

Spoon tilted her head and looked at him as if attempting to read the truth.

"The air is pretty thin in here," said John, disrupting her intent look, "And the water isn't getting any wetter, so we should go."

Both Immunes hyperventilated several times and pulled their heads from the air tube. John pointed to the siphon tube and began swimming along its path. He had an overwhelming urge to take a breath. The minimum oxygen in the air tube, coupled with the high CO_2, was causing his lungs to revolt. Spoon must have felt the same, because after less than ten seconds she took her first drag from the inhaler.

After thirty seconds, John began seeing spots dancing around his eyes. He knew blackout was only moments away. John took a deep heavy drag on the inhaler. His lungs filled, but not fully. He was out of oxygen. The mad desire for a breath went away briefly. He noticed Spoon had taken her second breath. After another ten seconds of swimming, they reached the end of the siphon tube.

Beyond the siphon end, it was stygian black. John pointed and they swam on. Spoon took another breath. Another twenty seconds of swimming and still no light appeared to direct them. The urge to breathe was overwhelming. Spoon took another breath. They swam on. Spots again appeared before John's eyes. He kept swimming. He pushed up on the ceiling of tentacles to see if any would budge, but none did.

He felt himself slipping away. A point of bright light appeared in the water deep in front, but it wasn't sunlight. John swam toward it. He heard of the bright light patients visualized when they became anoxic, millions of brain cells firing off in a panic. So this was it. *Swim into the light,* he thought. He had a vision of a moth in a bug zapper, then things went black.

CHAPTER 37

DEATH OF A HERO

J ohn coughed and gasped. His eyes opened to a fiery bright light. He was flying in hell. Demons were screaming at him. His brain did a reboot. No, he was floating, not flying, and he was looking directly into the sun. The screaming was from Spoon, who had him in the life-saving cross-chest carry. Her mouth was next to his ear, and her screams for help were like fingernails scratching across his eardrum. He struggled and she tightened her grip. He tried to say, I'm okay, but all that came out was a fit of coughing. Then he felt her grip loosen and several hands grab him.

"He's alive!" A face blotted out the sun and Suggs' happy countenance filled John's vision, "I guess I'm back to second in command."

"Waiter," said John, wheezing to Suggs, "can you move us to a different table? I'm feeling a damp draft at this one."

"Okay," said Suggs, releasing his hold, "he's fine. The comedian can swim back on his own."

The hands released John's extremities. John rolled face-down and swam to shore with Spoon, Suggs, Bob, and Dude. On shore the remaining Immunes were standing around the admiral, who was holding a flare gun. Several empty shells were at his feet. He was the only one smiling in the group and it was faint.

"So, John," said the admiral, "you go in for the rescue and end up the rescuee." John knew Spoon must have towed him out. He also realized Admiral Beckwourth must have had the foresight to fire flares into the water so they could find their way out.

"Last flare, John," said the admiral, holding up the flare gun. "You guys were just about out of luck."

John looked toward Spoon to thank her. She was whispering to two of the other Immunes. She suddenly fell to the ground in tears with Cupcake holding her. A clasp on his shoulder by the admiral stopped John's movement toward her.

"I sent Booboo to stop you," said the admiral softly to John, "He ignored my orders. He tried to rescue Spoon. I didn't know he and Spoon had a thing going. His heart monitor stopped transmitting two minutes before you appeared. I thought we were losing you, too, John."

John turned and looked at the lake, "Isn't there anything we—"

"No!" interrupted the admiral, "Booboo is dead and I have to take these airwars down now. This lake will be nothing but tentacles in a few minutes."

John couldn't help but notice the gunfire was getting close. The admiral nodded to Captain Howe. The touch screen tablet glowed green and red as Howe tapped instructions. Suddenly the remaining airwars began the death dance.

"Are we getting this?" said the admiral to Captain Howe.

"Yes, sir," replied Howe, "from the helicopter cams."

"Good," said the admiral, nodding, "So far, so good."

"What?" said John, "So far, so good—Booboo is dead, and you're saying things are good?" He was maddened by the cavalier comment. "What's gotten into you?"

John saw the admiral look off in the distance to avoid his glare.

"Look John," said the admiral, "we lost Booboo. It's a tragedy, but he was expendable. You're not. I do deeply mourn the loss, even though you may not believe me."

Bob and John looked at each other, shocked at the admiral's response.

"I'm just as expendable as Booboo," said John.

"No!" said the admiral, turning swiftly on John, "no, you're not—and you need to follow orders!"

"I'm sorry!" John said angrily, "What branch of the military did you say I was in?" He tore his video headband off and threw it at the admiral's feet.

"You're correct," said the admiral, his face contorted, "You don't belong to a military branch, and I have no legal right to order you. However, I'm in charge of the Immune Corps, so you should carefully heed my *recommendations*. That is, if you want to continue to down airwars or even think of getting a chance at Sengele. If you keep doing stunts like that, you'll die, and the psychological cost to the world will be irreparable."

"I think our friendship may be clouding your military decisions," said John, frowning.

"I think you overrate the importance of friendship," said the admiral, shaking his battle tablet at John, "The mission always comes first. You don't have—"

"Look!" shouted Dude. John saw him pointing toward the far right side of the lake. One of the Colossi hadn't gone down. It moved over land and was now passing adjacent to a wooded area.

"The TC is definitely not in place," reported Captain Howe after tapping on his battle tablet, "Its GPS shows it to be somewhere at the bottom of the lake."

"Who was the Immune responsible for that Colossus?" demanded the admiral.

Captain Howe looked first at the Colossus, whose tentacles were now exploring the edge of the woods, then to Suggs.

"I thought it was on secure," said Suggs with a shrug. "I was in a hurry. I was trying to down two. What can I say? I wanted to be the first Immune to take down two Colossi on the same day."

"You imbecile," screamed the admiral, "You've seriously compromised this mission with your egotistical child-like score keeping."

Suddenly, gunfire erupted next to the Colossus, and John heard screaming.

"Now," demanded the exasperated admiral, "who the hell is shooting?"

CHAPTER 38

REUNITED

J ohn saw Colonel Vickers look up from his battle tablet. "It's not the Grey Youth Guard or any of our team. It must be that breakthrough group from Mad Mike."

The reports from the shots indicated light automatic rifles were being fired, not heavy weaponry. Although machine guns are effective attacking common airwars, the sheer size of a Colossus prevented them from suffering takedown damage. As the Colossus shifted position, John could see the militia wasn't faring well. Several were visible, trapped in the outer curtain, and more screams came from within.

"Well, this is a surprising yet happy turn of events," commented Colonel Vickers to no one in particular, "We'll still have to down the airwar, but it can wait until our uninvited guests have expired."

"You can't be serious," said John.

"Consider this," said Colonel Vickers, "if these terrorists live, they'll be transferred to ASC city, then executed. This is a better scenario, and we're catching it on video. Mad Mike's men trapped in an airwar; what great propaganda for the admiral to use."

John looked toward the admiral, who was watching the struggle between the militia and the Colossus. Beckwourth looked stressed and was cursing softly to himself. John knew the admiral liked his plans to run smoothly and it was obvious he didn't care for this turn of events.

Except Spoon, who was sitting on the ground next to Cupcake sobbing, John realized the Immunes were looking at him for guidance.

"Let's save these guys," yelled John. He began running toward the Colossus, and the Immunes followed. John glanced back at Beckwourth to see if he would order them back. The admiral appeared to be concentrating on his battle tablet. He made no attempt to stop the Immunes. John hated running the 200 meters to the Colossus. This exhausted him more than a 200-meter swim. As the Immunes approached, the screams intensified and the number of gunshots decreased. It appeared the Colossus trapped the entire band of militiamen.

John watched the Immunes deftly climb to each trapped militia. Although a few of the militia were unconscious or semi-conscious, most were struggling and fighting back. They continued to fire rounds without any effect on the massive hydrogen sac.

Rescue harnesses worn by John and the Immunes allowed the injured to ride down on the Immunes' chests. The strapping reminded John of an early Strong Enterprises tandem-jumping parachute harness, but with two large Velcro straps in front to wrap around the victim. The Immunes secured the airwar's former prey onto his or her chest, cut the entwining tentacles, and slid down. The survivor would still receive stings, but once on the ground, the Immune would lay on top of the rescued person, protecting them from further contact until the airwar passed. The Immune would then ascend again for another victim.

John already arrived at the motion protuberances and was directing the Colossus slowly back toward the lake.

Suggs attached the TC to the air tube. John had an overwhelming urge to tell Suggs to make sure it was on secure, but suppressed it. It didn't matter because Suggs saw John's glance.

"Don't say a word," said Suggs, "it's on real tight." Both John and Suggs hung at the base of the hydrogen sac until they got the call of all-clear from the other Immunes. "John, you go on. I'll finish taking it over the lake."

John started to prepare for his slide down, but then he heard a whimper and a soft cry for help. He thought at first he overlooked a small woman in fatigues, but then realized it was a prepubescent boy. The tentacles were carrying the boy toward the gastric sphincter.

John passed easily from tentacle to tentacle and sliced the boy free, attaching him to his harness. He marveled at his own skills now, moving within the airwar as if he belonged. He had to admit he no longer felt an adrenaline rush each time he passed through the outer curtain. Now it seemed like a familiar job, like a framing carpenter who walks across beams forty feet in the air and thinks nothing of it.

"Son," said John, "everything's going to be fine." John gave the child the most reassuring look he could muster.

"Thanks, Dr. Long," the boy said with a small sob.

John was shocked. It had been months since anybody called him Dr. Long in a familiar way. The stings caused such swelling of the boy's face he was unrecognizable. John wanted to ask how he knew him as Dr. Long rather than The Immune, but the lake was approaching fast. Soon they were lying flat on the ground and the Colossus passed. Bob ran up with a panicked look.

"Call a medic," yelled John, "I have an injured kid."

Bob shoved John out of the way, scooped up the boy from the ground, then kissed his swollen forehead. John abruptly made the connection. Although John was shocked to see the boy alive, this was clearly Bob's son, Daniel.

"Bob," said John, "Daniel's going to be fine. We're much better at treating airwar stings than our first little go round. He only needs medical attention; you won't even have to roll up your sleeve. A medical evacuation unit will be here shortly."

Bob turned, looked at John, and said, "He can't go back. You know ASC policy on airwar terrorism."

"Daniel's a child," said John reassuringly, "I'll intervene."

"No," said Bob, shaking his head, "It's best this way. I'll be leaving with him. Mad Mike has got as good, or better, care for stings as ASC, and without the required execution."

John thought for a moment, then climbed up from his knees. He brushed off dirt and bits of airwar tentacle adhered to his harness.

"The admiral will be pissed if you rejoin Mad Mike's group. It'll be a public relations nightmare. I see the headlines now, *First Immune Attack Force loses member to Mad Mike's Militia.*"

Bob looked at John while rocking the softly crying boy in his arms.

"Were you not listening to what the admiral said today? John, the admiral has changed. In the beginning, I thought he was on our side. Now it's all about him keeping power within ASC. He's clearly bucking for first tier and he's afraid any screw-ups will ruin his plans."

John moved to Bob. He began examining the stings on Daniel's face. Bob continued speaking, "Did you see how he's out of sorts today? He's been giving us the old FS maneuver for his own advancement. Now he's stressed out because ASC's making him squirm. I doubt my defection will ever see the light of day in the news. Remember, we're dealing with the PR king of the world. Besides, I'm not rejoining Mad Mike. I've never left."

"You're a mole for Mad Mike?" said John, his jaw dropping.

"Yeah," said Bob, grinning, "Something like that. The admiral was so focused on getting Immunes in the news, he neglected security measures. You may remember I wasn't part of the original indoctrination. I arrived that night. When Mad Mike got wind of the admiral forming an elite team, he wanted someone on the inside. Mad Mike wasn't on board with me at first because I had Daniel, but the Big Zee, his most trusted advisor, pushed for it—"

"Ow! Ow! Ow!" Daniel hollered. John pulled a fragment of tentacle off the boy's neck.

"Sorry," said John, "I'll stop." He threw the piece to the ground.

"No," said Bob, "go ahead, it needs to be done." He looked down at Daniel. "Daniel, let Dr. Long clean you up."

"Okay," whimpered Daniel.

John nodded and returned to tending Daniel's wounds.

"So," Bob continued, "The Big Zee volunteered to watch over Daniel and be my contact. Mad Mike reluctantly agreed I was perfect; I was an Immune, a swimmer, and knew you. Zee drove me all night and he was amazing as he talked his way through the checkpoints to get to the admiral. I told Beckwourth my family was dead. He was so eager to assemble a cohesive team he got lax on his obsessive background checks."

John pulled another fragment off Daniel. The boy twisted in his father's arms. He buried his face in his father's chest and cried.

"I think this can wait until later," said John.

Bob nodded and continued, "Our perfect leader made other mistakes, too. He had a high-tech handprint reader operating his office door lock, but no alarm. How stupid. Through my contact with the Big Zee, Mad Mike's engineering geeks figured out how I could jimmy the lock without anyone knowing. The admiral even once upgraded the handprint reader and installed a new door, but never alarmed it."

John thought back to when Flinch busted into the admiral's office.

"How else do you think our fledgling militias so easily avoided the world's militaries, especially in the early days when militaries were fully armed?" Bob smiled mockingly, "All the military intelligence was right there on his computer unencrypted. Of course, anything to do with the Immunes had eight layers of security. He was so focused on his little squad, he lost sight of the big picture. I know—"

"Dad!" said Daniel, pulling on Bob's rescue harness, "Can we go?"

"In a minute. John, I know you have high regard for the admiral, and so do I in some ways, but he's human and has his own foibles. I must say I've enjoyed downing airwars with you. I wouldn't mind staying on and killing a few more, but I have to find out why the Big Zee let my son go on a combat mission, then kick his ass."

At that moment, a militiaman with a shaved head hobbled up. He was weaponless. His face and entire scalp glowed red from welts and bruising, but appeared okay otherwise, except for the sprained ankle.

"Bob!" the militiaman said, "the Big Zee's dead. Daniel snuck in during the deployment. Zee caught up to us. He was crazy out of his mind when he found the kid gone. Zee reached us immediately before the battle started. He was screaming at Daniel, 'what were you thinking?'"

Bob frowned down at his son.

"Dad!" said Daniel, looking up at Bob, "Honest—Mr. Zee told me it was okay to go."

"Yeah," said the militiaman, "that's exactly what your boy said to Zee. Zee screamed, 'that's crazy,' then hugged him. He took charge of our squad and let Mad Mike know we were returning

Daniel to safety. The Big Zee kept complaining his battle tablet's GPS was malfunctioning. Zee got us lost, and somehow we ended up here."

"So," said Bob, surprised, "you didn't fight your way through the battle lines?"

"Hell, no," he said with a grimace.

John saw the man stagger on his injured leg. He grabbed the man's arm firmly and helped him to the ground. John nodded to him to keep speaking.

"We heard radio reports of a group breaking through. We didn't know they were referring to us until we saw the Colossus. We must have accidentally walked through an opening in the battle lines. Even though—"

"Dad!" whimpered Daniel, "*really*, Mr. Zee said I could go."

"Daniel!" said Bob with an exasperated look, "it doesn't matter now, let this soldier finish talking—please!" Bob gave an apologetic shrug to the soldier.

"That's okay," said the man, "I've got kids myself. At that age, boys hear what they want to hear. Even while we were lost, the Big Zee was real calm and cool; that is, until the Colossus appeared, then he freaked out. He screamed at Daniel to run, then started shooting. We joined him." The man hung his head. "Didn't make much difference; it ended up nailing us anyway."

John looked around at the injured militiamen. All had bright red welts on any exposed skin. Two were clearly deceased, and three others were comatose and had irregular gasping breaths. John doubted they would last the hour without immediate attention. Several others, although conscious, didn't look like they could ambulate. The rest, even though standing, looked as though they'd been dragged through a briar patch.

John said, "Do you think there's any way you can get these men through the battle line back to your people?" He motioned with his hand to the militiamen lying on the ground.

"John!" the angry voice of admiral Beckwourth came from behind, "Nobody's going anywhere. These men are under arrest. They're airwar terrorists and will be turned over to ASC."

CHAPTER 39

AIR SUPERIORITY

The admiral was standing with four heavily armed servicemen and four staff with weapons aimed. Both the admiral and Captain Howe's side arms remained holstered. Three of the militiamen who still possessed rifles aimed them weakly at the admiral. John doubted if there were any rounds left in the guns.

"You might as well surrender," said the admiral, "Resisting might delay your arrest momentarily, but please look."

He pointed to six specks in the distance. The flying objects were clearly troop transport helicopters from Central.

"They'll be here in less than two minutes. You've lost! Surrender, and it'll go better at your hearings."

"Notice what he said, hearings?" Bob whispered to John, "Not a trial of peers, yet another liberty lost, justified by crisis."

"Who's the leader of this group?" demanded the admiral.

The bald-headed man replied, "The Big Zee," and he pointed to one of the dead bodies. The corpse lay spread eagled on the ground. The face was one giant bruise with a non-bleeding gash across the forehead.

"Damn!" swore the admiral, and he stomped the ground. He bent and checked for a pulse just to be sure.

"See how upset the admiral is that he can't get an interrogation?" whispered Bob again to John, "I'm telling you, the admiral is looking out for his own skin."

John saw Admiral Beckwourth notice Bob's whispers. The admiral's eyes shifted to Daniel. The admiral walked to Bob and in a hushed voice said, "What's this boy doing here?"

"He's my son," said Bob, seemingly resigned to his fate, "He was with the militia."

"Admiral, why don't you let these men go?" said John before the admiral could respond.

The admiral rubbed his chin, then said, "I can't do that; too many witnesses. I'd have to explain to ASC."

John watched the admiral pause as if pondering his options.

The admiral whispered to John, "Walk Bob and the boy to the tree line and let them escape. It saves our butts, and no one will know. I'll say Bob defected. That's an easier spin than dealing with his son in custody."

Before John could respond, Beckwourth, in a booming voice, shouted, "I trust you all see the necessity of surrender. Line up here." He pointed so everyone's view directed away from John, Bob, and Daniel.

A report of a single rifle shot crackled through the air. John ducked instinctively.

"The only surrender I see happening might be your own," thundered a voice from behind the trees. John saw approximately forty men step out of the woods to their left. One of the militiamen had his gun aimed toward the sky and was obviously the source of the shot.

"The battle is finished," said an elderly silver-headed man. He, like the other men, was wearing camouflaged fatigues. There was no evidence of ranking insignias on any of the uniforms. John did notice a small caduceus on the old man's collar, and he was carrying a battle tablet.

He, like the admiral, had a side arm, but it, too, remained holstered. All the other men were heavily armed and looked like former military. John noticed the sounds of gunfire and explosions, which had been a constant background noise since their arrival, had stopped. Only the smoke spires from the woods gave any indication a sizable battle occurred only minutes before.

"We pulled back since the airwars were downed," said the silver-haired man, "but I may have acted too soon." He pointed to the airwar streaking across the lake that Suggs was controlling.

"Sir," said Bob, "it has a TC attached. As soon as the Immune gets out, it'll be downed."

"That's good," said the old man, smiling.

The helicopters were closing in. John could hear the thumps from the rotors now faintly in the distance.

The admiral spoke up, "Listen, whoever you are—"

"How's your son, Bob?" interrupted the old man, ignoring the admiral. He looked at Daniel. "And where's Zee? He radioed me about your boy."

"Daniel will be fine, but the Big Zee didn't make it," Bob said and pointed to the prostrate body.

The old man moved to the body and kneeled. He reached into his pocket, and a small penlight appeared in his hand. He opened each eyelid and shined light in the pupils one at a time. The pupils remained fixed and dilated. The old man's face saddened.

"He was a great commander and a true friend. Such a pointless loss. Zee pressed me hard for this Colossi attack against my better judgment; I should've listened to my gut instincts."

"I guess I can't blame anyone but myself," Bob mumbled. "Daniel is a stubborn, reckless, impulsive kid, just like his old man."

"Dad!" said the boy, "why won't you listen to me? Mr. Zee said I could go."

Bob gave the old man a *see what I mean* look and said, "I'll kick his butt when he's better. Currently, I'm just grateful he's alive. Thanks once again to The Immune."

John felt a small flush come over his cheeks and a warm glow of pride fill his chest. John was used to receiving a thousand accolades a night on the evening news. Never once did he feel emotion, but this was special.

The old man turned to John, "Dr. Long, we're colleagues in a fashion. I'm a pediatrician. I've always admired your character. I realize much of your fame is a creation via the admiral. Peel away the hype and one really does find a great man, which is so unusual with celebrity."

John thought, *Well, everyone has me pegged wrong. Pull back the hype and one finds only a void filled with vengeance.*

"Hold on, hold on," interrupted the admiral, "Hate to disrupt the little chat fest here, but we've got many men with guns pointing them at each other. Doctor, you need to surrender before somebody starts shooting."

Colonel Vickers slowly drew his gun out of his holster. He manually chambered a round.

The old man smiled, then said, "Admiral, take a glance at your battle tablet. Your ground troops began leaving the area as soon as ours did. If you remember, their mission was to prevent us from downing the Colossi."

John watched as the admiral began furiously tapping on his battle tablet. His brows furrowed as he appeared to absorb the reports flashing across the screen. He looked up at the old man with a puzzled gaze.

"General Cleevus started retreating immediately after he thought all the Colossi were killed," explained the old man, "Oh, you might be able to muster a few of your Grey Youth Guard, but not enough to stop this crew." He nodded toward his rugged men who encircled the small group.

"Our helicopters will be here in less than a minute," retorted the admiral.

The old man pointed across the lake, which currently appeared more of a deflated Colossi graveyard than a body of water.

"Actually, you don't," he said, "We won the battle for air superiority. Our pilots were some of the best of the former US Air Force. Our jets control the air, and they have radar missile locks on your Chinooks. That's why your helicopters wisely chose to land on the other side of the lake."

CHAPTER 40

MAD MIKE

John watched the admiral swing around. The admiral's skin paled as he saw the Chinooks landing on the opposite side of the lake. The admiral pulled out his pearl-handled revolver and offered it to the elderly doctor. "Please accept my surrender, but I would strongly advise you to set the Immunes free. Your militia's low popularity ratings would hit a new nadir, and you would virtually eliminate remaining community support."

The old man waved the gun off. "We're not interested in prisoners or surrender. What we'd like is a truce." He then motioned with his hand. Several medics appeared from the woods and immediately began tending to the injured. Several of the men were covered in soot. It appeared they passed close to some of the small fires burning in the woods.

John noticed the truce offer seemed to have caught the admiral off-guard. The admiral stood in silence for what seemed several minutes.

"Well," said the admiral, "under the circumstances, I think I can work out an amnesty agreement for you and these men. ASC would be fine, but I seriously doubt Mad Mike would approve."

"Well, I think I can speak for him," said the old man, letting out a small laugh and giving the admiral a smile. There were scattered laughs from several of the militiamen.

"Admiral," said Bob, smiling, "you're speaking to Mad Mike." He was still holding Daniel in his arms, and the boy seemed to have a smile on his swollen face as well.

"Impossible!" said Admiral Beckwourth with a startled look, "I have a complete file on Mad Mike, and you're not him. We had the best intelligence in the world on you."

"You also had a mole in the First Immune Attack Force," said Mad Mike with a smile.

"But you're a pediatrician?" said the admiral with disbelief.

"True," said Mad Mike, "but consider this statistic. Airwars are the number one killer of children, who better to lead the battle. Plus, I have a master's degree in military history and back in the day I was a navy seal—that helps."

"Points well noted," said the admiral, "So, you want a truce. Does this include the Mad Mike allies around the world?"

"Yes," said Mad Mike. He began moving around his injured men, shaking their hands and patting them on their backs. The most severely injured were already being moved by stretchers toward the woods.

"I've got to ask why the change in strategy?" said the admiral, raising his eyebrow and following along after Mad Mike.

"Well, several reasons. First, airwars seem to have a sixth sense for avoiding our recon teams. We don't seem to be making an impact anymore. Second, losing Big Zee today has taken the wind out of my sails. He was my right-hand man since day one. He had an uncanny ability to ferret out military intelligence even before Bob became our mole."

The admiral gave Bob a frown.

"Sorry, admiral," said Bob, "I was following my heart. I had no intention of hurting you or the Immunes."

Mad Mike continued, "Third, human deaths from airwar attacks are down dramatically. The coastal safe zone tactic seems bogus to our scientists, but it's difficult to argue with success. But sometimes strategies don't make sense to those on the outside. For instance, why wouldn't ASC share information with other scientists? After all, we're fighting the same evil enemy. Finally—"

"Bull!" interrupted the admiral, "Check your history books for how many times the United States has been burned using the same thesis 'the enemy of my enemy is my friend.'" Then he laughed, "Of course, a government's typical reaction to failed policy is to repeat it, only with more money — sorry I interrupted; please continue."

"Finally, many of my people are tired. Some of my most loyal followers want to take their families to the coastal safe zones." He looked at the corpse of the Big Zee. Two of his men were zipping him up in a black body bag. Mad Mike let out a sigh of weary resignation.

John watched with astonishment as the admiral's demeanor abruptly changed.

"You will immediately disarm," commanded the admiral in a draconian voice, "Your people will go to re-education camps, then to safe zones, in that order."

Mad Mike looked stunned.

John cringed and thought, *For being such a brilliant public relations man, the admiral is certainly blowing this negotiation.* John noted Captain Howe's birthmark was now shining red. The admiral's reaction seemed to have an effect on him as well.

"Admiral," said Mad Mike calmly. He appeared to have regained his composure almost immediately. "You're not in much of a position to be making demands. To show good faith, we'll agree to a cease-fire for six weeks. Then you'll let those who wish to migrate to coastal zones, migrate directly, no camps. They'll abide by ASC rules on entering the Coastal Safe Zones, but will leave weapons with those who remain inland. There won't be a confiscation of weapons. The remaining militias will keep their weapons, but refrain from attacks."

The admiral appeared in deep thought. Before answering, he took a long pause. "Agreed, but we'll need to make the cease-fire three months before I can get ASC to admit any of your group into safe zones."

"My people are tired," countered Mad Mike, "Two months."

"Done," said the admiral, "but for those who don't migrate to the safe zones, I can't grant amnesty."

"Those of us who choose not to relocate aren't looking for amnesty," said Mad Mike, "We're tired of killing those young misguided zealots in the Grey Youth Guard. We'll refrain from seeking airwars, only killing those attacking us or blocking supply routes. If ASC doesn't assault us with their adolescent boys, we'll keep to ourselves and watch how things transpire in the coastal safety zones. Perhaps later, others will join the rest in safe zones. More immediate, I would hope we could share information on airwars. We've discovered one fact that ASC appears not to be knowledgeable of."

"What's that?" inquired the admiral.

"Not all airwars have juveniles," said Mad Mike in a grave tone, "Our men have killed several without releasing offspring. Airwars have an uncanny way of avoiding my men, but on occasion, we'd stumble on one unexpectedly. On no account did any release juveniles. We never could dissect one to discover why, as curiously, a downed airwar was like a guaranteed ticket for an ASC airstrike. The Big Zee thought the Colossi might be absent juveniles. He convinced me we needed to test the theory. This is the sole reason for our presence: to determine if Colossi release juveniles. Sadly, I agreed."

The admiral paused, then seeming to have made a decision, said, "I'll pass your findings to ASC, but council members were already cognizant of that fact. For your edification, ASC knows with certainty Colossi contain juveniles. It's sad to think this entire escapade was avoidable. I'll see what I can do about information-sharing in the future."

"What about their propaganda?" asked Colonel Vickers, turning to the admiral.

"Yes," said the admiral, "good point. Following the two-month cease fire, will you agree to stop propaganda against coastal migration?"

"Our members have always been able to come and go as they please," said Mad Mike, "They personally decide what liberties they're willing to sacrifice for safety."

"Okay," said the admiral, smiling, "We have a deal. I'll get the High Council to draw up a truce agreement. We'll do a press conference and sign the historic document in front of billions of people."

As the admiral was speaking, Mad Mike looked straight into his eyes. He shook his head slightly in the negative. He then held his hand out to the admiral. The admiral shook it and Mad Mike said, "This is our agreement. Nothing else is needed."

Mad Mike motioned to one of his men, who began tapping on a battle tablet. "In less than ten minutes," said Mad Mike, "worldwide, Mad Mike's militias and allies will back down. I hope, for all of us, this is the right decision."

"It's absolutely the right decision," said the admiral, now grinning, "Are you sure we can't do a signing? The PR would be great!" John thought the admiral seemed to have returned to his old self.

"Sorry," said Mad Mike, "no. All I want is peace and quiet. Good luck to the Immunes and ASC. If we can be of help, let us know."

As he said this, he and his men began dissipating into the woods. Bob followed alongside Mad Mike, with Daniel in his arms. The boy shifted in his father's arms, waved, and smiled at John. John knew the boy would be okay, but he was worried about Bob leaving the Immunes.

Bob appeared to sense John's concern, "I'll keep the same cell number unless the admiral cuts me off," shouted Bob, "We'll keep in touch."

"Good luck!" said John, feeling relieved.

John turned and looked toward the lake. Suggs had taken the Colossus and put it in a slow spin over the lake. He slid down and now gripped the end of an outer curtain tentacle. The tentacle was arcing through the water, and Suggs unbelievably managed to barefoot ski from the spinning force of the tentacle. He found a patch of water not filled with previously downed Colossi and was able to ski toward the shore and run up on land in one move.

John saw Captain Howe touch his battle tablet, activating the TC remote, and the Colossus began its dance of death in the background. Suggs screamed, "Woooo haaaa! Did you people see that? I hope someone caught me on video. It'll lead the evening news." As he ran up toward the Immunes, he saw Spoon, and without a word, sat down and began to cry.

CHAPTER 41

THE GREAT SUCCESS

The admiral made sure Booboo's death and the truce led the evening news. The world's population mourned in unison at the loss of one of its most celebrated heroes. Booboo's death even overshadowed the announcement of the truce, which illustrated the tremendous worldwide following the First Immune Attack Force carried.

The importance of the truce wasn't lost with ASC, though. The High Council was ecstatic, and the admiral knew his political influence had risen to its apogee. Unlike his previous visit with the High Council, the admiral was pleased to be greeted with smiles. The exception was Captain Stewart.

"The High Council is delighted with your resolution of the militia problem," said Senator Snivaling.

"Thank you," said the admiral, in a serious tone, "I've never forgotten who I serve, and I'll always do so to the best of my abilities."

Snivaling continued, "Yesterday there were no reports of militia-sponsored airwar attacks, and the human death toll fell to its lowest point in nearly a year. Public attitudes are at an all-time high since the crisis began."

She began clapping her hands lightly. The rest of the High Council joined her applause except for Captain Stewart, who scowled. The scowl of Stewart gave the admiral a nice warm feeling inside.

As the clapping subsided, the admiral leaned close to the microphone and spoke, "Due to the outing of Bob Rund as a mole for Mad Mike, I would assume there's no further need to investigate my department. It would distract me from other—"

"You assume wrong," interrupted Captain Stewart viciously, "My investigation continues regardless."

The admiral noted there were murmurs of disagreement throughout the High Council hall.

"Captain," said Senator Snivaling with a slightly surprised look, "I think that the admiral has certainly earned our trust."

"What he's earned is a suspension for being so ignorant as to let a mole access critical ASC information," said Stewart maliciously, "I'd like the High Council's authorization to personally interrogate the admiral."

"Captain," said Snivaling firmly, "there's not a member of the High Council unaware of your interrogation skills. I'm quite sure you could make the admiral confess to being a duck-billed platypus given enough time. This would *not* serve any purpose other than resolving your own personal vendetta."

The captain looked around the room as if to see if he had any followers. Every council member turned away from his demanding gaze.

"Glavin, are you with me?" asked Stewart, apparently trying to drum up support.

The admiral watched intently as Glavin, stood, then looked at Chairperson Snivaling. Snivaling slightly arched her right eyebrow at Glavin, adding a slight frown. Glavin sat down without speaking.

"Ah, Spokesman Glavin," said Stewart, "and I thought that was a suntan on your nose." Stewart appeared to realize he lost the debate, then he stalked from the hall.

"Well," said Snivaling sweetly, "again, thank you, Admiral, for helping us change the world circumstances to the positive. You *are* fully aware stability is critical for the next several weeks. I *would* like to discuss the Immunes' continued role in this endeavor. Would you please meet me in my chambers after we adjourn this meeting?"

John was amazed how much the world changed in a year. Over ninety-five percent of the world's population now resided within eight hundred meters of a shoreline. Glavin was constantly crowing that success replaced a crisis of disaster. War between men, for the first time in history, had all but ceased.

A few of the most passionate socialists were even suggesting this was Sengele's master plan. They, along with the Sengele Cult, called for his release and justified the deaths of millions as a necessary step for a better world. Of course, the majority of the population didn't share the feeling. The website *ExecuteSengele.com* was one of the most frequently visited sites on the Internet. Execution suggestions had grown to over twenty-three thousand descriptive options. John visited the site multiple times and even posted a few proposals of his own.

John now spent more time doing public relations visits in safe zones than downing airwars. No longer sequestered at Central, he was shocked to see how much personal freedom had eroded.

During this post-militia period, John and the admiral had time for many political discussions. John noted the admiral believed ASC would solve the airwar threat with a subsequent return to normalcy. The admiral remained adamant that any attempts to change political direction at this point would be irresponsible. He was constantly admonishing John not to challenge ASC, as it would be bad for the Immune Corps.

Since ASC controlled the media, news and reality were radically different. John realized the admiral had no problem with media FS maneuvers. The admiral believed these were necessary to prevent chaos until the crisis ended. Titled "The Great Success," media constantly pounded the audience with evidence for the improvement of the human condition.

The most lauded "Great Success" was the banishment of hunger. Free ASC loaves contained all essential nutrients a healthy adult needed and had an acceptable taste even with its greenish tinge. Much to the consternation of the High Council, the Internet sites darkly nicknamed the loaves Soylent Green after the classic movie.

One late night comedian joked, "The good news is only Tuesday is Soylent Green Day; the bad news is ASC has renamed all days Tuesday."

On one of John's frequent flights with the admiral he noticed vast areas of farmland were returning to the wild.

"Admiral, how can ASC continue to supply the world with food with the cessation of agriculture? Are the High Council members tapping emergency food reserves?"

"No," said the admiral, "ASC tells me they have food supplies under control. ASC loaves are simple and easy to produce." He pulled a greenish object from under a seat next to him that looked like an uncut loaf of bread wrapped in clear plastic.

"How long has that been there?" said John with a slight grimace.

"Three weeks," said the admiral, smiling. He peeled back the plastic wrap and tore a hunk off the loaf. It was the same color on the inside. The admiral then held the piece to his nose. "Smells like it came straight from the bakery. These loaves don't go stale. It says so right here on the wrapper."

John noticed a strong musty odor wafting over from the loaf. "Well, the loaves have to be produced from something."

"There are farms in the safe zones," said the admiral.

"Not many I've seen," said John with a frown, "Farms all appear to be ASC controlled. I notice ASC officials and other fortunate individuals like the Immunes still get bacon and eggs for breakfast."

The admiral rubbed his belly and gave John a knowing smile, "All societies have a ruling class, and all ruling classes have privileges. The certainty of this fact ranks up there with death and taxes." Seeming to like his maxim, he pulled out the children's book he always carried and began scribbling in it.

"I spoke with a farmer in the safe zone the other day," said John. "He said 'I'd like to farm, but ASC's compassionate gift of free food means there's no one to sell to. Not much incentive to work a farm.'"

"True," the admiral looked up from his writing, "But ASC likes the hype for its compassion in providing free food. There's no PR points or control in telling folks to work hard growing food for the future."

"Sounds like an example of reckless compassion Bob's always speaking of," said John, "I think ASC is tapping world food reserves, and there will ultimately be a catastrophic shortage."

"Interesting thought . . . I mentioned the same to an ASC official. He said, 'If food costs go up, we'll just print more money.'"

"That's not a solution. That's—"

"Absurd," said the admiral with a twinkle in his eye, "Please remember I said I was speaking to a government official. You might want to hang on to this just in case." The admiral tossed the loaf to John.

Another highlight of "The Great Success" was gun control. Gun confiscation led to a highly celebrated all-time low in firearm deaths. Missing from the report was overall murders, muggings, and home invasions were at an all-time high. Previous firearm death statistics didn't separate justifiable deaths from the accidental, suicidal, and nefarious. The safe zone was full of thugs, now fearless, as they preyed on the defenseless.

John also noted "Great Success" included the solution for the world's healthcare crisis. ASC banned insurance and private fee-for-service medical practice. ASC was compassionately providing healthcare to all comers. John's medical colleagues reported this was possible due to the suspension of high-tech services, except for those needed by ASC officials and their families.

As during China's Cultural Revolution when leaders advocated replacing western medicine with traditional Chinese therapies, ASC was requiring homeopathic care as first-line therapy for all medical conditions. Even if one had a myocardial infarction, homeopathy was attempted. If you lived, great; if you died, it was even better because the health care costs were extremely low. Cardiac catheterizations, stents, bypass operations, transplants, implantable defibrillators were procedures of the past unless you were an ASC member. ASC took great delight in promoting healthcare was free for everyone.

The euphoria surrounding the "Great Success" led ASC to decree a holiday called the Festive Holiday Month. Extravagant events designed without regard to expense were the rule. Of course, the most lavish and ostentatious functions were ASC events, where John was a frequent guest of honor. He was the recipient of every award known to mankind and, of course, thanks to the admiral, the world was always watching.

The President of the United States commissioned John the Field Marshal of the Immunes. The title gave him command of all remaining functioning U.S. military forces, if needed, by the Immune Corps. The ASC High Council largely ignored the honor, but it was an extremely popular pronouncement among the general population. Many other countries awarded him a similar rank with their militaries. John couldn't have cared less. His thoughts centered on returning to downing airwars and getting his hands on Sengele.

The Festive Holiday Month did have a theme, "The Salvation Wall." ASC's idea was to build a giant barrier immediately inside the oscillating wire as a back up in case of a breach by airwars. The Colossi all but replaced the common airwar along the oscillating wires. Their numbers reached over a million. In highly populated areas, aerial views of the Colossi looked like a pool lane line, all the floats lined up in a row. Movement was minimal; Colossi always hovered a few hundred feet from the protective wire.

The concept of the Salvation Wall was to pile rubble and debris to the height of thirty to forty feet. Contests were set between coastal areas to see who could set up the highest, most impenetrable barrier the fastest. Anyone working the contest got lavish food and alcohol rations beyond the standard ASC loaves. John thought the Salvation Wall was ridiculous and expressed his judgment to the admiral, who agreed.

John's low opinion of the wall created an interesting situation early in the Festive Holiday Month. John was attending a High Council meeting, as he was to be a recipient of yet another award. He was the only non-ASC member to enter ASC City in the last six months.

Before John's award presentation, a short ceremony honoring the admiral was held. John and the admiral stood at the small desk with the one microphone. The High Council was recognizing his role in the development of a new defensive aerosol dubbed "greens." The admiral privately contracted with non-ASC scientists in the development of a non-Immune derived protective spray. Its production effectively ended the discussion of the need for Immune extractions. The first shipment arrived for members living in ASC City that morning. ASC members traded in their blues and browns for the new, more powerful, and longer lasting green.

"I must remind High Council members to turn in all their blues and browns when you receive your green," announced Senator Snivaling, "Blues and browns will be recycled into antitoxin.

Should you ever get attacked without your green you *will* be glad you did, because our antitoxin supplies are currently limited." Around the room most of the council members could be seen with their little green aerosol canisters already holstered to their belts.

"No worries for other ASC members. We have just enough greens to supply every resident of ASC City," said the admiral, bending to the microphone on the desk.

Snivaling stood. "Admiral, I think I speak for the entire High Council when I commend you on such an extraordinary job. Your service to the High—"

"Oh—pleeeease!" cut in Captain Stewart, who appeared irritated by the accolades. He stood next to Snivaling.

"The greens are all about saving the skins of his precious Immunes. They're not even ASC so I don't even know why he gives a damn." Then he glared at John, who was standing next to the admiral.

John noted Stewart had his green holstered to his belt, but a cylindrical bulge in his pocket revealed he didn't feel obligated to recycle his old canister as did the others.

"Captain," said Snivaling "I believe that—"

"Enough about the admiral," said Stewart scornfully, "The impressive progress in the Salvation Wall construction is vastly more important. As you know I'm in charge of this undertaking and it has advanced faster than naysayers predicted. Largely due to my extraordinary efforts we believe some areas will be completed in less than two weeks."

John might have held his tongue if it had been anyone else speaking. John picked up the microphone, and interrupting Stewart's self-congratulations, addressed the High Council.

"Excuse me, but I have concerns about the Salvation Wall. I'm experienced as anyone dealing with airwars, and I assure you if Colossi breach the wire, the Salvation Wall won't be a barrier."

Stewart looked enraged. John thought he might leap from his upper level row. Snivaling put her hand on Captain Stewart's shoulder and whispered something in his ear which seemed to mollify him.

John continued, "I've personally seen the common airwar easily cross obstacles more formidable than your wall. The Colossi tower above it. The Salvation Wall construction makes absolutely no sense. Furthermore, I don't see construction of a Salvation Wall around ASC City. Why's that?"

John noticed the ever-present camera recording lights clicked off as he addressed the council. John also observed the admiral was now hunched over, his right hand on his forehead, covering one of his eyes and shaking his head back and forth.

Senator Snivaling leaned to her microphone and addressed John in somewhat of a sweet, slightly condescending voice, "John; may I call you John?" she didn't wait for a reply; she just continued speaking, "I *am* Senator Beulah Snivaling. We wish to commend you for your magnificent service to the world. You *are* indeed an inspiration. Unfortunately, your entertaining daily activities do *not* allow you to be privy to the subtleties of the global picture. This is why we exist."

She smiled around the room at the other High Council members.

"The wisdom of the ASC High Council has catapulted the world from its biggest crisis to this grand level of improvement of the overall human condition. The sage advice we impart may befuddle one that *is* more physical than cerebral."

John could feel his face flush.

Most of the other High Council members were nodding agreement and Snivaling's voice became even more patronizing, "Issues such as this should be left to elite social planners and scientists who have high intellect and can spend their days thinking and studying. I certainly don't mean to diminish the wonderful contributions you've made, but I think you *will* agree that policy-making should be left to those who have special intellectual talents, which sadly you and the rest of the population do *not* have." She then smiled sweetly at him.

"I'd think the input of the Field Marshal for the Immunes might be worth something," John retorted sarcastically.

"A pathetic pronouncement made by a President and other former leaders who irrationally believe the previous archaic political system still confers them power," replied Snivaling, with her most patronizing voice, "This is not a game of chess where pawns can be promoted to queens, so please do *not* take that honorary label too seriously. The High Council recognizes the title solely for the pleasure of the populous. ASC does *not* acknowledge its function or otherwise we *would* have invited you to vital ASC meetings which you *have* clearly not been in attendance."

She then addressed the admiral. "Admiral Beckwourth, I would suggest you apprise The Immune, whom we all love and respect, with the rules of decorum so that he will *not* be put in a position of embarrassment like this in the future. Admiral, I'll see you in my office after the presentation, and we *will* discuss this further."

John was about to explode. The admiral walked up, put his hand on his shoulder, and whispered, "I can explain. Please don't blow up."

John received his award in silence and was unceremoniously whisked from the High Council Hall.

An hour after the episode, the admiral rejoined John, who was fuming. As the admiral passed through the doorway, John said, "I think I may call my own little press conference and let the world know how I feel about things."

"Calm down," said the admiral. He handed John a pink envelope that had a perfumed smell of lilacs. *Dr. John Long* was handwritten in script on the outside.

"John, open it. It's a letter of apology from Snivaling. She's a nasty lady under a lot of stress, but I worked everything out."

He read the letter, which was fully contrite and he felt less perturbed.

"Let me now explain to you about the wall," said the admiral, "You know as well as I do that the wall is worthless for its stated purpose. Its construction is unmistakably another FS maneuver. ASC City doesn't need a wall because the High Council knows it's useless, plus ASC members all now own greens for protection.

"So why the FS maneuver?" asked John.

"Regardless of my cheery media reports, ASC is highly nervous about maintaining the social fabric in the safe zones. The Salvation Wall is a great way to distract the masses."

"Until what?" said John sarcastically, "The wall is nearing completion, what then? Dig giant holes for airwars to trip and fall into? Give me a break."

"No," said the admiral, "just to buy a little time. The High Council says they've a major announcement in two weeks. They're referring to it as *Fulfillment Day*. The security on this is so tight I don't even know the details. Apparently it's a crisis ender."

"Again, why the wall?" said John, confused.

"ASC needs to prevent anarchy for two more weeks. So think about it, John, the wall is perfect. The masses are distracted because working people aren't rioting people. The artificial sense of security makes everyone feel calmer and safer. Finally, it gives a place to store trash and debris collecting in the safe zones."

"Are you sure about this major announcement?" said John skeptically.

"That's the scuttlebutt. Two, three weeks tops. We have Fulfillment Day, and the airwar crisis ends."

"It sounds too good to be true—I guess I can keep my yap shut for a couple more weeks. I suppose, in that respect, this bizarre FS maneuver makes some sense, but if everyone is migrating back out in a few weeks, it'll take days to dig enough exits to handle the exodus."

"Yes, but what's a future minor delay if in the grand scheme of things it prevents injuries and deaths?"

"I suppose you're right," John paused, "This smacks of your planning."

"Well, yes," said the admiral with a little laugh, "I'd like to think I'm the world's greatest PR guy, and I sincerely hope someday everyone believes it, but this wasn't my idea. It was our favorite High Council member Captain Stewart's plan. As I said before, the only people better than me at FS maneuvers are politicians."

"It's hard to believe Stewart could make any plan not involving pain and suffering of his fellow man." Then John changed the subject. "So what about the greens? Is everyone receiving them?"

The admiral shook his head, "No, only those in ASC City. The first run had enough to give each resident one can. Not even ASC members out of ASC City are receiving greens. They'll have to make do with whatever they already have, browns or blues. After Fulfillment Day it'll be a moot point."

"You're so politically connected," said John, "I can't imagine you not knowing what happens on Fulfillment Day."

"Nah, you give me too much credit. There's an inner circle within the High Council I can't penetrate. I view these last two weeks with excitement and trepidation. I only hope that this horrible year of FS maneuvers, extreme stress, and moral compromise is ending satisfactorily for humanity."

CHAPTER 42

A SHOT AT SENGELE

During the period of waiting for the announcement of Fulfillment Day, John was occupied attending ceremonies, meeting politicians, accepting awards, and promoting the Salvation Wall. After many days of pampering, fawning, and having every title and accolade bestowed on him, it was with great relief he returned to his quarters at Central.

The team was immensely glad to have him back, as Suggs presumed he was team leader in The Immune's absence and was driving everyone crazy. The only way they survived his pomposity was with endless pranks.

Today Suggs awoke sans bathroom mirror. His threats regarding a hasty return of his mirror were met with laughs and Prof's heckles.

"The mirror ran away to a safe house. It couldn't stand the abuse," and "the standard mirror is only good for a million views, you exceeded its capacity." The missing mirror was an FS maneuver for the primary prank, which was the painting of Suggs' upper eyelids neon purple during his sleep. The absent mirror served to prolong the team's enjoyment of Suggs' new fashion statement.

A betting pool was ongoing throughout Central to see how long it would take Suggs to learn of the prank. As John and the admiral arrived in the common room, John was able to assess the situation immediately and kept his mouth shut.

"Suggs," said the admiral upon entering the common room. "Have you gone completely out of your gourd? Get that paint off your eyelids. You look like a freaking idiot. Have the rest of you not ..." He stopped mid-sentence as he noticed fully half the team had fallen to the floor, unable to breathe from laughing.

After looking through several pages on a clipboard of names and times Prof said, "Someone run and tell Sergeant Clark he just won a pot full of money." DS, laughing, skipped out of the room.

"Sorry," said the admiral, looking sheepish, "My bad."

John approached Suggs with a smile. Suggs was trying to see his reflection in the bowl of a spoon.

"I'm upside-down," mumbled Suggs.

John took the spoon, reversed it to the convex side and Suggs gazed at himself closely, first one eye, then the other. The irregular crimson of Suggs' flushed face made him appear smeared with lipstick, which made the purple eyelids appear even more bizarre.

"The command is yours," said Suggs turning to John. Then he stalked out of the room.

Following John's return, the routine changed for the Immunes. In the subsequent days, only one mission transpired. The admiral left Central for business at sea and wasn't heard from.

Most of the team enjoyed the break, but John spent his time alone in his apartment. The crisis happened so fast, the demands on his time were so immense he never had opportunity to grieve properly for Cassandra. Now immersed in delayed grief, his only respite was the waves of anger at Joseph Sengele. Without the release valve of daily airwar battles, pent up emotions left him exhausted. Externally, he was a living legend as "The Immune." Internally, he was a seething, despondent being. In the giant theatrical show of the airwar crisis he felt cast as an actor, a talking prop. Others were the writers and directors. He sensed The Immune was another's creation; it wasn't him.

While John greatly anticipated the end of the crisis, he knew it would be a hollow victory as he lost his one love. He secluded himself, mourning. Occasionally, team members would check on him, but he was frank about his grief.

"Strong trees fall hard," said Dude, quoting a proverb, "John, please, let us know if we can help."

Early one morning, following several days of isolation, a firm knock rapped on his door.

"John," bellowed the admiral's voice through the door, "Dude has apprised me of your situation, but nevertheless, I need to speak with you—immediately."

John cracked the door. Admiral Beckwourth was in a full military dress uniform, sidearm at his side and a newspaper and manila folder under his arm.

"John, word from High Council is Fulfillment Day will be announced within forty-eight hours. Salvation Walls are complete and the population is restless. We need one last FS maneuver to keep folks on the tube, not in the streets. ASC needs breathing room, so you and the First Immune Attack Force are assigned a special mission."

John squinted from the light suffusing from the hall into his darkened room.

"Nobody's watching us down another airwar," mumbled John.

"Yes, I know," said the admiral, "but ASC has discovered a new airwar called the Red Zeppelin. The High Council wants the team to down it."

"Oh, come on—a Red Zeppelin?" John felt the fog lifting from his mind.

The admiral smiled, apparently happy that John appeared out of his stupor. He opened the manila folder and removed an eight by ten inch photograph, handing it to John.

"It's more magenta than red. It's a genetic aberration occurring one in five-hundred thousand. ASC says they're not poisonous, but they're not telling anyone until after the mission."

"Well . . . that's somewhat different," said John, slightly perplexed, "The novelty will attract a few viewers, but not blockbuster ratings," said John, now getting dressed.

"True; that's why you're not going. As the team downs the Red Zeppelin, you, Prof, and Sumo will be noticeably absent on a 'secret' mission. That'll keep people watching as we leak out details."

"What could we possibly do that would keep people glued to the tube?" John started pulling up his pants.

"I know you've been in mourning and not up on current events," said the admiral.

He held up the morning newspaper. The headline in bold black letters read SENGELE TO BE EXECUTED NEXT WEEK. John snatched the paper from the admiral's hands, letting his pants fall to his ankles.

"Yesterday," said the admiral, "ASC announced the execution of Sengele. In one week they're feeding him to an airwar. ASC thought the announcement would captivate and subdue folks, but it only agitated them. The general populous doesn't want to wait a week. Small riots have broken out—High Council is letting you meet Joseph Sengele."

John was silent.

"The High Council wants two meetings, the first immediately after we arrive at his location. You'll meet privately with Sengele. This was reportedly his only last request. ASC wants you to forgive him publicly after the meeting, but approve the punishment. The next morning you'll serve as a commentator during his execution. Prof and Sumo will accompany you for show."

"You know I'll kill him on the first meeting," said John, his lips pressed together tightly.

"Yes," said the admiral, "but by my reckoning, if anyone deserves the honor, you do."

"Is ASC okay with this?" said John, rolling up the paper.

"ASC needs a distraction. If you kill Sengele prematurely, they'll forgive you, even if it's a surprise. It still gets them out of a pickle. The High Council is desperate for things to stay status quo for the next forty-eight hours."

"You still don't know the big announcement?" asked John.

"Not a clue—other than it's a crisis-ender."

"Admiral, you sure you're okay with me killing Sengele? No trial, no public hearings?"

The admiral looked away. "John, he wasn't getting a trial anyway."

"Well," said John, thumping the rolled up newspaper in his other hand, "I've all the facts I need. I only wanted your blessings."

The admiral was now back looking at John. John recognized the admiral's game face.

"Absolutely. In fact, I'm counting on it. I need the big distraction. After that, the announcement will occur, the hard work will have come to fruition, and I'll be a PR legend."

"I'll be happy to know Sengele is dead and the airwar crisis is over," said John, "I look forward to returning to a normal life."

The admiral gave John an amazed look, "John, you'll never be able—" He stopped mid-sentence and said quietly, "Sengele's death will be good for you."

He patted John on his shoulder and turned from the room.

John watched the rest of the team deploy on the Red Zeppelin mission with much fanfare. Dude replaced Sumo on John's mission. The admiral told John he overlooked an important detail and couldn't chance any flies in the ointment, but didn't elaborate further. The press went wild with questions regarding The Immune's "secret" mission. The admiral looked at ease as he parried question after question. John knew the admiral just bought his window of time. As they got in the transport plane, John asked, "Where are we going?"

"To the USS Acheson," said the admiral, "I visit every two weeks or so."

John's eyes narrowed and he said, "So you knew Dr. Sengele's whereabouts all along?"

"Yes," said the admiral, looking guilty, "but I never met him. I was conducting ASC business with another ship, but I berthed on the Acheson. Obviously, I could never tell you, John. It would have distracted you, and Sengele was politically out of your reach. The ship is currently in the Caribbean, over the Cayman Trench."

The mention of Cayman revived recollections of Cassandra and their engagement. Rage against Sengele being in the vicinity of his cherished memories overwhelmed John. It cleared any question in John's mind that he wouldn't have the mental fortitude to kill the man. Not only was he sure he could do it, he relished the thought.

The flight to the USS Acheson went smoothly, but there were two noteworthy aspects of the trip. First, none of the Immunes had flown in a seaplane. The flight was extra bouncy, and Prof, a poor flier even on a smooth flight, looked distressed.

"I wish Suggs was here to harass," said Prof, with the only smile he gave on the entire flight, "That calms me better than a Prozac."

Second, as they flew over the ship, it was obvious there were two airwars hanging onto the stern of the ship. Before John could get off a question, the admiral spoke.

"Those are the airwars planned for Sengele's execution. They hang on to the stern because there's no exit that's not salt water. An oscillating wire on the aft deck keeps them from moving elsewhere on the ship."

John thought, *Someone just wasted a lot of time setting this up. Sengele will never make it to the airwars alive.*

Upon their arrival the admiral told John and the other two Immunes to stay on the upper deck for an autograph and photo session. He warned them not to mention Sengele, as most of the crew didn't know he was a prisoner onboard.

John fulfilled his duties as The Immune, taking photos with beaming sailors, shaking hands, and signing autographs along with the other two Immunes. The autograph session went by quickly. The ship was operating on a skeleton crew, so there would be less of a chance for the secret of Sengele's presence to slip out.

Admiral Beckwourth had been in his stateroom for only a few minutes when his phone rang.

He looked at the caller ID, clicked answer, and immediately spoke, "Colonel Vickers, I emphatically told you not to call me except for an extreme emergency. My next hour is extraordinarily critical . . . What?" The admiral took the folder he was examining and hurled it against the wall. Papers flew across the stateroom.

He began screaming at Colonel Vickers on the phone, "That wasn't the plan. My orders were clear. I want to know who's responsible; I'll have their head. Take the Immunes back to Central and quarantine them all in the common room. Nobody goes in or out without my permission. Yes, use armed guards until I return. I don't care what you tell them, just do it." The admiral clicked the phone off, screamed expletives, and pounded the desktop violently.

CHAPTER 43

THE RED ZEPPELIN

S umo wondered what the reason was for the last-minute change in his mission. Whatever John was doing, it had to be better than listening to Suggs. Suggs became annoying the moment the First Immune Attack Force entered the Osprey. His questions to Captain Howe were incessant. Where was The Immune going? What kind of secret mission was John on? Why wasn't he selected to go on the secret mission with John?

Sumo thought, *How I miss Prof. He's the only one who can humiliate Suggs into silence.*

"Suggs," said Captain Howe, "Okay, you can be team leader for downing of the Red Zeppelin. Now shut up!"

"Good God, man!" said Mr. Eddie, "do you have any idea what you've done?"

Sumo watched the other Immunes all turn in unison and give Captain Howe incredulous looks.

It was a seven-hour flight to a remote area of Washington State, even with an in-air refueling of the Osprey. The first hour and a half was quiet as Suggs scribbled out battle plans. Things got out of control when Suggs insisted on prepping the team on the nine different attack plans he devised. All plans were a variation of the same theme, Suggs attacking and bringing down the Red Zeppelin single-handedly and the others helping him out of the water. Suggs droned on for several hours on the plans while most of the team ignored him or slept. Sumo felt like throwing him off the plane.

"Okay, I think we should now have a short oral exam on my mission plan," announced Suggs.

"That's it—I've had enough," yelled Sumo, "Cupcake, you grab his legs."

The two Immunes wrestled Suggs to the deck and using an opened parachute they wrapped Suggs up like a cocoon using the cords to tie him.

"Suggs, if you keep your mouth shut I won't gag you," said Sumo, "Do we have an agreement?"

Suggs nodded.

"I give him ten seconds," said Mr. Eddie, "Max."

There were several seconds of silence.

"Guys," said Suggs softly, "what if we do a written exam instead?"

"Mr. Eddie," said Sumo, "hand me the duct tape."

"Damn," said Mr. Eddie, "he lasted fourteen seconds. I'm glad I didn't make a bet."

Mr. Eddie tossed a large roll of shiny gray duct tape to Sumo.

"I didn't know how important Prof was to the team until today," said Sumo as he stretched duct tape over Suggs' mouth.

"Well," said DS, "I think you're being overly mean to Suggs."

"Yeah," piped in Spoon, "I agree."

"Ladies," said Sumo, "you're more than welcome to peel the tape off his pie-hole anytime you like, but you've got to promise to sit and listen to his yammering the rest of the trip."

DS and Spoon whispered among themselves briefly.

"We've decided not to remove the tape, as that would make us a party to the crime," said DS. "We refuse to involve ourselves in such testosterone-driven monkey business." Spoon nodded in agreement.

"Why, it's an honor to be in the presence of those with such purity of thought and action," said Mr. Eddie sarcastically.

The necessity for the Osprey became apparent to Sumo during the landing. A small field was adjacent to a two-acre lake. The Osprey, with its vertical landing capabilities, barely fit in the field. Except for gravel roads, there were no open areas in the woods for miles. A few photographers and video camera operators were positioned along the lake edge. The numbers were in no comparison to press coverage early in the First Immune Attack Force encounters.

Sumo decided to leave Suggs bound in the Osprey while the team formulated a plan. A water-based approach was designed, as the airwar was hovering above the small lake. The team huddled to discuss the downing.

"You know," said a photographer wearing a gray winter ski jacket, "the water temperature is fifty-two degrees."

Sumo noticed him smiling as he saw the reactions from the Immunes.

"Oh crap!" said Cupcake, "That's the same temperature as the Shamu tank at Sea World."

"I'd rather swim Alcatraz," said DS. "Look—where did he come from?" She pointed to the plane.

Sumo turned and looked toward the Osprey. He was surprised to see ASC spokesman Glavin exiting the plane with the pilots. Sumo hadn't seen him get on the plane.

Glavin was carrying an automatic rifle, which seemed out of character, especially since he was wearing a dress suit. He walked up to Captain Howe and began speaking quietly to him.

Captain Howe turned and approached the team.

"Okay, guys, this comes straight from Snivaling herself. The High Council wants the entire team to down the Red Zeppelin as a group."

"Well, I've got something to tell Snivaling," said Sumo, "If she would come blow some of her excessive hot air into the lake it would make our job a lot easier."

"Yeah," said Mr. Eddie, "couldn't Snivaling move this little show a little farther south? I think I see an iceberg in the lake."

"Can't Suggs do it himself?" added DS. "That's what he wants anyway."

"Okay, guys," Captain Howe looked toward Glavin, "I know the temperature sucks, but Snivaling wants a photo-op as a team."

"Chairperson Snivaling," said Glavin irritably.

"Cupcake," said Captain Howe, ignoring Glavin's correction, "go cut Suggs free."

Suddenly, a shrill scream came from the water's edge. Suggs had just dived into the water and was adjusting to the less than tropical temperature. A smiling Sergeant Clark was in the opening of the Osprey with knife in hand. He apparently freed Suggs without disclosing the lake temperature.

Everyone on the team was laughing except for Captain Howe. "You guys need to join him. I don't want to get my butt in a sling with ASC."

"Oh, the admiral will get over it," Sumo said.

"It's not the admiral I'm worried about. It's that witch Snivaling. Come on, guys, I'm on the spot here," Captain Howe pleaded.

"Now!" screamed Glavin, "you must go now!" His body jerked spasmodically as he yelled.

DS interjected, "Okay, okay, we'll all swim out for the photo op, but our favorite hotdog is almost to the curtain, and he's clearly downing it on his own. You've got to promise we'll stop for hot cocoa on the way home."

"You vexing bitch! Do as you're told!" screamed Glavin, spittle coming out of his mouth.

Before anyone could respond, the photographer in the gray ski jacket yelled, "What the hell is he doing?"

Sumo turned toward the airwar. Suggs was four feet off the water's surface wrapped in the outer layer of magenta-colored tentacles. He severed the tips of three tentacles, but at least six others were binding him. His face twisted with a grimace of intense pain. Suggs let go a scream resembling more of a battle cry than a yell of agony. He managed to free his knife-wielding arm enough to slash three other tentacles. However, more replaced these. Completely bound, he twisted his head to look at the Immunes on shore.

"Friends, *don't* rescue me," exhorted Suggs. With that ominous warning, he was yanked from view.

Sumo touched Cupcake on the shoulder and he pointed to the Red Zeppelin. Both Immunes began running for the water. Sumo felt an arm grab him as he was tackled from behind. He fell into Cupcake, knocking him down. Angry, he turned and glared at Captain Howe, who tackled them at the lake edge.

"I've got to try!" screamed Sumo.

"No," Captain Howe yelled back. "There's something wrong. We need to think, not act. This is all wrong, all wrong." The birthmark on his neck glowed red.

All three turned as they heard splashing in the water. A shirtless Sergeant Clark was swimming toward the Red Zeppelin holding the knife he'd freed Suggs with between his teeth.

"Stop, you'll be killed," screamed DS, horrified.

The sergeant ignored her screams and swam on.

DS ran up to Captain Howe as he was untangling himself from Sumo and Cupcake. "For God's sake, please order him back."

Before Howe could respond, Sumo watched in surprise as the non-Immune Sergeant Clark passed through the outer curtain without difficulties.

"Is Clark an Immune?" said Cupcake, looking at Captain Howe.

"No," said Captain Howe, looking perplexed, "but that's expected. The Red Zeppelins are reputedly non-poisonous, but apparently there's a paradox with Immunes."

After a few tense minutes, Sergeant Clark swam free of the outer curtain with Suggs in a cross-chest carry. Sumo swam with the other Immunes to help, but Suggs was covered with tentacle fragments, and everywhere the Immunes tried to touch him, they suffered severe stings.

Finally, Sergeant Clark, with the help of Captain Howe and the photographers, pulled the lifeless Suggs to the shore. It was clear Suggs was dead.

Sumo stood weeping over Suggs with the other Immunes and Sergeant Clark. Captain Howe moved toward the plane trying to get reception on his phone. A click of a gun's safety being released was heard by Sumo. Sergeant Clark's head snapped up. "Mr. Glavin, killing the airwar won't help Suggs," he yelled.

"You bumbling idiots!" screamed Glavin, "You smartass screw-ups! All you had to do was to swim out and die, but nooooo! Now I'm in danger of losing my reward. It's not happening I tell you. I've worked too long and too hard to be denied my reward."

Glavin raised the automatic rifle and aimed it at the group. Sumo felt a wave of panic as he realized Glavin's intentions. A shot rang out. Glavin toppled like a felled tree. He bounced once as his body hit the ground. Blood could be seen pumping from the back of his head. Sumo looked toward the shot. Next to the plane stood Captain Howe, pistol aimed. A small wisp of smoke curled from the barrel muzzle. His neck birthmark was now a dark purple coloration.

Captain Howe, walked over and removed the automatic weapon from Glavin's dead hands, and to the grieving team's shock, aimed it at the magenta hydrogen sac.

Sumo put his hand on the captain's shoulder and said, "Captain, don't. Snivaling will crucify you."

Howe looked down at Glavin, then at Suggs' body and said, "Screw Snivaling." And without even looking back at the airwar, he pulled the trigger.

CHAPTER 44

BURGEONING VENGEANCE

John, with Prof and Dude, eventually reported to the admiral. It was a small compartment, clearly not the admiral's stateroom. A solitary desk and chair were centered in the otherwise empty room. The admiral had Prof and Dude remain in the corridor.

John thought the admiral appeared strained. The admiral unlocked a drawer, withdrew a knife, and handed it to John.

"Sengele will be bound and gagged," said the admiral. "It should be straightforward. I'll, of course, take care of the media once you finish. One more thing, and Prof and Dude need to hear this."

When they were together, he told them he'd been informed of Suggs' death. He explained it was by one of Sengele's creations, and he would detail them later, after John met with Sengele.

Dude began cursing. John stood paralyzed with overwhelming rage, but Prof went berserk. He screamed and pounded the bulkheads with his fists until his knuckles began leaving red stains on the gray paint. Finally, he collapsed in an exhausted heap on the deck, sobbing.

The admiral stood in stoic silence. His only sign of emotion was the bulging veins on the sides of his neck. Finally, he walked to Prof, extended his hand, and said, "We have a mission to complete."

Allowing himself to be pulled to his feet, Prof mumbled to himself, "I should have never left that numbskull alone."

John walked in shock with the other two Immunes. As they followed the admiral down the corridor, John began to reflect. Of course, there was self-doubt. Killing a man would be different; would he hesitate? No, the loss of Cassandra, and now Suggs, ripped all compassion from his heart. Besides, millions would love to be in his position. Fortunately for Dr. Sengele, others would have extended the task as long as possible, taking pleasure in every scream.

Memories of Captain Stewart passed through his mind. John promised himself he would kill with compassion. It would be quick. He would cut the right carotid artery, then left, job complete. Sengele was a dead man anyway. The majority wanted him fed to the airwar. John had to agree this would be the most fitting execution, but vengeance was a harsh mistress John couldn't resist. He knew his actions wouldn't heal the black hole in his heart, but it might mute some of the pain.

The group reached a turn in the corridor. It widened into a large short passage with one door at the end guarded by four marines. Admiral Beckwourth stood beside John and gave him the slightest nod.

"You have five minutes," then as an afterthought, "please don't do anything foolish. The guards and I will be right outside. You have time to reconsider, John. You don't have to meet with him. He deserves no last request, especially from somebody as noble as The Immune. Feed him to the airwars, I say, today."

The four guards broke their emotionless stares fleetingly with nods of agreement and slight twisted smiles to their lips.

John knew the admiral's little speech was a show for the guards. It would only take twenty seconds to kill Sengele. His only concern was the two Immunes might storm in to avenge Suggs's death.

The admiral's statement was already prepared for when John completed dispatching Sengele; he read it to John previously.

"Ladies and gentlemen of the press, the notorious Dr. Sengele is dead. He died in one last craven act, the attempted murder of Dr. John Long, beloved and known worldwide as The Immune."

The admiral left a pause in his speech, allowing for the world-wide gasps that would occur at that point.

"Happily, I report The Immune is without harm. He single-handedly wrested the assassin's knife from Sengele and ended his ignoble life. Sengele knew he would suffer the same fate as millions, in the tentacles of the monsters he created. A fitting ending for the madman, but The Immune, being compassionate, agreed to a final request of listening to Sengele's confession and contrition. Fortunately, good, once again, won over evil."

John would then hold a press conference, and the admiral would slip off the USS Acheson to meet with ASC to placate their loss of the highly promoted execution.

John requested a fair fight to the death, but the admiral wouldn't hear of it. The admiral's one absolute requirement was Sengele would have no opportunity to harm John. John was to enter the compartment and kill him quickly. John would then remove the gag and cut the binds. It was the admiral's way or no way.

John's anger from Suggs' demise was such that he agreed without argument. It would all go efficiently. He did have one curious neuron firing off. *What does Sengele want to say to me alone? He'd probably beg for mercy knowing I have the power to stay the execution. The desperate fool; he'd be speaking to the one person most intimate with the destruction he'd caused.* John mentally agreed it was for the best Sengele would be gagged.

"Guards, open the cell," ordered the admiral, interrupting John's thoughts. John noticed Prof was sobbing again.

CHAPTER 45

DR. SENGELE'S LAST REQUEST

John looked at the four large marine guards standing to either side of the massive metal door bearing the sign RESTRICTED ACCESS. His hand entered the right front pocket of his faded green and brown fatigues. His fingers lightly touched the hilt of the knife. He had shoved the blade through the base of the pocket so the handle wouldn't show. Not that it mattered. The Pope would more likely be searched upon entering the Vatican than any guard would attempt to confiscate a weapon from John.

Beyond the door in an empty room, gagged with arms and legs bound to a chair, sat the infamous prisoner, Joseph Sengele: lunatic, unrepentant biogenetic creator of the airwars, whose continuing random attacks on humanity resulted in tens of millions, if not hundreds of millions, of horrific deaths worldwide. In a moment, John would pass through the door and kill Dr. Sengele.

John never killed a man before, but he had dispatched hundreds of Sengele's creations. Each represented to John a small step to the ultimate goal of Sengele himself. Should the family of deadly sins ever consider an eighth, vengeance would make a fitting brother. Vengeance is a powerful, life-altering emotion, and no one in history could claim more metamorphosis from this sensation than John. At this point, he knew not whether Sengele's death would alter the fate of the world, but he believed it would provide him some peace and certainly a degree of satisfaction. The guards stepped back and the heavy metal door, straining on its hinges, opened for John.

John stepped through into a medium-sized compartment, barren of all features, no portholes, no bulkhead coverings other than dull gray paint on all four sides, including the door. A chair in the middle of the room was the only furnishing. Ensconced in the chair was the most reviled man in the world, Dr. Joseph Sengele.

As John entered, his grip tightened around the knife handle in his pocket. He stepped forward, focused and ready to kill. Dr. Joseph Sengele sat with a calm expression. *Clearly, Sengele didn't realize he was seconds from death*, thought John. John pulled his knife.

John was immediately shaken by the realization—although Sengele was sitting in the chair, he was without restraints or gag. The glint of a knife blade flashed from Sengele's right hand. It appeared an exact duplicate of John's knife, although Sengele held it casually between the thumb and forefinger.

John was pleased. *So, the admiral caved to my wishes. It'll be a fair fight. I might need the whole five minutes after all.*

He had no doubt regarding the victor. His muscles contracted, waiting for Sengele to make his move, or at least to get out of the chair. Sengele did make the first move. He tossed his knife to the floor. The echoes bounced back and forth off the gray metal bulkheads.

"Cassandra is alive, and I'm her brother," said Sengele.

John paused, and in an instant knew hesitation was a mistake. The thought, *words can be weapons*, flashed through his mind. His reaction was reflexive, like moving the foot when scissors slip from the hand. John shifted to his right, spinning himself back and around. He waited for the slicing pain in his Achilles' tendon, which he knew would come if his hesitation had been too long.

During his spin, John could see Sengele in his mind. Sengele would be lunging forward, deftly snatching the knife from the deck in a shoulder roll, then slicing at John's vulnerable Achilles tendon. Sengele then would spring up, facing a now partially immobile opponent.

At the completion of John's defensive spin, he knew he negated Sengele's attack. He used his momentum to swing the knife in a horizontal arch, where Sengele's exposed abdomen would be. The knife moved so fast there was a swishing sound in the air. John waited for the feedback of the knife cutting cloth and flesh. It never came.

Damn, he's good, thought John, *I might need more than five minutes.*

John assumed a defensive position while trying to locate Sengele to his left, but he wasn't there.

CHAPTER 46

JUDGE AND JURY

John's head snapped around, looking back at the chair. Nothing changed except for parted lips of surprise on the face of Sengele. Both men stared at each other in complete silence for several seconds. A low mechanical rumble from one of the many machines imbedded in the bowels of the ship broke the silence.

"What?" said The Immune, his voice cracking from the adrenaline surge.

"Cassandra is alive," said Sengele, repeating his initial comment. He remained perfectly still as if any movement would provoke an attack. "Your fiancé, my sister, is alive, but she needs your help. With my fate sealed, time is of the essence."

"You're lying," said John, angrily, "You're as cunning as you are evil."

A sardonic smile crossed Sengele's lips, "Yeah, that's me, cunning, evil genius, mad scientist, cannibal, pedophile, torturer of virgins, drinker of blood, and half-brother of Satan himself."

"Well, the blood drinking is a new one, but the others appear to be fairly factual."

"Yeah," said Sengele, moving for the first time pointing at his Hitleresque moustache, "Well, propagandists said Hitler was a former housepainter."

John shuddered. Sengele unquestionably looked like a skeletonized Hitler replica. Sengele chose his likeness well if he wanted to create an image that imparted instant revulsion.

"Look," said Sengele, "regardless of what you may think you know of me, listen for two minutes, and if you still want to kill me, fine. There will be no resistance on my part. I suspect it'll only require a prick of your knife tip for the desired results." Sengele held out his index finger as if making an offering.

"You're completely insane," said John, "I'm planning a deep gash to the side of your neck. A finger prick definitely won't suffice." John made a cutting motion in the air with his knife.

"Whatever," said Sengele, "the result will be the same to me." Sengele sat in his chair intently looking at John. His clothes loosely hung off his emaciated body. He was certainly no physical match for John.

John scanned the floor for Sengele's knife. He stood between it and Sengele. The tenseness in his muscles relaxed.

"I won't give you two minutes," said John, "but I'd like to know how you discovered my fiancée's name. Although I shouldn't be surprised. The press has had me under a microscope for a year, but I've never mentioned Cassandra. She was supposedly off limits."

"I'll say it again, I'm her brother," said Sengele with a hint of frustration in his voice.

"And that's precisely how I know you're lying," said John with self-assurance. He pointed his knife at Sengele. "She has no brother."

"Ah," said Sengele with a look of understanding, "I should be more specific, her step-brother."

John frowned and said, "Your names are different."

"Yes, obviously, my father was a Sengele. Her father was a Shelley." Sengele now was looking intently at the knife in John's hand.

The emotionless expression on John's face belied the churning in his intestines. He new he needed to make a decision.

Sengele continued, "She spoke of you in nearly every communication we had. I know she loved you dearly. She must have spoken of me at some point. She said she wanted us to meet." He paused for a chuckle, "Ha . . . well, I guess we just did . . . small world."

Okay, The Immune thought, *he's three seconds from death, and he's cracking jokes. He's either mental or something is very, very wrong with the big picture.*

Sengele continued, "The last time I spoke to Cassandra, you proposed the night before. She was so excited and, moreover, she was concerned because you just impaled yourself on an urchin spine."

"Which foot?" asked John.

"I believe she said it was your hand," said Sengele, smiling at the ploy.

"Chunky?" said The Immune, his eyes wide in astonishment.

"In the flesh," said Sengele, "Or what's left of it." Sengele pulled his shirt away from his chest and let it drop. The shirt looked as if it were three sizes too large.

"I always imagined you a bit more portly," said John.

"I was, in my youth," said Sengele, "hence the nickname. I slimmed down as an adult, and the 400-calorie per day diet from my hosts continues to keep me trim and fit. Plus, the guards frequently urinate in my — "

"I suppose you're telling me you aren't responsible for any of this mess," interrupted John.

"Obviously!" said Sengele.

"I saw your confession," challenged John, "Everyone saw it."

He started tightening his grip on the knife. He glanced back to reassure himself that he stood between the knife on the floor and Sengele.

"And that's precisely why Cassandra is alive," said Sengele gravely.

"You were coerced?"

"Patently," said Sengele, nodding, "What would you say if Cassandra was behind the teleprompter, a knife to her throat, with a neurotoxin coated on the blade's edge?"

"I'd have read whatever came up," said The Immune, loosening the grip on his knife.

"And so did I," said Sengele, hanging his head.

The Immune took a moment to collect his thoughts. He turned and bent down, picking up the knife Sengele tossed to the floor. They were matching knives.

"As you may imagine," said John, with an element of distrust in his voice, "I'm experiencing exhilaration as well as considerable disbelief that Cassandra may be alive."

Sengele nodded. "I fully understand. For the moment, I believe she's safe, and I'll tell you what I know of her, but first we have many things needing to be discussed, like — "

"But what about the lab videos of you growing airwars?" interrupted John again.

Sengele nodded patiently, "Yeah, those airwars were real, but we didn't grow them. They just appeared."

"You didn't do the genetic engineering?"

"I couldn't genetically engineer a fruit fly," said Sengele, laughing. "I'm a marine ecologist. I swim around after porpoises all day."

"But . . . the video showed airwars at different sizes of development . . . you were there."

"True, but check the time code of the video, and you'll find it's after the appearance of the first airwar."

"Why didn't you report?"

"Report to whom?" said Sengele irritably, his arms gyrating, "Both our satellite links went out with most of our electronics the day before airwars appeared on our island. I believe it was a lightning strike. It was a small island with a makeshift research lab. We weren't worried since communications went in and out all the time. For us, two weeks without communication was no big deal. The supply boat would replace all the non-working electronics in our bimonthly supply runs."

Sengele stood and moved behind the chair. He was John's height, but due to thinness appeared taller. He stretched his calves one at a time, holding the back of the chair like a runner preparing to race. John watched him cautiously.

Sengele continued, "We thought we'd fallen into the biggest biological find of the twenty-first century. We were studying these things 24/7, and we didn't want anyone finding out early and beat our discovery to the punch. We thought the loss of communication was a godsend. There would be no accidental slips of the lip in outgoing messages. Our mood was ecstatic. We were sleeping with dreams of full professorships and speaking tours dancing in our heads."

"Why set you up, of all people?" said John. He felt anxious. He much preferred Sengele sitting. "It doesn't seem plausible."

"Plausible, plausible!" Sengele shouted. He stopped stretching. "We have a million plus airwars floating around the world, millions dead so far, and you have the audacity to say not plausible?"

The Immune thought, *The reality of everything I believed the last year has just been challenged.* "My head is swimming," said The Immune, now with a tone of trust.

Sengele smiled and said, "Well, if your head is swimming, get prepared, as you're about to enter a maelstrom."

CHAPTER 47

ENTER THE MAELSTROM

A clanking of the lock on the door broke the conversation. The Immune swiftly moved Sengele's knife behind his back as he approached the door. The admiral took a step back as The Immune's face filled the opened crack.

"John," said the admiral, with concern, "what's going on? It's been over eight minutes. I was beginning to worry."

"Sorry, the deed's not done yet," whispered The Immune, "He's trying to buy time through praying and begging forgiveness. He'll run out of things to say shortly, then I'll permanently end the conversation." The Immune held his knife up to the crack of the door. "By the way, thanks for not restraining him. It makes me feel less the butcher. Still not too late to give him a knife. There's no way he can take me in a knife fight. It would seem more civilized."

"Not restrained?" said the admiral with an incredulous look. "Guards, restrain and gag Sengele."

"No," said The Immune, sternly. The Immune pulled the admiral's ear to his mouth and whispered harshly, "If the guards know Sengele is restrained, word would get out. It would tarnish my image you've worked hard to create. Trust me, I can handle Sengele. The deed will be done shortly, but it may be another ten or fifteen minutes." The Immune stepped back and pushed the door closed in the admiral's face.

The admiral stood outside the door in disbelief. A chill ran down his spine. *This is unexpected*, he thought. He raised his arm to the door to enter, then dropped it to his side. "Not the plan. Not the plan," he mumbled to himself.

The four marines all looked at the admiral waiting for orders.

"Admiral, do you need Prof and me to do anything?" said Dude with a perplexed look.

"No—all will be fine as long as John follows through . . ." Then he thought, *But if John doesn't follow through, it'll be disastrous.*

Back in the room, Sengele sat again in the chair. He was pale and visibly shaking.

The Immune looked at Sengele and said, "Okay, I'm ready to plunge into the maelstrom. Why you?"

Sengele leaned forward, resting his elbows on his knees, and in a low voice as if he was afraid of being overheard, said, "It was the footprints." His eyes were wide, and he looked like a mad scientist revealing a sinister plan.

John started to believe he made a terrible mistake. Sengele was obviously psychotic and now rambling. John wanted so badly to believe Cassandra was alive, but he knew he'd been sucked into Sengele's schizophrenic delusion.

"Footprints?" said John, sarcastically, "What did you do? Walk on a covert military beach and spoil their dunes?"

Sengele seemed to regain his composure. He sat straight in the chair and cleared his throat. Then he began speaking in a normal voice, "No, we filmed footprints where there should be none. It was at the bottom of the Cayman Trench, and the footprints weren't human."

The answer did nothing to assuage John's belief that Sengele was psychotic. He knew, as a physician, psychotics could weave almost believable stories using components of both reality and fantasy.

"Why would a marine biologist who studies dolphins be filming at the bottom of the Trench?" challenged John, "Dolphins could never dive so deep. The pressure would kill them. Moreover, it's obvious the footprints couldn't be human. With the exception of research submersibles, no human could reach that depth. Footprints would have to be from some crab or something like that."

Sengele looked exasperated. "We were trying to film a dolphin carcass at the bottom of the Trench for a clip in a documentary we were doing. It would've been a big deal to us if we found one. To clarify, when I said the footprints weren't human, I meant not of this earth."

"Your story only gets weirder and weirder," said John, "You may be Chunky, but you're clearly psychotic."

Sengele ignored John's comment. "A large vehicle formed the footprints. The impressions appeared as circles fifteen feet in diameter. We believed it was some kind of ship, at least one hundred feet wide and possibly six hundred feet long. We concluded from the number of tracks there must be several ships."

"You saw them?" said John skeptically.

"Uh," said Sengele, "only the tracks, except—"

Sengele hesitated, and The Immune blurted, "Except what?"

"The last signal showed a partial image of an immense structure with a tread-like track. The track was covered with fifteen-foot diameter discs. After the last image, the reception went dead. Following that, we lost contact with the drone. One million in research grant money vanished in an instant."

"Military?"

"Oh, come on," said Sengele, "Nothing that size could withstand the pressure."

"Did you show the images to anyone?" asked John suspiciously.

"Yeah, Captain Logan on the Brittle Star."

"You mean there's someone sane who can corroborate your story?" said John with astonishment.

"Yes, Captain Logan's research vessel did runs near our island, so we were familiar. He was doing a government-sponsored sonar research project. We had meetings regarding his assignment. My concern was sonar testing might affect local dolphins. Captain Logan didn't know about the project details. He was more of a chauffeur than a researcher on the venture."

"Wait," said John, "So this Captain is alive and can be contacted?"

"As far as I know. My social schedule has been somewhat limited for the past year," said Sengele, smiling wryly.

"Understood," said The Immune, "Tell me more about Captain Logan."

Sengele closed his eyes as he tried to remember details from a year ago.

"We were in my lab. I was doing a necropsy on a dolphin we found floating dead near the trench. I had just made an incision in the ear canal. It was filled with blood and fluid. Captain Logan walked in my lab . . ."

"Ah, captain, you're just in time. I want you to see this."

Captain Logan was a thin man about six feet tall. He had red hair with touches of gray in the temples. He always seemed to maintain a weeks growth of beard which was almost all gray. Fine lines crisscrossed his face as a testament of his years in the sun.

"What the hell are you doing, Sengele?" said the captain, holding his nose, "I thought you studied the behavior of dolphins, not dissected them."

"Comes with the territory," said Sengele, "This is what I was talking about the other day." Sengele pointed into the dissected area. "Blood and fluid in the ear canal. It's exactly like previous reports of dolphins that have been damaged by sonar."

The captain peered over the stainless steel table into the dissected head. He grimaced.

"Not my cup of tea. Don't even know what I'm looking at, Sengele, but whatever I'm seeing you can't blame on me. We haven't started testing. I just received the submersible today, so I had to stop by and brag."

"How so?" said Sengele.

"Well, it turns out I not only get paid to ferry the submersible around, but I get to keep it after the project is over — free." The captain was practically dancing with excitement. "We do one sonar test. Which I'm being handsomely compensated for. Then I get the sub."

Sengele laid his scalpel down on the necropsy table and pulled off his gloves.

"Okay, I'll admit I'm green with envy. I lose a million-dollar drone last week and you get handed a multimillion-dollar, pilotable, deepwater submersible out of the blue. Life's not fair, but congratulations anyway. When do I get to see it?"

"How about now?" said the Captain, "I've got her on the Brittle Star. We're getting the sonar later today, and they're running the test."

The Brittle Star was the name of Captain Logan's ship. Captain Logan was a PhD marine biologist who did his dissertation decades before on the brittle starfish. Hence, the name of his ship.

They left Sengele's lab and took a skiff out to where the Brittle Star was anchored. The Brittle Star was a large ship for a research vessel. The twenty-two foot underwater submersible named Pathfinder looked small on the aft deck. It was sitting next to an all metal storage container which protected it from the elements when not in use. The hatch of the bright yellow vessel was open, and Logan invited Sengele to look inside. The submersible had two seats up front and a great deal of electronics. Two telescoping claws were mounted on the front of the vessel.

"The pathfinder will carry the sonar device out in its claws," said the captain. "The naval researchers float it with an inflatable raft. The Pathfinder returns, and they remotely set the sonar off."

"Why do they need a submersible for that?" said Sengele.

"In case the sonar sinks—it's reinforced. The Navy boys can pick it up from the Trench bottom if need be," said Logan, smiling. "Hey, I know it's crazy, but it's not my money. Now check this out. I get one more freebee."

Logan and Sengele climbed to the top deck of the Brittle Star, which was covered with antennae and satellite dishes. They moved to a silver cylinder, seven feet tall, mounted to a five-foot diameter brass disc in the center of the deck. Near the top of the cylinder was a ten-inch hole that looked like a large retractable telescope lens. The other side was a monitor encased in clear plastic. Off each side of the monitor were grips that looked like they were from a motorcycle.

"You'll not believe this," said Logan as he stood on the brass disc and grabbed the handles, "I'm getting you eye candy."

As he stepped on the disc, the monitor came on and prompted *Enter object scan.*

Logan spoke to the device, "Ship scan."

The entire apparatus spun with the brass plate as if it were on a dolly. The captain revolved with it, gripping the handles. He could apparently control the rate of spin by squeezing the handles. The spinning continued for twenty seconds and stopped. The screen displayed: eight objects identified, one cruise ship, one freight ship, two tankers, three fishing vessels, and one personal craft.

Sengele squinted. He could only see one tiny object on the horizon. He couldn't tell if it was a cruise ship or a tanker.

Logan smiled, and said, "Locate cruise ship."

The cylinder spun one quarter a turn and the monitor filled with an image of large ocean liner displaying a Norwegian flag.

"Incredible," said Sengele, "Nice boat, but not what I would call *eye candy*."

"I'm not done," said Logan, smiling. He touched the monitor, and the screen magnified.

Sengele could clearly see a row of deck chairs with several striking young women tanning.

Logan tapped on one of the women. The screen filled with a buxom blonde wearing a hot pink bikini and sunglasses. The straps of her top were pulled down, and Sengele could see the tan lines. "Eye Candy," said Captain Logan, grinning.

"Impossible!" said Sengele.

"No, possible, and right before your eyes."

The blonde rolled over and adjusted her bikini bottom.

"The image is rock steady," said Sengele, "There are big waves out there today." He could feel the Brittle Star pitch.

"It has advanced wave and motion stabilization," said Captain Logan with a happy look.

"I know video technology pretty well, and what we're seeing just doesn't exist," said Sengele with disbelief.

"Well, seeing is believing, and it's all mine when the project is completed," said Logan with a giant grin.

"But what does this have to do with the sonar test?" asked Sengele.

"Well, get this—nobody bothered to put a GPS in the submersible or on the sonar. So the government's fix was, instead of adding a couple hundred-dollar GPS to the sub and sonar, they bring out this phenomenal scanning telescope so the investigators can find it easily—their stupidity, my gain."

Sengele stood in silence as he mentally debated whether to trust the Captain with his Trench bottom images.

"Okay, Captain, it's my turn to try to top your incredible show and tell."

They returned to Sengele's research station and entered his small office. His desk consisted of a door laid on top of a pair of two drawer metal file cabinets. A fold-out lawn chair served as his chair. In the middle of the desk were several monitors. Journals and papers were stacked and scattered covering the rest of the desk. Sengele shuffled through files and pulled out a large manila folder.

"Check these photos out. This was taken immediately before we lost our drone."

Captain Logan looked through the photos in silence. He carefully studied each one, especially the final shot, which showed the large edifice. Without looking up, he said, "Where were these taken?"

"The bottom of the trench."

The captain looked up from the photos. "Now it's my turn to say impossible. There's no way a structure that size could withstand the pressure."

"I agree," said Sengele, "but as you say, seeing is believing. Perhaps this structure has something to do with your sonar test?"

"Perhaps. . . Who knows about these?"

"Only me and my research assistants."

"Well, my bet is this is Chinese military," said Captain Logan, "Scary if they're that far ahead of us in pressure technology. Keep this quiet until I bounce these photos off the navy boys. A few high ranking muckety-mucks are involved in the sonar test, and I'll show them."

Sengele opened his eyes and looked at John.

"Later that day we had the lightning strike, taking out most of our electronics. I never heard from Captain Logan again."

"Did you post the images on the Internet?" asked The Immune.

"Never did."

Sengele rocked back in his chair, balancing on the back two legs. He took a deep breath and let out a sigh. Then he continued speaking, "The next morning we discovered a variety of sizes of small airwars on the island. They ranged in size from one to twelve feet. We used long poles to push them into the lab. We began studying them 24/7. This was the source of the pictures and videos of me with the intermediate sized airwars in the lab. Fortunately, we'd stowed all the camera equipment in a solid metal trunk. It must have insulated them from the lightning strike. Of course, the media has never shown the video of us pushing them into the lab or discussed how we found them."

"Wait," said The Immune. He held his hand up like a policeman stopping traffic. He silently walked to the door and put his ear against it. After listening for a few moments he seemed reassured and turned back to Sengele.

"Sorry, I thought I heard something. Not so sure who I should be trusting at this moment. Please continue."

"One week later at our station, I awoke to three full-sized air-wars, and five missing research associates—sort of. My friends were all being digested by the airwars. A naval vessel I never saw before was anchored off our island. My captors forced me at gun-point to pose in front of the airwars entwining my colleagues. After taking videos, they arrested me for crimes against humanity.

"I was in solitary for several days. From what I could pick up from guards, ASC officials were announcing I caused the crisis, and I was to be executed. At some point ASC changed their mind, felt could be useful propaganda remaining alive, then they moved me to this floating spa."

"No phone call, I guess?" quipped The Immune.

Sengele smirked, "No need. The arresting officer informed me he'd also been assigned as my attorney."

"Based on your current situation, I'd say his legal talents are limited."

Sengele, dripping with sarcasm, replied, "Actually, he has great talents, such as applying electrical devices to testicles, should you ever wonder how my attorney located Cassandra so easily. Confessions to crimes against humanity can be resisted during physical torture, but add your sister and that works!"

"I see the urgency," said The Immune grimly, "When you're gone, Cassandra will have served her purpose."

"Yeah, I fear she'll disappear quite quickly."

"Do you know where she's being held?"

"No, but I suspect she's kept close, just in case they need a state-ment and I get uncooperative. I haven't seen her in person, though, in six months."

"Damn, then you've no idea whether she's alive or dead?" said The Immune. A wave of dread passed through his body.

"Yes," said Sengele, "she's definitely alive. My keepers have her read the morning headlines and the date each day over the radio. It keeps me submissive."

"Do you get to talk to her?" said The Immune anxiously, "How is she?"

"They won't let her say anything other than reading the daily headlines," replied Sengele, frowning.

"So, do you have a plan?"

Sengele got up from the chair. He started cracking his fingers one at a time.

"No, I only got as far as getting to speak to you. I figured I'd play it by ear from that point on."

"Fantastic!" said The Immune sarcastically.

"Hey, you're the hero of the world," said Sengele, mockingly, "I'm sure you can come up with something."

"Well, as of late, I've been kind of busy killing airwars and basking in adulation. Clearly you've had more time to think this through."

"True, there isn't much for me to do between the occasional testicular spa treatments." He patted his groin area and winced slightly. "Of course, I've received limited information, other than headlines, and it's hard to formulate a plan from a cell when you haven't a clue what's going on in the outside world."

"Okay," said The Immune, "anything I can update you on? It'll have to be the abbreviated version."

Sengele stood rubbing his temples in thought for a few moments, then said, "What were those ships or whatever in the Trench?"

"Well, they're news to me, and I'm pretty high up on the security updates."

"That's what I was afraid of," said Sengele, frowning, "I can't fit the pieces together yet, but I'm sure they're related to the airwars." Then he added, "Listen, the reality is, we don't have much time. We can do updates later. I think you need to concentrate on locating Cassandra."

"Admiral Beckwourth can help me with that," said The Immune, motioning to the door.

Sengele looked worried, "At this point, I'm not sure who you should trust," he said.

"The admiral has been with me for the last year," said The Immune with conviction, "He's saved my butt on more than one occasion, and I trust him with my life."

Sengele raised an eyebrow. "Did he give you the knife and arrange your visit?"

The Immune took pause to digest this. "Yes, but he wanted you dead as much as I did."

Sengele pointed to the knife in The Immune's hand. "See the greenish tinged residue on your knife blade edge?"

The Immune nodded. He held the blade up toward the light and examined it closely.

Sengele pointed to the other knife in The Immune's hand. "Well, it's on my blade, too. Look!"

The Immune held up both blades in the yellow light. Both had an oily greenish tinge, definitely coated on the blade edge. The knives appeared to be identical in all features.

"It's some kind of poison," elucidated Sengele, "We were both supposed to die in this little engagement. Hard to believe someone wants to get rid of the hero of the world at the same time as me."

"It doesn't make sense," said The Immune, looking puzzled, "Who gave you your knife?"

"My attorney," said Sengele with a derisive smile, "He told me you were coming to kill me and if I put up a good fight, he would release Cassandra. I wanted to use it on him, but I was bound when he gave it to me. He left as his goons were unbinding me. I suspect your admiral friend got yours from the same guy."

"How did you know about the poison?" The Immune asked.

Dr. Sengele felt his body shudder as his memory was reawakened. "I saw my attorney put it to good use many months ago. I'm sure he forgot. Shortly after my transfer to this ship. He was interrogating a Professor Koehler. I was there for demonstration purposes only." Sengele pointed to his groin area.

"After a few electrical conduction experiments in which the attorney volunteered my body as his assistant, the professor was reticent. Even with my sincere appeals to give up any information, it had no effect. Perhaps he felt I was faking, or maybe I was entertaining."

Sengele stopped for a moment as he could feel his body shaking. He closed his eyes and, when the shaking passed, he continued. "When the demonstrations switched to him, the entertainment value lessened. I think they kept me in the room for my words of encouragement. I begged him to give up the information. Why suffer so? I gathered from the conversation, as far as the public knew, Koehler had been dead for at least a week."

A pounding on the door interrupted the story. Sengele watched The Immune jump to the door. Without opening, it, The Immune shouted, "Three minutes more, admiral, and I'll be out." The pounding stopped, and The Immune motioned for Sengele to continue.

"I'll admit, Koehler was a tough old bird. He spat on my attorney, even after being treated to the ultimate in cutaneous testicular pleasure. It was what I refer to as the smoking jolt. It made me nauseous, though. I was used to smelling 'barbecue me.' Other peoples' flesh burning was a new experience. It must have trapped some of the smoke particles in my nasal hairs as I kept getting whiffs of him even hours later. For a second I thought Koehler might not break, but then guards wheeled in his wife and daughter.

"No matter what the torturer had done to him before, I could tell the sight of them in that situation gave Koehler more agony. My attorney pulled the knife and made a slight slice on the upper arm of his wife. Koehler screamed profanities at the attorney in both English and German . . .

"Dr. Koehler," said the attorney, "as much as I'd like to take your family apart piece by piece in front of your eyes, I don't have the time. I have an important meeting in twenty minutes, and they're expecting to hear everything you know and I mean everything."

The attorney took one-step back and motioned to the professor's wife. She was gasping, making choking sounds with spittle running from the corners of her mouth. Her face suddenly became cyanotic. Ten seconds later, she slumped over, and that was that. I thought for a moment the professor would break his binds. The lawyer calmly walked over and put the blade unceremoniously to his daughter's throat. The professor broke.

"You're a traitor to mankind," Koehler shrieked. "What could they possibly offer you to give up humanity? Where do you think you'll fit in the hierarchy when it's over? Sadly, the doctor included me in his sweeping accusatory stare of the lawyer. Clearly, my earlier sacrifice of future reproductive abilities didn't give me a pass on the accusations. Koehler's recognition of my continued presence resulted in my immediate dismissal with a flick of my attorney's hand.

"Since my nether-regions were aglow, making walking difficult, I was dragged to my cell by four charming attendants. All who interacted with me got fed the same crap filled story that I created airwars. The attendants were all clearly cognizant of this fact based on the several complimentary kicks I received in the short journey. I got them all in the end; I stiffed them on the tip. I strained to hear any other tidbit of information the professor might give up before I was out of earshot. The only word I heard clearly was 'colony.'"

"Oh, well," said The Immune, shaking his head, "that doesn't help. It's common knowledge airwars, same as Man O' Wars, are colony-based organisms."

"For some reason," said Sengele ominously, "I don't think he was referring to airwars."

"Any word on the professor and daughter?"

Sengele shook his head. "No, I asked my attorney in one of my biweekly photo-glamour shoots for crimes against humanity. He said the Koehlers were slow runner risings. He didn't elaborate, but based on his wicked smile, I assumed I wouldn't see them again."

The Immune confirmed this with a sad nod. "A 'slow runner rising' is slang for a dead person or someone whose death is imminent. If one runs too slowly, the airwar catches them, then the victim rises in the tentacles to the gastric chamber."

"I suppose I'm to be a slow runner rising shortly."

"Well, more like a tossed in and rising, but you get the point."

Sengele smiled. "I'll worry about that later," he said.

"What we need is a covert escape plan for you."

Sengele laughed, "Well, that should be simple. Locate and rescue your fiancé, solve the puzzle of the airwars, and plan a covert escape of the most identifiable villainous person in the world by the most recognizable hero in the world. Hardly a challenge."

The Immune tossed Sengele his cell phone and said, "I may need to call you, but I'd recommend you not call out."

Sengele nodded he understood, but added, "Does that include pizza delivery?"

CHAPTER 48

METAMORPHOSIS

A s The Immune reached for the door, he couldn't help but notice digestive juices coupled with residual particles of his breakfast moved from the stomach to the back of his mouth. When The Immune stepped from the room, it was clear he wasn't the only one under strain. The admiral looked extremely pale.

"What happened?" the admiral whispered, "You were in there over fifteen minutes — is Sengele dead?" He wiped perspiration off his brow with his sleeve.

"No," said The Immune. "All didn't go according to plan. Dr. Sengele let some fascinating facts slip about the airwars' siphon. I believe he may know more. I want to keep him around awhile in case he'd like to elucidate further."

The admiral gave The Immune an astonished look.

"John, how could he . . ." then he hesitated and said sternly, "Don't forget the point of us coming all the way out here."

"It'll have to wait," said The Immune, "I'd like Dude and Prof assigned to him at all times in case he has something to say."

"John, I don't want to guard the SOB; I want to kill him," interjected Prof with rage.

"I think our marines should suffice," said the admiral, nodding toward the four stone-faced guards standing at board like attention on either side of the door.

"No," said The Immune firmly, "If he speaks, I want it to be to an Immune. Prof and Dude are in a better position to determine its relevance as opposed to a guard."

The admiral began to protest, as did Prof, but The Immune interrupted, "Look, you keep . . ." The Immune looked at the name-plates of the two closest marines, "Keys and Howard. You'll assist the Immunes. Should anyone attempt to move, assault, or injure Sengele, shoot them. Are my orders clear?"

"Yes, sir!" replied both guards. Their eyes remained forward, but were widened.

"John," said the admiral, sputtering in disbelief, "you don't have the authority."

"Three weeks ago I was proclaimed Field Marshal of The Immunes. With this command, I have absolute power to control any U.S. military forces."

The admiral rubbed his temples in silence.

"John," replied the admiral in a soft voice, "you know that's a ceremonial title. You have no real military experience. That's why I'm here to guide you."

"Fine," retorted The Immune obstinately, "let's call the President and find out how ceremonial the title is."

The admiral took a step back from The Immune and rubbed his hands together nervously.

"Okay, okay, have it your way," said the admiral, "but there'll be hell to pay. John, your ass isn't crossing the river Styx alone, you know. I've got to say I'm a little . . . 'miffed' that you've lost trust in me." The bulging jugulars belied the word of his choice.

"Speaking of trust," said The Immune, "I happened to wrestle this utensil from Sengele's grip before our little discussion. When did the Navy start feeding prisoners steak?"

The Immune held the knife out toward the admiral. The admiral glanced down at the knife, raised one of his eyebrows slightly, and said, "That's the knife I gave you."

The Immune brought the other knife out. He held them side by side in his right hand. It was clear the knives were identical.

Disbelief spread across the admiral's face, "John . . . no, you're not suggesting? I would never . . . I assure you . . . there will be an investigation," said the admiral, clearly rattled.

"Why were there any knives in the cell in the first place?" said Dude with a bewildered look.

"Quiet, Dude!" snapped the admiral, "We have an exceptionally grave situation. I need a moment to think."

The admiral began rubbing his eyes.

John was at a loss on how to decide whether to trust the admiral. Then an idea flashed through his mind and he said, "Admiral Beckwourth, would you swear as blood brothers you had nothing to do with this?" He shook the two knives at the admiral.

The admiral looked up.

"What?" replied the admiral, looking perplexed "Sure? What the hell are you talking about, John?"

The Immune held out the knives. "Okay, slightly cut your palm enough to draw blood, and I'll do the same. We'll clasp hands, and we'll be blood brothers and all is forgiven."

Prof and Dude looked at The Immune slack-jawed. Even the granite-faced guards gave sidelong glances to each other.

"You can't be serious." The admiral looked at The Immune in disbelief. "What a sophomoric thing to do."

The Immune stared at him in silence.

"Look, John," said the admiral, "I'm pissed, too. This is a massive screw up, and I assure you heads will roll when I find out who gave Sengele a knife, but there's a bigger issue as well." He paused.

The Immune's face remained emotionless.

Finally, exasperated, the admiral said, "Well, for God's sake, if that'll bring back The Immune I know, give me the damn knife, and I'll do the stupid ritual," and the admiral reached for the knife.

CHAPTER 49

WHO'S WATCHING WHO

The Immune yanked back both knives. The thought of the medieval test for witchery passed through his mind. Tie a witch to a chair and throw her in the river. If she floats, she's a witch. If she drowns, she wasn't. It was a harsh price to pay to clear the accused of sorcery. The Immune thought, I could have accidentally killed the one person I can trust.

The Immune gave a smile, "Sorry. I may have overreacted a bit. Who did you say gave you the knife?"

The admiral gave The Immune a brief disapproving look, then thought for a moment, "Chief Childress, early this morning."

"Let's pay Chief Childress a visit," said The Immune.

"Why?" said the admiral, looking surprised. "I'd be more concerned with who gave Sengele his knife."

"Well, I know who gave Sengele his knife. I think both knives have the same origin, and Chief Childress knows the answer."

"Who gave Sengele the knife, John?" demanded the admiral.

"I think I'll keep that secret close to the chest. Don't want to have to use your rule and kill someone."

The admiral smiled and nodded, "Okay, okay, that makes sense. Let us give the good chief a visit." He looked at two of the marine guards and said, "Powell and Stoval, please accompany us."

"No," The Immune shook his head, "We need to do this alone."

A perturbed look from the two marines caught the corner of The Immune's eye. Dissed on the security detail, and now this, neither of the marines looked happy. The Immune knew he couldn't have them running around flapping their lips about what they heard. The Immune added, "I need these marines for a more critical venture."

Powell smiled and Stoval beamed. The Immune reached for his phone, then realized Sengele had it. "Admiral, may I borrow your phone? I seem to have misplaced mine." The Immune studied the admiral's face to see if it registered concern, but he detected none.

"No problem," replied the admiral, pulling out his phone, "Who do you want? I may have it on auto dial."

"Military resources on this ship," said The Immune.

The admiral tapped the face of the phone and handed it to The Immune.

"Hello, Resources, Seaman Withers speaking," came over the phone.

The Immune looked surprised as he recognized the name. "Is this Carol Withers who was at the Immune party at Parrot Joe's in Key West?"

A tentative, "Yes," replied.

"Well, this is The Immune. I met you a few months ago with fellow Immune Sumo. I hope you remember."

"You must be joking. How could I not remem— Oh, I'm sorry, sir . . . Yes is the answer, sir. I meant no disrespect . . . sir."

"Carol, you can drop the formality. Nice to hear your voice. I wondered where you ended up." The Immune gave the admiral a perturbed look, but the admiral couldn't hear so it didn't register why. "Could you do a favor and see if your computer has a Cassandra M. Shelley listed?"

"Yes, sir."

The Immune could hear the seaman's fingers tapping on her keyboard. "Sir," said Seaman Withers, "that information requires a level five security access code."

"I see," said The Immune softly in contemplation.

"Sir," she said, "you could come down here with your keycard and access this file. It was provided when you boarded the ship."

"Well, I'm a bit pressed for time," said The Immune, "I'll read you my access code and you punch it in." John pulled the dog tag chain around his neck and a credit card like object came out from the top of his shirt.

"Sir," said the seaman, with apprehension in her voice, "that's against protocol."

"But," said The Immune in a commanding voice, "this is Admiral Beckwourth's phone and a secure line."

"In that case protocol requires this be logged in as an emergency," replied Seaman Withers.

"Okay, do it," said The Immune.

"Sir," said Seaman Withers, "I'm entering your code . . . Oh my, I've never seen this before."

"What?"

"I've got a pop-up reading access to this file requires co-approval of Admiral Wilkinson. Should I contact him?"

"No, no," said The Immune, frowning, "That's okay. So, there's no other way to locate Cassandra Shelley?"

"Not unless she's on the Acheson," replied Seaman Withers.

"What do you mean?"

"Well, all dog tags or key cards, if you're visiting on this ship, have a GPS locator. We're the beta test ship for this locator system. It's a different program from personnel files. It locates you in real time." After a pause, The Immune could hear her again tapping the keyboard.

"Yes, well that's odd; she's in the steward's room adjacent to Admiral Wilkinson's stateroom and the COM. Strange, I haven't bumped into her. There're only a handful of women on this ship and her log-in says she's been on board for nearly a year without leave. That's got to be an error—buggy system. May I locate anyone else for you?"

"No. Thanks! Carol, you've been a big help. Wait—Chief Childress, is he on your screen?"

"Let me punch him up . . . Found him. He's in his berth, number 14."

"Great! Oh, one more thing. What happens if you toss away your tags?" The Immune started removing the chain from around his neck.

"Tags and keycards detect slight cardiac currents. If the tags are away from your body for fifteen seconds, an alarm sounds here. Alarms happen all the time. For instance, even though everyone is required to wear them during showers, people forget. Again, we're a beta test. All the bugs haven't been worked out."

The Immune put the chain back around his neck, then said, "Carol, who accesses this system?"

"Well, resources does, and anybody with a level five clearance, but I can't tell you who's logged in at any particular time."

The Immune glanced at the marines waiting for their critical mission. Covering his hand over the phone so he couldn't be heard, he said, "Carol, can you make a memo? Write the name *Cassandra* and her location, then write *I'll be in touch.* Sign it *The Immune*, seal it in an envelope, and give it to the marines Powell and Stoval on their arrival."

"Yes, sir."

"Many thanks, Carol."

The Immune tapped the phone off and handed it to the admiral. He then turned to the two marines.

"Go to resources and ask for Seaman Withers. She'll give you a message. Bring it back here and give it to Dr. Sengele. It's for his eyes only. Tell no one." The seamen snapped salutes and were off, brushing by the two Immunes.

The Immune made the admiral wait while he huddled privately with Prof and Dude whispering instructions. Suddenly The Immune wheeled and turned to the admiral. "Let's see the chief." He looked back at Prof and pointed, "Trust me."

Prof gave The Immune a bewildered look and nodded.

The admiral and The Immune went down three decks, then down a long passageway in silence. Finally the admiral stopped walking and said, "Damn it, John, since when do you keep secrets from me?"

"You mean me and the Immunes?" He said, nonchalantly, "Oh, that was just girl talk."

"I'm not laughing, John," said the admiral, frowning.

"Okay, truce until we see the Chief," said The Immune.

The admiral nodded as they stepped up to a nondescript metal door marked with a black number 14.

CHAPTER 50

POSTMORTEM

The Immune watched the admiral pound on the hatch. "Chief, it's Admiral Beckwourth. I need a word with you." The admiral pounded twice more. The echoes from the thumping reverberated down the passageway. A neighboring door opened. The Immune saw a head pop out of the threshold.

"For the last time, shut the fu—" A taken aback Chief Young stopped mid-sentence as he recognized the admiral and The Immune, then said, "Sorry, sirs," and withered back into his compartment.

The admiral tried the door lever. It clicked, and the door swung inward without a sound. Chief Childress swung slightly back and forth in the middle of the compartment, belt around his neck, attached to a single pipe jutting out from the overhead. The chair next to the desk was overturned.

"Good Lord, John!" said the admiral, staring in disbelief, "He's committed suicide."

The Immune reached over and examined the hanging man's hand.

"It looks like he tried hard to stop himself," said The Immune, "His hands are contused and lacerated, probably from hitting himself in the face."

The body slowly twisted in the light, showing the bruised, beaten face. The Immune dropped the hand, and the body swayed more. "No rigamortis yet. Must've happened within the last three hours." He noticed the chief seemed to be missing his dog tags. "Admiral, get me back to resources."

The admiral pulled his phone, tapped the face, and handed it to The Immune. All the while, the admiral's eyes remained glued to the bloated face of the former chief. Seaman Withers voice came over the phone. The Immune pressed the phone to his ear and spoke softly, "This is The Immune again. Did Chief Childress's GPS alarm go off?"

"Yes, immediately after you hung up, but only for a minute. He must have taken his tags off and put them back on. Normally we have to notify a watch commander if the alarm goes off, but this was under the three-minute protocol limit."

"Where's Chief Childress now?" said The Immune as he looked at the slowly twisting body.

"Level I, corridor A," said Seaman Withers.

"Thanks, Carol. I may be calling again."

The Immune tapped the phone off and looked around the compartment. It looked like there had been a struggle. Items were strewn around on the floor. The Immune picked an item off the floor near the bed. He held it up to the admiral. It was a wallet packed with fifties and hundreds.

"Well," said The Immune, "I think we can rule out robbery as a motive."

"John, you have to report this," said the admiral, "I, on the other hand, need to get off this ship now."

"Hold that thought," The Immune stepped from the room to the next compartment and knocked.

A pale chief petty officer in his skivvies opened the door. His head hung low, "Sirs, I can't begin to tell you how sorry I am. I was on the zero dark thirty watch, and I—"

The Immune put his index finger to the Chief's mouth.

"No worries," said The Immune, "I only need to know one thing. How many times did you get awakened?"

"Twice," said the Chief, "You, sirs, then about ten minutes before."

"Did you open the door like you did with us?" asked The Immune.

"Yes, sir. They were louder, but they were already leaving when I opened the door."

"What do you mean, leaving?" asked the admiral.

"Well, they were at the end of the corridor." The chief petty officer pointed down the corridor The Immune and the admiral had just come from.

"Do you know who they were?" said The Immune.

He nodded, "Simmons and an officer."

"Who's Simmons?" asked the admiral.

"He's a knuckle dragger engineering mechanic," replied the chief. "People use him to collect gambling debts. He takes thirty percent. You can't miss Simmons. He's a Neanderthal."

"Who was the officer?" said The Immune.

"Can't say. They were far away, and he was partially blocked from view by that hulk Simmons. I figured Chief Childress paid up, and the show was over."

"Chief Childress is a gambler?" questioned The Immune.

"Yeah. He was broke the day before, and all of a sudden he walks in with a wad of cash to play last night . . ." The chief hesitated, then quickly added, "So I've heard. I've never seen gambling on the ship, and I'd report it immediately should I discover first-hand evidence."

The Immune said, "I'm sure you would, Chief. One more thing. After you finish your sack time, would you please knock on Chief Childress's door and discuss the evils of gambling with him?"

Seemingly relieved a reprimand wouldn't be forthcoming, he beamed and said, "Absolutely, Sir."

CHAPTER 51

TIME FOR A DRINK

Admiral Beckwourth, perhaps we could retire to your stateroom for a moment," said The Immune. He grabbed the admiral's arm and gave it a tug. The admiral followed in silence. They passed through the corridors rapidly, then entered the stateroom of Admiral Beckwourth.

The office was standard. With the exception of wood paneled bulkheads and a small bar, there were no luxuries. The Immune noted a UV grow-light was on the admiral's desk, but no plants. He also observed a green bottle like the one Captain Stewart provided Captain Flinch many months ago. It sat on top of the file cabinet, filled with lima bean-shaped pills.

The Immune walked to the bar with his back to the admiral and began pouring a drink.

"I think this is a good occasion to break the no alcohol policy. Just don't tell Sumo."

"I could use one of those, too," said the admiral, leaning against the front edge of his desk, "I guess you've already figured out why I switched Sumo from this mission. I had Seaman Withers stashed out here and almost forgot."

The Immune turned to face the admiral. He held two glasses in one hand. The tainted knife was in one glass, swirling the light brown liquid, then The Immune dipped the knife in the next glass with the same swirling motion. The admiral's face screwed up. The

Immune noticed the admiral had taken his holstered pistol and placed it on the desk less than a foot from his right hand.

"Crap," said the admiral, "John, there are spoons. We're not in the wild."

The Immune turned his back to the admiral, but the glass of the President's photo on the wall reflected the admiral perfectly. The admiral sat on the desk corner, his fingers only inches from the butt of the gun.

The Immune turned around, holding the two drinks, one in each hand. Each now contained a red swizzle stick. The Immune handed the left one to the admiral and said, "Let's talk."

"Sure." The admiral grunted, and in one swift move, downed the drink and smiled. "I needed that. I could use another."

"I had to be sure," said The Immune, now smiling.

The admiral had a quizzical look. "Sure about what?"

The Immune moved aside from the bar, exposing two identical glasses on the bar, one with the knife still in it. The admiral slightly shook his head back and forth.

"John, I didn't mean you had to pour new drinks. I may be a bit picky, but I'll not waste good alcohol. Hand me one of those."

As he dropped his hand back to the desk, The Immune noticed the admiral's right hand was now fully resting on the gun butt. Suddenly the admiral's expression changed. He grasped the gun handle and raised it, still holstered.

The Immune reacted, twisting toward the bar in one swift move. He plucked the knife from the glass and ducked to the floor. Two shots rang out. The Immune felt no pain. He didn't know if his massive adrenaline release muted the pain of the bullet wounds or if the admiral missed. At that point, he didn't care. His entire focus was on getting the knife blade anywhere under the admiral's skin. He hoped enough residual poison remained on the alcohol-drenched blade to avenge his death. He was certain the next time the admiral shot, he would hit his mark.

As The Immune hit the floor, he shifted his feet flush with the base of the liquor cabinet and pushed off, same as he would push off any swimming pool wall. As he slid across the slick waxed deck, he pointed the knife directly at the admiral's calf.

Inches from impact, The Immune's momentum suddenly stopped with a crushing force on his back. Air was abruptly forced from his chest. He saw stars for an instant, but not long enough to black out, only long enough to lose the grip on his knife. He watched it spin on the deck, past the admiral's feet, clattering harmlessly against the baseboard of the opposite bulkhead.

A heavy weight pinned The Immune's upper torso to the floor. His first thought was, *He hit my spinal cord. I'm paralyzed. No, that couldn't be it.* He could move his legs. Then he felt a trickle of blood run down his neck.

The admiral looked down in disbelief. Lying on the floor in front of him was the lifeless hulking three hundred pound body of Engineer Simmons. The body rested on top of The Immune, who seconds before looked like he was trying to stab the admiral's leg with a knife.

The admiral knew, had the falling body not stopped, The Immune's slip and slide action, he would now have the knife blade hilt deep in his left calf. Fortunately, the admiral was a good shot, even shooting a holstered gun. The first shot grazed the massive man's left jugular. The second entered the forehead one centimeter above the left brow and was immediately fatal.

The admiral contemplated the strange sight for a second. The Immune's upper body was covered by the door-like torso of Simmons. Only his head and upper arms stuck out. Due to the transected jugular, blood was everywhere. The giant man's arm lay between The Immune's legs, his meaty calloused hand clutching a large knife with an oily greenish tinge on the blade.

"For God's sake," said the admiral as a sudden wash of realization occurred, "John, I wasn't shooting at you." He bent down, setting the holstered gun on the floor next to John's head and began struggling to free The Immune from the deadweight of Simmons' body.

As the admiral rolled Simmons' body off, The Immune twisted on his side, looked up, and with a grin said, "Oops!"

"Okay," said the admiral with a nervous laugh, "that's The Immune I know and love. Glad to have you back."

Both men looked up when they heard an unmistakable click of a cocking gun. Captain Stewart was standing in the doorway with his M-9 pistol pointed directly at the admiral. Panic seized the admiral's chest, but externally he appeared calm.

"Beckwourth, stand up and kick me your gun," said Captain Stewart with a snarl.

CHAPTER 52

STEWART'S REVENGE

U riah, what's the meaning of this?" demanded the admiral. The Immune's hair stood up on the back of his neck, giving him a prickling sensation. The pieces all seemed to be fitting together. The attorney who was torturing Sengele was the same man who nearly skinned John a year ago. Sengele never mentioned Captain Stewart's name.

"Shut up and do what I say," said Stewart furiously. The scar on his face flushed purple. "Put your hands behind your heads."

The Immune got up from the floor. The admiral kicked the holstered gun to the feet of Stewart. Both men, leaning on the desk, faced Stewart and put their hands behind their heads.

"Complicated, complicated," muttered Captain Stewart, "I need to think. How will this work now?"

"You gave Sengele the knife!" said the admiral, confronting Stewart.

"Shut up, you dim-witted buffoon. You're nothing more than an interfering tool who's been a complete pain in my ass for the last year. Happily, you've now become obsolete." He pointed to the admiral's hip pocket. "Toss me that book." The admiral pulled out the children's book, *Three Samurai Cats*, he always carried. Then he tossed it to Stewart. Stewart thumbed through each page using his free hand, then said to no one in particular, "Flinch was an idiot. There's nothing written in here."

"So, it was you who sent Flinch to break into my office?" said the admiral, "This book is only a remembrance of my dead nephew."

"Beckwourth," said Stewart with a sneer, "I never liked nor trusted you. I don't give a shit about your nephew, but your allegiance verification was difficult to confirm." He waved the book in the admiral's face, then tossed it to the deck at the admiral's feet.

"I didn't know it was under investigation," said the admiral in a cool voice, "I thought I was in good standing with ASC."

"Your ASC status won't help you now," said Stewart maliciously, "We've finally reached Fulfillment Day, and you've served your purpose. Your permanent absence will go unnoticed."

The Immune was clueless regarding the discussion, but he wondered if Stewart's hubris, if tweaked, might provide more information. The Immune, in a chastising voice, said, "Hey, that's no way to talk to a high ranking officer."

"Oh, pleeeease," replied Stewart contemptuously, "He's no more than a pawn for us chosen. Sometimes we have to sacrifice even chosen for the better good. Kind of like Boxer off to the glue factory. As for the rest of you, you're nothing more than offal that must be disposed of."

"I suppose I'm a pawn, too?" taunted The Immune.

"Clearly," said Stewart with disdain. "Not only are you a pawn, but you're a most magnificent one. Had you and Sengele killed each other with those poisoned knives—"

The admiral twisted and gave a shocked look at The Immune. The Immune responded with a shrug.

"You would've played from start to finish perfectly," said Stewart gloating. Then he mused to himself, "I only have to change a few moves and the result will be the same."

"I don't mean to sound trite," said The Immune, "but I don't think our deaths will go unnoticed."

"Ha," said Stewart, seeming to relax now he had a clear upper hand, "Oh, the good doctor is clueless and a fool. We *want* your death publicized on Fulfillment Day. We wanted your entire team, but apparently the village idiot Glavin can't follow orders. Well, I understand he got the just reward for bungling ineptitude."

Stewart threw his head back and laughed. Then he continued to address The Immune. "I see evening headlines now. The Immune is dead, hero of the world dies coward's death, hope is lost, humanity is doomed."

"You mean it's all about dealing a psychological blow?" said The Immune, looking perplexed.

"Yes, doctor," said Stewart nastily, "You're *very* dim, but it's finally sinking in. Although, that's only the icing on the misdirection, or if you prefer your admiral's nomenclature, icing on the FS Maneuver."

Stewart smiled with confidence. He moved to the bar, picked up a drink with his free hand, and took a sip. He then leaned back against the bar, always maintaining the barrel end of the gun pointed in the middle of the admiral's chest.

"Doctor, you were completely "FSed." The Immunes originally presented us with a minor problem. We couldn't have them joining militias killing airwars. Our initial plan was to kill them all, but how do you kill all those Immunes without revealing the bigger strategy? Well, thanks to the buffoon here . . ." Stewart pointed at the admiral, "ASC members became convinced Immunes could be used in better ways than harvesting their skins. I, of course, believe the only good Immune is one who's minus his skin, as you will be in a couple of minutes." Then he laughed maniacally.

The smugness suddenly drained from Stewart's face. His eyes began darting wildly. The Immune lunged forward, grabbed the gun holding hand, and forced it upward. The glass slipped from Captain Stewart's other hand, splintering into shards as it hit the deck. Stewart began convulsing. The Immune twisted the gun from his hand. Upon release of The Immune's grip on Stewart's arm, the Captain collapsed into a twitching pile on the deck. Fifteen seconds later he gave one final agonal gasp, and the attorney was no more.

"Well," said The Immune, with a small shrug to the admiral, "I'd rather be lucky than good."

The Immune spent the next ten minutes updating the admiral on his conversation with Sengele. Upon completion of the story, the admiral took a deep breath and gave a long slow exhale.

"Well, that explains a few things I always wondered about."

"In what fashion?" said The Immune.

"ASC endorsed my original plans for the Immunes more enthusiastically than expected. Promote the Immunes and give the world a rallying point, they agreed. ASC was adamant that I provide the world a singular hero. Develop and concentrate on one above the others, and protect him from harm."

The admiral smiled and patted him on the back.

"In that regard, you've been a total pain in my backside. How you stayed alive, I'll never know. You were completely emotion-driven. I registered protests that you were too reckless, but the High Council said you were perfect. Little did I know it was an FS maneuver to kill you in the end."

"It all sounds insane to me," said The Immune.

"John, the FS maneuver was brilliant. They distracted the public by creating a deity-like interest in you. Then, when it's time for them to play their hand, they'll deal a shattering psychological blow, killing hope. First destroy the will of your opponent to fight, then deal a crushing offensive attack."

"So," said The Immune, "I assume, since I was to die today, the crushing blow was to occur within the next day or perhaps hours?"

"If I were to do it," said the admiral, "I'd give it twenty-four hours so everyone would be at the peak of despair and mourning, but I don't know what *it* is."

"Well," said The Immune, "my guess is it has something to do with those vessels in the Trench."

"I agree," said the admiral, "Perhaps we should play along. Let folks think you died at the hands of Sengele. I'll get off the ship to my contacts while you hide. Then I'll figure out who's behind this massive FS maneuver."

"There may be somebody who already knows. It's time to rescue my Cassandra."

The Immune bent down, picked up the admiral's gun and handed it to him. He shoved Stewart's gun under his own belt.

The admiral's behavior suddenly changed. His eyes started darting, and he had visible perspiration on his forehead. "John, I need to get off this ship now," he paused and said, "I've important matters to take care of personally. You have to trust me on this."

The Immune looked surprised, but ignored his comment. "Admiral, get resources on the phone again." The Admiral handed John his phone. John hit the speaker button and the other end picked up.

"Resources, Blanc speaking."

"Seaman Withers? Where's Seaman Withers?" The Immune commanded. The force of The Immune's words startled Seamen Blanc.

"Two MPs just removed her from her station," Seamen Blanc stuttered. His voice cracked, "I don't know why."

He paused. The corpsman apparently regained composure, then demanded, "Who's this?"

The Immune punched the phone off.

"They must know Captain Stewart is dead," said the admiral, "It's imperative I leave the ship, but it'll have to wait. We have to get to Sengele before they do."

"Who's they?" asked The Immune.

"Captain Ames and Admiral Wilkinson. They're the only other ASC members on the ship. They had to know what Stewart was doing."

Both men dashed out of the admiral's stateroom.

CHAPTER 53

THE CONTROL ROOM

I n the control room, Admiral Wilkinson and Captain Ames stared at a fifty-inch monitor which displayed a three dimensional layout of the ship. Small red flashing dots each with a unique identification code could be seen moving throughout the ship.

Admiral Wilkinson was a heavy set man in his sixties whose abdominal girth hung well over his belt line. Gray-haired and bald on the crown, he was clean shaven except for prominent bushy sideburns. Admiral Wilkinson stood in stark contrast to Captain Ames, who was a gaunt man in his forties with a full head of dark immaculately groomed hair. Both men frowned as they followed two dots moving rapidly.

"Dammit," said Admiral Wilkinson, "they've gone back to Sengele. Redirect our men!" The captain immediately barked orders over the com. Admiral Wilkinson added, "Tell them to shoot to kill."

"What about Beckwourth?" asked Captain Ames with a startled look.

"The Immune must die without delay," said Admiral Wilkinson grimly, "Since Stewart didn't do his job, Beckwourth is now acceptable collateral damage!"

Captain Ames glanced again at the monitor and said, "Now, what's going on?"

"I think they're releasing Sengele," said Wilkinson, "The guards may be fighting them off . . . No, that's not it. They're moving as a group. Where the hell do they think they're going? Fools, there's no escape off the ship going that way."

The officers watched the group of red dots descend farther and farther into the bowels of the ship. After a few minutes, the dots stopped moving.

The captain spoke, "That's an engineering compartment. They're trying to hide."

"No," said Admiral Wilkinson, "I think they'll barricade themselves in and call for help. Those doors can be sealed and locked from the inside. Call communications and have them lock out that grid, both analog and digital."

"What about cell phones?"

"Won't work from that location, but just in case, institute priority one communications lock down. Nothing goes in or out of this ship. Send the packet before satellite uplinks have been dropped."

"But The Immune isn't dead yet," said the Captain with a look of concern.

"Dead or soon to be dead," said Admiral Wilkinson forbiddingly, "the media will never know the difference. Send the packet."

The captain moved to a large LCD monitor. His fingers ran lightly across the keyboard. He turned his head slightly to Admiral Wilkinson. The green fluorescence from the screen gave the side of his face an eerie ominous glow.

"Admiral, the packet has been sent. We're in communications lock down. I've locked out other level five clearances ability to override the lock down. Only ASC codes will work."

"Good," said the admiral, nodding to himself, "It has begun. Now let's have a check on our engineering room refugees."

The captain tapped the com, "Ensign Marcum, report."

A staticky voice came over the com, "They're holed up in engineering bay two. They've locked the doors and don't respond to orders."

"Blast the doors!" ordered the captain.

"Sir, that might kill them," replied Ensign Marcum.

"Blast the doors and kill everyone inside," commanded Captain Ames. "Take no prisoners. They've let Sengele escape."

"Aye, sir, you can count on us," replied the voice with an icy coolness at the mention of Sengele's name. The com clicked off. Admiral Wilkinson smiled at Captain Ames.

CHAPTER 54

LET'S MAKE A DEAL

The door burst open, men entered with guns waving, and someone screamed, "Drop your weapons!"

Admiral Wilkinson and Captain Ames stood there in obvious disbelief as they faced three Immunes, two marines, Admiral Beckwourth, and Dr. Sengele.

"Impossible," said Captain Ames, "You're in engineering."

"No!" said The Immune. Only marines Keys and Howard are in engineering. They're wearing added identification." The Immune pointed to the absence of his ID badge. The Immune was pleased he noticed Stewart wearing Chief Childress's dog tag earlier.

"I hope you're happy, smartass — you've just sent them to their deaths," said Captain Ames.

"Call your men and tell them to stand down," Sengele said to Captain Ames. "They're to remain in position and guard it."

"Screw you, Sengele!" said Admiral Wilkinson, with a hiss.

Sengele aimed Seamen Howard's pistol he was now carrying and pulled the trigger. Admiral Wilkinson fell back in the chair grasping his foot, screaming expletives. All eyes turned to Sengele. He gave a slight shrug and said, "Hey, ASC created me. I'm only trying to live up to my reputation."

He turned again to the captain and tersely said, "Call your men." Then he slowly and deliberately aimed the gun at the admiral's other foot.

"Call them off!" screamed Admiral Wilkinson.

Captain Ames grabbed the com and repeated Sengele's instructions.

"You've accomplished nothing!" said Admiral Wilkinson, looking up from the chair at Sengele, "Fulfillment Day's plan has already been initiated."

"What plan?" said Sengele.

"Screw you!" said Admiral Wilkinson with a malicious look. The Immune could see blood running from between Wilkinson's fingers from where he was squeezing his foot.

Sengele aimed his gun again, this time at Admiral Wilkinson's nether regions. The admiral made an attempt at a stolid face, but the widening maniacal grin appearing on Dr. Sengele's face shattered his fortitude.

"Okay, okay, I'll talk, but you're too late . . . Maybe we can make a deal." He cast an affirmative glance toward the captain, then to Admiral Beckwourth.

"Currently you aren't in a position to offer deals," said The Immune, "but go on and talk."

The admiral crossed his shot foot over the other leg to give it support.

"Two years ago several world leaders were contacted by an advanced race."

"What do you mean, advanced race?" said Sengele. "Aliens?"

"Yes."

"The airwars?" queried The Immune, looking puzzled.

"No," said Admiral Wilkinson, "The Krone. The Krone, in exchange for cooperation, offered opportunities beyond our wildest dreams. Krone selected several political leaders along with key military personnel, scientists, and their families as *The Chosen*. Initially a few thousand people worldwide made up *The Chosen*. With time the numbers grew. Careful research went into the selection of *The Chosen*, attitudes, intellect, political strength, compatibility —"

"Treachery," Prof broke in.

"Quiet," Admiral Beckwourth snapped.

Admiral Wilkinson gave Admiral Beckwourth an uncertain look and frowned, but continued, "Listen, the path was clear once you had the details. One way or another, they'd crush us. At least humanity survives by this path. The other option was complete obliteration in the hands of a far advanced enemy."

"I can't believe so many leaders agreed to go along with this arrangement," said The Immune doubtfully.

"Well, as I said, we carefully screened potential candidates before they were asked. A few whom we initially thought were good candidates declined enrollment after we disclosed the full plan. You may remember an extraordinarily large number of politicians around the world died of natural causes that year."

The Admiral stopped speaking and winced in pain. He squeezed his foot more tightly with both hands.

"Do you think we could call a medic for the admiral?" asked Captain Ames.

The Immune glanced at the small pool of blood on the deck collecting from the drippings.

"No," said The Immune, without even a hint of sympathy. "He's not in any danger of bleeding to death. You keep talking." He pointed at Admiral Wilkinson who had now stopped wincing.

Wilkinson continued. "The Krone, with their advance technology, had a device which, through voice patterns, could detect prevarication. This helped in the selection process. We have similar devices, but not as sensitive. With time, we got adept at whom to make an offer. It's a difficult process to fake deaths for world leaders. For instance, the President of the United States and the Prime Ministers of Britain, Canada, Australia, and Japan we had no chance of converting, so we didn't even try. In the United States, we had to settle for the Secretary of State, Defense, and some senators, even though we had to replace a couple."

He again stopped speaking. His face contorted with the pain radiating from the foot. Sengele stepped over and tapped the admiral's foot a couple of times with the barrel end of his gun. The admiral grimaced and twisted wildly in the chair.

"As my good friend Captain Stewart used to tell me," said Sengele coldly, "'You may stop talking only when I feel the pain'."

"When I'm done with my explanation, you'll regret your actions," said Wilkinson. His eyes hatefully glared at Sengele.

Sengele swatted the admiral's foot with his gun. This time the admiral screamed in pain.

"What's one more regret when I have so many?" said Sengele, smiling wickedly back at Wilkinson.

The Immune put his hand on Sengele's shoulder and gently moved him back from the admiral. "Chunky, he can't talk if he's screaming."

The admiral gave a nod of appreciation to The Immune and continued. "We had little trouble in countries controlled by dictators and despots. In democratic-capitalistic countries, we had to do the most replacements, but in all democracies, there's always a fifth column, which fully believes an all-powerful centralized government is best, just as long as they're running it. We just had to find those people."

"Surely someone would've spilled the beans," said The Immune, "There are too many in ASC to keep a secret, and I doubt your lie detecting device was accurate beyond fail. You were dealing with politicians."

"True," said Wilkerson, "they're all masters of the lie. We had a presumed fail rate of one tenth of one percent, which meant we accidentally terminated a few of the qualified Chosen. We sequestered almost everyone in ASC City, which by design had limited communication outside official channels. This greatly reduced the risks of accidental slips of the tongue. Keep in mind, the reward was beyond our wildest dreams, so we believed we had fewer false negatives than false positives in the test. Even so, there were a couple of false negatives, but we weeded those out with the allegiance test."

"What's that?" asked The Immune.

"You had to kill a family member," said the admiral without any evidence of remorse.

"No way," said The Immune, looking incredulous, "Everyone in ASC did that?"

"Yes," said Wilkinson, nodding, "All *The Chosen* without exception."

The Immune looked at Admiral Beckwourth in stunned disbelief, now realizing what happened to his nephew. The admiral avoided The Immune's stare.

Admiral Wilkinson continued, "Our best recruit was Senator Snivaling. Her husband, the original senator, refused our offer. She became livid. Right in front of him she asked if the offer was good for her if she performed the allegiance on him. Our recruiters said yes, and they held him while she injected several vials of concentrated potassium chloride to simulate a heart attack. Three weeks later, the governor, who was already a Chosen, swore her in to fulfill the rest of her husband's term."

"God, how I hate politicians," said Prof under his breath. Then he spat on the deck.

"It was obvious to the true Chosen what the wise choice was," interjected Captain Ames.

"But," said The Immune, "if airwars aren't the Krone, what are they?"

"The airwars are only a diversion," said Admiral Wilkerson, "an FS maneuver, if you like Beckwourth's label. The airwars were a distractive strategy while the ground work was being laid for the definitive attack. The Krone will be colonizing earth."

CHAPTER 55

THE KRONE

The room remained silent for several seconds as everyone digested the admiral's words.

"What else do you want to know?" said Admiral Wilkerson, breaking the silence.

"What are these Krone you speak of," said The Immune, somewhat dumbfounded, "and where are they located?"

"Well, I don't know much about them biologically, as I've only seen two in person on the Hiss. They're about six feet tall and look like walking sticks of celery with faces, if you'd call them faces. Krone have root-like appendages that move them around. Currently their location . . ." He paused to ponder if he should give up everything. Then thinking, *there's nothing they can do about it now*, he restarted, "Five miles below us are five thousand invasion craft. Twenty thousand Krone attack troops pack each vessel. In a Clarke orbit behind Mars is another flotilla with a hundred million colonists who'll be taking over after the shock troops remove all but *The Chosen*."

"Where will everyone be removed to?" asked Prof suspiciously.

"Actually," said Admiral Wilkerson, "recycled is a better word . . . than fertilizer, I think. Krone needs lots of CO_2 and fertilizer."

"My God!" exclaimed Dude.

"So we're to believe Krone are unbeatable with their advanced technology?" said Prof.

"Yes," replied Wilkerson, "in a sense. Plant for man, we fight comparably. Krone have a few advanced handheld weapons, such as pulse lasers, but reality is bullets are as deadly to them as pulse lasers to us."

"Well," said Dude, "then we'll fight."

"In twenty-four hours there'll be nobody in appreciable numbers left to fight," said Captain Ames with certainty in his voice.

"How so?" said The Immune, looking confused.

"Well," said Admiral Wilkerson, "this is where airwars come in. As you've already surmised, airwars weren't a creation of Dr. Sengele. The Krone produced airwars for two purposes. First, as a diversion. With the world's eye on airwars, nobody was checking for an alien strike force gradually building in the Cayman Trench. Second, airwars serve as herders. Ninety-nine percent of humanity resides within a half mile of coastlines."

"So the Krone control airwars?" asked The Immune.

"Yes," said Wilkerson, "They're part animal, part machine, and technically a cyborg. Satellite links direct where airwars go and what to attack. Otherwise, they move at random, attacking whenever hungry or taking on water when thirsty. Those metal wires which occasionally impaled Immunes were embedded electronics near the Long protuberances. Our biggest concern was airwars getting into non-ASC scientist hands. We lost a couple early on to guys like Dr. Koehler, but with time we became skilled at avoiding the militias and recovering downed airwars."

"You said the Krone produced airwars?" said Prof.

"Yes, airwars don't reproduce. With Krone technology, airwars were easy to manufacture. The release of the juveniles was another FS maneuver to make everyone believe they reproduced only when destroyed. Early in the crisis, most airwars were fitted with thousands of juveniles to prime the con. We tried to make sure every time a militia had contact with an airwar, the airwar was always fitted with juveniles. We weren't constantly successful."

A crackling of the intercom interrupted the admiral, "Captain Ames, this is Ensign Marcum. We are waiting on further orders from you."

"Tell them to remain guarding the door and not to contact you again," commanded Sengele to the captain.

The captain looked at Admiral Wilkinson, and the admiral nodded his approval.

After the captain relayed the orders, Admiral Wilkerson continued speaking, "The militias were a big headache. If that Immune hadn't been a mole for Mad Mike and given them all our Intel, we could've easily cleaned them up early in the plan. As it was, we needed the juvenile FS maneuver to keep militias from attacking airwars. The juveniles last twenty-four hours, and they decomposed rapidly wherever they ended up floating. Everyone assumed juveniles grew into bigger airwars, and ASC promoted the idea."

"Conventional wisdom is the most dangerous wisdom of all," mused Sengele aloud.

"Airwars planted at Sengele's lab were the only ones constructed of intermediate size. They had no electronics," continued Wilkerson, "The airwar lifecycle, published by ASC, was completely bogus."

"So," said The Immune, "I'm not getting this bizarre strategy. If the Krone are so advanced, why didn't they walk in and take over the planet without all these machinations?"

"Well, first off, we do have nukes. The Krone have them, too, even more destructive than ours. In a head-to-head battle, we'd ultimately lose, but the worldwide radiation damage would be immense. Who wants to colonize a radioactive planet? In addition, humankind is widely dispersed; we'd be able to keep up the fight for decades. The Krones' key advantage is their advanced application of unique force fields. How else do you think they could keep all those ships at crush depths? Even with advanced structural engineering, their vessels would implode without supplemental force fields."

"So, 'move not unless you see an advantage.' It's straight from Sun Tzu's *Art of War*," said Prof.

"Exactly," said Wilkerson, "Surreptitiously, Krone placed force generators off coasts worldwide. In a few hours the force generators will be creating sixty-foot high tsunamis, which will deluge the coastal areas with floodwaters ten to twenty feet deep, reaching over one mile inland. We're expecting an eighty-to-eighty-five percent kill rate.

"You bastards!" blurted the marine Keys, "My entire family is in the safe zone."

The admiral ignored the Marine's outburst and continued speaking. "Colossi will then cross the oscillating wire during the chaos and kill the unarmed survivors. A few hours later, the Krone strike force will rise from the trench and disperse worldwide. ASC will offer unconditional surrender of all remaining military forces. There'll be a transfer of the non-ASC populace to temporary holding facilities. After one month, most of humanity will be collected in these facilities, and they'll be terminated."

"Not everyone will drop their pants and bend over," said Dude.

"True, but almost all nukes are under control of ASC. Should the few bases under questionable control try to fire a nuke, force generators are in place in these areas. The nuke would explode on take off."

"Is there a way to counter the force fields?" asked The Immune.

"Yes, an electromagnetic pulse from a nuke fries them and, based on the way the technology works, force generators can't be protected from the EMP, but it's a catch twenty-two. You have to explode the nuke first, which wipes out the facility, so no second nuke can be deployed after force generators are destroyed."

"Well," said Dude, "let's drop a nuke into the trench."

"That's why the Krone have stayed concentrated and hidden deep. Their laser satellite defense fully protects a localized area. They'd knock off any missiles or planes within a hundred miles."

"We could sneak a ship in and detonate a nuke on the surface," said The Immune.

"Won't work," said Admiral Wilkinson, shaking his head. They're protected by five miles of water. The force generators will block any pressure changes should they even reach."

"There's got to be a way to fight these SOBs," said Dude.

"Trust me, the Krone have figured out every angle. The Krone owned this planet before the first ship ever hit the Trench. Currently, the entire world is grief-stricken from the death of The Immune at the hands of Dr. Sengele. Hope is dashed and, in a few hours, eighty percent of the world's population will be under water. This is Fulfillment Day. In a month, ninety-nine point nine percent of humanity will be gone. However, it doesn't have to include you people. I'm offering you a chance to be one of *The Chosen*."

The admiral carefully examined everyone's faces to see if he was making headway.

"Admiral, tell them the reward," interjected Captain Ames.

The Admiral nodded. "Gentlemen, I'm talking immortality. Not only surviving, but immortality. This is the reward of *The Chosen*. All *The Chosen* have been taking treatments for months. It's as simple as swallowing a big green pill. With immortality as the reward and the looming futility of resistance, your decision should be quite clear and easy." Wilkinson noticed The Immune was finally nodding agreement.

"The decision *is* quite clear and easy under the circumstances," said The Immune.

"I knew you'd come around, once you understood the facts," said Admiral Wilkinson, smiling.

"I think I speak for all of us," said The Immune. He lifted his pistol and shot Admiral Wilkinson and Captain Ames each once in the chest. "Do not pass go, do not collect immunity on the way!"

CHAPTER 56

WHERE'S JOHN

J esus, John," said Admiral Beckwourth, appearing visibly shaken, "We could have gotten more information."

"Sorry, I was pissed," he said, flashing a smile. Then his forehead furrowed. "Admiral, I do have a couple of questions for you—"

A banging on the door, which led into the steward's compartment, interrupted him. Dr. Sengele lifted the bulky metal latch locking the door. The marines aimed their weapons as the door swung open with a metallic squeal.

Standing in the threshold, holding a chair above her head, was a sweat-drenched Cassandra. Within was a padded compartment with a thick soundproof insulation, including the inside of the door. A hole in the padding and lagging on the door was apparent where she had been repeatedly pounding the chair.

The Immune was thrilled at the sight of her. He opened his arms and waited, but he was denied the expected embrace. Instead, Cassandra dropped the chair, stepped over the coaming, and snatched Sengele's pistol. She took several strides across the room and, with determination in her eyes, pointed the muzzle directly between the admiral's eyes.

"Drop it!" she said, nodding toward the admiral's gun in his right hand.

"No, Cassandra!" shouted The Immune, "He's one of us . . . the good guys . . . I *think*—"

"The hell he is!" yelled Cassandra, "Drop it, Beckwourth, or so help me I'll shoot!"

"Admiral," said The Immune, trying to intervene, "put your gun down. I'm sure we can resolve—"

"John, I love you, but shut up," interrupted Cassandra firmly, "You have no clue what's going on. Don't think of trying to stop me!" While saying this, she never once took her eye away from the admiral. "Now tell me where John is or I'll start shooting off body parts."

The Immune and Sengele watched the drama unfold with mouths slightly agape. Neither had seen Cassandra act with such ferociousness. The admiral appeared at extreme risk. The Immune wondered if she cracked under the pressure of her prolonged captivity. He didn't want to subdue Cassandra, but he felt he would have to, and quickly, if he was getting any further answers from the admiral. The Immune began a slight turn of his body to get a better angle to lunge at Cassandra's gun-wielding arm. He stopped his movement when the admiral dropped his gun to the deck.

"He's okay," said the admiral, "Now, put the gun down."

"I want him NOW!" shouted Cassandra, without moving her weapon.

"That would be impossible, but as long as you don't kill me, the boy will be fine!"

"Boy?" asked The Immune, clearly confused, "What boy?"

Cassandra's lips curled into a slight smile. She slightly glanced at The Immune as she said, "Your son, John, Jr." Then, after a moment's hesitation and a bigger smile, she said, "Surprise!" The Immune and Sengele both gasped.

"Impossible!" said the admiral with a baffled expression.

"Admiral," replied Cassandra coolly, "meet my fiancé, Dr. John Long." She looked at Sengele and said, "They wouldn't let you see me when I started to show. I couldn't find a way to let you know." She then turned back to the admiral and harshly said, "Now! Take me to my son."

For ten seconds the compartment was silent without movement, then the admiral spoke, "He's safe with a keeper."

"I don't see that filthy psychopath Stewart," said Cassandra, glancing down at the two bodies, "If you left my son with him, I swear I'll shoot you now."

"No, no," said the admiral quickly, "Stewart's dead. I'd never let Stewart around a child."

"I almost regret hearing he's dead," Cassandra mused, "I wanted to add a bullet hole to the previous scar I gave him. He deserves it for what he's done to Chunky." She glanced at Sengele.

"You were the one who gave him that scar?" interrupted The Immune, feeling stunned.

"Yeah," said Cassandra. "I should've poked instead of sliced. He and a jerk called Flinch grabbed me in my apartment. I got the carving knife to them both." Then it looked like she was ready to cry. "They took my engagement ring, John." She immediately regained her composure, moved the gun closer to the admiral's face, and with forced inflection said, "WHERE'S MY SON?"

"You have two choices," replied the admiral with an unruffled look. "You can kill me." His hands swept down, outlining the bodies of the slain admiral and captain. "Upon doing so, your son will certainly die, and ultimately you won't change the course of world events and . . ." He paused. "Please aim your gun elsewhere as I say this. I have the power to make you part of *The Chosen* and to give you all immortality, including your son."

"I think I've made my answer clear on that subject," said The Immune, pointing his gun at the two bodies. A wave of anger washed over his body.

"Please remain calm," said the admiral. "John, I'm clearly in favor of the continuation of the human race, although my actions may, at first blush, seem to reflect otherwise. Realize, a good soldier knows when to surrender even if the terms may not be to his liking. My only request is you let me off the ship immediately. Should you take a little time to reflect on the subject, I think you'll find my actions have been reasonable."

"Torture, kidnapping, sedition, genocide!" spit out Sengele, "You call those actions reasonable?"

"Yes," replied the admiral with a stone face, "The circumstances warranted overlooking others' actions."

Sengele blurted, "Well, then, I think circumstances warrant these actions." But before he could attack the admiral, The Immune grabbed his right arm, restraining him.

"Sengele, wait!" said The Immune, "We've got a bit of a situation here, and what we need is as much information as we can get. Killing him at this point will serve no purpose. I may have acted a bit hastily with the former captain and admiral. Admiral Beckwourth obviously knows things we don't know, so we need him if we're to stand a chance."

"Have a chance at what?" said the admiral with disbelief.

"Beating the Krone," replied The Immune.

"World's hero to the end," said the admiral, smiling, "Look, John, you're a product of my creation. You're the world's biggest FS maneuver, a distraction used for military purpose. Quite well, I might add. I can offer you hope. It's only a simple matter of letting me off the ship."

"Admiral, you have no idea how this rips me to my core," said The Immune. "It's like discovering your wife is sleeping with your arch enemy and enjoying it. I admired you. I always thought in the battle of good and evil you would always side with good no matter the personal cost. Your actions disrespect your purported philosophical principles."

"John," said the admiral, "don't take this wrong. You're The Immune now, someone I think I could've confided in, but it's too late. I had to do my job. It was a tough one. I could've used help, but you were too reckless. You were a figurehead who ran on emotions of anger and vengeance. From the outside looking in, you appeared the hero. But I also know a man who was hollow on the inside who didn't care what happened to him. Courage isn't action, but action with the risk of losing something."

"Beckwourth," said Prof disapprovingly, "you're the last person on this world who should be lecturing The Immune on courage. Bob was right about you."

The admiral ignored Prof and continued. "John, your efforts weren't your own, only a manipulation by others. Like a man who goes to work every day for forty years and receives great accolades for doing everything expected of him. In the end, he realizes he's achieved nothing of his own; just fulfilled others' expectations. A legacy of fulfilled expectations of others is no legacy at all.

"I not only had to make you a living legend, but protect you until we could use your sudden demise for our benefit. I must admit, though, you're clever and brave in a foolhardy sort of way, but you're in no position to be the savior of the world. You're just a well-done marketing campaign. Further information from me won't help. I've considered all possibilities, and this is the only reasonable action. If not for yourself, consider your son, which I might add, I had no idea of the link here. Again, all I'm asking is to let me off the ship so I can speak to the Krone on your behalf. I believe you've awakened from your stupor. Trust me now."

CHAPTER 57

THE BARGAINING CHIP

The Immune slipped away in deep thought. Prof and Cass-andra both looked as if they wanted to kill the admiral on the spot.

"Admiral," said Sengele, "you speak like a politician. Everything is done in the name of 'the people,' then politicians reap the rewards. You excuse your behavior as just doing your job. That's not a suitable defense for blindly ignoring and not speaking out against evil. Evil is pernicious and devious. Ignoring evil is the first foothold in acceptance of it."

"I agree," piped in Dude, "Sengele, for a guy portrayed as the antichrist, you're alright by me."

Sengele continued, "It's personal self-interest, which is human nature, that's the foundation for building strong societies. The irony is the same quality of human nature in government has the opposite effect. I fear we're too late in recognizing, for every law passed restricting personal rights, ten should be passed restricting government's power."

The admiral looked at his watch. "Are you done?"

"No," said Sengele, "your faulty logic that we shouldn't fight, because the greatest military minds were selected from a pool of those most inclined to surrender, gives me no confidence. Perhaps selecting the recommendation of the most intrepid leaders instead of the most craven would've resulted in a different strategy. Should we lose, you'll get your fitting punishment — immortality as a coward."

The admiral looked at his watch again.

"If you let me off the ship, I can save you all, but we're running out of time. I need to get to my political contacts."

"Who's that?" interrupted Cassandra, "Senator Snivaling, the one who wanted John skinned alive? We're supposed to trust her?"

"Cassandra," said The Immune, "the admiral can't stand Snivaling anymore than I. He hates her. He couldn't fake that all these months."

"Well, maybe he's faking his orgasms with her, too, but he's sure making her chimney smoke. I've heard the admiral discussing her with his two former immortal friends in this very room." She pointed to the dead bodies of Wilkinson and Ames.

"That's impossible," said the admiral, with wide eyes, "That used to be a soundproof room." The admiral motioned to the hole in the padding on the door. "You could scream all you want in that room, and I believe you did for the first two weeks, and a person in this room wouldn't hear a peep."

"Clearly the greatest military minds knew this to be true," responded Cassandra sarcastically, "Nevertheless, if a woman cuts a hole in the insulation and presses a simple water glass to the metal door, she hears every traitorous word said on the other side. If she has nothing better to do for ten straight months except to listen, she learns a lot. Had John not discovered a way to bring airwars down without ruining ASCs' FS maneuver, he'd be in a blue spray can with the rest of the Immunes. John, you were a useful tool for the admiral, but he's all about political positioning. Currently I just want my son."

"You're absolutely correct about one thing," said the admiral confidently. "Every action I've done is about positioning. That's the singular reason I can save you all. Just let me off the ship."

"Give me a break," said Cassandra with a roll of her eyes, "You're not about what's best for us. It's about saving your sorry ass. Now, where's my son?"

"The boy is my only bargaining chip," said the admiral, jutting out his chin, "and I plan to keep it until you release me. Just let me off the ship, and when I'm safely away, I'll tell you where your son is."

"Let's see," said Sengele, "thirty minutes ago you were having us all killed, and now we should trust you. I don't think so."

"It's the only thing you can do," implored the admiral. "Let me off the Acheson, and you can fight if you want. I'll give you the boy's location. I'd recommend staying here and doing nothing, and I'll smooth everything out with the Krone."

"Admiral," said Cassandra, "if you're so confident in the Krone's victory, why don't you give me my son?"

"Well, for one thing, you would have no reason not to kill me, and if you did, your son would die. I'm only trying to protect your son," he said with a priest-like smile.

Dr. Sengele walked over to face the admiral. "Restrain him!" said Sengele. Dude and Prof grabbed the admiral's arms, and Sengele bent over and snatched the admiral's gun from the deck. "It wasn't all tea parties and Swedish massages with your buddy Captain Stewart. I picked up a few conversation icebreakers along the way."

Sengele then shoved the barrel of the pistol down the front of the admiral's pants and pulled the trigger. The bullet ricocheted off the deck, then the far bulkhead. The admiral staggered, but the Immunes held him. The bullet passed through the base of his trousers. No blood was seen. Visibly shaken, the admiral appeared to be realizing he still had all of his anatomy.

"Well, it looks like I missed," laughed Sengele, "If at first you don't succeed, try, try again."

He shoved the gun barrel again down the front of the admiral's pants and cocked the hammer.

CHAPTER 58

THE BRITTLE STAR

W ait, wait!" screamed the admiral.

"Okay," said Sengele. "You've got three seconds to tell us where my nephew is located."

"I need assurance you won't kill me."

"Well, well, is this your right testicle I feel with the gun barrel? One, two . . ."

"Okay, okay. The baby is with Seaman Dobbs," said the admiral, shaking.

The Immune stepped to a monitor and typed in a few words. "She's not on this ship."

"That's because she's on the Brittle Star," said the admiral.

"I know this ship and the captain well," said Sengele turning to The Immune, "It's operated by Captain Logan, the one I told you about. I can't believe his ship is still in the area."

He looked back at the admiral for confirmation.

The admiral nodded. "Captain Logan is an unwitting Krone employee via Admiral Wilkinson. The Krone had a miniature electromagnetic pulse generator placed on board the Brittle Star. The EMP generator was five feet in size, but could generate an EMP of a hydrogen bomb. Captain Logan believed it was a sonar device for locating small underwater fissures deep in the trench.

"Why did the Krone need to test an EMP generator?" said Sengele, "Also, why did Wilkinson need Captain Logan's help?"

"Admiral Wilkinson wanted the Brittle Star because seven years before Captain Logan purchased it as a research vessel; it was a covert reconnaissance vessel used in the China Sea. As with most covert military ships, the electronic parts in the ship are hardened against a possible EMP. When the ship was decommissioned and sold, the hardened equipment went with it. He located the ship and paid Captain Logan handsomely for letting him run the 'sonar' test."

"So," said Sengele, "how does the submersible fit in."

"Yes, well, Wilkinson provided the Brittle Star with the Pathfinder, which they didn't have time to harden. Wilkinson built a large storage unit on deck, which Captain Logan thought was to protect it from the elements. But in reality it was a giant Faraday box to keep it from being damaged from any EMP. After the test we'd be able to recover the EMP device and any damaged force generators for the Krone to study. Wilkinson didn't put a GPS on the submersible because nobody wanted a record of where it would be going. Hence, the necessity of the optical telescope, so he could find the submersible and EMP device."

"So that's why we had the blackout on the island?" asked Sengele, "It was an electromagnetic pulse?"

"Correct."

"But why the EMP test?" asked The Immune.

"The Krone wanted to test the submersed force generators against a surface EMP attack. The Krone knew, up close, an EMP would knock out the generators. The Krone's biggest worry was a boat concealed nuclear warhead could be set off on the surface. They wanted to make sure the warhead's surface EMP wouldn't damage the force generators."

"What about an underwater missile?" asked The Immune.

"Nukes aren't designed for those pressures. Even the old nuclear depth charges can't go that deep, and ASC secured all of those early. Initially, the Krone deployed test generators and empty housing vessels. These produced the 'footprints' Dr. Sengele discovered. Remember those weird tidal waves in Cayman written off as seismic shifts in the trench? Well, they were from the first force generators revving up."

"So can I assume the surface EMP had no effect at the trench bottom?" asked The Immune.

"Exactly, the surface EMP didn't affect the force generators at all. The Krone calculated, for the EMP to damage the generators, it would have to originate within a couple thousand meters of the units. Following the test, other generators were deployed. These obscured evidence of a space to earth landing channel."

"By my calculations this preparation has been going on for nearly a year," said The Immune, "Why so long?"

"The Krone could only obscure a tight landing channel, only a few housing vessels could land each day. It was a time-consuming process. Since then, there's been a slow build up of underwater units over the last year. Some Krone have remained housed on the trench bottom longer than ten months, but they're able to enter a torpid state so time is meaningless. They're now at full force and active. The entire endeavor was a complete success."

"That depends on your point of view," said Sengele, frowning.

The admiral looked at Cassandra. "I then did an FS maneuver. I moved your baby to the Brittle Star to prevent questions on this naval ship about a baby at sea. We told Captain Logan and Seaman Elisabeth Dobbs, who attends the baby, John Jr. was born on this ship to an obese seaman who didn't realize she was pregnant until she went into labor. To prevent scandal, we sent the baby to the Brittle Star until our joint research mission completes. When the baby visited you, it was under the guise of medical checkups."

"So Captain Logan has no clue about any of this?" said Cassandra.

"None. After I was recruited to ASC and learned about the FS maneuver with the EMP test, I expanded the FS maneuver. I provided Captain Logan another grant to be on call for me for the use of the submersible. He had all the original test equipment, the 'sonar' in the ship's hold, the submersible, and the telescope. Captain Logan thought it was a continuation of the original testing. I'd come out every couple of weeks to go down in the Pathfinder, purportedly to check the accuracy of the initial 'sonar' test."

"What were you actually doing?" asked The Immune.

"In reality, the Krone wanted regular updates on the coastal migrations. I hand-delivered migration progress reports to the central commander every other week five miles below. Before their planned attack, the Krone wanted eighty percent migration completed. ASC did better than expected. We reached the population move goal before all the Krone vessels were in place. The death of The Immune by Sengele was to start Fulfillment Day. After the psychological blow, the tsunamis would start a few hours later, followed by a Colossi attack, then the invasion force would surface. Captain Logan, to this day, has no clue what's going on."

"What about the seaman who's caring for my baby?" said Cassandra.

"Seaman Dobbs has no clue either," said the admiral, "Your baby is in good hands."

"So nobody on the Brittle Star knows what's going on?" asked The Immune.

"No, they're all FSed."

"What about other researchers who used the submersible?" said The Immune. "They'd have seen things."

"I alone control the Pathfinder," said the admiral, "Matter of fact, I made sure I was the only one on the ship capable of operating the sub. I arranged to have any qualified pilots off the vessel. I didn't want any accidental runs occurring."

"Captain Logan can operate the Pathfinder," said Sengele.

"Yes, but he knew who was paying the bills. I made it clear I alone would operate the sub while the project was ongoing. He wouldn't dare pilot it when I might show up at a moment's notice requiring its use. Now what I—"

The Immune broke in, "So you were lying about the baby being in risk of dying?"

"What I said was, if you kill me, he'll die. There's a naval destroyer, the Hiss, within ten miles of the Brittle Star. The Hiss has on board the entire ASC High Council, as well as many Krone waiting for the start of Fulfillment Day. If Admiral Wilkinson, Captain Ames, or I don't perform the required check in, they'll know something is amiss. I assure you, the Hiss won't hesitate to destroy both ships. Clearly, the admiral or the captain won't be making that call." Admiral Beckwourth glanced down at the two dead bodies.

"Why's the High Council on the Hiss, rather than ASC City?" asked The Immune.

"The High Council didn't want to risk staying in ASC City during Fulfillment Day. If Mad Mike discovered the treachery, he might attack. Currently, ASC City is unprotected. The Grey Youth Guard who protects the city's perimeter is rewarded tonight with a hedonistic beach party. A thousand guards were transported to Chesapeake beach and are enjoying an open bar while waiting for the promised women. The only *reward* arriving for them are a series of tidal waves. Currently, ASC City's only protection from Mad Mike are thousands of Colossi which surround the city. Given time, Mad Mike could easily breach the airwars."

"Okay," said The Immune, breaking in, "Here's my plan. Rescue the boy, save humanity, and kill the entire Krone force." Then The Immune added, "But maybe not in that order," and smiled. From the expressions on everyone's face, nobody appreciated the added levity.

"Great, then you can end poverty, stop global warming, and rid us of taxes!" The admiral looked at his watch. "But in the meantime, I need to check in or you'll have even bigger problems."

CHAPTER 59

LATE CHECK IN

J ohn!" said Sengele furiously, "don't let him do it. It's a trap. He'll warn them."

"No," said The Immune, "I doubt it. He knows if he warns them, we'll kill him on the spot. He's trying to stay alive long enough for our position to be hopeless, then he'll try to stay alive long enough to barter our surrender without getting himself killed. If he doesn't report, he knows he'll die, because they'll blow us out of the water."

"Well," said the admiral, smiling, "you do have an uncanny way of figuring things out, John. Why not go the next step, let me off this ship?"

The Immune gave the admiral a disapproving look. "Perspective history may decide the traitorous, but a man's soul bears the burden regardless of historical approval."

The admiral snorted and moved to the monitor, slightly pushing The Immune out of the way. He tapped on a few keys, "Okay, no more communications lockdown."

He hit a few more buttons. "John, step back from the camera. I don't want them to see any of you on the monitor. They may sense something has gone wrong, and besides, you're supposed to be dead."

Other monitors in the room flashed on with the face of Admiral McCloy, an ASC High Council member. Admiral Beckwourth spoke, "Bill, how's it going? I'm just checking in." The man on the monitor looked stressed.

"Beckwourth, what the hell is going on over there?" demanded Admiral McCloy, "You've had communications lockdown for twenty-five minutes. The Krone are getting antsy."

"No problem now, only a little disturbance with a couple of the men after The Immune was killed. I didn't want anyone posting crazy ideas to the Internet at zero hour; it was only a precaution. All secure presently, though."

Admiral McCloy gave a cool smile to the camera. "Everything is going according to plan here. Couldn't be better than if the Mets won the World Series."

Admiral Beckwourth's face twitched. It looked like he was trying to make a decision. The Immune lifted his gun and pointed it at Beckwourth. Admiral Beckwourth returned to his previous facial countenance and said, "That's great, Bill."

Admiral McCloy then said, "One slight last-minute change. The Krone want you to bring the Acheson to us and have everybody disembark. They're doing that for the Brittle Star, too. You're ten minutes away. Make sure the men are unarmed."

"Sure," replied Beckwourth, nodding with a bland expression, "Understood."

The monitors clicked off. The admiral slumped over the keyboard with his head hung down. "Damn, damn, damn."

The room was quiet. All were looking at the admiral, who looked despondent for the first time. "Something's wrong," said Admiral Beckwourth. "Bill used the emergency code about the Mets. He also didn't inquire about Admiral Wilkinson, who should've been the one checking in. Additionally, the Krone have changed plans. The Brittle Star shouldn't be disembarking on the Hiss. Only ASC members were to leave our ship on a shuttle, and it was to be several hours from now."

"Maybe the Krone suspect we have you," said Sengele.

"No, they'd sink us immediately, not bring us in close." The admiral suddenly stood bolt upright. "I need to make another call."

"I don't like this," said Sengele.

The Immune's eyes narrowed. "Who are you contacting?" he asked.

The admiral's eyes shifted toward the deck, "Beulah Snivaling."

CHAPTER 60

THE SENATOR'S REWARD

Snivaling?" The Immune said her name with disgust, "Where is she and how could she help?"

"She's on the Hiss," said the admiral. "Cassandra was correct; we have a thing. Couldn't ever tell you because her politics weren't to your liking, but her urges were to my liking. She was one of the original chosen senators who brought me on board with ASC. I have a link to a monitor in her stateroom. In the evenings she would . . . umm . . . like to entertain me before bedtime."

"Go on and do it," The Immune said, "but leave out the entertainment part. If I witnessed that, I might have to kill myself."

The admiral ignored the barb and went to work on the connection. Two seconds later an image came on the screen. The admiral took two steps back in horror. All eyes in the room suddenly fixed on the monitors.

Lying on the stateroom deck, fully disrobed, was a screaming, begging Senator Snivaling. A desk was overturned. An empty green jar formerly filled with lima bean-shaped pills lay next to a green spray can and a blue-lidded spray can with the letters UW written on the side. Standing on top of her was a giant celery stalk with a face. Entwined in scores of roots, which were slowly moving around her body, lay Snivaling. Some clearly pierced the skin and appeared as if they were large, bulging veins underneath the surface. All orifices were penetrated, with the exception of her left ear and mouth. A large root was trying to enter the mouth, but her twisting face and neck were avoiding the slow jabs of the root.

Her horrible screams were punctuated occasionally by, "I'm a Chosen . . . I'm a Chosen." The celery stalk seemed to pause to contemplate the problem of the moving head. A metallic voice came from a small black translation unit strapped a third of the way down the stalk.

"Yes," said the celery stalk. Snivaling's head stopped moving and looked toward the celery face. "You Chosen."

"I've had the treatments!" screamed the senator. She started twisting. "You're killing me!"

"Nutrients provided, yes," responded the celery. Snivaling stopped moving again. "Nutrients assemble you taste pleasurable for Krone, yes." Her eyes widened in horror. "You absorb to society, last perpetually. Immortality, guarantee, yes."

A long piercing, "Nooooo!" came from her lips.

"Society important; you feces, yes." With this last statement, the root, which was being carefully positioned during her momentary pause, thrust forward into her mouth. A muffled scream was followed by gagging and choking. As the diameter of the root enlarged as it penetrated beyond the oral cavity, it began to collapse the trachea. Snivaling's face developed a dark blue hue. Her eyes bulged. One violent twisting convulsion shook the body, then she went limp.

Roots pulled the limp body a few inches from the deck while other roots in a centipede-like movement moved the celery stalk with Snivaling engulfed in its base toward the door of the stateroom.

The marine, Powell, began vomiting on the deck.

The admiral collapsed in a heap on the floor, sobbing. "What have I done? What have I done? I've gambled and lost. So close . . . so close!"

The Immune walked over, pressed a button on the keyboard, and the connection went blank.

"So, you gave Ube's extract to that wretched woman for sexual favors. You're a real piece of work, admiral."

The Immune walked to the whimpering admiral, grabbed him by the collar and, with a sharp jerk, lifted him to his feet. He leaned close to the ear of the admiral and said, "Have the Krone ever suffered a setback?"

The admiral, his collar in the grasp of The Immune, his head hanging, said, "No."

"Well, then, the Krone wouldn't be expecting an attack."

The admiral stood. The Immune loosened his grip.

"If you even started to radio for an attack, they'd sink us and the Brittle Star. Additionally, there are no weapons in the coastal safe zones, and the military would take hours to respond. By then the tsunamis would have hit."

"What if our ship attacked the Hiss?" said The Immune, "Could we destroy them?"

"Possibly, with direct hits from torpedoes," said the admiral, "but they'd have plenty of time to respond before they're hit. Their missile systems would obliterate us. It would be a pyrrhic victory even if we sunk them. We'd be gone and there would be no one to coordinate a response to the airwars, plus there are 100 million attack forces five miles below."

"But would the Krone fire on the Brittle Star?" asked The Immune.

The admiral put his hand to his chin and thought a moment.

"No, probably not. They'd be focusing all their efforts on us, and the Brittle Star is unarmed. But, even if the Hiss took torpedo hits, it might not go down, then they'd turn on the Brittle Star."

"Okay, here's my plan," said The Immune. He walked to the radar screen, which showed the destroyer and the Brittle Star nearby. Everyone in the room gathered around. Four minutes later, the admiral was barking commands.

CHAPTER 61

SIGNAL FLAGS

Cassandra, arguing with The Immune, interrupted the admiral's orders to the crew. "I want to ride to the Brittle Star with the Immunes. I must get to John."

"No," said The Immune, shaking his head, "You'll die. Stay with the crew."

The admiral pulled a blue-capped spray can from his pocket marked UW on the lid and sprayed her down. The Immune started to question the admiral, but the admiral cut him off, "There's no time. I'll explain later." Beckwourth then searched Admiral Wilkinson and Captain Ames's pockets, retrieved two browns, and tossed them to the two marines.

Sengele looked at the can the admiral had in his pocket and said, "You have too many hidden toys I don't understand. I'd feel more comfortable if you'd get undressed."

The admiral glanced toward The Immune for support. He saw he wasn't getting it, so he began stripping down to his underwear. He stood wearing only white briefs looking un-Navy like, being tattoo-less except for a small omega-shaped scar on his shoulder. He took the children's book from his pocket and slipped it under the elastic band of his briefs. As he stood, he said to The Immune, "I guess you'll have to hang on to my phone a while longer."

On the Brittle Star, Captain Logan was within a few nautical miles of the destroyer. He was fuming mad. Never in his career had he been talked to that way, especially not as a ship's captain. Admiral McCloy said, "Meet with the Destroyer Hiss and have all personnel disembark from the Brittle Star to the Hiss."

McCloy ordered him like he was a miscreant junior officer.

Captain Logan thought, *Admiral Beckwourth has been easy to work with, but this McCloy is a real peckerhead. I may be a research scientist, and McCloy may not respect me as a ship captain, but I'm not some scutboy for him to order. I'll tell him where he can put the Navy's grant money.* He was thinking of a few choice words he would relay to Admiral McCloy when he got aboard the Destroyer.

"Sir," said one of the crew, interrupting Captain Logan's thoughts, "We've got a strange message from the Acheson. It said, 'Captain Logan, bow eye candy, check it out'."

"Did you ask what the hell that meant?" said Captain Logan, feeling confused.

"Yes," replied the crewman, "several times. The Acheson didn't respond."

"This day is just getting worse and worse," said Logan to himself. "Turn the optical scope on and point it toward the bow of the Acheson."

One minute later, they were looking at the monitor of the optical scope and saw Admiral Beckwourth in white briefs using signal flags.

"Is this some kind of joke?" said the crewman, "What the heck is the admiral doing signal flags for, sir? Should we radio them?"

Captain Logan thought for a moment. "No, don't radio anyone before we figure out what the hell Admiral Beckwourth is doing. Who knows how to read signal flags?"

"Stevens does, sir," said the crewman, "He's a Chief Petty Officer loaned to us a couple of days ago from the Acheson. He agreed to work on the backup radio, which was on the fritz. He's a flag wagger."

"Get his butt up here—now!"

Moments later, clearly perturbed at being rushed along, Chief Stevens was on the Brittle Star's top deck. His face was like wrinkled leather, and bright red vessels crisscrossed his bulbous nose.

He took one look at the screen and said, "Well, hell has frozen over. I'm seeing an admiral in his skivvies doing signal flags."

"What's he saying?" asked Captain Logan.

Chief Stevens paused a few moments as he watched the flags. "Admiral says if you understand, change course two degrees for ten seconds, then resume back."

The captain looked to the crewmember to his left. "Okay, do it."

Thirty seconds later the admiral resumed signaling from the deck of the Acheson.

"I'll need a pencil and paper," said Stevens, his eyes remained transfixed on the monitor. Four minutes later, the captain was reading the sheet of paper, mouth agape.

CHAPTER 62

PREEMPTIVE STRIKE

On board the Acheson, the admiral walked back into the control room with Sengele. Sengele had a gun on the admiral and said, "I don't trust him. We've no idea what he told the Brittle Star."

The Immune stared at the monitor without looking up. "They've adjusted their speed. We'll pass them and be 1800 meters clear. We've cut it close going at full speed. We'll just make it if everything goes perfect. We took too long with our crew."

"No, we'll be fine," said the admiral.

The Immune spoke without lifting his eyes from the monitor to the others remaining in the control room, "Okay, you've got four minutes—get going."

On board the Hiss, the leader of the Krone's advanced team, the "Surface Director," had just begun enjoying his initial feeding on Admiral McCloy. He was pleased. The admiral had just the right nutrients to make him taste good. This was one of the few rewards of the advanced team. All the others would have to feed on unfortified bodies. It served everyone's needs, but the flavor wasn't there.

The admiral was a large man. He would get eight to ten months of feeding off him. Then he would join the feeding fields with the others. There would be billions of bodies to lie out in the feeding fields. What a great planet this was.

The Chief Colonizer himself would probably give him a two rank party elevation for the acquisition of this planet. He loved planets with centralized world governments. It made progress simpler.

"Sir," said a smaller stalk, breaking his daydream, "The Acheson needs to slow down."

The surface director looked at the monitor and pushed a button.

On the Acheson, The Immune and Admiral Beckwourth could see the Hiss was signaling them. The Immune said, "Hold five seconds to answer. Every second counts from here on out."

The surface director was becoming impatient. He was considering calling an alert when the screen came on with Admiral Beckwourth's face.

"I'm Admiral Beckwourth, one of *The Chosen*. What can I do for you?"

A slight pause occurred as the interpreting device computed the plebeian language usage. The box two-thirds of the way up his stalk said, "Admiral, slow ship. You approach much fast, yes."

"We're trying to reach you before the Brittle Star," said the admiral, "It would be better for my men to disembark first. Less time my crew has to think, the better. I might have officers get suspicious seeing the Brittle Star crew disembarking, but if you want, I can give orders to cut our engines."

The surface director thought for a moment, then said, "No, catch ship Brittle Celebrity, diminish velocity, Acheson disembark primary, yes, yes, exceptional."

The screen clicked off and The Immune looked at the admiral and said, "Strong work," with a sigh of relief.

"The world's greatest PR guy," replied the admiral with a small shrug.

The ship sped along at full power, now bearing down on the Brittle Star. One minute later, the larger Acheson passed the Brittle Star, and an airwar left the stern as it passed. The Brittle Star's engines cut off, and the ship rocked heavily in the wake.

On the Acheson, the control room received several signals that the Destroyer Hiss was trying to contact them.

The admiral's face smiled toward the cam. "Almost there, Surface Director." The Immune had his eyes on a countdown timer, which read thirty-seven seconds.

"Incise Acheson engines back, Admiral," demanded the voice box in high volume.

"But our engines have been cut," said the admiral with a look of surprise, "We're approaching at only ten knots."

The Surface Director lightened for a moment. "Good, yes."

Two more seconds ticked by, and the clock read twenty-one. The admiral watched another celery stalk appear behind the Surface Director.

"Informed I Hiss coming much propulsion forty-five knots," said the Surface Director.

The admiral calmly looked on the screen and said, "No, your instruments are incorrect. We're now doing five knots."

On the Hiss, the Surface Director glanced at his screen and thought, *well, these devices are not as advanced as ours. Maybe the outputs are wrong.* He looked around at the cabin with eight stalks at the controls, each with a High Council member entwined in their roots at the base of each stalk. He looked at the screen filled with the reassuring face of the admiral. Then he looked up from the instrument panel. He looked to the port side. Bearing down on the Hiss, five hundred meters out, was the Acheson, with a huge bow wave spilling over the sides. The stalk translator unit screeched in a high volume, "Incise Hiss engines immediate or Chosen admiral denied reward, yes!"

"I'm afraid my reward will be limited to watching you go to hell," said Admiral Beckwourth, with scorn.

The admiral looked toward The Immune, whose eyes hadn't left the countdown timer. The digital one flashed to zero, and The Immune punched a button.

On board the Hiss, a junior stalk informed the surface director the destroyer was under attack. A salvo of three Mark 46 torpedoes had been released from the Acheson. The Surface Director looked toward the screen.

"See you in the compost pile!" said Beckwourth's image, smiling. The screen went blank.

If the battleship wasn't sitting dead in the water, there might have been a way for the Hiss to take evasive action. Lacking that ability, a barrage of missiles was sent toward the Acheson. A decoy blew up one of the torpedoes one hundred meters out. The surface director watched the monitors as the other two torpedoes smashed into the sides of the Hiss.

Two giant holes formed in the ship's bulkhead as it rocked from the explosion. Several celery stalks with dead sailors attached to their roots fell into the sea. The Surface Director's middle orifice crinkled in what would be considered the human equivalent of a smile. The Hiss had taken severe damage, but wouldn't be sinking.

The Surface Director looked up again from his monitors to see the Acheson bearing down on him. Smoking, and on fire, with several gaping holes in its side and command tower, the Acheson was coming. The crushing impact of steel on steel followed. The Hiss rocked sixty degrees toward the starboard side on impact. The Acheson pierced one third of the way through the mid-section of the ship, yet both vessels floated.

Three hundred meters away from the entangled ships floated a solitary airwar. Tentacle tips were touching the water's surface, slowly moving it toward the Brittle Star. Inside the airwar, sitting on the coiled suction tube was The Immune.

The Immune looked at his watch and said to himself, "We calculated ten seconds after impact and it's been twenty. It's not happening. We're screwed."

The Surface Director ordered the targeting of the Brittle Star with all weapons. It would be his last command. The jarring impact of the two ships caused a small-computerized self-destruct mechanism to re-boot. This took twenty seconds and the countdown resumed from the last number before shut down. The self-destruct code of the missile deep in the bow of the Acheson hit zero, and the bow of the Acheson and the mid-section of the Hiss were no more.

The Hiss split in two pieces and the remains of the Acheson's stern all turned on end as one. Like a drowning man holding three fingers up, it slipped slightly below the oily debris-ridden surface.

"Now that *was* satisfying," said The Immune to himself.

CHAPTER 63

DOWN WITH THE SHIP

The Immune's thoughts returned to moments before. He was leaving the near-naked admiral on the deck of Acheson as he climbed into the airwar. There were no other aerosol cans of Immune extract left on the ship.

"Admiral," said The Immune, "grab a lifejacket and jump. We'll pick you up after we retrieve the crewmembers who exited two miles ago."

"I'm going to stay with the ship," replied the admiral.

"You'll die in the collision," retorted The Immune, "It's a senseless tradition to stay."

"It's my choice as senior naval officer to go down with the ship," replied the admiral, "My only request is my nephew's book and a pen to write some last confessions for myself. Good luck with your plan."

The Immune lost sight of the admiral as he entered deep within the tentacles. His last vision of Beckwourth was him standing next to the outer curtain, scribbling madly on the inside back cover of the book.

Twenty minutes later the Brittle Star's bow was beneath the hovering airwar's tentacles. The Immune slipped down to the deck below. The airwar slowly floated off the starboard side of the deck, hanging on to the deck rail with its outer curtain.

The Immune smiled at a sailor holding a machine gun and motioned he'd like to borrow it. The seaman handed him the gun, eyes fixed on the airwar. The Immune aimed at the hydrogen sac and pulled the trigger. Several short bursts came from the gun's muzzle. The central sac shredded with the impact of the projectiles. One of the last rounds was hot enough to begin combustion of the hydrogen. From within, a fire lit up the central sac, spreading peripherally to engulf the entire bag. The tentacles collapsed down on themselves, floating on the water, finally covered by the burning, smoking, residual hydrogen sac. There wasn't a juvenile seen.

"My, that's so much simpler," mused The Immune aloud. He handed the weapon back to the sailor, who was eyeing the smoldering carcass of the airwar.

Wasting no further time, he ran up to the bridge of the Brittle Star. On the bridge, Sengele and Cassandra were already with Prof, Dude, and Seaman Keys. Both Sengele and Cassandra had a few nasty welts, but otherwise were fine.

"Where's Powell?" asked The Immune.

"One of the Browns was a dud," said Dude, shaking his head, "He didn't make it."

"We tried to help him," interjected Prof, "It just wasn't possible. We've filled Captain Logan in on details. He already has Bob and Mad Mike on the line. I've updated them, as well as Colonel Vickers back at Central. The rest of our team is safe."

Prof handed The Immune a headset.

"Bob," said The Immune, "you'll have to wait for my humblest apologies, as you were right and I was wrong about the admiral."

"Well," said Bob, "it's good to hear The Immune is alive. I have to say I shed a tear when I heard of your demise. As far as airwars are concerned, our boys are already chewing through them like maggots on a rotting rat. Regarding your apology, I'll take it over a beer. You'll be buying."

"Fair enough." The Immune disconnected Bob and seconds later he was broadcasting worldwide. He didn't need to mention how to handle the airwars, because as soon as the general population learned of the FS maneuver, all wanted to down an airwar.

It was a wildfire spread by hurricane force winds. Mad Mike's militia trapped airwars on one side. The other side was an angry boiling mass of humanity. Anyone with a strong arm was pitching every sharp object found toward hydrogen sacs. It became immediately apparent the ASC confiscation of guns was of limited success. Those lacking a forceful throw or firearms used homemade slings to hurl burning items into the sacs. Although many airwars fell to earth in spectacular fiery deaths, most slowly deflated from multiple puncture wounds.

Accidental injuries occurred from people shoved into airwar tentacles as the crowds around airwars became massive and uncontrollable. The screams of these victims infuriated the masses more. Within ten minutes of The Immune's broadcast, close to a million airwars and Colossi had been grounded and were on fire, having been doused with a variety of flammable materials.

A withdrawal from all coastal areas began. Those living at the water's edge already noticed a receding of the water line. In another hour hundreds of extra feet of beach would be showing, then the tsunamis would start.

The early warning would save billions from a violent drowning death. However, due to the vast numbers needing relocation in such a short period, complicated by the Salvation Wall, it was clear hundreds of millions would die. Even more would die once the Krone's attack force surfaced.

The Immune stood before the captain of the Brittle Star and made his request known. The EMP generator had to be loaded, and the Pathfinder needed a pilot. Captain Logan looked away from The Immune toward the sky.

"Yeah," said Captain Logan, "I see there's no other way, and no, I don't need you along. As much as I admire your offer, it would be a waste of life." He looked at his watch, then The Immune. "We've wasted a good fifteen minutes of time discussing this, and there can be no other action on my part."

"Thank you," said The Immune softly.

"Please prepare the Pathfinder," said Captain Logan clicking on the com, "I'll be taking her down."

After a brief silence, a voice came over the com, "Captain, we can't do that. The Pathfinder has been descending for the last ten minutes."

"Who ordered that?" demanded the captain, "No one, I mean no one on this ship is authorized to operate that vessel."

Chief Stephens entered the control room as this was being said and interjected, "That would be Admiral Beckwourth." He went on to say, "It's been a weird day. First, an admiral doing signal flags in his skivvies, then the same admiral floats in hanging on the bottom of an airwar wearing the same."

CHAPTER 64

DOUBLE CROSS

That's impossible," said The Immune, looking at the Chief in disbelief. "I left him on the deck of the Acheson immediately before it crashed. He had no extract spray; the airwar would have killed him if he grabbed it."

"Well," said the chief, "I don't know anything about that, but he's an admiral, whether in skivvies or not. The boys all did as he said. We loaded the sonar thing in the Pathfinder's claws, and he took off."

"Why didn't you stop him?" demanded Captain Logan.

"If the admiral wants to prance around in skivvies," replied the chief, looking confused, "I guess he can. He's an admiral."

"No," said Captain Logan with frustration in his voice, "I meant why didn't you stop him from taking the Pathfinder?"

The Chief looked even more confused. "Why, Sir? He takes it down every two weeks. Didn't know there was a rule he couldn't do it in his skivvies."

"Did he say anything else?" said Captain Logan.

The chief nodded, "Yes, said he had a gift for friends, and he still had a chance for immortality, whatever that means."

"Oh bloody hell!" said the captain with a horrified look.

Stevens turned to look at The Immune. "One more thing, Sir. Can I ask you about your phone?"

The captain turned and snapped at Stevens, "We're in crisis mode here. You're excused from the control room—immediately." The chief, taken aback, quickly exited the control room.

Captain Logan took three long strides across the control room and flicked a switch. Only static came over the speaker above his head. He jabbed his thumb in the microphone switch and said, "Beckwourth! What the hell do you think you're doing?" He waited for a response, which was lacking.

The Immune was now focused on a tracking screen and said, "He's descending quite fast. Can the craft take that speed?"

The captain, without acknowledging The Immune's comment, said, "You're descending too fast. I demand you return the Pathfinder to the surface."

This time the com crackled, and the admiral's voice, in a harsh tone, said, "I'm going to the Krone. I've cut a deal to deliver the EMP generator, and I live. If I stay with you, I die. Easy choice."

Captain Logan began pounding the control panels in front of him in a mad rage. The captain screamed into his microphone the admiral was a coward and a traitor, followed by punishments the admiral would receive that weren't biologically possible.

After the captain's rant ended, the admiral's voice was heard again over the speaker, "I'm not a bad guy. I'm just making the right choice for *me*."

"I hope they blow your ass out of the water and your carcass serves as nematode food for the next twenty years," said the captain, in a rage.

"If the Krone wanted to blow me up," said the admiral, "they would've done it when I first contacted them immediately after I started down. They've been tracking me the whole way. Why destroy something if you can get it given to you?"

He paused.

"Look at your monitor," said the admiral, "You can see the Krone's housing vessels." The Immune glanced at the monitor which was being fed video signals from the Pathfinder. It looked like an aerial view of a city glowing green. There were hundreds, maybe thousands, of what looked like windowless buildings as far as camera could focus. "What you see before you is the future of the world."

"Beckwourth, you're a real bastard," yelled Captain Logan.

"John," said the admiral, "if you're listening, as I trust you are, congratulations, I'm proud of you. You're now The Immune. This is what I always wanted you to be. Man defines his life by choices—some good, some bad. I made my choice early, and I never wavered. I believe my choice will give me perceived immortality, and now to my friends one thousand meters below: Alpha Mike Foxtrot."

With those words the speaker crackled and went to static, the lights flickered, and the monitors clicked off and turned on again.

The Immune reached down to the admiral's cell phone. It had a dead screen. He pushed several buttons without response, smiled, and said, "Best PR guy in the history of the world."

CHAPTER 65

THE CENTRAL COMMANDER

Five miles below, the central commander of the Krone assault force was monitoring the descent of the Pathfinder. He had concerns when he lost contact with the Battleship Hiss. Although disturbed by the attack on the Hiss, he was reassured because the attacking ship sunk, and one of the Chosen intervened.

It was an extreme oversight on his part to overlook the test EMP generator as a potential weapon. Once the Chosen One, Admiral Beckwourth, delivered it into his hands, no one would be the wiser. He initially considered blowing the submersible up when the admiral first contacted him, but knew if he fired and destroyed the vessel, high command would want to know why. His superiors might uncover his mistake with the EMP generator and that could darken an otherwise perfect colonization. In addition, he knew the admiral well; they met every two weeks for the last ten months.

Up to this point, even the Chief Colonizer couldn't have done the operation smoother. The central commander was in for great rewards. The first would be feeding on Admiral Beckwourth, who was bringing down the EMP generator.

He was perturbed the surface advance force was already dining on supplemented Chosen Ones. Once the attack force surfaced, he knew he'd be too busy to acquire a nutritionally enhanced Chosen One. He'd hoped the admiral might come down on Fulfillment Day as he provided the admiral a special supplement he personally liked feeding on. After promising delivery of the EMP generator, the admiral confirmed he just finished taking the last pill. The central commander was overjoyed he wouldn't get stuck feeding on a common, and he would begin to feed even before the strike force started their ascent. It was turning into a great day.

The central commander carefully monitored communications from the Brittle Star to the submersible. The voice analysis recorded a definite positive on stress and anger in the captain's voice. Unquestionably the captain believed the traitorous admiral's intent. The admiral's voice had been analyzed multiple times over the year, and he was always truthful, including today.

The submersible Pathfinder was now on the video screen, and the admiral just finished speaking with the ship. The Krone commander was wondering whether an admiral would have better flavor than a common man. A stalk interrupted his thought, handing him a read-out of the possible meanings of Alpha Mike Foxtrot or AMF. The commander didn't know the meaning of either, so he requested further analysis. Deeper analysis showed in the less than one percent probability the American Machine and Foundry, AMF bowling lanes, and the Arab Monetary Fund. Two percent was Action Method Protocol, and finally ninety-seven percent probability was an American acronym for Adios Mother Fu—

The electromagnetic pulse waves spread out on the bottom of the Cayman Trench. The force generators stopped. Within seconds, thousands of housing vessels lining the bottom began to implode. Their under-supported metal walls crushed with five miles of water pressure sitting on their backs. In twenty seconds, it was all over, the greatest military force in the history of the earth eliminated without firing a single shot.

CHAPTER 66

TRAGIC LEGACY

B ack on the surface, it would be thirty minutes before the first
sign of victory would appear in the form of a few small bubbles breaking the surface of the water, most having been dis-
solved and absorbed by the water in their five-mile ascent to the
surface.

With the loss of the controlling signals from the armada, the
force generators unleashed the waters building up along the safe
zone coastlines. Not enough time passed for the force generators to
release a giant sixty-foot wall of unstoppable water. Instead, the
coastlines were treated to a sudden nine foot swell. Fortunately,
there were no deaths and little destruction.

Celebrations were spreading around the world as the last airwars were shredded. Even more intense celebrations would have
occurred if the world knew of the now vanquished invasion force
crushed five miles below.

The world's most important war ended, and at that exact
moment the world was united and in peace. For the first time in history, men weren't fighting each other. This lasted thirty-seven minutes and twenty-two seconds. Unfortunately, celebrating Southern
République de Côte d'Ivoire, non-Muslim citizens ran out of beer
and borrowed kegs without permission from nearby partying
Muslim Northern République de Côte d'Ivoire citizens.

The southerners rationalized their acquisition as a good deed because Muslims shouldn't be drinking anyway. The Muslims didn't recognize the charity in the action and several armed men deployed on a rescue mission. The result was twenty-eight dead on one side and twenty-one dead on the other. Escalations of violence quickly developed along religious lines, and within a few hours, civil war once again embroiled the Ivory Coast. Two of humankind's most dubious creations, beer and religion—the causes and alleged solutions for all of man's problems—allied themselves to return the world to pre-airwar days.

Back on the Brittle Star, the captain was agitated and said to The Immune, who was smiling and staring at the admiral's dead phone, "What was that all about? Why are you smiling?"

"The admiral set off an EMP," said The Immune with a grin.

"How could you possibly know that?" said the captain with a bewildered look.

The Immune held up the admiral's phone, "It's fried," he said.

Captain Logan gave an unconvinced frown. "But the Brittle Star; nothing happened to it." He looked around confirming to himself that all electronics were working. The Immune relayed the covert history of the Brittle Star before its purchase by Captain Logan. Captain Logan reached down and brought out his phone. After he pushed buttons without response, he held the phone up to The Immune and smiled.

"Fried. Did you know he was doing it?"

"I'd hoped," said The Immune, "but I wasn't sure until the phone went dead."

"Why didn't you stop my tirade?" asked the captain.

"Well, it wouldn't have changed his plans. He'd have wanted it that way. You demonstrated real anguish from his presumed defection. To anyone monitoring the conversation, as I suspect it was, you were believable. I'm sure Admiral Beckwourth was worried about destruction before reaching an effective range. I suspect in some way you helped achieve his goal. He FSed us all the way to the end, and although I can't forgive his past misdeeds, I do feel his final choice has given him some redemption."

"You speak as if he were dead," said the captain, looking perplexed.

"The Brittle Star is hardened. The Pathfinder is a research submersible and not hardened for an EMP. Its electronics, power, everything was wiped out."

Captain Logan shrugged, "Nevertheless, the EMP shouldn't have killed him. The pressure wouldn't collapse its shell like the Krone's vessels that required supplemental force fields," he said.

"True. He's sitting in absolute pitch black without communication on the bottom of the ocean floor. The vessel's oxygen recirculation and CO_2 scrubber systems have stopped. The temperature is dropping. He'll die from lack of oxygen or hypothermia in a few hours. You know as well as I, there are no local underwater rescue vessels capable of reaching him."

"I guess I knew that, too," said the captain, "You said it was a suicide mission when I was planning on going. The slow death never occurred to me."

"The admiral knew this would happen," said The Immune, "He's accepted his punishment. The admiral finally realized his choices had always been wrong, but ultimately he did the right thing. He was correct about his immortality, but it'll be only in the history books. His final act will be immortalized, as well as the vessel he guided, The Pathfinder. However, he won't go down in history as a great man, for which I sadly mistook him. His legacy is a tragic character whose final redeeming act was to free himself from his flaws."

The grizzled old chief came back in the control room. He looked at The Immune and said, "Sir, sorry to bother you again, but I'm under orders to ask about your phone."

The Immune, with a surprised look, said, "Sure, what do you want to know about my phone?"

"Is it working?" said the chief.

The Immune smiled and gave a knowing look at Captain Logan. "No."

"Good," Stevens replied, "Then I can give you this and be done with it." He handed The Immune the rolled up book, the *Three Samurai Cats*. "The naked admiral ordered me to give it to you when your phone went dead, but not before; said he wanted you to pass it on to his nephew."

CHAPTER 67

THE SAMURAI CAT

C aptain Logan looked as confused as The Immune felt at the moment.

"What did he say to do if the phone kept working?" said The Immune.

"Strange, I asked him that, too," said Chief Stevens, "He said it wouldn't matter then. It's been a weird day — admiral using signal flags, giving orders in his skivvies, carrying around kids' books, and taking joyrides in the Pathfinder. I get drunk and do crap like that, I end up in the brig; he'll undoubtedly get a promotion and another star on his sleeve."

Stevens wandered out of the room, continuing to mumble the unfairness of it all.

The Immune shook his head and said to Captain Logan, "But his nephew is dead. He killed him."

He began thumbing through the story in the book. The core of the Japanese fable was patience for the right moment to attack. Two strong and able samurai cats were previously humbled when they directly attacked a giant rat. However, an old worn and weak samurai cat with the power of extreme patience waited and waited. During the wait, he took abuse, watched others being abused, and overlooked intolerable behaviors from the rat. Finally, the cocky rat made a mistake, placed himself in an indefensible position, and suddenly found himself at the mercy of the old samurai cat. It was-n't strength and power that led to victory, but patience.

The Immune smiled to himself. "An FS maneuver; no wonder the admiral liked the book."

The Immune thumbed to the front of the book. The inside cover had several childlike crayon drawings. In the top left corner was an inscription, *To my favorite Nephew, John Smith*. The Immune thought, *what the heck*. The admiral used this same name for The Immune's fictitious cousin. The Immune then flipped to the inside back cover, and there were several hastily written paragraphs.

To my dear friend, The Immune. I hate filling you in this way, but there isn't time. As you've probably surmised, I'm an Immune as well, but not a swimmer. I'll write the best as I can as I hold onto the tentacles on our trip to the Brittle Star.

I wish to make what I'm sure would be your perspective history of me a little closer to physical history. You'll find in the blank margins of the book my notes and plans I've recorded the last year. If I'm successful, I hope these will be regarded as the world's greatest FS maneuver. These are written in UV ink and are readable only under UV light.

The Immune immediately understood the purpose of the UV plant grow-lights on the admiral's desks. He made a mental note to pick up a UV light when he reached shore, and he continued read-ing.

When I was "invited" to be a Chosen, I was given two choices, join or die. My recruiters apparently didn't appreciate the third option, an FS maneuver. During the indoctrination, Admiral Wilkinson made me privy to EMP testing details. The Krone were proud of their invincibility and used that image to help recruit The Chosen. With a little checking, I found out the EMP test generator remained in the hold of the Brittle Star. I rec-ognized its one-time potential use, but I had to endure and patiently wait until the entire Krone force completely deployed in the trench.

I was forced to watch, tolerate, and even participate in many disturb-ing, morally reprehensible activities in my year of patience. I devised a plan early to save Immunes from extractions. I would use their attributes as an FS maneuver to keep The Chosen and Krone happy.

Ironically, the Krone executed their own FS maneuver on the Chosen with the promise of the immortality treatments. I thought the Krone were serious, as obviously did all the Chosen. I must admit the Krone "FSed" us well. By the way, I never took the treatment. Didn't figure the treatment would do me much good. All my plan variations ended with me stuck in the Pathfinder on the bottom of the Cayman Trench. It would suck being immortal in that situation, ha.

I convinced The Chosen that creating a hero and killing him immediately before the invasion would deliver a brilliant tactical, psychological blow. I previously saved Sengele from execution when I proposed using him for propaganda. When you appeared on the scene, I presented the psychological blow option to ASC. Lionize you, then have Sengele kill you for added effect. I knew this would keep you both alive until the end. If you stayed alive, I could keep all the Immunes protected as well. I was also worried I might not be privy to the timing of Fulfillment Day. However, with your death planned as a first strike, it would be a good marker.

I knew the Krone would wait until they positioned all strike forces before ASC would call you to meet Sengele. I had no intention of letting you die, but I knew Sengele's sacrifice was necessary. I had no idea he was your future brother-in-law and Cassandra was your fiancé. My extreme apologies to them both.

The original ASC plan was two sham meetings with Sengele. You never were to actually speak with him for obvious reasons. He was to remain gagged. I was to make sure you gave the needed post meeting statement. After the first 'meeting,' you were to announce in a press conference you heard his confession and forgave him, but punishment would proceed. This would maximize public presence and confer you a cleric-like quality. Then, hours later in a second meeting, Sengele would kill you, or rather ASC officials would kill you and say he did it.

I knew you'd kill Sengele on the first meeting because you were consumed with vengeance, but I told no one. After you killed Sengele, I would use the confusion to slip away to the Brittle Star and take the Pathfinder down. The sacrifice of Sengele was necessary for this FS maneuver to work. This is why I never spoke to him. I couldn't face the man I knew I was condemning to die to save the world; again, my sincere apologies to him.

I'd planned to approach the Krone under the guise of having a backup plan for your unanticipated killing of Sengele. As you now know, I carried out repeated submersions with the Pathfinder updating the central commander. The Krone were comfortable with my appearance every other week. Now, on this final visit, with the entire Krone force in place, I would set off the EMP.

Captain Stewart's attempts to kill you and embarrass me blew my plans. You may remember I stopped his extractions and he was such a sadistic psychopath he wouldn't let up until he had revenge on me. He was the one who sent Flinch to my office to get dirt on me. Flinch found this book, and by chance, happened to open the front-page close enough to the grow-light to read my hidden notes. I had to kill him, and I took the can of Ube Extract from him. I always kept the book with me from that point on.

Stewart suspected I was giving Intel of military operations to Mad Mike. He was correct. Initially, I was providing the Big Zee all the information directly, but I got nervous. If caught, my FS maneuver was finished.

The Big Zee arranged for Bob to be a mole. By letting Bob break into my office and download the files, I had a pawn to sacrifice, if needed. Bob and Mad Mike never knew I was working with the Big Zee the entire time. When Stewart started getting too close for comfort and called for an investigation, I had to give up Bob to take off the heat.

The Big Zee and I arranged the Colossus affair. He told the boy, Daniel, it was okay to sneak along with the mission. Zee followed the boy, then acted as if the boy had done it on his own. Who were folks to believe? A ten-year-old kid or one of the most trusted advisors of Mad Mike?

I used my battle tablet to spread our forces thin, allowing Zee and the boy to make it through without risk. The Big Zee pretended his GPS malfunctioned, but I directed him the entire way. The plan was for Bob to find Daniel, exposing his link to Mad Mike. This would force him to "escape" back to Mad Mike's group.

I gave Bob the central planning speech pretty hard. I needed him to badmouth me when he got back to Mad Mike to keep my ASC image intact. I would then expose him as the mole getting me off the hook with Stewart's investigation, and Bob would be safe with Mad Mike.

However, neither the Big Zee nor I anticipated the Colossus attack, and nobody expected Mad Mike to show up and ask for a truce. With the Big Zee's accidental death, I was forced to wing it. Mad Mike was too accommodating with his truce requirements. I had to get real demanding because I wanted the militias armed and out of the safe zones until Fulfillment Day. My authoritative demands worked. Mad Mike wanted more time to trust me, and that's all I needed.

Stewart also suspected I was using Senator Snivaling. I got her to change her vote on the Immunes fighting militia by giving her Ube Watabee's blue extract can. You may remember me removing it from

Flinch's body. Flinch hadn't turned it over to Snivaling at Stewart's request. Stewart wanted to use it later as a bargaining chip with Snivaling.

Actually, it was a small can of shaving cream I removed the label from, then added a blue cap. I figured she'd never get close enough to an airwar to use it. If she did, even better.

The greens I provided the Chosen in ASC City were fakes as well. During the time you're reading this, all the Colossi surrounding ASC City will have crossed the wire. The Chosen will be frantically spraying themselves with the green-capped cans, which are in reality roach spray. I believe this to be a fitting end to The Chosen in ASC city.

Regarding the original Ube extract, I saved the can and used it on Cassandra for her exit from the Acheson. At least the final memory of Ube ended up for good use.

I couldn't predict your metamorphosis when you bonded with Sengele, although I heartily approve. I tried to convince you to let me off the ship. I couldn't reveal the plan, because if the Krone thought for a moment I wasn't with them, they would never let the submersible close. My job is public relations, so I easily passed their lying analysis tests from the beginning. I could maintain cover, but I knew others wouldn't if they knew my plan.

My situation worsened when Cassandra showed up. I thought I could use your son to bargain my way off the ship and do the deed, but that clearly didn't work either.

After my conversation with Admiral McCloy, I got panicky; events weren't following original plans. I thought I could use Snivaling's influence to get me on the Brittle Star and in the Pathfinder. I previously forced myself to develop an intimate relationship with Snivaling to gain favor. It was a sickening task at best. A session with her was less enjoyable than a skinning session with Captain Stewart. Although I had to tolerate the deaths of thousands of innocents, the memories with her torture me more.

When I witnessed her being consumed by the Krone, I wanted to cheer, but overcome by the realization my FS maneuver was ruined, I collapsed. It's overwhelming when you believe you're the last hope for humanity and you've failed. The Krone's FS maneuver trumped mine. I had no idea the Krone were killing The Chosen, too. Humanity had lost.

Your suggestion of an EMP sneak attack gave me one last hope of getting to the Brittle Star. I knew you would fail since the Krone would never let you close enough in the Pathfinder, but I could do it. I couldn't confide *because the Krone getting any hint of others working with me would be suspect. I trust my traitorous Chosen One charade has pissed off someone enough, and he or she will berate me all the way down; that can only help.*

I'll tell the central commander I've finished all my treatments when I offer up the EMP generator. I hope he's like most politicians and will put his personal interests before the entire Krone force he's leading. This is my last FS maneuver. I hope it works. If it does, let my epitaph read, "Liberty is a fragile gift, take one vial of fear, add three drops, lust-for-power, and it's easily poisoned."

Your Friend, Beckwourth

PS By now, you know my nephew is safely playing with your cousin.

The Immune stood in shock as he finished reading the note.

Captain Logan, looking over the Immune's shoulder, read the last line and said, "So your cousin and his nephew are alive?"

The Immune shook his head in amazement. "No, they both never were. He FSed the death of a nephew he never had."

The door of the control room sprung open, and Sengele walked through. The captain started reaching for the knife sheathed at his side, stopped mid-move, and withdrew his hand. The movement caught Sengele's eye, and he looked at the knife. The captain's neck flushed. "Sorry, it'll take some getting used to, thinking of you as a good guy."

"Yeah," said Sengele, giving him a sad smile, "I fear I'll have to watch my back for a while, until everyone gets the notice."

"Sengele, where's Cassandra?" said The Immune.

"I'd prefer to be called 'Uncle Chunky' when your son is around," said Sengele with a smile.

The Immune heard a baby crying outside the compartment. Cassandra walked in with a beaming smile, which was impervious to the red-faced screaming baby she held in her arms. He was wrapped in a pure white blanket. The Immune reached in his pocket.

As Cassandra walked up to The Immune, she bent her face close to the screaming child and said, "John, I want to introduce you to the hero of the world, your dad."

She gently handed the baby to The Immune, while kissing him on the cheek. In the same movement, The Immune slipped the heart-shaped diamond ring with the two rubies on her finger.

Cassandra glowed, and tears ran down her face. The Immune looked down at his crying son, cradled him in his arms, and rocked him back and forth.

"Hi there, big fellow. I'm your dad, and everything's alright. One day I'll tell you the story of the greatest public relations man ever to live, the real world's hero. Would you like that?"

The baby stopped crying and smiled.

THE END